Date Due

JAN 30			
FEB 13			
FEB 20			
APR 2 9			

PRINTED IN U. S. A.

MIDCENTURY JOURNEY

MIDCENTURY JOURNEY

THE WESTERN WORLD THROUGH
ITS YEARS OF CONFLICT

By *William L. Shirer*

FARRAR, STRAUS AND YOUNG

New York

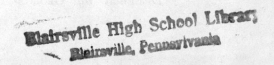

TO EILEEN AND LINDA

*—This particle of light
on the world in which
you were born*

Designed by George Hornby

TABLE OF CONTENTS

NOTE

WILLIAM STYRON, who wrote a discerning first novel the mid-century year and who was born at the quarter-century mark, stated in the New York Herald-Tribune Book Review of October 7, 1951:

"I am pretty much in the dark about the future. I would like to go to Europe, and to read a lot more. I would like to discover the moral and political roots of our trouble, and to learn why it has come about that young men . . . have to suffer so endlessly in our time."

Turn to the opening quotations of this book and you will find another and older and also very discerning writer, Katherine Anne Porter, reflecting in 1940 that all the conscious and recollected years of her life had been lived under the "heavy threat of world catastrophe" and that most of the energies of her mind and spirit had been spent in an effort to grasp the meaning of that threat and "to understand the logic of this majestic and terrible failure of the life of man in the Western World."

It is with these things, the moral and political roots of our trouble, the logic and meaning, if any, of our majestic and horrible failure, and with the great changes that have taken place and the prospects for the future, that this midcentury journey through the Western world and back through the fateful years is principally concerned.

W.L.S.

"We are in the midst of a period of revolutionary change that is likely to be as profound as any in the modern history of the human race."
—HAROLD J. LASKI in *Reflections on the Revolution of our Time.*

"To live in a revolution is a dubious privilege, and to live in this particular revolution is in some respects particularly unpleasant."
—JULIAN HUXLEY in *On Living in a Revolution.*

"The period through which we are living presents itself as one of unmitigated confusion and disintegration . . . a period whose evil fulfillments have betrayed all its beneficent promises."
—LEWIS MUMFORD in *The Condition of Man.*

"We can assert with some confidence that our own period is one of decline; that the standards of culture are lower than they were fifty years ago; and that the evidences of this decline are visible in every department of human activity."
—T. S. ELIOT in *Notes Toward the Definition of Culture.*

"We none of us flourished in those times, artists or not, for art, like the human life of which it is the truest voice, thrives best by daylight in a green and growing world. For myself, and I was not alone, all the conscious and recollected years of my life have been lived to this day under the heavy threat of world catastrophe, and most of the energies of my mind and spirit have been spent in the effort to grasp the meaning of these threats, to trace them to their sources and to understand the logic of this majestic and terrible failure of the life of man in the Western World."
—KATHERINE ANNE PORTER, June 21, 1940, in the introduction to the Modern Library edition of *Flowering Judas.*

"Those who do not remember the past are condemned to relive it."
—SANTAYANA.

1. THOUGHTS IN A PLANE

OVER THE OCEAN

THE CENTURY was half over and I, who happened to be born in its fourth year, was setting out again for Europe, to which I had first gone in 1925.

It was not in my mind this time to seek out prime ministers, kings, or commissars for interviews. What concerned me immediately was whether the Communist aggression in Korea, which had just occurred, would plunge us into a third World War. It would not be necessary to go to the heads of state and government to ascertain that. One had only to pause for a bit in Berlin or Vienna to see whether the Russian Red Army marched westward. Everyone knew that if it did Continental Western Europe would fall in a few weeks and that the third war would be on. In twenty-four hours the plane I had boarded in a rather jittery New York would be in Vienna.

But there was more to this particular little journey than the quest for the answer of peace or war. I wanted, if I could, to find out where we stood at the midcentury mark. If one could travel back and forth not only in space but in time, perhaps some perspective would develop and some bit of understanding. It might be easier to perceive where we were if one could recall honestly and accurately the road we had taken, the wrong turnings as well as the right ones, and what of significance—for good or evil—had happened along that wearying, tortuous route soaked with so much blood after such cruelty and suffering.

Exactly twenty-five years had raced by since my first journey in this direction over these gray, northern Atlantic waters. It was a mere speck of time in history. Yet in one's mind the gulf between now and then seemed almost impossible to bridge. The Europe I had first approached with a raw American youth's high hopes no longer existed. That I knew, for I had chanced to live through, and partly share, its incredible convulsions. Even the America from which my plane had just taken off, though it had escaped the full impact of the violence that had uprooted Europe and Asia, bore little resemblance to the nation of the irresponsible growing-up days of the mid-twenties. In the relatively brief period between these two ocean crossings my own country had come of age, suddenly emerging from the Second World War as one of the two superpowers in the world. It had not sought this position; indeed its citizens and its leaders had shied away from the responsibility. Greatness had been thrust upon it.

All this had come about, if you considered the world as a whole, in a time of unparalleled violence, revolution, war, bloodshed, tyranny, confusion, and strife. My own generation had known little else. It had lived from early youth entirely in an Age of Conflict, as the historians were beginning to call it. Even in the intervals between the wars and the revolutions and the harrowing crises, one felt one was living in, as the poets and psychologists said, an Age of Anxiety, with the threat of a new war, a new revolution, a new bomb, another aggression, another crisis frightening the frenzied mind and exacerbating nerves already frayed.

A man of the right or of the center could agree with Leon Trotsky, an uncompromising man of the left, when he said some time before he was murdered by Stalin's agents: "Anyone desiring a quiet life has done badly to be born in the twentieth century."

We had not had, of course, much choice in the matter; and the parents of those of us who had been born toward the beginning of the twentieth century had not the slightest inkling then of what lay ahead for their children or, if they should live on awhile, for themselves.

It is difficult for those of my age to fathom the mood of these first years of the century; one can feel it but dimly from the writings of those who were old enough to experience it. There is a vast abyss of what someone has called "empty space and empty time" which separates us from the world that died in 1914 but which still flourished in a wonderful state of peace, faith, innocence, and equilibrium when my generation was born.

The flavor of that time in Europe, the grace and beauty and gaiety and abandon of living—at least for the well-off— has been preserved for us in the long novel of Marcel Proust, in the recent memoirs of Osbert Sitwell, and in countless other works. It was also an age of confidence, when men had faith and a sense of security, and if it could be said that in America the art of living was not quite so exquisitely refined as in the great cities of Western Europe because our society was newer and rawer, it could also be said that Americans were even more certain than Europeans in the belief that progress was the eternal law of life and that despite a few flaws here and there the human race was moving rapidly along a splendid road that led inexorably toward a promised land where all men would be free, happy, harmonious, and rich.

Science, technology, invention promised a millennium. Machines would liberate human beings from drudgery and

give them a life of abundance, freeing them for the pursuits
of leisure. The advances of medicine would ensure longer
life and a healthier one. Public education, making all men
literate, would widen their horizons. The rapid development
of long-distance transportation and communication by the
railroads, fast trans-Atlantic luxury liners, the telegraph,
telephone, and wireless, and the promise of automobiles
and even airplanes would bring men together from the far
corners of the globe and make them good neighbors if not
brothers. Electricity was coming in too, with possibilities
that stretched beyond the imagination; the motion picture
promised to bring fine entertainment to the remotest village
and the filthiest slum.

And if the conquests of science and technology concerned
mostly the improvement of the material side of life then the
good folk at the turn of the century could point with pride
to the fact that the spiritual life had not suffered in the least.
Almost all citizens, rich and poor, placed their faith in Al-
mighty God, and even the heathen in Asia and darkest Africa
were being led by the zealous missionaries toward the light
of Christianity. Doubts were few and Sitwell later, in our
own age of doubt, could look back and claim that before
1914 there was no disillusionment—as if it were beneath
man's dignity. He might have added that there was no concern, either, with the "crisis of civilization" and the "atomiz-
ing of man." Civilization and man were doing quite well.

Never since the Renaissance, it seemed, had man's creative
genius flowered so richly. The arts thrived like everything
else. In music, painting, drama, poetry, the novel, the ballet,
philosophy, new heights were being reached and for the first
time in history art was being shared, appreciated, and enjoyed by everyone, or nearly everyone.

Above all, it was an era of Peace. Some nations, it was

true, maintained great armies and navies. But Americans did not think an expenditure of money and men on such things was necessary for the security of their own country, protected as it was by the oceans. For many decades there had been no serious wars, so that by 1914 few could recall what war was like; Americans and Europeans alike had come to accept the idea that future disputes between nations would be settled by peaceful means. Institutions such as the International Court of Arbitration, housed in the Palace of Peace at The Hague, had been established on this assumption; and the man who had developed dynamite as a weapon of war had given his fortune to perpetuate the Nobel prize for peace.

It seemed indeed to many in the West that human society had reached a state of equilibrium that might well be permanent. Some changes there would always be in human affairs, but from now on they would be invariably for the better. And they could be wrought peacefully, without commotion, without revolution and bloodshed, without war.

As my plane droned over the ocean it occurred to me that my father, who had died in 1913 at the age of 42, must have known no other concept of life. In his lifetime, so full of faith and hope and optimism, there had been: no world wars nor even cold wars; no important revolutions, no genocide, no communism or fascism, no totalitarian dictators of left or right, no Soviet Union, no atom bombs (or hydrogen bombs)—none of the things that had dominated my own life and times. He had, no doubt, believed in the inevitability of peace, progress, and prosperity—and in the essential goodness of man.

He died, I am sure, in complete peace of mind and soul, just a year before the Archduke Ferdinand, of whom he had probably never heard, was assassinated at Sarajevo, a faraway Balkan town of whose existence he undoubtedly was totally unaware. I could only know much later that his world died with him, so to speak: the world of McKinley, Taft, and the G.O.P. Old Guard (he was a staunch Republican), of Victoria and Edward, of the Hohenzollerns, Hapsburgs, and Romanovs and of the wonderfully civilized, if fickle, early Third French Republic. It was soon in shambles, its venerable institutions, which must have seemed to him so stable, and all. Certainly he could not have faintly imagined that his body would hardly be cold before the earth he thought so reasonable and good would be littered with the shattered corpses of millions of men who had been as decent, as innocent, as full of faith and hope as he.

Nor could he have had the slightest foreboding that this senseless mass slaughter would be repeated on an even greater scale a quarter of a century later, nor that at the century's halfway mark, despite the incredible carnage of two world wars, the children of his planet would be living again in abject fear of a third savage conflict and that peace, which had meant to him such a reasonable state of affairs, could at the midcentury be such a damnation, compounded of such hatred and violence, intolerance and hysteria, full of so much degradation of the human spirit.

No doubt if he had looked searchingly enough he might have discerned before he died the sprouting of the seeds of destruction. It is easy to see now that they were there. There was the powder keg of the Balkans. There was the revolutionary ferment in Czarist Russia. There was the militarism in Germany which indoctrinated a virile but unstable people with the idea that war was a desirable, noble thing, the finest and highest law of life. There was the evident decay in the multinational Hapsburg Empire. And between the great

powers there was the growing rivalry for markets and overseas possessions.

But that was not all. Despite so much progress and prosperity, there was widespread poverty and economic-social
maladjustment. The economic system that had transformed
the Western world and brought so many benefits to so many
people had also made life a mean, monotonous, inhuman
ordeal for millions upon millions. In Europe, there was a reaction to this in the rise of socialism and in the growing influence of Karl Marx. In America the reaction was weaker
because the opportunities for the masses still seemed bound-
less.

But even in America voices of warning were raised. They
were to be forgotten quickly or ignored in the wild scramble
for riches; but they were raised.

I had come across some of them in a patch of desultory
reading I had done on my farm just prior to taking this plane.
It might well be, as Brooks Adams said to Justice Holmes,
that philosophers were men hired by the well-to-do to prove
that everything is all right. But around the turn of the century
a remarkable group of writers and philosophers rose to proclaim that in America, despite its blessings, things were far
from right.

Had not William Dean Howells, the dean of American
letters of his time and, for most of his long literary career,
an incurable optimist, come to the bitter conclusion in the
evening of his life that civilization was coming out all wrong
in the end and that he abhorred it? Had not his friend Mark
Twain in the very midst of his own glittering success as the
country's most popular and loved writer privately put down
his opinion that "the damned human race is a race of cow-
ards," that civilization had been corrupted by the grab for
wealth, that the American dream had collapsed, and that

"none but the dead have free speech, none but the dead are permitted to speak the truth"?

It was a tragic confession for a writer who was the toast of presidents and corporation magnates as well as the favorite of the masses. Mark Twain's obsession that writers in America could not always afford to tell the truth reminded one of the advice Henry Adams gave to his brother Brooks not to publish a book in which the latter had lugubriously predicted disastrous wars and revolutions and the collapse of civilization, which he believed were certain to result from the inequalities and the greed and the cruelty of the industrial age. It would be monkeying with a dynamo, Henry advised; the author would never be forgiven by the "goldbugs," the bankers, the industrialists, and their political stooges.

Even William Graham Sumner, that massive apologist for the Gilded Age and for the American way which had made it possible, had begun to have his doubts toward the end. In an outburst against those who claimed to lay down the law as to who and what was American or un-American, he exclaimed: "Who dare say he is not 'American'? Who dare repudiate what is declared to be 'Americanism'? Those who have Americanism especially in charge have repudiated the doctrine that 'governments derive their just powers from the consent of the governed' because it stood in the way of what they wanted to do. They denounce those who cling to the doctrine as un-American. Then we see what Americanism and patriotism are. They are the duty laid upon us all to applaud, follow and obey whatever a ruling clique of newspapers and politicians chooses to say or wants to do."

The very aspects of American life which he had spent a lifetime praising and defending as inevitable and good—the practice of laissez faire, the privilege of wealth to dominate society, and the worship of financial success—seemed to him toward the end of his days to be leading only to disaster. "I have lived through the best period of this country's history," he remarked. "The next generations are going to see war and social calamities. I am glad I don't have to live in them."

One who did live through to see them was John Dewey. Late in his long life he, too, became a prey to doubts until he was forced to come to some somber conclusions: that the mass of citizens in America had needlessly surrendered their liberties to a few, that rugged individualism had become ragged individualism, that to talk of free individuals, equality of opportunity, the automatic blessings of democracy, was to overlook certain facts, and that actually genuine liberty had been greatly diminished in America as the result of the concentration of economic power in the hands of the few. In short, Dewey could not help but feel that there had been a tragic breakdown of democracy. Millions of Americans, he felt, were forced to lead lives that were personally frustrated, economically precarious, and socially sterile. In a corporate age they did not have the means nor the opportunity to achieve economic success. The constant propaganda which said that they did was merely a myth to lull them into accepting their plight without protest. The few who possessed the economic power in the nation also controlled the organs of mass communication: the press, the radio, the movies. Thus, Dewey thought, the people were often fooled.

But of all Americans who had begun to question the American dream at the turn of the century, Henry and Brooks Adams, whose illustrious forebears had twice occupied the White House, became the most disillusioned. Conservative by nature and education, inheritors of enough wealth to enable them to escape the trials of having to earn a living, they nevertheless took a dim view of the state of

American life. Brooks, though less known as a sage than his older brother, seems to have been the more radical thinker. In time he came to believe that democracy in America "had conspicuously and decisively failed" and that, though it retained the outward forms, it had given way to the tyranny and abuses of money power.[1]

(Brooks Adams made one prediction that kept bobbing up in my mind in the plane: "My conclusion is that our so-called civilization has shown its movement, even at the center, arrested. It has failed to concentrate further. Its next effort may succeed, but it is more likely to be one of disintegration, with Russia for the eccentric on one side and America on the other." He foresaw these two nations emerging as the colossi of the world.)

Of these views of civilization in America I, like most Americans, had been blithely ignorant. My father probably would have dismissed such talk as "radical" and therefore not true; and I heard little or nothing of it during my high-school and college days in Iowa. We believed in the American dream out there: in American democracy, American progress, in unlimited and equal opportunities for all Americans. Every Fourth of July amidst a flood of bellowed oratory and pink lemonade we renewed our faith.

During my junior year in college I began to have a vague feeling that the America of Calvin Coolidge was not going to be a very exciting place to start an adult life in. Life was getting awfully smug. It might be true, as Scott Fitzgerald was to say, that America in the early twenties was "going on the greatest, gaudiest spree in history," but we only *heard* about that in Iowa.

[1]The foregoing has been based largely on *Postscript to Yesterday*, by Lloyd Morris; New York, 1947.

For a long time in later years I tried to convince myself that I had fled America in 1925 to escape its Babbittism, Coolidgeism, puritanism, its Prohibition and the pathetic "booster" atmosphere of the Chamber of Commerce and Rotary. The truth, however, was that I intended to take my chances in that kind of an American world, however youthfully disdainful of it I might be, and that when I set out for Europe in a cattleboat, following my graduation from college in 1925, I intended to return in two months. Thousands of other Americans, mostly writers and artists, fled America in those days because they felt it had become a spiritual desert and that Europe, in comparison, was a green paradise. But I was too raw and young to know much about these things, or at least to feel them deeply.

At any rate, at about the time the Scopes "monkey" trial started in Dayton, Tennessee, and Coolidge was beginning his first elective term of office and the stock market was blazing and the boom was on in Florida and Bruce Barton's *The Man Nobody Knows* was at the top of the best-seller list (the man nobody knew turned out to be Jesus, "the founder of modern business" . . . "the most popular dinner guest in Jerusalem" . . . "an outdoor man" . . . "a great executive" . . . whose parables were "the most powerful advertisements of all time"), I set out for Europe. My two months' visit was to stretch into two decades and encompass many sad and awful changes: the decay of the Western democracies, the rise of the Soviet Union and the world Communist movement, the rise and fall of fascism and nazism, the death of the League of Nations with all its hopes, and, at the end, the bloodiest and cruelest war the earth had ever seen.

It cannot be said that a young American arriving in Europe in 1925 could foresee what lay ahead. To be sure, Mussolini had established himself in Italy, and the tyrannical grip of the Communist Party on Russia was complete. But both countries seemed, for the moment at least, to lie outside the main stream of European history. Italy, because of its inherent weaknesses, was a Big Power only by courtesy; the Soviet Union, though potentially the most powerful nation in Europe, held back from intercourse with the rest of the continent.

The Europe one saw at the beginning of the second quarter of the century was dominated by the two great Western democracies, Great Britain and France. Victorious allies and (with American help) conquerors of Germany, with immense overseas empires as sources of wealth and strength, their power was unchallenged in Europe and dominant throughout the world. It was they who had largely made the peace and who had the means to maintain it. How and why they failed to keep it, and what the consequences were, I was to see for myself in the years that followed.

———————

In the fading darkness just before dawn the plane set down on the airstrip at Shannon, Ireland, and after refueling continued on to London. By five o'clock that afternoon I had reached Vienna. All day we bobbed down at scheduled stops: Brussels, Frankfort, Stuttgart, Munich, and Prague. At each, as at Shannon and London that morning, it was easy to give in to memories. This journey, I could see, was going to carry me not only forward into space but backward into time, and even though it would be in both cases over familiar paths it might lead in the end to a destination a little beyond any I had yet reached.

———————

I had first gone to Ireland in the early, heady years of the Free State when the Irish—the majority, anyway, for they are not a people given to unanimity—were full of hope and confidence in the renaissance which political freedom, won after such heartbreaking struggle, would bring them. Already this tiny corner of the English-speaking world could boast, in William Butler Yeats, the finest living poet, and, in James Joyce, perhaps the foremost novelist writing in the English language. Now that its great political struggle against Britain had been won there was every reason to believe that a free and independent Ireland would flower as never before.

But somehow, even after a new constitution, hammered out by De Valera in 1937, proclaimed Ireland to be a sovereign, independent, democratic state, cutting off almost the last slender ties with the British Commonwealth and king and re-establishing the old Gaelic name of Eire, and even after the last threads of connection were severed and Eire became, on Easter Monday, April 18, 1949, "the Republic of Ireland," the dream faded, the great objectives were lost sight of and Ireland struck even such a sympathetic observer as this one as a community whose vision had narrowed, a parochial place preoccupied with pettiness, content to remove itself from the major currents of Western life and thought, intent on censoring good books and denying many of its greatest writers. Freedom, by some queer quirk of reversal, appeared to have dulled the fine creativeness of a poetic and imaginative people.

I did not stop over in London, for I intended to return here after the Continent had been visited. It would take some time, I knew, to get clear in one's mind the measure of events which had so transformed England from the prosperous, conservative, complacent seat of empire I had first seen exactly a quarter of a century before. It had been my initial stop then, but now I was pushing on to Vienna.

The American plane from London descended first at Brussels, and here, though we remained but half an hour and I never got beyond the airport, one was forcibly reminded of an unpleasant matter of some importance in Western Europe. There was a grim atmosphere about the airport that morning. This was in itself unusual since airfields are usually the most colorless of places. There seemed to be an unnecessarily large number of police and even troops about. I bought a batch of the local French-language papers.

King Leopold III, it developed, had returned to Brussels from his long exile in Switzerland three days before, and there was trouble in Belgium. The capital itself had been transformed into an armed camp to protect the King. Some 8,000 troops and police had been assembled at the military airdrome of Evere, outside of Brussels, the morning he arrived and had escorted him through streets filled with angry, resentful citizens to the royal residence of Laeken.

What was the cause of the trouble, of the anger and resentment? The heart of the matter went back to a spring day just ten years before. On May 28, 1940, the thirty-nine-year-old king, without consulting his hard-pressed allies and in defiance of his own government, surrendered unconditionally to the Germans, thus rendering even more desperate the already precarious position of the trapped French and British armies which at Leopold's frantic appeal had gone to his aid when the Nazis attacked Belgium.

The Belgian cabinet, sitting in Paris, had promptly declared the King's action illegal and unconstitutional, approved an order depriving him of his throne, and resolved to continue the war. From this arose a tragic split in Belgium that had now, as I was passing through, reached an ugly climax.

The issues went deeper than the question of Leopold's person and whether his surrender and his subsequent behavior in relation to the German conquerors were becoming to a king of the Belgians. One question involved his mistaken judgment, and I could not help recalling that it had a decisive bearing on the early part of the war and had served as a lesson to the little nations of Europe.

Despite what had happened in 1914, Leopold believed that in the second German war Belgium could remain neutral. Three other sovereigns, the Queen of the Netherlands and the kings of Denmark and Norway, shared similarly erroneous views in regard to their own countries—as did their governments and parliaments. Not even when Allied intelligence tried to warn them in advance of what Hitler had in store for them would they budge from their stubborn position. They coolly rebuffed all the efforts of the British and French to consult about mutual defense against the Germans. I recalled a broadcast we had heard in Berlin by the Dutch premier, De Geer, on April 9, 1940, exactly three weeks before the German hordes poured into his country, and nine days after they had overrun Denmark and invaded Norway: "We rely solely upon ourselves. In addition, we have a promise from both sides that our neutrality will be respected. Therefore we do not want any arrangements. We even shun them." Such inane thinking—and it was fully shared by King Leopold—was a good example, when it was put into words, of what Winston Churchill later would describe as the "ceaseless chatter of well-meant platitudes" which filled the smug air of the Western world (including the United States) right up to the last second before catastrophe came. It took Nazi conquest and a barbarian Nazi occupation to prove to the little nations that neutrality was an old-fashioned luxury they could no longer afford if they wanted to

survive. In the struggles of our day you had to choose sides;
you could no longer sit on the sidelines. This went for individuals as well as nations.

It may be that even Leopold learned this lesson. What he
did not learn was that he had forfeited his throne for good
when he capitulated against the advice of his government
in the spring of 1940. For five years he had waited with growing impatience in Switzerland to be called back to the throne.
Finally on July 20, 1950, the call had come. The Christian
Socialist Party, which had a small majority over all other
parties, had finally put through parliament his reinstatement
following a referendum on March 12 in which 57.7 per cent
of those voting had approved this course. But the ruling party
had failed to realize that, in democratic countries at least,
kings are supposed to have the allegiance of all the population, not just a bare majority of it. The Christian Socialists—
actually not socialist at all but conservative—also had failed
to judge the temper of the country.

As I raced through the headlines of three or four Brussels
newspapers that morning it was clear that the King's return
had brought Belgium to the verge of a civil war. Crowds
were beginning to riot before the royal palace. Violence was
spreading to the provinces. The police were beginning to fire
on unruly mobs. People were getting killed and hurt, and in
their resentment they were getting out of hand.

At the bottom of it all, I think, was the feeling of nearly
half the Belgian population, concentrated in the French-
speaking, industrialized Walloon district and in Brussels, not
only that the King had been a bit of a collaborationist himself in the days when Hitler's victory looked like a sure thing,
but that his return was something of a vindication of collabo-
rationism, an encouragement to those who had accepted
German domination in the mistaken belief that it was per-

manent, and under which they sought personal profit as vassals of the promised Germanic New Order.

The survival of those who co-operated with the occupying Germans, indeed their return, in many instances, to high place in politics and business, I was to learn on this trip, was a sore that festered in all the lands that had been overrun and ruled by the Nazis. This was especially true in France, which had two sorts of collaborationists to deal with: those who had aided the Hitlerite masters in the occupied zone, and an even greater number who had faithfully served Pétain and Laval in the unsavory regime of Vichy.

The case against Leopold which impressed nearly half the Belgians (the Walloon half, that is; the Flemish half of the population supported him fanatically) was this: Perhaps his surrender to the Germans could be forgiven. But why, on November 19, 1940, had he gone to Berchtesgaden to talk with Hitler? He claimed his only purpose in seeing the Fuehrer was to try to obtain the release of Belgian prisoners of war and to get better food rations for the hungry Belgian people. But many Belgians believed that his true intent was quite different. They were inclined to think that by the autumn of 1940 the King had convinced himself, as so many others had done, that Germany had won the war and that his real reason for journeying to Berchtesgaden was to beg the Fuehrer to grant some sort of "independence" to Belgium within the framework of the New Order, as Hitler had done with Vichy. Of this new vassal state, Leopold would be king.

The more one peruses the record the more one is forced to conclude that Leopold was chiefly concerned at this time, as later when the fortunes of war changed, with keeping his job as king. As long as the Germans seemed to be the victors he would make his peace with them.

There is, for instance, a damaging piece of evidence, which

came to light only recently. When the Germans were on top, Leopold resumed his family's German titles which his illustrious father, King Albert, had renounced after the first German war. Leopold began to attach to his title of king that of "Duke of Saxony and Prince of Saxe-Coburg-Gotha," apparently on the assumption that this would improve his position with his German masters.

He did another thing early in the war which displeased many Belgians. On September 11, 1941, he married a beautiful commoner, Marie Liliane Baels, daughter of a Flemish official whom the King himself had had to dismiss from his office as governor of West Flanders for deserting his post in the face of the German advance. An American observer may safely refrain from trying to answer the riddle of why the common people of the few remaining monarchies resent their king marrying a commoner; but many do. Besides that, what the Belgians especially resented was that Leopold thought it necessary to ask Hitler's permission to marry the lady, and that the Fuehrer quite ostentatiously sent the King his congratulations and a fine bouquet of flowers for the wedding. Nor were many Belgians pleased to learn that their king, who made much of his role as "the prisoner of Laeken, sharing the fate of his people," took his honeymoon in Nazi Austria, and thereafter, when life in Brussels became too boring, went off with his bride on trips to Munich, Vienna, and other German spots. Finally, some resented the propriety of the King's choice of a title for his bride, "Princess de Réthy." It happened to be the title his late wife, Queen Astrid, had used when she traveled incognito.

As the tide of war changed, Leopold, like others who had banked on German victory, began to change, too. But he was not one to risk jumping too soon. As late as 1944 the Belgian Resistance suggested to the King that he slip away from Brussels and go into hiding with them. This he would not do. He was also urged by some of his well-wishers to remain in the capital and await there the entry of the Allied armies toward the beginning of September. At this point, his opponents charge, Leopold made a curious decision. In the belief that it would help to mitigate the hostility of his people, the government-in-exile, and the Allied governments if it appeared that the Germans had forcibly removed him from Belgium in the wake of General Eisenhower's rapid advance, he requested—so the charge goes—the Germans to transfer him and his family to Germany. He hoped that at the war's end the Allied governments, as well as his own, would quickly restore him to his throne. But the call to return did not come, and for this he blamed the British.

And so after the war he settled down in exile in Switzerland, still awaiting the call, and as the months passed into years, fretting at the delay. When the summons finally came on July 20, 1950, when he was 49 years old, he hastened home—but not to stay for long. On August 1, as tens of thousands of aroused citizens marched on Brussels to depose him, defying the troops, the *gendarmerie,* and the police to stop them or shoot them down, with Belgium paralyzed by a general strike, and civil war already under way, the obdurate king yielded at last to the frantic entreaties of his own frightened supporters who had brought him back. He stepped down. He agreed to abdicate in favor of his son, Crown Prince Baudouin, when the latter came of age September 7, 1951. But the Belgians did not want him as king even during the year's interim. They forced him to turn over his constitutional powers forthwith to the Prince Royal.

Belgium, rid of its king, quickly settled down to peace.

———————

We flew on to Frankfort, to which I planned to return in

a few weeks to look into the state of West Germany. When last I had seen the vast airport, in 1948, it was humming with activity. Giant C-54's were taking off every three minutes with provisions for beleaguered Berlin. In the confusion wrought by subsequent Communist aggression and the West's reaction to it, one tended to forget that the airlift had not only saved Berlin but that it had administered the Soviet Union one of the few decisive defeats it had suffered in the cold war. Even more than that, it had shown the Russians the scope of American air power and thus acted, it seemed to me, as a deterrent to the men in the Kremlin. They had not imagined that airplanes could feed and fuel a city of nearly two million people. When that happened it must have struck them that such air power, if it were used in transporting other objects, such as, say, atomic bombs, might well bring disaster to their own land.

We came down next at Stuttgart, and after a brief stop continued on to Munich. I could never return to Munich or even pass through the old Bavarian capital, as I was now doing, without remembering as if it were yesterday the night Chamberlain and Daladier capitulated to Hitler and surrendered Czechoslovakia to him. I can still see the late prime minister, looking like some evil bird, like one of the vultures one had seen in Bombay after a heavy feast on Parsi remains, striding into the Regina Palast Hotel after his dirty deed with Hitler (Mussolini had also been present) and smiling pleasantly at the correspondents who were so sick at heart that night.

Before he left for London, he would have another talk with Hitler, the following morning, and sign with him a communiqué that dared to say: "We regard the agreement signed last night [destroying Czechoslovakia, that is!] and the Anglo-German naval accord [which allowed the Germans the submarine tonnage which scarcely a year later would bring England so close to disaster] as symbolic of the desire of our two peoples never to go to war with one another again. . . . We are determined to continue our efforts to remove possible sources of difference and thus to contribute to the assurance of peace in Europe."

The credulous old man with the umbrella had flown back to London that afternoon and from the balcony of 10 Downing Street had smugly declared: "My good friends, this is the second time in our history that there has come back from Germany to Downing Street peace with honor!" Only a handful in the House of Commons, Eden, Duff Cooper, and Churchill, who, it is difficult to recall now, had been a voice in the wilderness for a decade, dared to expose Chamberlain. Said Churchill: "We have sustained a total, unmitigated defeat." This was a minority view not only in Western Europe but in the United States of America.

The greatest irony of Chamberlain's surrender at Munich was only to be revealed to us seven years later. In late November 1945, while attending the Nuremberg trials, I came across a secret memorandum which General Halder, chief of the German General Staff at the time of Munich, had drawn up after the war for the Allied High Command. He disclosed that, had Chamberlain not come to Munich, or had he even delayed his coming, a group of German generals, under the leadership of General von Witzleben, would have carried out a well-planned attempt to dispose of Hitler. Of Witzleben's serious purpose there can be no doubt, for later, after becoming a field marshal, he was a ringleader in the plot to assassinate Hitler on July 20, 1944, and was tortured and hanged for it. The plot at the time of Munich, as disclosed by Halder, called for Witzleben to march on Berlin with a panzer division and arrest the Fuehrer. Hitler, lingering on at Berchtesgaden, did not arrive in the capital as soon as expected, but when he finally did come, the conspirators decided to go through with their plans immediately. Then, as Halder puts it: "The execution of the plan was about to begin when news came, as a complete surprise, of the imminent meeting with Chamberlain in Munich. The foundations for the planned action had therefore collapsed."

Thus we may speculate that, had Chamberlain not come to Munich, there would have been no abject surrender of Czechoslovakia, a deed which made World War II inevitable. There might not have been thereafter any Hitler to launch a war. On such tiny threads as this the fate of mankind sometimes hangs.

Munich is a rococo town of great charm, where the arts have flourished and living has been highly civilized, but over it in our time has hung a curse. It was here that Hitler rose from the gutter to create his barbaric nazism, of which Munich was always the center; and in this pleasant Bavarian city at the foothills of the Alps, the only two great surviving democracies of Western Europe came to Canossa and nearly sealed their doom.

I went to sleep, and when I awoke, the plane was on the ground and through the window I could see we were not in Vienna, as I had expected, but in Prague. Once a week, it seemed, the plane from Munich veered north to the Czech capital for a quick stop before flying on to Vienna, a practice that was discontinued on this particular American line a few months later.

No one got on or off. Red guards with tommy guns strapped to their shoulders glared at the plane. It was a sunny, warm summer day and the restaurant terrace was crowded, but the people looked glum and scarcely spoke to one another, as if they were afraid they might attract the attention of the guards. Often, in the days before the war, I had stopped to have a drink on this terrace, a place, then, of wonderful animation and gaiety.

The Czechoslovakia of that so recent time, like so much else that was good and decent in Europe, had been destroyed first by the savagery of the Nazi Germans and finally, after a brief resurrection which followed Allied victory, by the unspeakable tyranny of its own Communists, egged on by the commissars from Moscow. No country in modern times had suffered such an appalling tragedy, and when one heaped the blame on the Germans and then on the Communists one could not entirely forget that it was Chamberlain, abetted by Daladier of France, a gallant ally of Czechoslovakia, who at the Munich I had just passed through first sold the democratic little country down the river and thus made certain the agony which was to follow. No one, no country, had entirely clean hands in the crime.

Still, despite Munich and Hitler's attempt to destroy the nation that Thomas Masaryk had built, it seemed for a short time after the war that Czechoslovakia was destined to live again in the finest liberal and democratic traditions of its illustrious founder. Moreover, by the very course it took under the leadership of Eduard Benes it gave hope to many that here would be the proving-ground which would show that the East and the West could meet and that Communists and non-Communists could live together within a single nation in tolerable harmony.

As late as 1947 the correspondent of a magazine of which I was an editor had been assured by President Benes that "Czechoslovakia is perhaps the best example that there can be co-operation between Communists and non-Communists." And he had continued: "For more than ten centuries we have been part of Western civilization and culture. On

the other hand, the Soviet Union is our neighbor and ally.
We have a coalition government with the Communists as the
strongest party, and you have seen for yourself that Czechoslovakia has not betrayed a single principle, a single idea, of
true democracy. We have no censorship and no police state.
The West and East can live together. . . . The co-operation
between the two ideologies which we have brought about in
our state—it must and can succeed on the international
scene."[2]

Within a year the democracy of which the ailing president
spoke with such fervor would be destroyed by the very Communists he had trusted to "co-operate" and he himself would
be in his grave, a victim of a broken heart, following into
death his foreign minister, Jan Masaryk, son of the founder
of the Republic, who a month after the Communist *coup
d'état* had jumped, or been shoved, from his bathroom window in Czernin Palace.

I had no visa that would permit me to leave the plane, but
I admit I had no heart to go into Prague as I had done so
often in other days. A blood bath, I knew, was on. Trumped-
up charges of "treason" and "sabotage" were being brought
against some of the finest citizens of the land; and after ludicrous trials these men and women were being executed. I
would learn in the next few weeks that more people were
being put to death by the Communists in Czechoslovakia
than in all the other iron-curtain countries put together.

Here was an example, for all to see, of how the communism of our day, with its technique of terror and brutality
devised by Moscow and adminstered under its strict and ex-
pert guidance, could destroy a decent, democratic people
and all that they had built. Russia had been a backward,
feudal, misgoverned land in 1917 and no doubt needed a rev-

[2] *The Nine Lives of Europe*, by Leo Lania; New York, 1950.

olution. But Czechoslovakia, a progressive and cultured community, did not need one in 1948, nor did the large majority of its citizens desire one. It had been staged by a minority of ruthless men backed by the threat of the use of the Russian Red Army on the borders of Bohemia. Within a few weeks the Communists destroyed the freedoms, the institutions, the fine culture of a noble little land.

"The land is there, the men are there, but the nation has been lost."[3]

[3]*The New Europe,* by Stanislas Wyspianski.

2. GLIMPSE OF AN
INDESTRUCTIBLE CITY

"If Austria did not exist, it would be necessary to invent her."

—PALACKY.

IT TOOK ONLY a few days in Vienna to learn from Allied intelligence that the Russian Army was not going to march despite the golden opportunity offered by America's being tied down in Korea and by the fact that Western Europe lay utterly defenseless. The Allied generals admitted ruefully that the Red Army could occupy the rest of the Continent up to the Channel and the Atlantic Ocean within three or four weeks. But it made no move to do so.

There would be no third Big War, then, to mark the beginning of the second half of our century of conflict. The Kremlin, at the moment anyway, propitious as the moment seemed, did not want to risk it.[1]

In the meantime, reassured that this time I would not, as in the fateful summer of 1939, run into the beginning of a world war, I was free to roam through a great city I had long loved and to ponder the indestructibility of a civilized people who in a brief lifetime—thirty-two years, to be exact

[1] For several reasons: fear of America's atom bombs; realization that such a conflagration might, in the end, destroy the Soviet Union; and perhaps a feeling that it was doing quite well for the time being in advancing its interests by provoking local wars, such as that in Korea, in which it forced the United States to commit large numbers of troops in battle far from their base without Russia having to sacrifice the life of a single Red Army soldier.

—had seen one world after another come crumbling down upon them amid revolution, invasion, Nazi savagery, Fascist oppression, Russian occupation, starvation, bombing and bombardment, and who yet survived, their spirit unbroken, their dignity as human beings preserved, their lust for life after such hardship and sorrow still magnificently strong.

Often in the days between the wars I had climbed to the summit of one of the hills of the Wienerwald and there, above the forests and the yellow-green vineyards, gazed down upon the magic city. The Gothic spire of St. Stephen's Cathedral rose gracefully from the center of the landscape, but even it, a man-made object of exquisite beauty, seemed a puny thing against the background of an overpowering nature. Off to the east one could see the Danube, not blue but silver, trailing off like a ribbon toward the endless expanse of the Hungarian plain. Southward loomed the Alpine peaks, their snows pink in the afternoon sun. On a good day you could look north, beyond the Marchfeld plain, and see the dim outline of the Carpathians that stretched eastward toward the enigmatic Slavic world. Westward lay hills of beech trees, hills running unbroken to the turbulent Germanic world, across the border, that stretched to the Rhine and beyond.

Cradled in so much earthly beauty and looking out on all of Europe from its center, Vienna took naturally to the cultivation of the arts which reflected what was beautiful and what was genuinely European. Of these arts music was the greatest. Here beneath the Vienna Woods, Haydn, Mozart, Beethoven, Schubert, Johann Strauss, and many lesser men composed, having found in this place some of the deep wells of their inspiration.

As one looks down from the green hills, the sound of a special music which came, in the eyes of the outside world, to stand for Vienna seems to float across the air. It is the waltz.

It is more particularly the waltz of Johann Strauss, who expressed more typically than any other the mood of the capital in the last days of its greatness: its gaiety and laughter; its abandonment to the lighter pleasures of life, to wine and song and dance and beautiful, elegant, flirtatious, frivolous, fickle women, of whom Vienna was then—and still is—so full.

Over the centuries at this European crossroads of north and south, east and west, life took on a soft and dreamlike quality that was never experienced, I believe, in any other city. The style that expressed it was baroque, both in the arts and in the pattern of living. Baroque was the key to the character and the life of the Viennese.

In Vienna, at least, it made for a special and peculiar vision of life, at once spiritual and material. It managed through the harmony and fantasy of form to bring heaven and earth together, to abolish the boundary between life and the dream, between the real and the unreal, and to reconcile for man the antagonisms of pain and joy, death and life, nature and man, faith and knowledge. It was a dynamic thing, full of passion and sensualism, for it recognized the human longings and the deep creative urges as well as the frailties. Above all, it was a call to dream.

Its influence on the Viennese temperament before the old world collapsed was expressed by Hermann Bahr, one of Austria's most representative writers, toward the beginning of the century:

Life is postponed until after death. It begins there; here all is unreal: the serious business is on the other side. Here we only dream. Life itself is a dream. This whole baroque is a play on a word: the word "world" is reversed in meaning. Baroque has one more message: it cries to the penitent who has turned his back on the world: "You recognize that life in this world is but a dream. Now turn again, back to life, for it has no perils for you now that you know it to be a dream. Dream on, dream on — but never forget that you are but dreaming!"

They dreamed on in Vienna, the imperial capital of the sprawling Hapsburg Empire, passing the pleasant days and nights waltzing and wining, in light talk in the congenial coffeehouse, in listening to music and viewing the make-believe of the theater and opera and operetta, in flirting and making love. An empire had to be governed, to be sure, an army and a navy manned, communications maintained, business transacted, and labor done; but as little as possible of the mind and the energies was devoted to such things. The real life of the Viennese began with the fun and the pleasures and the dreams.

Even those born at the beginning of the century in Vienna must have taken for granted that this charming civilized world would go on forever and no doubt would become even more charming as time went on. As the bells rang in the twentieth century, the good citizens recalled that the Emperor Franz-Josef had been sitting on the throne for fifty-two years and seemed destined by God to go on sitting on it for many years to come.[2] Life in Vienna seemed to have even more permanency than elsewhere in the glittering, prosperous Western world.

Then on a summer day in 1914, the shots at Sarajevo rang out, felling the crown prince and propelling Europe into war. Four years later, on a chilly November day, the ancient house of Hapsburg came tumbling down, bringing with it the end of a golden epoch and of a way of life which neither this city nor any other was ever to see again. Within the ensuing three decades these lighthearted and attractive people would go through a damnation unique in our time.

[2]For sixteen more years. He died in 1916.

It fell to me, as a newspaper and radio correspondent from the other side of the world, to whom the brilliance of the Hapsburg Empire was only a dim memory of something read from a chapter in an Iowa college history textbook, to come to the city during its agony. Now, in the summer of 1950, as I poked among its ruins and walked its still proud streets, I kept thinking back on what had happened here and on how it had led to this day.

The bleak winter of 1918-1919 and the two years that followed were a horror and a nightmare. There was desolation, starvation, humiliation, and hopelessness.

The revolution which overthrew the Hapsburgs and established the Austrian Republic in the bitter hour of defeat was itself bloodless. And for a few days the Viennese, despite the shock of the lost war and the sudden dissolution of the Empire which they knew meant the end of their glory, clung to a thread of hope for the future.

Monarchy and absolutism were dead, the subject peoples —the Czechs, the Poles, the Yugoslavs, and the others—had gone their own free way, but in what was left of Austria, a miniature land of six and a half million people, the spirit of republicanism and democracy filled the new air. Something of the same spirit, the Austrians knew, had abruptly come to life in Germany, which also had been defeated and whose emperor, too, had been deposed. Since Vienna, a city of two million people, which had administered to the needs of a nation of fifty millions, could not possibly exist as the head of a tiny state, nor that state, which had prospered only as the leading unit in a large Danubian economic entity, be either self-supporting or really independent, the Austrians turned quickly to the only solution in sight.

They decided to join with their blood brethren in Germany. On November 12, 1918, the Provisional National Assembly in Vienna in proclaiming the Austrian Republic went on to affirm that "German Austria is a component part of the German Republic."

The Allied Supreme Council in Paris, flushed with victory, would have none of it. Republican Austria was heir to the hated Hapsburgs. It must take its humiliation and its punishment. It must not dissolve. It must live. Whereupon the Allies did their best to kill it—to starve it to death. It was bad enough, though understandable, that the former oppressed nationalities, the Czechs, Poles, Yugoslavs, and Rumanians, who had now founded new, independent states, should withhold the food and fuel they had formerly sent to Vienna. But now the Allies in Paris clamped down an iron blockade on Austria. No food or coal or oil was allowed through from anywhere. Austria, which, like Britain, only raised a fraction of its own food and had no coal or oil, quickly went to pieces. Starvation set in at once. Homes were without heat. Electricity and waterworks ceased to function. Trains, streetcars, and buses stopped running. In the provinces, where some food was available from the fields, and the forests could be cut down for fuel, Austrians managed to exist. But in Vienna two million people were being smothered to death.

They were saved in the end largely because of American concern and charity. The American Relief Committee, under Herbert Hoover, came in with food enough to prevent a catastrophe. But even two years after the war, hunger was still widespread. Coningsby Dawson, an American, found 340,-000 children—96 per cent of all the children left—pitifully undernourished in 1920. The sight of tens of thousands of them dying from hunger, he reported, "was a disgrace to civilization . . . the stench from the starveling bodies was nauseating."[3]

With starvation came inflation, which wiped out the economic foundation of the middle class, reducing to pauperism the old officials dependent on their pensions, the professors, the lawyers, the men of science, the artists and writers. And because there were neither raw materials nor markets, the workers in the industries, which had been geared to supplying a whole empire, had nothing to do. Unemployment soared. Bankruptcy flourished. Misery for nearly all became complete.

On August 7, 1922, after four years of desperate effort, the Austrian government threw in the sponge. It notified the Allies through Mr. Lloyd George that unless they were prepared to guarantee a loan for Austria, the Austrian government would no longer be able to function. In that case the Allies would be responsible for the country's complete collapse. Thus, as the Vienna government put it, it "laid in the hands of these powers the future fate of Austria."

The British prime minister, who earlier had fought and won his "khaki" election with the slogan "Hang the Kaiser," would not accept the responsibility. But when the conservative Austrian chancellor, Dr. Ignaz Seipel, a Catholic priest, turned to Italy and Germany for help, the Western Allies and Czechoslovakia finally bestirred themselves. They arranged through the League of Nations for a loan to Austria of $130,-000,000.

Among the conditions attached in the Geneva Protocols governing the loan was one which forced Austria to promise never to give up her sovereign independence. Once again the Allied powers insisted on a country which could not be self-supporting agreeing to continue to exist. This it could only

[3] *It Might Have Happened to You,* by Coningsby Dawson.

do through outside charity. It was almost as if the victors
were reiterating Palacky's dictum in the time of the Hapsburgs: "If Austria did not exist, it would be necessary to invent her."

Actually, as the years between the wars unfolded it became clear that Austria, small as it was, was a key to the
creaking structure of all Europe. It was the crash of a Vienna
bank, the Credit-Anstalt, in 1931, which started the chain of
events that brought about the financial and economic crisis
of Europe in the early thirties. It was the bloody destruction
of democracy by little Dollfuss, a clerico-fascist, on February 12, 1934 which paved the way for the Nazi invasion of
March 12, 1938. And it was this invasion which forced on the
Austrians the *Anschluss* they no longer wanted and which,
by giving Hitler Austria, emboldened him to embark upon
that course of further conquest which led to the Second
World War.

———————

To see democracy and the decencies of life it stood for
destroyed became a rather common, if heartbreaking, experience for those of us who covered middle Europe during the
years between the wars. I had seen the Fascists at work in
Italy, but somehow there the pompous tyranny of Mussolini
was leavened by his own weaknesses and by the inherent
good sense of the Italian people, who had known many
would-be oppressors and learned down the centuries how to
circumvent them in many ways. The destruction of democracy in Germany had been a crueler thing because of the
nature of the Germans, and in the thirties nazism came to
stand in our minds (we tended to overlook Russia) for the
evil force that seemed determined to wipe out human freedom not only in Germany but everywhere else in Europe

In our obsession—and I myself was for years possessed by

it—we forgot that in the most sensitive spot in Europe, in Austria, whose troubles so easily and quickly spread to the outer world, like ripples in a pond, democracy was murdered not by the Nazis but by a group of men who were rabidly anti-Nazi, who called themselves Christians, who said prayers in the Cathedral even as they prepared to turn their cannon on the people for whom the democratic way had become a deeply felt and cherished pattern of life.

Democracy and the freedoms it gave to men were wiped out in Austria by devout clerico-fascists. Their assault began in Vienna three months after Hitler came to power in Berlin and terminated in complete victory a short year later. Be it remembered that when Hitler's legions crossed into Austria in the spring of 1938 and overthrew Chancellor Schuschnigg and his clerical authoritarian regime, democracy had been dead there for five years.

To the credit of its defenders, it had not gone down, as it had in Italy and Germany, without a fight. The pious Chancellor Dollfuss had had to slay more than a thousand men, women, and children in their homes with his artillery before he and his henchmen could clamp on the people of Vienna their miserable brand of despotism.

In these days when we are struggling to preserve democracy in the face of the deadly threats from the Communists, it may be instructive to recall the technique by which the dictators of the Right destroyed democracy between the wars; for our memories are short, and many, obsessed with today's menace from the Left, seem to have forgotten.

Dollfuss' first move began with a trivial incident which struck most people, until they realized the seriousness of its consequences, as little more than a joke. On March 4, 1933 (the day Roosevelt was being inaugurated amid panic and fear in America), the Austrian parliament happened to take a vote on a routine government motion to discipline some railroad strikers. A socialist deputy noted for his weak bladder had to answer a call of nature. He asked a colleague to hand in his vote. The government was defeated 81 to 80. But Dollfuss, its head, refused to accept defeat. He claimed the absent member's vote was void. In protest, the president of the Chamber, the socialist Karl Renner, resigned his chair. The two conservative deputy presidents did likewise. Parliament found itself without a speaker. The wily, unscrupulous Dollfuss saw his chance. He insisted that parliament could not be called again since only its president or deputy presidents could legally convoke it and they had resigned. When the members tried to meet again, Dollfuss, who had long been a friend and admirer of Mussolini, ordered the police forcibly to prevent them from gathering.

They never met again.

Dollfuss, who next proceeded to promulgate an authoritarian constitution modeled on Mussolini's Fascist state, though he claimed his inspiration came from the *Quadragesimo Anno* papal encyclical of Pope Pius XI, was determined to stamp out the principal source of democracy in Austria. This was the Social Democrat Party, which polled 42 per cent of the votes in Austria and had an overwhelming majority in Vienna, whose municipality it ran to some extent on socialist lines. The party also dominated the free trade unions, which in any country are anathema to would-be tyrants.

Dr. Dollfuss' determination came to fruition in the blood bath he provoked on February 12, 1934. This provided one more ordeal, though not by any means the last, which the unfortunate Viennese would have to go through between the wars, and one could see that even in 1950, sixteen years later, its scar had not entirely healed despite all the other savagery that had been visited upon this city in the years that followed.

Since the fall of the Hapsburgs and the end of the First World War, Austria's internal politics had been dominated by a struggle between the "Reds" and the "Blacks." It was a battle between Vienna, which was socialist, anticlerical, democratic, and highly sophisticated, and the provinces, which were conservative, Catholic, authoritarian, and backward. The capital drew its main strength from the workers and the lower middle class, and from the intellectuals, many of whom were Jews. The hinterland's strength came from its peasants, mostly Alpine mountaineers, who had a deep suspicion of intellectuals and who were anti-Semitic. Beginning in the early twenties, both sides maintained private armies. The Social Democrats had their republican Schutzbund; the clericals had their fascist Heimwehr. All through the first years of the Republic there were clashes between the two, though the casualties were surprisingly small, reminding one of the "battles" between the Chinese warlords. But as the conservative forces under the clerical Christian Socialists came into control of the federal government after 1922, they tended more and more to lean on the power of the Heimwehr and to suppress the republican Schutzbund.

In consolidating his dictatorial power, Dollfuss found the armed force of the Heimwehr an increasingly useful instrument. He took its two leaders, the irresponsible Prince von Starhemberg and Major Fey, a hatched-faced, narrow-minded army officer, into his government. In February 1934, with a little prodding from Mussolini, the three of them decided their moment had come.

On February 10, they deprived the socialist mayor of Vienna of his authority over the city's police and assumed it themselves. On February 11, Fey, addressing a Heimwehr parade, said: "I have seen Dollfuss, and I can tell you that he is now our man. Tomorrow we start to clean up, and we shall make a full job of it."

The next day, February 12, 1934, they did. They wiped out the last vestiges of democracy in Austria with field artillery. In doing so in the name of one form of authoritarianism, they dug their own graves (Dollfuss would be murdered by a Nazi assassin within five months) and made inevitable the coming of another, and even sterner, authoritarianism from across the German border.

The story of the fascist Heimwehr *coup d'état* which Chancellor Dollfuss led that day has been too often recounted to bear repeating here.[4] Suffice it to say in this brief account of Vienna's tribulations that for four bitterly cold February days and nights a government force of 19,000 regular troops, police, and Heimwehr laid siege to the working-class districts of the city, blasting the laborers' model apartment houses with howitzers and killing more than a thousand men, women, and children and wounding three or four thousand more. Entrenched in public parks, in the gardens of their homes, and behind sand-bagged windows in their flats, the Social Democrat forces resisted desperately with a few rifles and machine guns. They, and later the Spaniards, were the only democratic people in Europe who went down fighting before the assault of fascism.

The people of Vienna found themselves deprived of all the political freedoms they had won by overthrowing the Hapsburgs. Indeed the tyranny of Dollfuss was much worse. During the last years of Emperor Franz-Josef there was at least some political suffrage, considerable freedom of speech, and a system of justice based on law. In the few sorry months

[4] See *Fallen Bastions,* by G. E. R. Gedye; London, 1939; and *Inside Europe,* by John Gunther; New York, 1936.

there were left for him to live, Dollfuss stamped them all out, and his successor, Kurt von Schuschnigg, who later was to suffer such personal indignities from the Nazis, kept them suppressed. The human spirit, as I was to see in the bleak years that followed, takes a lot of crushing before it is broken. The Viennese were not broken, but one heard few songs in that period, and the lightheartedness gave way to a sullenness such as the great city had never known.

Though Dollfuss and the clericals around him were too stupid to realize it until too late, their destruction of the Social Democrats played directly into the hands of the Nazis. Together the "Reds" and the "Blacks," with at least 80 per cent of the electorate behind them, could easily have squelched the Nazis. Had they combined to do so, burying for the moment their bitter enmity, as the socialists proposed, there would have been no Nazi invasion of Austria in 1938 and quite probably no Munich and therefore—we may speculate—no destruction of Czechoslovakia, and therefore no World War II.

The Austrian Nazis, whose spirits had risen with the fortunes of Hitler in Germany, only became seriously troublesome after the Fuehrer came to power in Berlin at the beginning of 1933. During the February 1934 slaughter of the socialists the Nazis stood aloof. But they and their German masters in Munich and Berlin understood better than the narrow-minded Austrian clerico-fascists that by destroying Social Democracy and the trade-union movement Dollfuss had removed the one popular, democratic force in Austria that stood in their way.

The bodies of those killed in the February massacre were hardly cold before the Nazis set to work. They began a reign of terror from one end of Austria to another. Railways, power stations, telephone cables, post offices, and the houses of

Dollfuss' supporters were bombed. Police, Heimwehr, and Catholic groups were ambushed and slain. German radio stations poured forth a ceaseless stream of propaganda toward Austria designed to incite the population to revolt. An Austrian Nazi legion, 50,000 strong, was drilled and armed in Germany and then deployed along the border, ready to march into Austria. In Munich the self-exiled Austrian Nazi leader Frauenfeld went on the air night after night inciting the Nazis in Vienna to murder Chancellor Dollfuss.

This deed was accomplished on the afternoon of July 25, 1934. Once again the citizens of Vienna lived through the terror of threatened civil war.

Fortunately it was short-lived because the Nazi *Putsch*, backed by Hitler and the might of the German Reich, failed of its main purpose: to overthrow the clerical government and replace it with a National Socialist regime. The plotters, disguised as police and regular army troops, succeeded in occupying the federal chancellery, and one of their number, Otto Planetta, a discharged army sergeant, shot Chancellor Dollfuss twice at a range of two feet, once in the armpit and once in the throat, and left him to bleed to death in an agony that lasted three hours.

Through a tragi-comedy of errors the conspirators failed to take advantage of the initial success of their *coup* and Dollfuss' followers, led by Dr. Kurt von Schuschnigg, quickly regained control. The 144 Nazis who had seized the chancellery, though promised safe conduct to the German frontier, were arrested and the thirteen ringleaders, including Planetta, were hanged.

When Hitler entered Vienna in triumph four years later, after his second plot to take Austria succeeded, he glorified the assassins and caused monuments to be erected in their sacred memory. But for the moment this further tragedy for

Austria could not be foretold. For the moment the long-suffering Viennese, recovering from the shock, knew only that they had personally witnessed the first example, in modern times at least, of the head of a great state personally plotting the murder of the head of another state. And they knew they had escaped becoming nazified by a hair's breadth.

But escaped for how long?

If few Americans had bothered to read the Nazi bible, *Mein Kampf*, by Adolf Hitler (the first English version had been published only the year before, in 1933, and contained less than half the original German text), the same could hardly be said of the Austrians, for whom the Fuehrer, after all, was a fellow countryman, born in the Austrian town of Braunau on the Inn on the border of Bavaria. They must have recalled that in the very first paragraph of his book Hitler had stated that for him the reunion of Austria with Germany, was "a task to be furthered with every means all our lives. German Austria must return to the great German motherland. . . . *Common blood belongs in a common Reich.*"

The italics were Hitler's own.

Dr. Kurt von Schuschnigg, scholarly, devout, politically aware, and only 37 when he succeeded Dollfuss as chancellor on that tense July evening, must have known those lines, but he does not seem to have pondered them nor a great deal of additional evidence of Hitler's real intentions. His one chance of saving Austria from nazism was to come to some sort of a *modus vivendi* with the 42 per cent of the population whom Dollfuss had suppressed five months before. But this he could not bring himself to do. He was too narrow-minded; his clerical background (he had been educated at the renowned Jesuit college of Stella Matutina in Vorarlberg) was too deep-rooted. He would treat with the

hated Social Democrats in the end and indeed implore their
support, but this would be eight days before Hitler marched
into Austria! By then it was much too late.

As it was, Schuschnigg in the nearly four years he was in
office, built up a personal autocracy much more complete
than that of Dollfuss. And though as a man he had a sense
of decency and a probity lacking in Hitler or Mussolini, this
did not restore political freedom to the Austrian people. In
later years, when he came to America to live, Schuschnigg
achieved a good deal of popularity among Americans, who
were naturally sympathetic to a man who had been so ill-
treated by Hitler. But an American might be pardoned for
remembering that Schuschnigg, in the days of his power, had
nothing but contempt for the democratic freedoms so dear
to Americans. As minister of justice under Dollfuss, he bore
the main responsibility for writing the clerico-fascist constitution of May 1934, which deprived the Austrian people of
their political liberty. I remember a proud boast he made of
it at the time:

"It deliberately turns its back on formal democratic principles and on universal, equal, and direct suffrage. It lays
weight on independent and strong leadership; hence the
providing of emergency powers and the right to alter laws
by decree."

Not content with crushing men's democratic rights and
privileges, Dr. von Schuschnigg went on to violate one of
the great concepts of Western civilization bequeathed to it
by the Romans: life under law. As he said, he reserved the
tyrant's right to alter laws by decree whenever it fitted his
purposes.

———————

Such was the state of human existence in the great city
when I returned to it in the fall of 1937 after a lengthy

interlude in Spain, France, and Nazi Germany. Vienna had a desolate, forlorn, dejected air. The workers, even those who had jobs—and tens of thousands were unemployed—were sullen, and they were ill-clad and looked ill-fed. Beggars in rags stretched out their palms at every street corner. The middle class did not seem to be much better off than the workers. It was evident at once that they were turning to the Nazis. Schuschnigg's drab authoritarianism was losing its following to Hitler's more colorful and dynamic kind. Vienna had a deadness, a gay hopelessness about it that numbed the soul.

One winter night—February 11, 1938—Chancellor von Schuschnigg slipped secretly out of the forlorn capital and sped by special train to Berchtesgaden. The next day, February 12, the fourth anniversary of the massacre of democracy in Vienna by the government of which he was a member, he was received by Hitler. In a session marked by what must have been the most insulting and outrageous outbursts and threats ever meted out by the head of one government to another (until Hitler gave similar treatment to President Hacha of Czechoslovakia on the eve of the Nazi invasion of that country) the Fuehrer pronounced Schuschnigg's doom and the end of an independent Austria.

The insults and the vilification aside, Hitler issued an ultimatum to the Austrian chancellor consisting of eleven demands. If they were not immediately accepted, the German Army, which he had secretly mobilized on the border, would invade Austria and crush it. The detailed demands need not concern us here. They included turning over the key Ministry of Interior, with its control of the police, to an Austrian Nazi, Dr. Seyss-Inquart, who turned out to be a quisling before Quisling; and the release of all imprisoned Nazis, including those implicated in the murder of Dollfuss. All in all, fulfil-

ment of Hitler's demands would have quickly brought
Austria under Nazi control, preparatory to its coming under
direct German control.

By evening Schuschnigg capitulated. He returned to
Vienna at 3 A.M. the next day, February 13, a broken man.

During the next four weeks he tried desperately to find
a way out—some way that would preserve Austria's independence. He appealed to his old friend Mussolini, who had
mobilized 200,000 Italian troops on the Brenner when the
Hitlerites assassinated Dollfuss in 1934, but the Duce now
was vague and not inclined to interfere. Schuschnigg turned
to the West, but France was going through one of its frequent
cabinet crises and at the crucial moment would not even
have a government. In London the blind and bungling
Chamberlain assured the Commons that he had no reason
to believe that the Berchtesgaden agreement endangered
Austria's independence. His faith in Hitler's word was still
immense.

Finally on March 4, eight days before the end, Schuschnigg turned in desperation to the Austrian Social Democrats
and former trade unionists for help to stem the inevitable.
Despite the hounding and the persecution to which they had
been subjected by Schuschnigg's government, they agreed to
come to his aid; for a Nazi dictatorship, they knew, would
be even worse than his. But it was too late. Hitler was already
determined to annex Austria.

Schuschnigg played one final card. On Wednesday, March
9, he took to the radio in Innsbruck and announced that on
the following Sunday there would be a plebiscite. "I must
know," he said, "whether the people of Austria want a free,
German, independent, social, Christian, and united Fatherland."

Hitler, driven to sudden fury at the very thought that his

detested opponent should employ a device which he himself had used (though dishonestly) to impress the outside world that his people were behind *him,* never gave the people of Austria the opportunity to decide whether they wanted to remain independent. He knew what their decision would be. Within forty-eight hours he had his goose-stepping armies marching into Austria. Schuschnigg yielded to German force without a struggle, because, as he said in his radio farewell— the most moving moment on the radio I have ever experienced—he was not prepared, "even in this terrible situation to shed German blood."

This terrible situation would lead shortly to the shedding of rivers of German blood and even greater rivers of non-German blood in a new German war; but Schuschnigg perhaps, in the terror of the moment, as his world crumbled down upon him, could not foresee this clearly.

Few Austrians foresaw what lay ahead of them. On the evening of March 11, when the Nazis took over the government and waited for Hitler's triumphant arrival, there was hysterical rejoicing in the Vienna streets such as I had never seen in Germany itself. It would be short-lived, I knew. There would soon be a rude awakening, even for the enthusiastic, deluded minority. Anyone who had lived in Berlin under Hitler could tell these people that. But for the moment they were in no mood to listen. They were riding, they thought, the wave of the future.

Indeed when I left the city the next morning on my way to London to do some uncensored broadcasts, I noticed that the swastika was flying atop the high spire of St. Stephen's Cathedral. The great bells were ringing in celebration—on the orders, someone said, of Cardinal Innitzer. The Cardinal-Archbishop, like others, would learn in time what the coming of Hitler meant. Before the year was up, in fact, his palace

across the street from the Cathedral would be sacked by
Nazi thugs and he himself would narrowly escape with his
life and, for a time, be held in "protective custody," as the
phrase went.

———————————

And so Austria, as Austria, passed for a moment out of
history, its very name suppressed by the revengeful Austrian
who now ruled iron-handed over the expanded Third Reich.
The ancient German word for Austria, "Oesterreich," was
abolished. Austria became the Ostmark and soon even that
name was dropped and Berlin administered the country by
Gaue (districts) which corresponded roughly to the historic
Austrian *Laender* such as Tyrol, Salzburg, Styria, and Carin-
thia. Vienna became just another city of the Reich, a provincial district administrative center, withering away.

Hitler had always hated the old Austria, and particularly
its capital, for not appreciating him when he went to Vienna
in his youth seeking, without success, a career in the arts.
Now his revenge was complete. He had wiped the very name
of his native land off the map and deprived its once glittering
capital of its last shred of glory and importance.

Seventeen months later he plunged the Austrians into his
war, and in time, Vienna, like most other cities of Hitler's
Reich, became the object of Allied bombing. It did not suffer
as badly as Berlin, but the destruction was considerable,
particularly in the old, historic inner city. The spring the war
approached its end the inhabitants spent most of their days
and nights quivering in the cellars. The bombs were bad
enough, but there was the "liberation" by the approaching
Russians to ponder too.

On the eve of the seventh anniversary of Hitler's annexa-
tion of Austria, March 12, 1945, Vienna was in flames from
one end to the other from the bombing. Building after build-

ing toppled over into the street. Buses and streetcars came to a halt. The great city seemed doomed. That afternoon a rumor began to spread. To the Viennese, it was too terrible to believe.

"The Opera has been hit!"

From all corners of the burning city the citizens converged on the Ring, unmindful that their own homes might be going up in flames or that they might get killed in the street from collapsing walls. All through that evening and through the next day and night thousands stood in anger and sorrow as the stately Opera House, which had received four direct hits from American bombs, burnt out. You could pulverize their homes and offices and the great state buildings, but to destroy this temple of music was a mortal blow.

The frightfulness was not yet over. Less than a month later, as the Red Army fought its way into the heart of the city, a retreating Nazi S.S. division deliberately turned its artillery on St. Stephen's Cathedral. It, too, in part, went up in flames.

In this April month of the war's last gasp, the hated Nazi Germans were finally gone but the Russians were there, and there was rape and looting that the Viennese will never forget nor forgive as long as they live.

The war, however, had come to an end and the irrepressible inhabitants of Vienna, though they were hungry and ragged and either completely homeless or without roofs over their heads, began to let their hopes rise again. At least, they thought, they would escape the shame and hardship of foreign military occupation which would be meted out to their German brethren. Had not the United States, Russia, and Great Britain solemnly sworn at a meeting of their foreign ministers in Moscow in the middle of the war that Austria would be "liberated from German domination" and that the Allies wished "to see re-established a free and independent Austria"?

The Austrians soon found to their sorrow that the Allies had no intention of keeping their word. Instead of being treated as a "liberated" nation, as promised at Moscow, Austria was militarily occupied by the four Allied powers in much the same manner as Germany. As long as the occupation continued, it was obvious that Austria could be neither free nor independent, though that was just what they had been specifically guaranteed in the Moscow Declaration of October 1943.

For a couple of years after the end of the war, the Viennese lived on the verge of starvation, as they had after the First World War, and during the winters they again shivered in their unheated dwellings, for there was no fuel. Despite aid from UNRRA, supplemented by extra grants from the United States and Great Britain, the U.N. at the end of 1947 found Austria to be one of the worst-fed nations in Europe.

Once more it was saved by American generosity, this time in the form of aid from E.R.P. From 1948 to 1950, E.R.P. furnished Austria 170 million dollars' worth of food, including more than a million tons of wheat and flour. Some 70 per cent of what Austrians ate came from America. Without this American aid, half of the Austrian people would have faced starvation—though I found few of them either in Vienna or in the provinces who realized this.

Between 1945 and 1950 America's gift to Austria amounted to nearly a billion dollars. Not only did we feed her but we revived her industry and agriculture. In the dry language of an official Austrian government report handed to me by a grateful official of the federal chancellery, American aid during the first two years of E.R.P. (1948-50) enabled Austria to increase "industrial production by 82.5 per cent; industrial productivity per employee by 51.7 per cent; exports (by volume) by 132 per cent; agricultural production (from 1948 to 1949) by 27.4 per cent; real national income by 13 per cent; real gross investments by 30 per cent; total consumption (and thus the general living standard) by 9.5 per cent.

By the spring of 1950, industrial production in Austria was 142 per cent of that of its last prewar year of independence in 1937.

That summer the Austrians relaxed. For the first time since long before the war there was plenty of food and it was good and it was cheap. My wife, who was Viennese, and I used to gather on an early evening for dinner on the broad terrace of the Kursalon on the edge of the lovely Stadtpark in the heart of the city. Despite the poverty and the broken lives from three decades of misery and terror the Viennese seemed, on the surface at least, to be more animated, to be fuller of their special lust for life, than at any time I had observed them—at least since the days of Dollfuss.

The wine from the vineyards on the nearby hills was mellowing and it made for high spirits and laughter. Whatever their woes—and we have seen in this chapter what some of them were—the good people seemed to be able to push them from their memories and to live for this pleasant and civilized moment over the food and wine. To be sure, those with whom we mingled on the raised terrace may have been relatively well off, for the price of a five-course meal with wine came to all of one dollar. But on the ground terrace below, where the citizens could gather at bare tables and buy only beer and wine to go with their homemade sandwiches, which they carefully unwrapped from old newspapers, the spirit was equally buoyant and gay.

As evening came and the lights went on, music began to fill the air. A symphony orchestra which had assembled without our noticing it in the creeper-covered bandstand facing the terrace slipped easily and gayly into a Strauss waltz. To me the Stadtpark had always been Johann Strauss' preserve. From where we sat I could just glimpse the whimsical little gilded statue of him which I had passed almost daily on the way to my office in bygone days. It showed him in a frock coat, violin in hand, leading an orchestra through what surely would have been one of his great waltzes—perhaps the one that was being played this moment on this summer evening of 1950. Strauss had died in time, in the last year of the old century, before catastrophe overcame the Vienna he immortalized. He had cast an enchanted light over the city on the Danube, added new color and substance to its dreams, and given it the last fine fairy tales it would ever know. Of him it did not seem banal to say that of all the artists who had lived here his spirit had most survived. Nothing that had happened here—wars, revolutions, suppression, hunger—had dimmed it.

The waltz, one felt, would go on here to the end of time, mingling in the blood and the rhythm of these people; and the haunting melodies of "The Blue Danube," "Tales from the Vienna Woods," "Wine, Women, and Song," and "Vienna Blood," all from Johann Strauss, would remain as much a part of the good life to the Viennese as love and bread and wine.

———————

Part of the time that summer I roamed about the city to see what had happened to the old places where much of my own life had been lived. Many of them, I found, were gone.

Like the Viennese, I had frequented the cafés, which were

unlike any others in the world. In Vienna life centered about them. The *Kaffeehaus* was not only a place to meet your friends but about the only spot in which you could transact business. It served a third purpose. It was a place where you could sit quietly at a table over an excellent cup of coffee and peruse the newspapers and periodicals of the Western world. Every café subscribed to scores of them from at least a dozen countries, including England, France, and the United States, and the waiter would bring you with your coffee, and thereafter every ten minutes with a fresh glass of water, whatever papers and magazines from whatever capital you wished. No people that I have ever known were such avid readers of newspapers and periodicals as the Viennese. Few of them could have afforded to subscribe to the dozens of publications they read daily or weekly. But in a café these came, neatly attached to a bamboo frame which kept them unrumpled (and prevented you from carrying them away) with the price of a cup of coffee.

In summer, and in the wonderful spring that came in April in Vienna, the cafés functioned outdoors, so to speak. At the end of the day or in the cool of the evening one could gather at a table on the broad terraces facing the wide boulevard of the Ring and watch the throng pass by.

Most of my favorite cafés, I found, had either been bombed out of existence or were out of bounds—that is, taken over by the Russians, who excluded the public from them. The Imperial Café, on the corner where the Ring sweeps into the Schwartzenbergplatz, which had been a hangout of writers, journalists, and Balkan spies, was a part of the Imperial Hotel, which was occupied by the Russians as was the Grand Hotel across the street. Red guards with fixed bayonets kept foreigners such as myself strictly away. The Herrenhof Café, where many artists and theater people used

to gather, had become a Russian army club. The Central
Café, where Leon Trotsky had plotted and played chess on
the eve of the First World War and where the psychoanalysts,
modernist architects, and champions of atonal music as well
as painters, poets, actors, and writers had met in my own
time, was a mass of wreckage.

The café which I had frequented most had been the
Louvre, where, until the Nazis came, the foreign correspondents hung out. Quite a few of them worked there, scribbling
their dispatches at one of the tables near the corner and sending a waiter to file them at the cable office nearby.

There at the Café Louvre, Robert Best of the United Press
had reigned supreme. In all the time he was in Vienna, from
1923 on, he virtually lived there. It never would have occurred to anyone to telephone or meet him anyplace else—
at any time of day or night. I knew him well over the years
and saw him frequently but I was never in his home or ever
had the faintest idea where it was. He must rarely have gone
to it except to sleep. The café was not only his office but his
real home.

A big, genial, somewhat portly fellow who never lost his
native Carolina accent whether he was speaking English or
German, Bob Best was well liked by the other correspondents, for whom he was never too busy to do a good turn. His
tragedy, it always seemed to me, sprang from the fact that
he never went back to his native land, even for a brief visit.
It was a tragedy that befell a few other correspondents too,
and in time they became a rather pitiful lot, their native
American roots up-yanked and no genuine new ones to replace them.

I suppose it is true to say that in Bob Best's case other
roots did replace the original American ones. And this led
to his ultimate end. Some time after the Nazis came to Austria

he got the Nazi bug, and when the war came and we got into it, he elected to stay behind to broadcast Hitler's propaganda against his own land. In going Nazi he also went violently anti-Semitic, which surprised his old colleagues, who knew that during most of his long stay in Vienna his closest friend had been a Jew and who could not recall Best ever having uttered a word against a Jew as a Jew.

When he went on the air in Berlin for Hitler, however, he tried to outdo his master in his ranting against the Jews. His attempt to get an American audience for his short-wave broadcasts from Berlin during the war was pitiful; he had been away too long to remember what his fellow Americans were like.

After the war, Best was picked up by the American authorities in Austria, tried in Boston for high treason, convicted by a jury there, and sentenced to life imprisonment. I saw him at his trial, but he was a mere shell of the very decent man we had all liked in the days in Vienna which now seem, for so many reasons, so far off.

One warm afternoon my wife and I sauntered over to the Café Louvre. We had asked some of the new generation of foreign correspondents what had happened to it but they did not know. We came to the familiar corner but the Louvre was gone. In its place was a savings bank. The building had been bombed, someone said, and recently rebuilt. The bank needed the space; there were too many cafés anyway.

Too many cafés in Vienna! That is what the Nazis had said when they came in 1938. They had had scant sympathy for the civilized life that centered about the Vienna cafés —it could not be easily regimented—and had forced scores of them to close. During the war many more were bombed out.

And now, in 1950, the one thousand two hundred coffee-houses which had survived were threatened with extinction.

The reason was horribly prosaic. The price of coffee was up 700 per cent compared to 1937; and other costs—rent, heat, food, newspapers—had risen astronomically too. The owners protested they could not go on unless the government came to their aid with tax relief and cheap loans.

Some people said the Vienna cafés, like so many other venerable institutions that had flourished in the old imperial city, were bound to pass from the scene. But I could not believe it. Some way would be found, I knew, to preserve them. The Viennese in the last thirty-two turbulent years had been forced to give up a great deal that made the kind of life they wanted worth living. But they could not go on without their coffeehouses.

And without their music. On our way back from where the Café Louvre had been we stopped at the corner of the Kaertnerstrasse and the Ring to watch the workers restoring the bombed-out Opera House. They were working like beavers, as if the very existence of the city depended upon their labors. Indeed to them, and to their fellow Viennese, it did. They themselves could live awhile longer in their patched-up dwellings; but the beloved center of music must be made whole again immediately.

There was much to live for here after all, then, I began to see, despite the vicissitudes through which these people had gone in our time. They might not have—they didn't— most of the things that many of us in America kidded ourselves into believing made life a more pleasant experience: motorcars, refrigerators, washing machines, air-conditioners, television sets, and a host of other gadgets. They might not have—they didn't—our feeling of security, for an "independent" Austria would always be bankrupt and, as it was now, the danger of the Russians taking over the moment a new war came was ever present in their minds and naturally made them uneasy. Personal experience with the partial Soviet occupation had destroyed whatever illusions about the Russians they may have had. They knew that the Muscovites, if they once got complete control, might quickly succeed in doing what the Turks, the Nazis, the Fascists, and, at times, the Hapsburg tyrants had failed to accomplish—to destroy them entirely.

As we have seen, it takes a lot to destroy human beings. The Viennese had survived three decades of horror. As they moved into the last half of this tragic twentieth century they still managed to make life livable. The Catholic Christian Socialists had shed their infantile fascism and now, as the People's Party, pursued a policy of democratic compromise which, had it been adhered to two decades before, would have spared Austria much of its misery. They shared what political rule the Allied occupation left them with the Social Democrats, who had risen from the ashes Phoenix-like. Dollfuss, Schuschnigg, and Hitler had not been able to exterminate them after all.

The indestructible spirit of Vienna was rising. In fact, the people felt themselves rather well off. Once again they had domestic political peace and democracy, the freedom to think and say and write what they pleased; and they had enough to eat, and music again and wine. In the beautiful city so beloved by them and in the lovely hills above the Danube they seemed to find a fair measure of happiness.

Vienna that year was a good place in which to reflect on the freedom of the good people who lived to the east. After the First World War the subject peoples of the Hapsburgs— the Czechs and Slovaks, the Croats and Slovenes, the Poles and several million Rumanians had been freed. Hungary had achieved absolute independence. But, except for the Czechs, the aspirations of these Eastern Europeans for political freedom had not been realized.

Between the wars I had reported on these countries from my headquarters in Vienna and recounted the tyranny and the cruelty in each. But American readers were not interested.

Now, after the Second World War, these peoples had been forced to exchange one form of tyranny for another. The present form, no doubt, was worse—but perhaps not much worse, at least for the masses. I had been somewhat puzzled therefore to see how horrified our press and some of our congressmen were at the present enslavement of the satellite peoples inasmuch as we Americans had been uninterested in their freedom when it was being denied by Horthy in Hungary, King Alexander in Yugoslavia, King Carol in Rumania, and the "colonels" in Poland.

I would have thought that Americans were opposed to brutal tyranny. Period. Did it make a difference whether it was exercised by the Right or the Left? Apparently it did, for were there not some in America who seemed to be against tyranny only when it was red, and who in the same breath could denounce Stalin while praising Franco? Perhaps I was duly naïve; perhaps there were varying degrees of oppression that should be noted and even appreciated. But in my own experience the white terror and the brown and even the black had robbed men of their freedom and degraded them as human beings, and I did not like them any better than the red terror.

I did not journey into these eastern countries that summer, lacking the necessary visas, for one thing, and not feeling in the mood to risk arrest and imprisonment in case the Communists needed a hostage—the first time in twenty-five years of journalism that such a thought had ever clouded my mind.

But one did not have to travel to them to realize the tragedy of their citizens. It was not, except in Czechoslovakia, a new tragedy, as so many Americans believed, but a very old and continuing one in which the freedom these people had so long sought still eluded them and which, no doubt, under the Communists seemed farther away than ever.

3. THE WANING STAR
OF FRANCE

Star crucified — by traitors sold,
Star panting o'er a land of death, heroic land,
Strange, passionate, mocking, frivolous land.
Miserable! yet for thy errors, vanities, sins,
I will not now rebuke thee.
Thy unexampled woes and pangs have quell'd them all,
And left thee sacred.
                    —WALT WHITMAN, O Star of France.

No one who came back to Paris in 1940 during the June
days that would have seemed so lovely in any previous year
can ever forget the shattering spectacle of the fall of France.
It was not so much that she had been defeated in battle by
Germany, the hereditary enemy, and been occupied by the
hated foe. That had happened before.

What overwhelmed an American who loved this country
and had even known it in one of its moments of power and
glory, after the victorious First World War, was that it could
fall so low from so high so soon. For fifteen years I had been
watching and chronicling the decay of the western lands of
Europe. One could perceive the rotting away of France. Its
sickness—the corruption, the confusion, the class divisions
and antagonisms—was there for all but the most casual Yankee tourist to see. But I was not prepared to see a nation
which had dominated the continent of a Europe that was

59

still supreme in the world when I first came to Paris in 1925, suffer so quickly the most humiliating and catastrophic downfall in her long and, until now, proud history.

Dazed, I scratched into my diary that first evening of my return, June 17, 1940, as the German tanks rumbled past below my hotel window on their way south to crush the retreating remains of the French Army (the traitorous Pétain would ask for an armistice the next day): "What we're seeing here is the complete breakdown of French society—a collapse of the Army, of government, of the morale of the people. It is almost too tremendous to believe."

For a good many years it was too tremendous for me to comprehend. I believed it because I had seen it with my own eyes. But I kept asking: How did it come about? And why?

The year France was liberated from the Germans, 1944, and the next year, 1945, when the war was won, and again in 1948, when the French Communists made their bid for power with strikes and sabotage, I returned to Paris in search of answers. And now, in the summer of my midcentury journey, I was back in the city again, still seeking for light. It was August and hot, and Paris, as always at this time of year, was half deserted. There was time and opportunity to consult a few old friends, delve into what records there were, and refresh one's memory on the spot.

I was surprised to find that the French themselves could furnish little help. The subject—the quick, disastrous military defeat, and worse: the degradation of the collaboration in Vichy and Paris with the Nazi Germans on the part of an astonishingly large number of hitherto eminent Frenchmen—seemed to be too painful to go into. A few participants in the drama had, it is true, rushed out with books exonerating themselves; but these apologies were of little value in my own search for as much of the truth as one man in these times could find.

Even the scholars of France were avoiding the subject. Lack of funds for the necessary research, said some. There had not been time enough to acquire the necessary detachment and objectivity, said others. Even if you found the truth and published it the consequences might be harmful, still others explained. Many collaborators and traitors, they said, were back in power. They might ruin a poor professor. It was safer, most agreed, to stick to subjects such as the great Revolution of 1789 or the reign of Louis XIV and leave the unpleasant contemporary era to historians yet unborn.

Saul K. Padover, Dean of the School of Politics, New School for Social Research, who was in Paris the year before, gathering material for the Hoover Institute's study, *The World Revolution of Our Time*, tells of his experience in trying to collect simple data on the French generals from 1900 to 1940. Since France has no *Who's Who*, it was necessary to do some digging in the archives. After some negotiations and careful explanation of the Institute's project, he was refused permission to use one of the Paris archives by an eminent French general, who wrote him:

This project is not only pretentious but almost inconceivable for us; it shows a total ignorance of military problems not only in regard to France but also in general . . . That [project] is a typical American idea. The United States is a young country, for which the military problem is relatively recent. From the point of view of combined historical and statistical research, the United States could start at a point zero . . . But we, in France, cannot go back to the origins of our army, even to please our best American friends. We have a very heavy military past, let us not forget it. France was once the most important and the most mighty land force in Europe, which is no longer the case today . . . It would be much more important to study, for example, the reasons for the rivalry between the cavalry and the other services . . . A scientific interpretation [of the statistical material asked for] is not merely a danger but a heresy, the more so since it would involve interpretation by men who are uninformed about and foreign to our Western military conception. It is an extremely interesting project that you propose, but one that is extremely dangerous.[1]

The disintegration of the French Army in the May and June days of 1940 was an important part of the story of France's fall, and though I am not a military man I am sure that one can scarcely find the reasons for it by delving, as the general suggests, into the ancient rivalry of the cavalry with the infantry and artillery.

The National Assembly made what at first seemed a promising effort to get to the bottom of the reason for France's disaster. On August 29, 1946, it voted unanimously to establish a committee composed of sixty members of the Assembly and eighteen representatives of the Resistance to look into what it called "the ensemble of political, economic, diplomatic, and military events which, from 1933 to 1945, preceded, accompanied, and followed the armistice in order to determine the responsibilitites incurred and to propose, if necessary, political and judicial sanctions."

The committee opened its investigation on February 11, 1947, but has not yet reported its findings, if any, to the Assembly.

The more I brooded on it that summer of my journey, the more I realized that the story of France's fall from greatness could not be told merely in terms of documented events and statistics or by recounting the failings of the miserable in-

[1]"France in Defeat: Causes and Consequences," by Saul K. Padover; *World Politics*, April 1950.

dividuals who for brief intervals seemed to hold the destiny of the nation in their hands. These facts were of extreme importance, it is true, and I shall duly note some of them, incredible though they may sound. But there were in this French tragedy, I saw, many imponderables which it would be difficult for an American reporter to assess. For in the last analysis, it seems to me, the sickness of our present Western civilization infected the French more deeply than most of the other democratic people of the Occident, weakening their spirit and their morale and their morals so that in the end the virtues which had made them great were no longer strong enough to enable them to withstand the evil pressures which confronted them in the turbulent and corrupt time between the world wars.

That summer of 1940, with France under the heel of the barbarian Nazi, when conservative middle-class Frenchmen sighed and said to me: "Well, better Hitler than Blum!" (Blum, a Socialist, a patriot, and a Jew, had been premier of the Popular Front government), and when the Communists, who had captured the fanatical allegiance of the majority of the organized workers, justified to me their opposition to defending France against the Nazi invasion (because that was what Moscow had ordered in line with Stalin's pact with Hitler of August 1939), I began to comprehend the depths of confusion and treachery to which the French, as a people, had fallen.

It would have been better, it seemed to me, for France to have lain prostrate for a time under the Prussian jackboot as Poland had (there were no Pétains or Lavals in Poland after it fell), until her people had recovered their senses and their pride. But to the horror of their friends and admirers too many Frenchmen sprang to their knees, in Vichy and in Paris, and remained on their knees before the once hated

Germans until the Allied liberation four years later showed them that France was not destined, as they had not minded believing, to be a slave state in the service of Hitler's monstrous New Order.

How, in God's name, one asked, had the French come to this degrading state in so short a time?

So far as I could see, there had been little inkling of it when I first came to work in Paris at the end of the first quarter of this century. France then was supreme upon the Continent. She alone in Europe had a great army, and her navy was second only to Great Britain's. French diplomacy and French finance had wielded the new nations of Eastern Europe—Poland, Czechoslovakia, Yugoslavia, and Rumania —into potentially powerful friends and allies who would be of great value should Germany ever rise again to challenge French hegemony. But Germany lay prostrate, or so one thought, and the Germans never tired of saying so themselves. Italy was bogged down with Mussolini. Russia was just beginning to get back on its feet after the savage blows which had almost destroyed it as a nation: the lost war, the two revolutions, the civil war, and the impact of the Bolshevik regime. Even Great Britain, which had emerged victorious with France from the German war, was beginning, by 1925, to suffer economic stagnation, with its curse of mass unemployment. And a more acute observer than I might have detected even then in London signs of stagnation in British political thinking, especially in foreign affairs, which so soon would lead the nation to the brink of disaster.

But France, with the finest balanced economy of any nation in Europe, seemed prosperous even though the franc was beginning to fall and the government budgets were becoming more unbalanced than usual. French diplomacy was vigorous and far-sighted, the Quai d'Orsay never losing sight of the cardinal fact, as did the British Foreign Office in those days, that if the peace of Europe was to be maintained, Germany would have to be kept within reasonable bounds.

Paris was the intellectual and art center of Europe and—as most Americans who migrated to it thought—of the world. No Yankee who dwelt on the banks of the Seine in those days will ever forget the magic and light of the great city nor the wonderful freedom enjoyed by everyone, regardless of race, creed, party, or economic status, and whether French or foreign, to say and think and do what he pleased. Men were wonderfully free, and they were free of fear.

If ever a great nation seemed destined to continue on its glorious and civilized course for centuries to come, France was it.

And yet, even then there were signs of approaching catastrophe that one can only appreciate today—with the benefit of hindsight. That summer of my journey in the fourth year of the Fourth Republic, I mulled over them in my own mind and in many heart-to-heart talks with my French friends in Paris.

The troubles of France, it became evident, went back to the French Revolution of 1789, which had given birth to the nation we came to know. There the deep fissure developed which has divided France to this day. It was an unfinished revolution in that the old order was never really liquidated or even converted, and therefore survived to combat the republican idea right up to Hitler's entry into Paris, which it welcomed and which brought the Third Republic to an end.

For a hundred and fifty years two Frances which lost no love on each other, as Pertinax has said,[2] lived side by side. They never fused. Under the leadership, in the last century,

---

[2] *The Grave-Diggers of France,* by Pertinax; New York, 1944.

of kings, the Church, Napoleon III, and even of a general or two on horseback, the powerful minority which had not been destroyed in the blood bath of the 1789 Revolution constantly opposed the conception of the Republic, taking a strong stand against parliamentary democracy, the separation of Church and State, and social and economic reforms.

Often it was eminently if briefly successful. Thanks to the Congress of Vienna, which liquidated Napoleon, it enjoyed the restoration of the Bourbon monarchy under Louis XVIII. But the forces released by the Revolution, the bourgeoisie and the peasantry, were strong too, and when Louis' brother and successor, Charles X, tried to strengthen the monarchy's absolutism he was deposed in the "bloodless" revolution of 1830. This did not mean that the rising middle classes necessarily wanted a republic. They were willing to continue with a monarchy if it granted them a written constitution which would protect and augment their rights. Thus Charles' cousin Louis-Philippe was given the throne, and recognizing somewhat the spirit of the times, became the "bourgeois king," making of France a paradise for a middle class which, as later in America, was to worship the making of money and make a lot of it for itself. Much of the corruption in government and business which was to render France so weak on the eve of Hitler's attack stems from the reign of Louis-Philippe, which came to an end in 1848 when a new revolutionary tide swept through the continent of Europe and brought down the house of Bourbon-Orleans for good.

The ensuing Second Republic lasted but four years. Born amidst the revolutionary enthusiasm of 1848 which demanded not only universal suffrage (the property-owning middle and upper classes had alone enjoyed the vote) but, as de Toqueville reminded Frenchmen, a more equitable distribution of wealth and goods, the Republic floundered in a rising fear which has haunted the solid bourgeoisie of the Western nations ever since: fear of social disorder and communism. (The Second Republic had scared the daylights out of most Frenchmen by proposing—though unsuccessfully—the adoption of the red flag as its emblem.)

As in the case of Italy and Germany in our own time (and as might happen in America if we lost our heads), this fear of the Reds in France led quickly and directly to a dictatorship, that of Louis-Napoleon Bonaparte, who, at first elected president of the Republic, became dictator in the *coup d'état* of December 1851. It was on the ruins of his disastrous nineteen years of absolutism, culminating in the invasion and defeat by the Prussians in 1870-71 that the French built once more a republic, the Third, which restored France to greatness and gave her the strength to fight (and with powerful allies) to win the First World War.

Perhaps the Third Republic was ill-fated from the first. It had a freak birth. Its constitution was actually devised for a monarchy. Two-thirds of the members of the National Assembly, all freely elected, were monarchists. And it was the Assembly which was to choose the new form of government. After a bitter four-year struggle in which the agreed candidate for the throne, the Count de Chambord, unexpectedly weakened the monarchist cause by insisting on the restoration of the *fleurs-de-lis* flag of the old regime, the Assembly finally, in 1875, decided on a republic by a majority of one vote, 353 to 352. "The Republic divided us least," remarked Thiers, one of its principal architects, thus noting its essential negative and compromising character.

But that was not the only drawback. The birth of the Third Republic left France with its old divisions. On the one side was the democratic, republican Left, drawing its spiritual support from the *mystique* of the 1789 Revolution, and its popular support from the little tradesmen, the peasants, and the workers. On the other side was the authoritarian Right which looked backward with nostalgia to the *ancien régime,* still yearned for a monarchy, and drew its strength from the upper classes, the Church, the Army, big business, and high finance. Both sides were evenly matched at the polls and both were uncompromising.

It was this situation which led to the instability of the Third Republic, the constant shifting from Left to Right and back to Left, as the terms were understood in those days, and brought about the numerous coalitions and blocs, the frequent fall of cabinets, and a political atmosphere so charged with uncertainty that foreign observers came to refer to the republican regime as the "fickle" Third Republic. From its birth in 1875 until 1920, the Republic had fifty-nine different ministries; and after the First World War the changes came even more rapidly—from 1920 to 1939, there were forty-one French cabinets. At more than one moment of international crisis, such as in March 1938, when Hitler annexed Austria, France was temporarily without any government at all.

Looking back now, one can see how Renan, one of France's most renowned writers and intellectuals, could exclaim in 1888 to a youth who sought his counsel: "Young man, France is dying, do not trouble her agony."

She was dying, it seemed to me the longer I pondered it, largely because of what might be called her unfinished revolutions. The Revolution of 1789, as Padover[3] noted, failed to solve the social problem; the industrial revolution, by remaining uncompleted, failed to solve the economic problem; and the revolution which brought forth the Third

[3]France: *Setting or Rising Star?*, by Saul K. Padover; New York, 1950.

Republic failed, as we have seen, to solve the political problem.

There was a fourth failure which greatly weakened France: the decline of her population in relation to the other countries of Europe, especially Germany. As recently as the time of Napoleon, France was the most populous country in Europe outside of Russia. There were 25 million Frenchmen then, as compared to half that number of Englishmen and 5 million Americans. But about 1875 the French population became stationary at just under 40 million. The other peoples of Europe, however, continued to increase. Taking the whole nineteenth century, in which the French population increased by only 12 million, or 44 per cent, that of England trebled (a rise of 26 million) while the increase in Germany was 32 million, and in Russia 70 million.

The failure of the French birthrate to keep up with that of other nations was disastrous enough. (At the outbreak of the Franco-Prussian War in 1870, the French of military age equaled the Germans in numbers, but in 1914 the Germans had an advantage of 7 millions to 4 millions, and in 1939-40 the Germans had more than twice as many men.) But what doomed France was that in the First World War she lost not only the flower of her youth (as did England and Germany) but a large percentage of it. There were 1,320,000 men killed, and 57 per cent of them were under 31 years old. Moreover 700,000 Frenchmen were permanently maimed in the war. Such losses out of a male population of only 20 millions were not only in themselves a mortal blow but, because they concerned men who, had they lived, would normally have fathered children, further reduced the population drastically. The French indeed estimate that the deficit in births in the war years equaled the number of men killed. It was little wonder that at the outset of the Second World War,

France had fewer men of military age than it had in 1914. Germany, as we have seen, had many more.

World War II dealt a further blow to France's population. Fortunately the number killed in battle was much less than in the first war. Some 92,000 Frenchmen were slaughtered in the 1939-40 campaigns, and 58,000 in the war of liberation from 1940 to 1945. The French Resistance lost 20,000 killed, another 30,000 were executed by the Nazi barbarians, 60,000 civilians lost their lives in the bombings, and 280,000 prisoners, deportees, and forced laborers died outside of France. But the Germans kept nearly 2 million Frenchmen (one-third of those between the ages of 18 and 50) as prisoners of war in Germany for five years, and another half-million as slave laborers. They could not reproduce in those years, and the French birthrate as a result suffered appallingly.

There was an even worse consequence of this forced absence in Germany of so great a proportion of France's manhood. Coupled with the Nazi occupation of the country and the defection to Hitler and Pétain and Laval of numerous Frenchmen of the upper and middle classes, it led to a sickening degeneration in the morale and the morals of the French people. The family, the backbone of the nation, disintegrated with its menfolk absent year after weary year. In order to thwart the conqueror and at the same time eke out an existence, the French at home resorted to every form of trickery they could conceive. Thus the peasants developed a fine art of withholding food from the public markets, and the tradesmen and consumers in the cities and towns collaborated with each other and with the peasants to set up widespread black markets. It was considered patriotic to do so; it upset the German arrangements for milking the French economy dry; it kept food and goods from being siphoned off to the Reich. And it enabled Frenchmen to live.

The trouble was that after the Germans had been driven from the land in 1944, what had been a patriotic (and for a few a profitable) undertaking became a settled practice. The French could not rid themselves of the "black market" habit and its necessarily shady dealings. And the disrespect for authority which had been a fine thing under the Germans persisted after the French began governing themselves again. For a short time, to be sure, from the liberation in the summer of 1944 through 1945, the splendid fervor of the Resistance, with its spirit of self-sacrifice and its passion for French unity regardless of class or party, appeared to be sweeping France clean, uplifting the morale of the people and preparing them for a fresh and encouraging start in a nation reborn. But its surge was short-lived. The fissure dating from the Revolution reappeared and began to widen again. The French reverted to their old divided ways. The workers, cheated by high prices and low wages, went over, in the main, to communism, whose policies were laid down by the Soviet government. The middle class once more took fright of the future.

For a century this class, which had made the French Revolution and formed the backbone of the nation, had been slowly declining—in strength and in wisdom. It had once been, as even the Socialist Léon Blum[4] admitted, "upright and honest, patient and prudent, modest and decent, thrifty and reasonable." But its greed for money and property, its obsession with clinging to them, its passion for evading taxes, its lack of civic-mindedness, and its stubborn refusal to adjust itself to the changing times, especially to the consequences of the industrial revolution with its need for capital investment and the improvement of the lot of the growing

[4] *For All Mankind*, by Léon Blum; New York, 1946.

proletariat, gradually undermined it. "For more than a century," Blum concluded, "everything that has happened in
France suggests that the bourgeoisie has been using up its
sap." By 1940, when I returned to Paris, it seemed to me that
the sap had run completely dry. The demoralization of the
middle class was a fearful thing to see as bankers, tradesmen,
and businessmen turned desperately to the senile old Marshal Pétain, the sinister Laval, and even to Hitler, to save
what could be saved of their bankrolls and their worldly
possessions.

They had prospered mightily for generations. A cabinet
minister under the "bourgeois king," Louis-Philippe had
launched the slogan: *"Enrichissez-vous!"* and that was exactly what the good burghers had done. As fortunes, great
or modest, were made, the desire grew to preserve or to increase them, to avoid any risk that might jeopardize them,
to cheat the government out of taxes that might diminish
them, and to put down social disorder which even faintly
threatened the possession of them.

Thus it came about in the revolution of 1848, and in 1851
with Louis-Napoleon, and in 1940 with Pétain, that the
middle-class Frenchman, fearful for his possessions, would
not shrink from turning to a dictator to protect his pocket-
book. Nor, in his blindness, did he seem to learn any lessons
from these disastrous experiences. I thought I detected during my midcentury journey through France the return of the
old yearning in the men of means for still another dictator—
in this case General de Gaulle—to protect their lucre from
the dire threats of "Reds."

The old saying that a Frenchman will die for his country
but won't pay for it was unfortunately all too often true. In
no other modern nation of the West has there been such a
scandalous evasion of taxes. Just as the black-market habit

continued after the Nazis had departed, so the aversion of the middle classes to paying the king's taxes continued after the kings were no more. The dream of every Frenchman, as Charles Péguy noted, was to avoid paying taxes.

For two decades prior to the First World War the conservative classes in France blocked in parliament the imposition of the income tax. One of France's most distinguished economists, Paul Leroy-Beaulieu, predicted in 1907 that "a tax of this kind would poison the whole life of a democracy; it would spread defiance everywhere, cause capital to flee . . . it would be the onset of a struggle to the death between the treasury and the taxpayers. . . ."

A small income tax was finally imposed midway through the 1914-1918 war. The "struggle to the death" did not go so far as predicted. It ended in an easy victory of the middle-class taxpayer over the Treasury. He simply got around paying his rightful share of the burden. Salaried employees and wage earners were not so fortunate. The State could check their income at its source and did. It made them pay to the full. But it was common knowledge that the peasants, the tradesmen, and the businessmen went so far as to falsify their books in order to cheat on their taxes. As one Parisian explained the situation to me that year of my journey, many a proprietor kept three sets of books: the first to defraud the tax collector; the second (somewhat more honest) to deceive his creditors and investors; the third (completely honest) to show himself how much money he had really made. My friend, of course, was exaggerating, though not, I suspect, by so very much. The farmer not only avoided full taxation by refusing to keep books (there was no law compelling him to) but benefited by a ridiculously low tax rate in the first place. It was based on an assessment of his land made under Napoleon! It was an extremely low assessment at the time, and a century and a half later, when land values had increased many times, it was absurdly low. In some fertile districts it came to a few cents per person per year.[5]

If the French bourgeoisie and peasantry refused to pay their share of the taxes, how could the French state obtain the revenues needed? The answer is it did not obtain them. Even in 1914, on the eve of the war, revenue amounted to only 40 per cent of the total state expenditure; in 1918, at the war's end, it came to only 12 per cent.

Among the *unfinished* revolutions which, by remaining unfinished, contributed to France's decline was the industrial revolution. The French never completed it, as did the Germans, the British, and the Americans. From the very beginning the two classes which had made the great political and social revolution of 1789 looked upon the coming of the machine age with great suspicion and even hostility. They contrived not only to deprive industry of the capital it needed to keep pace with that of other Western countries but to keep labor in such a state of wretched poverty that it constantly rebelled against its lot. Instead of investing their savings in new business enterprises or at least putting them in the banks, where they could be siphoned off for investment, the tradesmen and the farmers preferred to keep their surplus cash in stockings hidden under the mattress. Even in our own times, between the wars, the French put into industry only about a quarter of the capital the British put into theirs. Today in all of France there are only 55,000 machine tools compared to 2,000,000 in Great Britain. Horsepower of machinery per head in France is a third of Britain's, a fifth of ours.

Smallness and even pettiness of outlook prevailed in

[5]*The State of Europe*, by Howard K. Smith; New York, 1949.

France. It was the paradise of the small merchant, the small manufacturer, the small farmer. They dominated French economics as they did politics. They instinctively recoiled from the technique of mass production which was being so successfully developed in the United States, in Great Britain, in Germany, and often used their power to hamper the growth of big business.

In many ways, of course, their outlook had its advantages. Certainly it was a civilized view in a world that was rapidly making men the slaves of machines and profits. The French prided themselves on the skill of individual craftsmen. Quality of the product, not quantity, was the thing. Dislike of conformity, horror of regimentation, were deeply rooted in these individualistic, creative, artistic people. The modern corporation, which enabled industry to expand at a breathless pace in Britain and America, was too cold and impersonal to suit a Frenchman. At the end of 1939 there were only 43,000 corporations in all of France compared to a half million in America.

The closely knit family was the proper unit to conduct a business enterprise, in the opinion of the French. What if it was woefully inefficient and made but a modest profit? It gave honor and reputation to the family and enabled its members to live decently well, free from the fears, the frenzies, the worries, the instabilities of the go-getters in the teeming business world of more "advanced" lands. The ulcered, nerve-wracked Madison Avenue radio or advertising executive would have seemed a ludicrous and barbarous creature to the steady head of a French family enterprise.

Thus it was that even as late as 1931, 64 per cent of the registered industrial establishments in France had no paid employees at all. Services and labor were supplied exclusively by the owner and the members of the family. A further

34 per cent of French "industries" had less than ten paid employees each. Exactly 98 per cent of the manufacturing concerns, then, were distinctly small businesses.

The fearful wear and tear of modern industrial life on the human being was thus spared most Frenchmen. But the cost to the nation of its failure to industrialize sufficiently was great. Wealth increased less in France than in other countries struggling to maintain or achieve a major place in the sun. And until it was too late, the French did not fully realize that in our time military power was coming to be based largely on industrial strength. In the fall of 1938, just a year before Hitler launched his war, French production was 25 per cent below that of 1930; German production was 30 per cent above.

The French military mind, for centuries the superior of any on the Continent, also began to lag in the years that followed the victorious First World War. In my own early days in Paris one became aware of a sort of hardening of the arteries in the French High Command. Its doctrines were rigid, its thinking unimaginative, its concepts outworn. Above all, it became obsessed with the idea of the superiority of the defense in contemporary warfare—had not the glorious defense of Verdun proved this for all time? This obsession led to the Maginot Line complex which was to prove so disastrous to France in the spring of 1940.

"The defeat of 1940," concludes a French writer,[6] "has its roots . . . in the eclipse of French military thought during the twenty years between the two world conflicts."

I remember becoming especially conscious of this when I moved from Paris to Berlin in the summer of 1934, a year and a half after Hitler had taken power. The German officer

[6] *"Appel à l'imagination,"* by Tony Albord; Revue de défense nationale, IX (August-September 1949).

caste, egged on by the Fuehrer, was already busy reorganiz-
ing and enlarging the General Staff, and even a civilian
correspondent could sense the new and daring ideas beginning to emanate from the Bendlerstrasse, where the War
Ministry was housed. It soon became evident from my own
cursory studies of the German military publications as well
as from talks with German officers that the successors to
Hindenburg and Ludendorff had already decided that, in
the next war, campaigns could be won quickly by a new and
ingenious use of tanks and planes as the spearheads of the
offensive.

Now the French High Command, so far as I could learn
in Paris, did not believe this. Pétain, Weygand, Debeney,
Gamelin (who was commander-in-chief of the Franco-Brit-
ish armies on the western front in 1939-40), and others in
the top rank of the French military hierarchy were sure that
the weapons of defense had become so superior that no German attack, no matter with how many planes or tanks, could
break the continuous front. After all, the solid front had not
really been broken by either side in four years of massive
warfare in 1914-1918.

With the exception of De Gaulle, then an obscure junior
officer, though a pestiferous one, none of the military men
in France thought very highly of the value of the tank and
plane in warfare. Both had been of some value in the First
World War, to be sure, but neither had been decisive. As
late as 1935, when Goering was already feverishly building
the Luftwaffe, Marshal Pétain expressed the belief that it
would be wrong to expect a great deal from an air force
used in independent operations. General Weygand clung to
similar old-fashioned beliefs even longer. At a meeting of the
War Committee on April 3, 1940, just five weeks before Hitler hurled his army and air force against the French (but

seven months *after* German war planes had paralyzed the
Polish Army in the first week of a three-week campaign),
Weygand stated his opinion that air forces would not fulfill a great role in the war! "You can't hold the ground with
planes," he said on another occasion, as if that dismissed the
little matter of air power.

On armored warfare, which the German General Staff
was developing into a new high military art, the French were
equally blind. Pétain believed the value of the tank had been
overemphasized, especially by those, like the Germans, who
wanted to use it independently—an armored division or corps
for the break-through. General Georges, the commander
of the French forces against the Germans in 1940, had
believed, until the German armor hit him in May, that the
German panzer tactics were quite wrong. "Their tanks," he
boasted, "will be destroyed in the open country behind our
lines, if they can penetrate that far, which is doubtful."[7]

The French intended to use *their* tanks in support of infantry, not to make a break-through for the infantry—a conception that was to lead to disaster when the Germans came,
though, contrary to the general belief, the French were *not*
outnumbered in tanks, there being about 4,000 vehicles on
each side.

But all that I have recounted here—the incompleteness of
the political, social, and industrial revolutions, the fissure
that separated the two Frances, the decline of the bourgeoisie, the instability of government, the dodging of taxes, the
failure of the population to increase, the failure to industrialize, the deterioration of French military thought—did not
explain, in my mind, as I tried during my journey that year
to fathom the French tragedy, one development which, more

[7]Pertinax, *op. cit.* (p. 11).

than any other, brought the great nation down. This was the treachery in high places.

When I first lived in France, in the middle twenties, the conservative classes, though they might distrust the Republic or even hate it, were at least staunch in their patriotism to the nation. Even the die-hard royalists of Action Française, who demanded nothing less than a restoration of the old monarchy, had rallied behind republican France when it went to war with Germany in 1914. No Frenchmen had hated the *Boches* with more venom than the two great royalist spokesmen, Charles Maurras and Léon Daudet. None had been more noble in their patriotism in 1914 than conservative writers such as Albert de Mun and the novelist Maurice Barrés. To defend the sacred soil of France against the German invaders was for the conservatives the first and highest duty of the citizen. Indeed on the eve of the First World War it was the Socialists of the Left (among whom was a young lawyer named Laval) who faltered in backing the nation against the German threat.

We have seen that in 1939-40 their successors, the French Communists, took a similar attitude. But this was because they made themselves subject to orders from Moscow. The conservatives were under no such compulsion. And yet the frustrations of the years between the wars had so poisoned their hearts and minds that they, with men like Maurras in the forefront, betrayed their native land shamelessly and actually welcomed the Nazi invaders. It was a reversion to more than a century before, when the French Legitimists, sickened by the Revolution of 1789 and its Napoleonic sequel, had enthusiastically greeted foreign kings and their invading armies, cheering Wellington at Bordeaux, and Emperor Alexander of Russia and King Frederick William of Prussia at the gates of Paris.

What made it fatal was that the treachery and subversion spread to the armed forces, to the intellectuals, to the great middle classes, and even to the non-Communist Left. In the Army, Weygand himself was anti-republican, as were Pétain and a number of other generals. These high officers were heirs to those who had fabricated the case against Dreyfus in the closing days of the nineteenth century; they had never forgiven the Republic for exposing the crime and insisting that even in the Army justice be done. The French Navy too was full of admirals who detested the Republic. After the Second World War two generals, Dentz and Bridoux, and two admirals, Platon and De Laborde, would be condemned to death for treason.

They, like many intellectuals and writers and bankers and businessmen, managed to work themselves into such an outlandish state of hysteria that they succeeded in convincing themselves that their position and interests were gravely threatened by the "Reds"—a term which came to include the most moderate of French liberals and republicans. Even some of the French leftists lost their heads, a group of them, led by Marcel Déat (who on the eve of World War II penned his famous editorial: "Why Die for Danzig?") and Adrien Marquet, the mayor of Bordeaux, breaking away to form a "neo-Socialist" movement, which became remarkably pro-German and, in the end, landed most of its members in high offices in Vichy and a few in collaborationist posts with the Germans in Paris.

As the Hitler war approached, many French conservatives concluded, as we have seen, that they would be better off under a Nazi order imposed from without than under their own "Reds." But before this they had tried to found their own branch of fascism in the numerous leagues which sprang up in the thirties: the Croix de Feu, originally an élite veterans' organization; the Solidarité Française, financed by the perfumer François Coty, and the Cagoule, a sinister secret society infiltrated by German and Italian agents, which carried out numerous murders and with which Pétain was connected.

French fascism never developed a leader of the capacity of Hitler or Mussolini nor did it ever fire the imagination of the masses. Perhaps it was its failure to catch on in France as it had in the two neighboring countries of Italy and Germany that made so many French conservatives, in their desperate foolishness, turn to Mussolini and Hitler in the end, as possible saviors.

Contributory to France's sickness was the venality of the press. Its corruptness had no equal in any free country of our time. The sinister influence of the press in a totalitarian land, where the dictator has the power, as Hilter and Stalin and Mussolini demonstrated, to poison the minds of the masses is one thing. It is an awful evil. But the poison administered by a supposedly free press in a democratic country is even worse, for the readers do not always know how they are being swindled and moreover there is no excuse for it except man's greed carried to a point of depravity. In France a "free press" meant a press free to be bribed. The news and editorial columns in nearly every Parisian newspaper were for sale. And not only to the French government and French politicians and French financial and economic interests. They were for sale to foreign interests, to foreign governments, no matter how hostile these might be to the French Republic.

Before the First World War the leading dailies of Paris— *Le Temps, Le Matin, Le Figaro, L'Echo de Paris*—were subsidized by the Czarist government. This was bad enough, but at least Russia, at the time, was an ally of the Republic. Before the second war however, more than one French publication had sold its editorial policy to Hitler and Mussolini. It did not matter that the two Fascist dictators were plotting the destruction of France. They paid the French newspapers or their editors hard cash, and this was all French journalism lived for. It has been estimated that between 1935 and the outbreak of World War II, the Duce's government spent at least fifty million francs a year bribing the French press. Some think the figure was vastly higher—accurate statistics are hard to track down since such dealings are always underhand. But sometimes an exact figure comes to hand to give an idea of the extent of the bribery. Shortly before the Hitler war began, two French journalists, Louis Aubin, an editor of *Le Temps* (the *Times* of Paris), and Jules Poirer, publicity director of *Le Figaro*, a leading conservative morning newspaper of Paris, were arrested and after questioning confessed to having received one million and three million and a half francs, respectively, from the Germans. Otto Abetz, the notorious Nazi German agent in Paris in the years before the war, was said to have had a payroll that included the names of some of the best-known journalists and writers in France.

Though years of working in Paris had acquainted me at first hand with the corruptness of the press, I did not know, when I returned to the city from time to time in the last feverish years before the second war, the extent to which Hitler and Mussolini had purchased it. Hence I was consternated to find the Parisian newspapers and magazines full of the most blatant Nazi and Fascist propaganda and equally full, it seemed to me, of outbursts against the only friends France had left in a world speeding toward war: the democracies of Great Britain and the United States. It was with more than astonishment that I, who had just come in to Paris from Berlin, where I was stationed, saw how the French journalists were parroting the insulting lies of Josef Goebbels, even to using the Nazi propaganda minister's choice language. I was used to it in Berlin, but to read in a Paris publication that President Roosevelt was "of Jewish extraction," that he was "the century's most conspicuous noodlehead," and that he wanted "to start a war so as to re-establish Jewish power and deliver the world to Bolshevism" puzzled me until it dawned on me that French journals were still for sale to the highest bidder and that the Nazi Germans had bought a few.

One can only understand the confusion and the defeatism of the French people on the eve of the war when one realizes how they were shamelessly betrayed by their "free" press. For years their minds had been poisoned, their once fine patriotism diluted, their judgment perverted by newspapers and magazines in the pay of France's enemies without and her traitors within. The pollution of French journalism is one of the darkest chapters in the life of France between the wars.

Finally—a bizarre story—one must recount briefly the way the French war veterans were taken in by Hitler as part of his strategy to weaken France for the kill. No more patriotic Frenchmen existed than those who had fought in the trenches between 1914 and 1918, and generally their feelings toward the Germans were just what might be expected: they disliked them, distrusted them, feared them. Unfortunately their leaders, the men who wormed their way to the top of the ex-servicemen's organizations, were of mediocre caliber, vain for publicity, ambitious for political power, but politically naïve. This was true of the leaders of the "leftish" veterans' groups as well as those of the Right, for in France, as in Germany, the ex-soldiers tended to organize on political lines. But right or left, they became easy prey for Hitler.

Less than two years after he assumed office, the Fuehrer began inviting them to Berlin. Jean Goy, head of the reactionary National Union of Combatants, made his pilgrimage to the Nazi capital in November 1934. His rival, Henri Pichot, leader of the Federation of Wounded Veterans and a genuine leftist, followed a month later. George Scapini, moving spirit of the blind veterans, himself blinded in the war, followed, as did Albert Delsuc, the secretary general of a special group of ex-soldiers who had been gassed. The Fuehrer, an ex-soldier himself, wined and dined the "comrades" of the front and then, with his undoubted gift for arousing the emotions, solemnly assured the French veterans that never again would Germany go to war against France. The French ex-servicemen took him at his word. They returned to Paris to tell their comrades the glad tidings. Never were the seeds of doubt about Nazi Germany's true intentions sowed in more fertile soil. Many of the veterans' organizations began to plump for an "understanding" with the hereditary enemy. Some of them, such as the Croix de Feu under Colonel de la Rocque, became outright fascist groups and strove to start a movement comparable to that of the Nazis in Germany. In the end men like Goy and Scapini became eminent collaborators under the German occupation.

I had come back to Paris in January 1934 from a year off in Spain just in time to witness an event that marked a turning point in the life of the Third Republic, indeed foretold its doom, exposing the corruption in high places that was now beyond hope of cure, demonstrating the timidity of liberal democracy, the cupidity of the Communists, the potential threat of the Fascists, and revealing not only the unbridgeable abyss which now divided Frenchmen but for the first time putting the finger on the very men who would betray the nation in its agony of defeat in 1940.

The event took place on the Place de la Concorde on the evening of February 6, 1934. A mob, whipped into frenzy by the irresponsible exhortations of the fascist leagues and extreme right-wing demagogues, got out of hand. Taking possession of the historic square, setting fire to autobuses, automobiles, heaps of park benches, and the lower storey of the Ministry of Marine on the northeast side of the Place, it tried three times to sweep south across the Concorde bridge to the Chamber of Deputies on the other side of the Seine. It was stopped, a hundred yards or so from its goal, by a hail of machine-gun and rifle bullets from the Garde Mobile. Mingling with the mass of infuriated Frenchmen that night as best I could, I thought for a time that it would succeed in breaking through the police and mobile guards and storm the Chamber. There was no doubt in my mind what it would do if it did get across the bridge. It would set fire to the Chamber and kill every nonrightist deputy it could get its hands on. And in so doing, it would bring down the Republic.

As it was, it failed by a narrow margin, by a scant hundred yards. By midnight the inflamed rioters had been repulsed at the Concorde bridge for the third and last time. Nineteen of them and one policeman lay dying or were dead. Some 1,300 were wounded, more than half police or guards. But from that midnight moment on, as we can see now, the days of the Third Republic were numbered. Thereafter its descent was to be steep and rapid.

What caused this savage outbreak, the like of which had not been seen in the streets of Paris since the Commune?

The immediate cause was the *affaire Stavisky*, which burst upon the land in the closing days of 1933 and rocked it to its foundations. But since Stavisky himself was a petty character and his financial swindles were on a relatively modest scale—there had been far bigger ones in France, as in other countries—one had to look deeper to understand why his exposure produced repercussions that were to lead so quickly to the rioting of February 6, the overthrow of the Daladier government the next day, and the hatching of a sinister relationship between Laval and Pétain and other enemies of the regime which six years later would bring about the overthrow of the Third Republic at Vichy. My first assignment when I returned to newspaper work in Paris in mid-January of 1934 had been to cover the Stavisky scandal.

Serge Alexandre Stavisky, a native of Kiev, the son of a Russian-Jewish dentist who emigrated to Paris, had long been known to the French police for a number of reasons. A rather small fry in the Paris underworld, he trafficked in drugs, prostitution, blackmail, forgery, and stock manipulations. But he was arrested only once, in 1926, at the instance of a couple of stockbrokers who charged he had swindled them out of some seven million francs. He was arrested, but never tried. And that, for the French, was where the real scandal concerning Stavisky began. Obviously he had "connections." And "protection." He was released "provisionally" from jail. His trial was postponed nineteen times by the Paris public prosecutor, who happened to be the brother-in-law of Premier Chautemps. In the meantime Stavisky quickly became prosperous again, promoting various bogus enterprises, buying a Paris theater, controlling two daily newspapers (one leftist, the other rightist), making friends with politicians, especially in the Radical Socialist Party, which dominated the French parliament and the various French governments, and occasionally, just to cover his traces, acting as a stool pigeon in the underworld for the French secret police. He became quite a man about town, a racy frequenter of the fashionable resorts, the race tracks, the bars, and the boulevards.

Late in December 1933 the storm broke over his head. He was exposed for fraudulently floating a few million francs worth of bonds of the municipal pawnshop of Bayonne—bonds which he got a minister in Premier Chautemps' cabinet to recommend. His connections with leading politicians, high government officials, and the police came to light. But this time they could not save him. The country literally exploded with anger at the scandal. Stavisky fled Paris, though not without a false passport provided him by the police which would have enabled him to get across the frontier and escape arrest. He waited in the fashionable French winter resort of Chamonix over the holidays and then, on January 8, 1934, police, who had been spurred on by the popular indignation to find and arrest the criminal, reported they had located him in a villa near Chamonix with a bullet through his head—a suicide. Most people in Paris however were sure that the police killed him to prevent him from talking.

And they were outraged against a government, its politicians, its officials, its police, even its courts, which could connive with such a rascal. Their natural rage was further inflamed by the wild charges hurled by the reactionaries, the Fascists and—it must be noted—the Communists. The extremists thought their hour had struck. It was the moment to take advantage of a general disgust among the people at the corruption and incompetence of the government. It was the opportunity they had been waiting for to attack the whole principle of liberal democracy. In this the Communists made common cause with the Fascists for they too wanted to over-throw the "bourgeois" Republic. After all, had not the Ger-man Communists joined the Nazis to ferment strikes in Berlin in the last days of the tottering Weimar Republic?

But the attempted *coup* of February 6 was mainly a Fas-cist enterprise in which the Communists, in their stupidity, rendered what aid they could by sending several thousand rioters into the streets. Moreover the Fascists were able to use right-wing war veterans, not all of them Fascists by any means, to do the dirty work on the Place de la Concorde.

While the Place de la Concorde echoed that evening of February 6 to the crack of rifles and machine guns and the roar of the mob, the elected representatives of the people in the Chamber of Deputies, a scant two hundred yards away, were giving Edouard Daladier, who had just been named premier to replace the compromised Chautemps, a vote of confidence by a large majority—360 to 220. Daladier, a Radi-cal Socialist (despite the name, the party was neither radical nor socialist but conservative middle-of-the-road), had been gaining a reputation as a "strong man" in France. But on this crucial night, as later in the even greater crisis of the war in 1940, he faltered. The next day he resigned. "The govern-ment," he said, "which has the responsibility for order and security, refuses to assure it by exceptional means which might bring about further bloodshed. It does not desire to employ soldiers against demonstrators. I have therefore handed to the President of the Republic the resignation of the Cabinet."

When I read that, I could not refrain from noting in my diary: "Imagine Stalin or Mussolini or Hitler hesitating to employ troops against a mob trying to overthrow their re-gimes! . . . To resign now, after putting down a fascist *coup* —for that's what it was—is either sheer cowardice or stu-

pidity." And it was a confession of the frightening weakness
of French democracy.

At this juncture the sinister figure of Pierre Laval reappeared. This depraved peasant from the Auvergne, as Pertinax[8] called him, who had started his political life in 1914
as a left-wing Socialist and pacifist and then had drifted
steadily to the Right, who, beginning life in sheer poverty,
had used political power to become a millionaire, who had
first entered the cabinet in 1924 in a leftist coalition and next,
in 1930, as a member of the conservative Tardieu's government and finally become premier in 1931, had long been
biding his chance.

He, more than any of the other unscrupulous politicians
who dominated French politics between the wars, saw with
an ambitious peasant's shrewdness how to take personal advantage of the contemporary condition of France: its confusions and divisions, the hysterical fears of the wealthy
bankers and businessmen, the resentments of the impoverished workers, and the very general and genuine hatred of
war in a people who had been bled white by the previous
one. By the time of the riots of February 6, 1934, he already
was plotting a course that in the end would enable him almost single-handed to destroy the Third Republic six years
later and to become France's first servant in Hitler's short-
lived totalitarian New Order.

In a way, the events of that February night provided Laval
with a rehearsal for the greater treachery he was to engineer
with Pétain in 1940. Daladier had resigned. The insurrec-
tionary fever was still strong in the streets. Even the uneasy
moderates were demanding a "strong government." The
timid and colorless President Lebrun was floundering about
wondering what to do, whom to call upon to form a new

[8]Pertinax, *op. cit.* (p. 387).

government. At this moment, the afternoon of February 7, Laval called on the President in his palace. He quickly realized the President's indecision. He then made a decision of his own. He asked to be permitted to make a telephone call. He was soon in long-distance communication with a faraway village called Tournefeuille, where a forgotten former president of France was puttering away the last years of a mediocre life. This individual was Gaston Doumergue, a vain, pompous, senile old man. The next day, to this reporter's astonishment, Doumergue was being welcomed at a Paris railroad station by the cheering crowds as the savior of France. He quickly formed a government of "National Union," consisting mostly of former premiers and cabinet officers of all parties except the Socialists and Communists. But Laval, working in the background as he always preferred to do, was its guiding spirit.[9]

Doumergue's secretary of war was Pétain, the hero of Verdun. With his appointment there began an association between the Marshal and Laval that was to culminate in their collaboration with each other and with Hitler in the hour of France's humiliating defeat of 1940. This was Pétain's first taste of public office and he liked it—a circumstance that was to prove disastrous for the country.

Doumergue lasted but a few months. He resigned in November after a futile and rather silly attempt to strengthen the powers of the presidency, a move which the moderates suspected was designed to pave the way for an authoritarian regime. But when he left office he saw to it that the reins of power were turned over to Flandin and Laval, who were to do so much to bring France down.

[9]The story of Laval's telephone call to Doumergue is told by Fernand Laurent, a conservative deputy and financier, in *Gallic Charter;* Boston, 1944 (p. 127).

France had one more golden opportunity to stave off the catastrophe which eventually engulfed it. That was in 1936 when Hitler reoccupied the Rhineland. Being in Berlin at that time I learned that, had the French Army made the slightest move to oppose the German troops, the Reichswehr would have hastily withdrawn its forces across the Rhine. Hitler could not have survived such a blow to his prestige and knew it. But the French cabinet, in which Flandin was foreign minister, and the French High Command hesitated to move. That their vacillation was due in part to the asinine efforts of the British government to hold the French back does not absolve the Paris government of much blame. France had the necessary military strength alone to halt Hitler; and she was entitled by the Locarno Pact to do so and in so doing to receive British backing. It was one of the last chances the Western democracies had to forestall the enemy across the Rhine, who was systematically plotting their downfall. The French were too confused, too divided, to realize it. And in the cabinet and in the Army the defeatists and the pro-Fascists regarded France's failure to budge on the Rhineland occupation as a great victory!

They were temporarily sidetracked a few weeks later when the Popular Front, which had been organized in 1935 by the Radical Socialists, the Socialists, and the Communists when they realized where the country was drifting after the February 6 *coup,* scored a surprising election victory. Léon Blum, the Socialist leader, became prime minister, and the conservatives and the reactionaries became thoroughly frightened. All that Blum and his associates tried to achieve was a delayed French version of Roosevelt's New Deal. But the workers, who had helped put the Popular Front into power, were not disciplined. A month after Blum took office there were 12,142 sit-down strikes by some 1,830,938 workers. The flight of capital, which had begun under Flandin, continued at an increased rate as the conservatives began to chant: "Better Hitler than Blum." The 40-hour week was introduced in industry. If the times had been ordinary this would only have been elementary justice. But in 1936, with Germany beginning to rearm at an alarming rate, the shorter working week was disastrous to French production, and the employers, by their sabotage, made it even more disastrous. To make Blum's task even more difficult, the Spanish civil war broke out, and he had to make the unpopular decision for a premier swept into power by the working class to submit to British pressure for "nonintervention" in Spain at the very moment Mussolini and Hitler were pouring troops and planes and tanks into Spain to help Franco.

No one who did not visit Paris in those days can imagine the hatred of the possessing classes for Blum. Actually, as all who met him knew, he was a man of great cultivation and culture, a writer and intellectual of eminence, possessed of considerable charm and absolute integrity and honesty. He was also a staunch French patriot. But he was a Jew. All the anti-Semitism of France, which had lain dormant since the end of the Dreyfus affair, was kindled against the new premier. I was shocked at many of my own French friends. "That Jew!" they would mutter, as if he were the devil himself.

Though Blum's regime, short-lived, as it was, did a great deal to cleanse the Augean stable (he abolished the fascist leagues, reformed the Bank of France, ousting the "200 families" from their control of it and of the country's whole financial structure, instituted collective bargaining, etc.), it also, unfortunately, united all the forces in France which were working for the downfall of the democratic Republic and for collaboration with Hitler and Mussolini. From 1936 on they became bitter, desperate men, biding their time, which, they felt, not without reason, lay just ahead.

———————————

In the imbecile scramble of French politics after the demise of the Popular Front, Daladier had become premier again in April 1938. On the night of September 29-30 of that year, I saw him in Munich a few minutes after the abject surrender of Great Britain and France to Hitler over the Sudetenland—a vile, cowardly, stupid, unnecessary submission which not only destroyed Czechoslovakia but made a German war inevitable. France had just sacrificed her whole Continental position and had lost, in Czechoslovakia, her main prop in Eastern Europe. For the French the evening's capitulation had been disastrous, and Daladier, judging by his demeanor, knew it. As he lumbered into the lobby of the Regina Hotel to say goodbye to Chamberlain, he looked a beaten and broken man. French correspondents whispered that he feared to return to Paris, that he was almost certain a hostile mob would get him.

This fear, at least, was without foundation. The next day he would get a delirious welcome in Paris and be hailed as the savior of peace. After briefly witnessing the Wehrmacht's occupation of the Sudetenland I went on to Paris for a few days' rest. It was a sorry place. Even the most intelligent Frenchman of my acquaintance had no idea of what had happened to France at Munich. In the great Champs-Elysées restaurants fat bankers and businessmen toasted peace with rivers of champagne. Even the humble, the waiters, the taxi drivers, the people in the streets and down in the subways and out in the Red factory belt that surrounded the great city had been taken in. They made you sick with their senseless clatter about how wonderful it was that war had been avoided. They had fought in one war, they said. It was enough.

To one who had just come from across the Rhine, this defeatist and pacifist talk sounded like a death knell. The Germans had also fought in one war, the same war, but now they were ready for another. Hadn't the French heard? Apparently not. Utterly disheartened, I sat in my hotel room in Paris on the night of October 8 and scribbled in my diary: "The guts of France—the France of the Marne and Verdun— where are they?" They had departed. All the glory of this great race and nation had departed. "France," I wrote that gloomy evening, "makes no sense to me any more."

I would be in and out of Paris during the eleven months of peace that remained, but each time I was there, France seemed to me to have edged a little further toward disaster. On March 15, 1939, the day the German Army occupied Bohemia and Moravia and destroyed what was left of Czechoslovakia, I noted in my diary: "Complete apathy in Paris tonight about Hitler's latest *coup*. France will not move a finger." A week later, still in Paris: "France has lost something she had when I arrived here fourteen years ago: her taste, part of her soul, the sense of her historical mission. Corruption everywhere, class selfishness *partout* and political confusion complete. My decent friends have about given up. They say: "*Je m'en fous*—to hell with it."

And so in the spring, a year and a half later, at the first impact of Hitler's mechanized army, France went down. Being stationed in Berlin, I had followed the panzer divisions as they raced through Belgium and northern France. At first, I admit, I had hoped against hope that the French would hold as they had a quarter of a century before against this same Germanic foe at the Marne and Verdun. Contrary to the general belief, they were not inferior to the Germans in tanks and guns. Only in the air were they at a disadvantage. Perhaps impressed in my memory was a speech which one of France's greatest soldiers, General Weygand, had made at Lille on the very eve of the war. "You ask my opinion of the French Army and I will tell you frankly and in all truth . . . I believe the French Army has greater value than at any other time in its history; it possesses matériel of first quality, fortifications of the first order, an excellent morale, and a remarkable high command. No one among us desires war, but I affirm that if we are forced to win a new victory, we will win it."

Less than a year later, as commander-in-chief of the French Army, he would sing a different tune. Turned defeatist himself, he heartily agreed with another famous soldier, Marshal Pétain, who, on the night of June 16, had become head of a government of defeatists and traitors assembled in Bordeaux and who the next day asked the Germans for an armistice.

I was in Paris, which already had been occupied by the Germans, and the news of Marshal Pétain's capitulation was not at first believed. That the beaten and demoralized French Army must surrender was clear. But most of us had believed it would capitulate independently, without committing the nation, as had the Dutch and Belgian armies, and that the French government would go, as Premier Reynaud had promised, to North Africa, where France, with a powerful navy and considerable troops and with the help of the British, could hold out indefinitely.

Here we come to grips with the shameful, treasonable nature of Pétain's surrender. Unlike Germany in 1918 and 1945, which sued for an armistice because all was lost and there was no other alternative, France, in June 1940, still had a vast, nearby empire in North Africa from which to continue the struggle against the Germans. (Algiers was an integral part of metropolitan France.) It had a powerful ally in Great Britain, and a potential and even more powerful one in the United States. The perfidy of the traitors in Bordeaux, led by Laval and Pétain, lay in their surrendering the nation's independence not because it had been forced upon them but because they saw in it a golden opportunity to destroy the democratic Republic, to reorganize the country on a fascist foundation, and in doing so to enhance their own personal power and protect their pocketbooks and those of their reactionary and misguided friends. To achieve this they showed no qualms at betraying a nation's honor which through the centuries had stood so high. Nor did they shrink from the final degradation: of seeking the friendship of the enemy who had just attacked their native land and laid it waste—and, even worse, of seeking the counsel and aid of that enemy in destroying the nation's honored institutions so that they could replace them with cheap imitations of the evil ones their barbarian conqueror had clamped for a brief moment on the pitiful "Master Race" beyond the Rhine.

I cannot say that I realized fully the infamy of the traitors as I paced about the little clearing in Compiègne Forest on the afternoons of June 21 and 22 and watched the sad proceedings in the ailing old *wagon-lit* car, where Foch had laid down the armistice terms to the Germans twenty-two years before. All I noted at the time and place was the humiliation to France and the French of the surrender. It would be some years later before the full light of day would be shed on the incredibly shameful behavior of Laval, the chief architect of the surrender, and Pétain, its chief executor.

Three weeks later, on July 10, at Vichy, the Third Republic died an ignoble death. Perhaps the abject way it passed into limbo was in keeping with the new times, marked as they were by the collapse of the old virtues: courage and integrity and a sense of honor. The hour admittedly was black. France was prostrate. A million and a half Frenchmen were prisoners of war. German tanks stood only 25 miles away on the line of demarcation between occupied and unoccupied France as the members of the Chamber and the Senate assembled in Vichy to consider the proposals for the nation's future advanced by the new premier, Marshal Pétain. The senators and deputies were heartsick and confused. Many of them recognized the Republic's responsibility for the awful collapse. They knew the regime must be reformed but beyond that their minds were vague or numb.

At this disastrous moment, the oily Laval saw a further opportunity and quickly seized it. Less than a month before, at Bordeaux, he had intrigued to put the doddering marshal into power as prime minister, sweeping away Reynaud and the more patriotic ministers who had wanted to move the government of the Republic to North Africa. Now in July, in Vichy, he would, by hook or crook, sweep away what remained of the democratic, republican regime. Then he might achieve his ambition: to become Hitler's little Fuehrer of France in the obscene Nazi New Order.

On July 9 the Senate and Chamber met separately. About two-thirds of the members had contrived to get to Vichy on forty-eight hours' notice. The Senate voted 225 to 1, the Chamber 393 to 3, to recognize that there was "reason to revise the constitutional laws." Practically alone, Léon Blum made a last-minute effort to put some courage into the frightened legislators. The vote showed the magnitude of his failure and the extent of the panic among his colleagues.

The next day, July 10, when both houses convened jointly as the National Assembly, Laval made the rout of the democratic forces complete. A good many of the members—perhaps a majority—had decided to support the so-called Taurines project, which would have granted Pétain power to legislate by decree until the end of the war and authorized him to establish committees to draft a revised or new constitution to be subjected to popular referendum whenever a free vote became possible. The idea was to let Pétain rule by decree for the duration of the emergency and postpone the drafting of a new constitution until the end of the war.

Laval would have none of it. He had other ideas and he immediately made them known. "Since parliamentary democracy chose to fight against nazism and fascism," he said, "and since it lost this struggle, it must disappear. A new regime, audacious, authoritarian, social, and national, must be substituted for it." He was careful to get Pétain's backing for his substitution. The aged marshal's prestige in the legislature, as in the country, was still immense—a fact which must be kept in mind if one is to follow at all the folly which now took place in the National Assembly, assembled in secret session in the Hall of the Grand Théâtre in this provincial watering place.

The Pétain-Laval proposal simply granted to the "government of the Republic"—which was now Pétain himself—"full power to promulgate the new constitution of the French state." By use of parliamentary trickery backed by threats, Laval succeeded in getting the mild Taurines plan, which legally should have come up for vote first, shoved aside in favor of his own proposal. It was adopted by the overwhelming majority of 569 to 80. Nine-tenths of the democratically elected legislators present thus abdicated and deliberately killed the republic they had sworn to preserve. Not a single party dared to defy, as a party, the would-be French dictators. The Socialists under Blum came out best, supplying nearly one-half, 39 out of 80, of the No votes, but even they were hopelessly divided, for they numbered 172 in the National Assembly and most of this number presumably was present.

In Berlin, a few years before, I had seen the Reichstag commit suicide at the bidding of Hitler, but democracy in Germany had never been more than skin-deep. For the French parliament, with all its genuine democratic traditions, to have emulated the sorry Reichstag was a disgrace that will forever remain a blot upon the name of a great nation.

In the end France was saved from extinction as a nation not by herself but by her friends, the United States and Great Britain, which, exactly four years after the ignominy at Vichy, liberated her from the Germans. I was in and out of France at this time, in 1944 and 1945, and for a couple of exciting years of promise saw a remarkable group of Frenchmen, though unfortunately only a minority, try to make up for all the shortcomings and all the evil deeds of the past which, they realized, had nearly destroyed their country.

They were the men of the Resistance, who, after the first shock of disaster had worn away, had taken up arms against both the German occupiers and the Vichy traitors. Their guerrilla battles with the Germans, their sabotage of German military communications and installations, the intelligence which they obtained for the Allies, played no little part in the swiftness with which the Anglo-American armies drove the Germans out of France in the summer of 1944, as General Eisenhower freely acknowledged.

Their nonmilitary contribution to the saving of France was

even greater. They resurrected hope in the French people, restored a sense of national honor, and by their fine spirit of self-sacrifice, the nobility of their purposes, the breadth of their views, and an inspiring—if unprecedented—tolerance for the conflicting beliefs amongst them, set out to purify France and regenerate it. In this they quickly failed, and their failure constitutes another tragic chapter in the modern history of the land.

Looking back during the summer of my midcentury journey I could see that perhaps the Resistance was destined to fail. Possibly its numbers were too small. De Gaulle, after his return, soon turned against it. The collaborationists and Vichyites managed to retain too much financial and economic power. And as François Mauriac, the great Catholic patriot writer, remarked: "We have been poisoned, and we have still not got the poison out of our systems." Léon Blum saw that too when he returned from German captivity a year after the liberation. "I have not found," he said sadly, "what I expected. I expected to find a France that had been purged and retempered, and I find myself in a country that in many ways seems corrupted."

But in the late summer and fall of 1944, immediately after the liberation, the spirit of the Resistance seemed to many of us who returned to Paris to be nothing less than magnificent. The Resistance program had been laid down in a remarkable paper drafted under the very noses of the Germans in Paris on March 16, 1944, by the National Council of Resistance, the supreme organ that united the various underground movements. That Frenchmen of such widely divergent faiths—political, economic, and social—for they ranged from staunch conservatives to Communists, could agree on so much augured well, I thought, for the future of a country that had disintegrated largely because of its internal divisions.

Among the "indispensable reforms" in the new France, the program listed:

"Establishment of a veritable economic and social democracy, involving the eviction of the great economic and financial feudalisms from the direction of economy."

(It seemed strange when you thought about it halfway through our century that the great Western democracies had obtained *political* democracy only, not economic and social democracy, and that at home, in the United States, democracy in the latter two fields, especially in economics, was regarded in many conservative quarters as a radical and even subversive idea.)

"A rational organization of economy which assures the subordination of particular interests to the general interest while avoiding the professional dictatorship set up in imitation of the Fascist state . . .

"The return to the nation of the monopolized means of production, fruit of joint labor, sources of energy, the riches of the subsoil . . . Participation of the workers in the direction of economy . . . The right to work and the right to repose . . . Guaranty of a wage level which assures to every worker and his family the security, the dignity and the possibility of a really human life . . . The effective possibility for all French children to benefit from education and to reap the benefits of the highest culture regardless of the fortune of their parents . . .

"Thus," the Resistance program concluded, "will be founded a new republic, which will sweep away the regime of vile reaction instituted by Vichy and which will render to democratic institutions the effectiveness which was lost by the corruption and the treason which preceded the capitulation. Thus will be rendered possible a democracy which will unite the continuity of government action to the control exercised by the elected of the people . . . Forward . . . so that France May Long Live!"

But France did not move forward very far. Disillusionment in the Resistance soon set in. The purge of collaborators lagged. In the end France brought to trial for collaboration only a third as many as did Belgium, a much smaller country. "France has need of all her children," De Gaulle declared in putting the brakes on the purge. Many Vichyites were soon back in business and even in office. In the first year after his return, De Gaulle did almost nothing to stem a disastrous inflation. The other liberated governments had immediately called in the inflated currencies of their countries and by re-stamping them had not only deflated them to normal pro-portions but had deflated the profiteers who had amassed millions in collaboration. De Gaulle hesitated to take this step until it was too late.

The Resistance, embittered by the treachery and the fas-cist sympathies of so many army and navy officers, had sought to sweep clean the old officer corps and found a new one based on the officers of the *maquis,* who had fought the underground's guerrilla war with the Germans. De Gaulle, who, it must be remembered, was virtually a dictator during the first year after the liberation, gave in to the extent of admitting 5,000 *maquis* officers into the regular army. Within a few months however he connived to retire 3,000 of them to the reserve. The old order in the Army, as in other fields, thus quickly rewon its traditional place in France.

And yet in the first election (it was also a referendum) held in France since before the war, in October 1945, the influence of the Resistance was strong enough to defeat over-whelmingly, 19,000,000 votes to 800,000, a project to main-tain the old Third Republic, and to elect to the Constituent Assembly, which was to draw up the constitution for the

Fourth Republic, 400 men and women of the Resistance out of 586 members. Moreover the three main parties of the Resistance, the Catholic Popular Republicans, the Socialists, and the Communists, had an overwhelming majority in the new Assembly.

They soon fell out. The constitution which the Assembly finally managed to write was rejected by the Popular Republicans, the conservatives, and by Gen. De Gaulle, who had resigned as provisional president in January of 1946. Given the opportunity of the hour, the chance to make good so many of the shortcomings of the previous Republic, the members of this first Constituent Assembly had fumbled badly. They had turned out a pretty shaky document, one that seemed sure to make the governments of the Fourth Republic even more unstable, if possible, than those of the Third had been. On May 5, 1946, the people in a national referendum rejected the proposed constitution by a vote of ten to nine million, with 21 per cent of the eligible voters staying away from the polls. It was the first time in history that the French people had ever said "No" in a country-wide referendum. They apparently agreed with the columnist André Stibio, who had written: "The Assembly's work will always give the impression of having been written on the margin of the nation's existence, of its misery, its confusion, the vital problems which it must face."

More than half a year's work to give France a new constitution was wasted. Nearly two years after the liberation France still had no regular system of government.

The second attempt succeeded, though the new draft constitution seemed to most Frenchmen to mark little improvement over the old one. It was ratified on October 13, 1946, by nine million votes to eight million, but another eight million Frenchmen, a third of the electorate, abstained. Little wonder that under a system of government which, in effect, had not been accepted by two-thirds of the people France was destined for still further difficult, uneasy times.

That was the state I found it in when I came to Paris on my midcentury journey. I had paused briefly there in 1948 when the country was nearly paralyzed by Communist-incited strikes. It was at a low ebb then and one's French friends, regardless of party, saw little hope. But there had been a good harvest that year and large funds from the Marshall Plan began to revive the country's sagging economy. The Third Force, wedged between the Communists on the left and the De Gaullists on the right, had begun to generate a little confidence after a precarious four years' hold on the government.

Most of the French friends I sought out were skeptical however that this moderate, republican, democratic center united in an uneasy coalition of Socialists, Radical Socialists, and Catholic Popular Republicans could survive the approaching elections in the face of the pressure from the Left and the Right. They were wrong. Though the general election of June 17, 1951 gave the Communists and De Gaullists nearly half of the votes cast, their combined representation in the National Assembly, due to a complicated electoral law which favored alliances of the moderate parties, came to only 221 members out of a total of 627. Thus the moderate groups still had a majority though the seemingly irreconcilable differences between them made it doubtful whether they could form a very stable government or one which could really tackle the fundamental problems which remained to be solved and which would have to be solved if France were ever to climb back to its former greatness.

The Communists and De Gaullists in the meantime remained a very real threat to the continued existence of the enfeebled Fourth Republic. Though the Communists polled more votes than any other party in the only two national elections since the war (28.6 per cent of the total in 1946, and 26.5 per cent in 1951) it seemed doubtful to me that they could ever come to power in France by legal and constitutional means, that is, by rolling up a majority of the votes in a national election. But it had to be remembered that the Communists had not gained power in any country, including Russia, by a majority vote in free and secret balloting. They had gained it, as recent events in Czechoslovakia showed, by an armed *coup d'état,* and this would be the only way they could gain political control of France. That a party which in 1951 could still poll five million votes out of nineteen million in an absolutely free election and which controlled the bulk of organized labor and even enjoyed considerable support among the peasantry and the intellectuals would continue to exert influence in French affairs was obvious. Its power to sabotage the economy was great.

The impact of its superbly organized propaganda on the French people was very evident. It still frightened or persuaded many Frenchmen to refrain at least from taking sides in the ideological conflict between East and West. Even the Catholic Church, bitter foe of communism that it was, declined to join unreservedly in the cold war. In 1949 the nation's four cardinals in a joint letter formulated its position as follows: "The Church refuses to join a 'Crusade' in which are intermixed so many temporal and economic rivalries and interests . . . In condemning the action of the Communist parties the Church does not take the part of capitalism. It is necessary to know that there exists in the very idea of capitalism . . . a materialism rejected by Christian teaching."[10]

The principal menace to the Fourth Republic and to de-

[10]Saul K. Padover, *op. cit.* (p. 56).

mocracy in France came, it seemed to me, from General de Gaulle and his new-founded party, "Rally of the French People." He had resigned suddenly as provisional president and premier in January 1946 when he saw that the Constituent Assembly was determined to give parliament, not the president, the exclusive authority to rule France. Five months later, having failed to receive the recall he evidently expected, he set out to regain power. The day I arrived in Paris in the late summer of 1950 he issued a bombastic statement warning his countrymen of the danger of the hour and —characteristically—offering to take over the reins of government himself. "He talks a queer kind of pseudo-authoritarian jargon," I noted in my diary that evening. "I doubt if many Frenchmen will take his declaration seriously." Yet a year later, in the election of 1951, his party would poll over four million votes, only a million less than the Communists, and actually elect more deputies to the Assembly—118—than any other party.

What did the man want, and what was his appeal?

To put it bluntly, he wanted the power to rule France himself, as a "strong" president. And he believed fanatically that such was his destiny. Gordon Wright[11] relates that De Gaulle, before the age of 12, when most boys are playing marbles and struggling with arithmetic in school, had reached the conclusion that fate had chosen him to guide the nation in a future hour of crisis.

History appeared to bear him out. Almost alone among the rising officers in the French Army he had predicted in two books written between the wars, *The Edge of the Sword*, in 1932, and *The Army of the Future*, in 1934, the form of future warfare, which he foresaw would be dom-

[11]*The Reshaping of French Democracy*, by Gordon Wright; London, 1950 (p. 42).

inated by armored, mechanized, highly mobile troops. Unfortunately he saw his ideas developed by the Germans, not by the French. A week after the German attack on May 10, 1940, he was named a general, the youngest in the French Army, and a few days later became under-secretary of defense under Premier Reynaud. Risking charges of treason, he flew to London when Pétain sued for an armistice, and there on June 18, 1940, made his famous broadcast to the French armed forces urging them to continue the fight and reminding them that France had lost a battle but not a war.

Whatever the destiny in which he believes so strongly holds for him, France and the French will always be indebted to him for his bold and courageous stand in the dark days of the June capitulation and for his founding of the Free French movement which preserved the true spirit and the honor of France and under his stubborn leadership paved the way for a rebirth of the nation. But many Frenchmen remembered that Pétain, a much more illustrious soldier, had also saved France in the dark days of Verdun, midway through the First World War, and then had forfeited the gratitude of his countrymen by instituting his vile pro-German dictatorship at Vichy in the hour of France's humiliation and fall.

There is no doubt that De Gaulle is a fanatical believer in the leadership principle—as obsessed with it as was Hitler. Even before Hitler became Fuehrer of the Third Reich, De Gaulle was writing down in his books his own conception of the leader. "All the credit that position and birth formerly enjoyed among the masses has now been transferred to those individuals who know how to impose their authority . . . Men need organization—that is, orders and leaders . . . The leader is distant, for authority cannot be without prestige, nor prestige without distance . . . Confident in his own judgment and conscious of his strength, the leader makes no attempt to please . . . All that he asks is granted."

Only such a leader, he holds, can meet the demands of the present era. "Our age," he has written, "will not long endure the delays, confusions, and weaknesses which softer times accepted . . . Every group, party, and leader calls for reconstruction, the new order, authority."

His contempt for political parties is complete: "Everything that comes from political parties—hypocritical passions, competitive demagogy, political patronage—had had the effect of corrupting the Army."

Today he would no doubt add that they corrupted the country. In so far as he has enunciated any program at all, De Gaulle leans toward a corporate structure for the French state not unlike that which Mussolini tried to set up in Fascist Italy. Whether he would attempt to abolish the present parties if he came to power is a question. He could scarcely do it constitutionally. When I asked Gaston Palewski, De Gaulle's right-hand man, what his chief would do if he got a majority in the Assembly he answered forthrightly: "Abolish the constitution." He admitted that meant abolishing the Fourth Republic too. Indeed De Gaulle's followers already speak of the coming Fifth Republic.

Saddest of all to that mass of French republicans who long hailed De Gaulle as a hero is the nature of the following that the General has now attracted to his party. There is no doubt that the majority of former Pétainists, the men of Vichy, who during the war would have condemned him to death as a traitor, are now behind him. As H. Stuart Hughes has written: "Those who had never accepted the Republic had again found their man. The classes, the interests, the social leaders that at moments of crisis have sought a solution in military authoritarianism, by the summer of 1947 had rallied to De Gaulle."[12]

A French editor spoke to Leo Lania more bitterly: "De Gaulle has become the leader of a party which rallies the traitors of yesterday, the grafters of today, and the Fascists of tomorrow under the cloak of patriotic slogans."[13]

In the late summer of that midcentury year I wandered through the narrow, winding streets and up and down the broad tree-lined boulevards of the great city I had first come to work in twenty-five years before. It was a magnificent city still, without equal in the world, and as you looked into the faces of the passers-by you wondered how these people, so richly endowed as human beings, could have faltered so in this brief time, could have failed to live up to this matchless monument to the glory and the worth of their splendid civilization which Paris was.

Exhausted by the savagery of two world wars, sapped by the corruption of the period between those wars and of the Nazi occupation, confused and depressed by the course of events which had brought about the most humiliating and catastrophic defeat in the nation's long history and reduced France to the rank of a second-rate power, the people, when they talked with you, saw little hope for the future. Certainly they saw little hope of solving by political means the problems of living in this tortuous age.

Had they not in the last century and a half tried every conceivable form of government? One evening, during an exhaustive and enlightening conversation, Pertinax had recalled to me that they had, and had referred me to a passage

[12]*Modern France*, edited by Edward Mead Earle; Princeton, 1951 (p. 253).
[13]*The Nine Lives of Europe*, by Leo Lania; New York, 1950 (p. 12).

in his book[14] in which he had enumerated them: ". . . an absolute and (for a few days) a liberalized form of imperial power, constitutional monarchy inclining to despotism, parliamentary monarchy, an almost socialist republic, a reactionary republic degenerating into dictatorship, an authoritarian empire, a liberal empire, a government of national defense imposed by the Parisian mob under the fast-growing shadow of German invasion, a National Assembly with the Commune at its heels, a conservative republic, a radical republic, a popular-front republic, and, under the fire of the enemy, a counter-revolution. Leaving the revolutionary period of 1789 aside, and counting only the nineteenth century, there are months, weeks, or days of civil strife to be found in 1815, in 1830-35, 1848, 1851, 1870, 1871."

Pertinax then posed some questions: "Behind all these phenomena is there not to be detected an increasing debility of the spirit of sacrifice, of the collective resolve not to allow a great inheritance to perish, which are the true foundations of any commonwealth? . . . Are we then at the end of France's history?"

He did not think so; he could not believe it.

It had been for a sympathetic foreigner from the New World a crushing experience to witness personally the downfall of such a great and civilizing nation. It was saddening to see her so prostrate, so divided still, so groping, her citizens so despairing of the future, that midcentury year.

But most sobering of all for a man of this sorry century was the realization that France, in a way, was only the clearest mirror of our outrageous times, the victim, as were so many other countries and peoples, of what Katherine Anne Porter has called "this majestic and terrible failure of the life of man in the Western World."

[14]*op. cit* (p. 568).

Something had been ebbing out of life for all men in the twentieth century. Paul Valéry, the French poet, had sensed it: "The storm has ended, yet we are still restless and full of care . . . We have only vague hopes, but clear fears . . . We are aware that the charm of life and its abundance are behind us . . . There is no thinking man who can hope to master this concern, or avoid the darkness, or even estimate the probable period of deep-going disturbance . . . All the foundations of our world have been shaken . . . Something more essential has worn out than the replaceable parts of a machine . . ."

And yet another French poet had seen some light, some hope, if only men would seek honestly to discover the reasons for civilization's decline. The French debacle for Antoine de Saint-Exupéry was not to be explained in simple terms or in black and whites. "It is true," he wrote not long before he gave his life as an airman to his country, "that we can explain defeat by pointing to the incapacity of specific individuals. But a civilization is a thing that kneads and moulds men. If the civilization to which I belong was brought low by the incapacity of individuals, then my question must be: why did my civilization not create a different type of individual? . . . There was a time when my civilization proved its worth—when it enflamed its apostles, cast down the cruel, freed peoples enslaved—though today it can neither exalt nor convert. If what I seek is to dig down to the root of the many causes of my defeat, if my ambition is to be born anew, I must begin by recovering the animating power of my civilization, which has become lost."[15]

Lost? And forever?

As I made my way from Paris toward the Rhine to look once more upon the tragedy of another people I had also

---

[15]*Flight to Arras*, by Antoine de Saint-Exupéry; London, 1942.

come to know, I kept pondering the question. I could not answer it, of course, nor, I believe, could any other, however wise. Lost, it still was. But I could not believe that so fine a flowering could be lost forever, nor even for very long.

4. THE MASTER RACE

"The history of the Germans is a history of extremes. It contains everything except moderation, and in the course of a thousand years the Germans have experienced everything except normality . . . Nothing is normal in German history except violent oscillations."
—A. J. P. TAYLOR.

"They are not a lovable people; they even take a melancholy pride in the fact. But they are unmistakably and with all their faults a great people, and they can never remain a negligible factor in the future of Europe."
—J. H. MORGAN.

"The profound and icy mistrust which the German arouses whenever he gets power into his hands is the aftermath of that vast and horrible fear with which for long centuries Europe dreaded the wrath of the Teutonic blond beast."
—NIETZSCHE.

I CAME BACK to the ruins of Frankfort on the Labor Day week end that year, the very September week end on which eleven years before, in Berlin, I had seen Hitler launch the Second World War.

The vast beehive of the sprawling I. G. Farben building from where the Americans ruled the western part of Germany was deserted for the holiday, reminding one that on this day the good folks at home—so lucky in life and so complacent about it—were relaxing on the beaches, in the woods and hills and mountains, or at the ball parks, the race tracks, the tennis lawns at Forest Hills, and the county fairs. I had thought of them too on their last summer outings that week end that Germany went to war, wondering then if they fully realized what had happened and whether it in the least disturbed their pleasant holidays and whether any of them stopped to face the fact that in a relatively short time they too, whether they liked it or not, would be drawn in to the obscenity of destruction which Hitler had inaugurated.

Even today, on this Labor Day at the midcentury, did they comprehend what had happened in this distant land, which so many of their soldier-sons had come, briefly, to know, this troubled Teutonic land which had provoked two recent wars in which tens of thousands of those sons had been slain? Did the Germans themselves, desperate and downtrodden amid the shambles of this once great city, and humiliated at the presence of the troops of a foreign conqueror, realize what had happened and, perchance, why?

On the way from Paris to Frankfort these questions had crammed my head. The West that year, and especially the United States, was obsessed by the Russian danger and the world-wide Communist threat. Both were great, as the Communist aggression in Korea had just shown, and the Moscow-inspired *coup* that had destroyed democratic Czechoslovakia a couple of years before.

But how many Americans, I kept wondering, realized what the French knew and the British suspected: that in addition to the Russian problem and the Communist problem there remained a third one, which even our victory in two world wars had not settled: the German problem?

Or had the German problem, as so many Americans believed, been solved? I had been back in Germany at the war's end, in 1945, and again in 1948, during the Russian blockade of Berlin and the American airlift which eventually broke it, and the problem then had seemed to me no nearer solution than when I had known the country and the people in the Nazi time—despite the death of Hitler and the unconditional Nazi surrender, despite the ruin by bombing of the great German cities, the annihilation of the German state, and the pitiful condition of a people whom but a short time before I had seen march off arrogantly to conquer the world in the mistaken belief that fate had destined them to be the master race of this earth.

Sadly, as I made my way from the ruins of one city to another in that grim winter of 1945, I came to the conclusion that not much had changed in the heart and soul and mind of the German people. They had not drawn the lessons one might have expected from their shattering experience of Hitler and the lost war. Or so it seemed to me.

I realized, though, as I made my way back to Germany in this fall of my midcentury journey that I could be wrong. It was possible that I had been for long too close to the German picture to see the changes for the good which so many of my fellow countrymen said they saw—from the distance of Washington and New York, especially. As I crossed the Rhine and saw again the neat little houses in the villages and the clean-cut sturdy people in the streets, I hoped that I was wrong and that the others were right, for none knew better than I what a gifted people these were and what good they could bring our faltering Western civilization if only they could straighten themselves out.

I had never had Dorothy Thompson's love for Germany, which was passionate but—as she wrote once—frustrated. The country had attracted me for its natural beauty and during the Weimar Republic for the promise I thought it briefly held. I loved its woods and lakes and mountains, and its music and some of its literature; and I had found among a few individual Germans as good friends as I had ever had anywhere. Perhaps there was love there. But God knows there had also been hate when in the Hitler time I saw what collective barbarians the Germans could become. It was all very well for the learned historians to say that all peoples were fundamentally the same. In the personal experience of daily living through most of the days of the Third Reich I could see for myself that, during that short period at least, the German people became possessed of an evil spirit, which brutalized them and degraded them so that they justly earned—and deserved—and had—the hatred of every other people in Europe.

Such thoughts as these led to another as I approached Frankfort. It had seemed to me at home that our good people had become unduly downcast by the terrible failure of the peace after the Second World War. Certainly it had brought few if any of the sweet fruits we had expected from our victory. Most of its fruits had indeed turned sour or bitter. There had come no surcease from turmoil and tension and the outlandish hatreds of one people for another. Already—only five years after the shooting stopped—we were spending most of our fortune and our energies in rearming for a new war, this time against an enemy we had never fought nor feared before: Russia. Already Americans were dying on a faraway battlefield in the first *armed* round against the Communist world, dominated by Russia.

Yet despite all that, it seemed obvious to me that the peace we had, disillusioning and dreadfully disappointing though it was, was infinitely better than what we would have had if Hitler had won the war. The Poles, the Norwegians, the Dutch, the Belgians, the Russians, the French, who had been occupied by the Nazi Germans, could tell us that—if we would listen. Even I, who had seen a bit of the German occupation of Poland, of Belgium, of France, in the early days before it became completely vicious and barbaric could tell that. In addition, at the Nuremberg trial of the chief Nazi war criminals, I had had an opportunity to study the secret German archives, which had told of Hitler's diabolic plans for ruling over a slave world. At least our victory and his defeat had saved us from *that*. To my mind, it was something to be more thankful for than we were.

———

All that fall of my journey, I ruminated not only on what course the Germans would take in the immediate years to come but on what they had gone through and on how they had become what they were in the changing years of the quarter of a century I had known them. For we cannot make even an intelligent guess about the future of a people unless we understand at least a little of their past—a stale truism to be sure, but one which those of our statesmen in Washington and Frankfort who have recently had the power to shape Germany's future might have remembered with profit, but didn't. Without minimizing the difficulties which Russia's deceitful policies caused them, one could say that they were making the same mistakes which their British predecessors made after the first German defeat—and making them and compounding them out of the same inexcusable ignorance of German history and German character. It was not unreasonable to assume that the results would be similar and equally disastrous.

When I had first gone to Germany in the late twenties, the Peace of Versailles was supreme upon the Continent. The Germans, of course, did not like it, which was only natural. No people likes to lose a war, especially one which it provokes. But the Treaty of Versailles, as it was eventually observed, was not nearly as hard on Germany as the Germans and their many sympathizers in Great Britain and America made out. It left Germany geographically largely intact. Only a tiny corner in the west was occupied by foreign troops; and these soon departed. Not a cent of net reparations was paid in the end, for Germany's loans from Britain and especially from the United States, which she never repaid, more than balanced her reparation payments. And throughout the middle twenties the Reich enjoyed a prosperity as great as any of the victor lands. The chief accomplishment of Versailles in those days was to keep Germany, not completely disarmed, but at least incapable of military aggression.

Germany's relative disarmament was the cornerstone of European peace, and though it could not be expected that this condition could last forever in a world whose other powers remained heavily armed it would have been a simple task for the victors, as Churchill has said,[1] to keep Germany disarmed for thirty years and in the meantime build up the strength and authority of the League of Nations to such a point that no nation, not even Germany, could defy the peace or break it. Even after Hitler came it would have been easy for Britain and France, for two or three years, to insist on the enforcement of the disarmament provisions of the Versailles Treaty which Germany had signed. But the follies of the victors were too great to enable them even to accomplish this.

A sort of paralysis of the mind, and even more of the will, had set in, in the democracies of the West. Their political and economic leaders could not see that it was absolutely essential for the victors to stick together for at least a quarter of a century if the German problem was to be solved and the world spared of future German wars. Most of them did not recognize the danger even after Hitler withdrew from the League, in 1933, and began to rearm Germany in earnest, in 1934, and occupied the Rhineland, in 1936, without the shadow of a reaction from Britain and France, whose military

[1] *The Gathering Storm,* by Winston Churchill; Boston, 1948 (pp. 16-18).

power—even at this late date—could have crushed Nazi Germany within a few days. Perhaps in the French government there were a handful who saw the rising threat from beyond the Rhine. If so, they lacked the will to do anything about it.

In England, Churchill and a half-dozen of his friends alone saw the danger clearly and warned of its consequences. But they were out of power then, unheeded prophets wandering in the wilderness of British politics, scorned not only by their Conservative friends who, under Baldwin and Chamberlain, complacently ruled the Empire, but by the Labor Opposition, which was equally blind to the coming storm that was forming over Germany, casting ominous shadows clearly visible over London to those not afraid or not too smug to look up.

Nearly all of us were blinded in those days, and few, if any, of us who moved around Germany during the heyday of the Weimar Republic faintly imagined that in so short a time the democracies would willfully throw away their position of supremacy, which guaranteed the peace, and that this relatively decent and just ordering of Europe, established in the bloodshed and by the victories on the western front in 1918, would degenerate into the abject surrender at Munich a scant few years later and thereafter into another world war unleashed by the Germans. Already, no doubt, sinister and chaotic forces were stirring just beneath the surface and sometimes pushing through, but we did not sense them.

This was due, we can see now, in great part to our ignorance of Germany and the Germans. We had believed, naïvely, that the German revolution in the autumn of 1918, at the moment of defeat and the flight of the Kaiser, had changed Germany fundamentally, laying overnight the foundations for a true democracy and for a peace-loving community that never again would embark upon a war of conquest.

The fact was that there had never been a genuine revolution at the war's end. If we had understood this at the time we would have realized the consequences of that fact: that Germany and the Germans had not really changed at all.

Historians have spoken of two German "revolutions" during that fall of 1918: the "October Revolution" and the "November Revolution." The first was made in what we might call a rather typical German fashion. It was made on the orders of General Ludendorff, who as second in command to Hindenburg had been virtually dictator of Germany from 1916 until the defeat. On September 29, 1918, realizing that the war was lost and that the Allies would only treat with a "constitutional" and "civil" government, he ordered the immediate establishment of a constitutional monarchy with Prince Max of Baden as chancellor. The so-called "revolutionary" party in Germany, the Social Democrats, which had been hounded and persecuted by the Emperor, was perfectly willing for Wilhelm to remain on his throne if only he reigned "constitutionally" as did his cousin in England. In fact the socialists did everything they could to save his throne.

They were thwarted in the end by a bizarre happening on the day of November 9—the day of the November Revolution, as it was subsequently called during the Republic. On that day, with the news from the western front becoming darker every hour, the majority Social Democrats, under the leadership of Friedrich Ebert and Philipp Scheidemann, were meeting in the Reichstag. Prince Max's cabinet had just resigned after announcing the abdication of the Kaiser. Ebert, a saddler by trade, who could now become head of government if he wanted to—indeed there was no one else—was pondering with his colleagues what to do. Though he was the leader of the socialists he personally abhorred social revolution—the avowed goal of socialism—such was the confusion in the mind of the German worker! "I hate it like sin," he declared. What he wanted was a constitutional monarchy on the British pattern. That might preserve order which he, as a German, prized above all. The Kaiser was gone, the crown prince was impossible; perhaps one of the latter's sons might be propped up on the tottering throne.

But down the broad Unter den Linden a few blocks away, the Spartacists, under the left-socialists Karl Liebknecht and Rosa Luxemburg, were preparing from their citadel in the Kaiser's palace to proclaim a Soviet Republic. When word of this reached the socialists in the Reichstag they were consternated. Something had to be done at once to forestall the Spartacists. Scheidemann thought of something. Without consulting his comrades he rushed to a window overlooking the broad Koenigsplatz, where a great throng of socialists had gathered, stuck his head out, and on his own, as if the idea had just popped into his head, proclaimed the Republic! The saddlemaker, Ebert, still intent on keeping the Hohenzollerns on the throne, was furious.

That was the November German "revolution"—that was the way the German Republic was born. And Ebert, in spite of himself, would shortly become the first president of the Republic. If that seemed strange to him and to others, stranger things would come a few years later when Hindenburg, the avowed monarchist, the very embodiment of German militarism, would succeed Ebert as president of the Republic.

We know now that they were not so strange after all. They were symbols of a fact which should not have remained hidden to us as long as it did: that little had changed in Germany or in the Germans. A few of the imperial trappings were removed with the Kaiser. The General Staff was officially dissolved (though not in fact) by the Allies—not, be it noted, by the Germans. But behind the flimsy façade of the Weimar

Republic, on paper the most democratic and liberal in the world, the forces which had made imperial Germany and detested the Republic remained untouched and unhampered, only waiting to catch their breath before they would conspire to curb, and then destroy, the new, "democratic" Germany.

In November 1918, the Social Democrats, holding absolute power, could have made Germany over into a decent, democratic republic—a little radical by conservative American standards, but no more so than His Majesty's government which ruled Great Britain immediately after the second war. But to have done so they would have had to suppress permanently, or at least curb permanently, the forces which would not loyally accept a democratic republic: the feudal Junker landlords and other upper castes, the magnates who ruled over the great industrial cartels, the roving free-booters in the so-called "free corps," the ranking officials of the imperial civil service and, above all, the army caste and the members of the General Staff. They would have had to break up many of the great estates, which were wasteful and uneconomic, the industrial monopolies and cartels, and clean out the bureaucracy, the judiciary, the police, the universities, and the Army of all who would not serve honestly the democratic regime.

This the Social Democrats, who were in the main well-meaning trade unionists with the same habit of bowing to old, established authority that was ingrained in Germans of the other classes, could not bring themselves to do. They abdicated their authority to the force which had always been dominant in modern Germany, the Army. Long before the Weimar Republic collapsed, indeed almost from its birth, the Army became a state within a state, the real power in the "new" Germany, and deeply hostile to democratic and republican ideas. The Republic was thus doomed from the outset. Looking back, it seems strange now that so many from the outside world did not understand this until too late.

We were fooled, I think, by the phenomenon of prosperity and tranquillity which occurred in Germany during the brief period between 1925 and 1930. This was due, in large measure, to the achievements of Gustav Stresemann, the first German statesman since Bismarck. It was also due to the steadying atmosphere which the Peace of Locarno spread over all of Western Europe, during those few, fleeting years which now seem almost golden when we look back at them. For the Pact of Locarno, signed in 1925 between the victors and the vanquished, expressed the yearning of the Europeans, weary of war and of postwar strife, for a respite, for some peace, for some stability, so that they could live decently again and without fear as they and their fathers had lived before 1914.

Few of us who moved about in Western Europe in those days doubted that this center of our Christian civilization— for such it still was—had entered upon a long era of peace and progress and even reason in which the statesmen, profiting from the agonizing lessons of time's most destructive war, would compose the differences between nations around the conference table of the League of Nations at Geneva, leaving the citizens free to pursue their work, their leisure, their arts, their sciences, and their quest for happiness in a secure, warless, democratic world. Even for Churchill the year 1928 marked the end of the "world crisis."

Two years before, in 1926, Germany had been admitted to the League of Nations and given a permanent seat in the Council alongside the victorious Big Powers. Almost overnight, it seemed, the Germans had stumbled into the light after the dark, chaotic days of the defeat, the collapse of the old regime, and—what was worst of all—the inflation.

In January 1923, the month the American army of occupation began its withdrawal from Germany, the month French troops marched into the Ruhr on the orders of Poincaré, the mark began to collapse. It dropped to 20,000 to the dollar that month, in April to 100,000, in August to 5,000,000. By October it was exchangeable at the rate of 25,000,000,000 to the dollar and on November 15, a week after Hitler's comic-opera Munich *Putsch* stood at 4,200,000,000,000—four trillions, 200 billions to the dollar, that is.

The lifetime savings of the poor and the middle classes were wiped out. For the first time in their experience, money no longer had any value at all. A straggly bunch of carrots, a half-peck of potatoes, a few ounces of sugar, a pound of flour had more value than the largest bank account. To the middle classes especially, with their habit of saving and investing, this was a catastrophe from which they never recovered until Hitler came. To be sure, in Germany they had never formed the pillar of stability which the middle classes in England, France, and America constituted. But they were almost the only solid keel Germany had, now that the working classes had shown they were neither ready nor willing to rule. The inflation not only destroyed the middle classes financially; it destroyed their belief in the very economic structure of society. For what good were the standards and the practices of such a society, which encouraged savings and investment and solemnly promised a safe return from them and then proved to be a fraud?

The embittered burghers blamed the democratic Republic for their disaster and thus became ripe for the first demagogue of a savior (he would soon appear in the person of Adolf Hitler) who promised to redress the wrong done to them. As a matter of fact, the state was largely to blame for the inflation. In the beginning it could have stopped it by

merely balancing its budget. Later on, it deliberately provoked a runaway inflation in order to free the government of
its inherited debts, to escape from paying reparations, and
finally to sabotage the French occupation of the Ruhr. If this
pauperized the lower and middle classes, as it did, it also
wiped out the state's indebtedness and thus, on paper, paid
for the staggering costs of the war. Moreover it allowed German heavy industry to wipe out its indebtedness at no cost
at all, leaving it free to renew its machinery and rationalize
its processes and begin afresh. No wonder that German industry, when prosperity returned in the middle twenties, not
only was able to capture great markets in Europe, Asia, and
South America but to give Hitler, a few years later, the guns,
tanks, planes, and transport which enabled him to come
within an ace of conquering Europe.

And the irony was that those who forced the state to encourage and then provoke inflation were the enemies of the
democratic Republic, the great industrial magnates and the
feudal landowners, who possessed property and plant and
goods and therefore personally profited from the inflation.
The members of the disguised General Staff also were
pleased to see the war debts wiped out so easily and so thoroughly, for this left Germany unencumbered for a new war.

The German people, always quick to find a villain or two—
however innocent—not only blamed the "democratic system"
of Weimar for their plight but also the Allies, arguing that
reparations had brought about the ruinous inflation. The argument was false. Between 1921 and 1923 reparation payments dwindled to almost nothing. That was why Poincaré
sent French troops into the Ruhr. Even during the six years of
blossoming prosperity between 1924 and 1930 the Germans
paid but 1.7 per cent of their national income in reparations.
This slight burden was more than offset by foreign loans to

Germany, which amounted to two and a half times the sum paid out in reparations and which were never repaid.

Thus the very conception of reparations as a ruinous, unjust burden on the German people was a myth, as was the belief, so sedulously cultivated by Hitler, that Germany had lost the war because of a "stab in the back." People in all countries at all times subscribed to many myths. But the widespread belief in these two particular ones by so many Germans paved the way for their deliverance to Hitler and their eventual fall. Their capacity for self-deception in the period between the wars, when I was observing them, was tragic to behold.

———

For awhile, in the last half of the twenties, the resentments, and the frustrations, real and imagined, of the Germans seemed to be forgotten in the sudden appearance of general prosperity, domestic political tranquillity, and the very real successes of Gustav Stresemann in foreign policy. Stresemann was a curious but towering figure in Germany in those days. Burly, bald, and with eyes that gave him the misleading appearance of a pig, he possessed a fine intelligence and considerable character and charm. As the years passed he seemed to be one of the few German political leaders who learned from experience and increased in wisdom, though there were many, in and out of Germany, who questioned his sincerity and who suspected that his genius lay in his expediency.

During the First World War he had been a violent annexationist, a fanatic for unrestricted submarine warfare, and as a whip of the High Command had become known as "Ludendorff's young man." At the Weimar National Assembly he voted against acceptance of the Versailles Treaty. After the war he formed and led the so-called People's Party, the party of big business, the successor to the old National Liberal Party, which had been not liberal but national and expansionist. The People's Party at first accepted the democratic Republic only as a temporary expedient. Until his death, Stresemann kept up a personal correspondence with the former Crown Prince, to whom one day, he seemed to think, would be given back the Hohenzollern throne.

Yet in the catastrophic days of the inflation and the French occupation of the Ruhr he saw clearly that further blind resistance to the Allies would only bring the German nation closer to destruction. In August 1923 he became chancellor in a coalition government of "fulfillment" which called off the struggle in the Ruhr and resolved to fulfill its engagements under the Versailles Treaty. He lasted but three months as chancellor but remained as foreign minister in ten successive cabinets until his death, from strain and overwork, on October 3, 1929. In those six years he restored Germany to a high place among the Big Powers and by the force of his personality and intelligence helped to guide the Germans toward economic and political stability. His successes in foreign affairs were prodigious: the Dawes Plan, in 1924, which reduced reparations to a level which Germany could easily afford to pay; the Locarno Pact in 1925, which stabilized the peace of Europe; the admission of Germany to the League of Nations as a Big Power in 1926; and the Young Plan of 1929, which further reduced reparations and provided for the evacuation of the last Allied troops from the Rhineland years ahead of the Versailles schedule. Stresemann's personal achievements in foreign affairs brought him, in 1927, the award of the Nobel peace prize along with Briand, with whom he worked so doggedly for a new era of peace and understanding in Europe.

It did not take, however, a very astute reporter to note in

those days that Stresemann was far from having either the
gratitude or support of the overwhelming majority of the German people. The Left distrusted his conservatism and his ties
with big business. Big business itself and all the parties and
classes of the Right grew to regard him somewhat as reactionary circles in America later would view Franklin Roosevelt:
as a traitor to his class. They welcomed his victories in foreign affairs but resented his means of obtaining them; they
accused him of truckling too much to Germany's enemies;
they began to suspect that he really had become converted
to a belief in a democratic republican Germany and the concept of Germans becoming good Europeans and men of
peace.

Actually, Stresemann, staunch German patriot that he was,
but less befogged in his thinking than the politicians on the
Right and Left, merely saw that for the time being, in a world
dominated by Allied military power, Germany could only win
back its old position of strength through diplomacy. But his
policy had one fatal weakness. For Stresemann, like Bismarck
before him and Hitler after him, had to go from one foreign
success to another in order to maintain his regime. He was in
the position of a bicycle rider who could not stop for fear of
falling down. No sooner did he ask for and receive one concession from the Allies than he was forced to ask for another
in order to maintain himself in power. The threat was always
there, as it was immediately afterward with Chancellor Bruening, that if the Allies did not give in to him he would be replaced by the reactionaries and militarists. It was a form of
blackmail, but once given in to, the Allies could not abandon
the game. To do so, they feared, would be to invite the worst:
the replacement in power of the "good" German by the "bad."
Thus even when Stresemann brazenly lied to them in denying
that Germany was secretly rearming after the withdrawal of

the Allied Control Commission in 1927, they had to accept the falsehood.

They might have taken an event that happened in 1925 as a warning of the real forces which were gathering strength behind the façade of Stresemann's "fulfillment" policies. On February 28, 1925, Ebert, the first president of the Republic, died. The German people elected as his successor Hindenburg, symbol of the old Germany, a true representative of the monarchy and of Prussian militarism, and moreover seventy-seven years old. Would it not have been reasonable of the Allies to ponder, at least, the durability of the young republic which would elect to its highest office an aged and nearly senile field-marshal who stood for all that the outside world believed had been discarded or given up when the "new Germany," as Stresemann called it in his Nobel prize address at Oslo, was born in the "revolution" of November 9, 1918?

What kind of a revolution was that and what kind of a democratic republic was this to go back to Hindenburg? It was a fair question, but it does not seem to have been asked very often by the victorious Allies, who then, as now in the very year of my journey, complacently convinced themselves, despite the growing evidence to the contrary, that the Germans had changed and would henceforth be peaceful and democratic like themselves.

Perhaps Stresemann, with his intelligence, saw that foreign success was not enough to save the Republic and that it would have to be buttressed from within if it were to survive. At any rate, he tried to create a great coalition of the moderate middle-class political parties and the Social Democrats which would eliminate the frequent changes of government that resulted from the ceaseless maneuvering and horse-trading of the parties, and thereby give the republican government the political stability that it lacked. In this effort he failed. It was perhaps not fully realized outside of Germany that the parties represented in the Reichstag were little more than pressure groups, more concerned with extracting concessions for the special interests they represented than with governing a great nation. This conception of parliamentary politics they had inherited from before the war when a party judged itself successful if it wrung a few concessions from the Imperial chancellor—as Bismarck, who was contemptuous of parties, quickly learned, and to his advantage. Not all the persuasive powers of Stresemann, which were considerable, could induce the parties which formed the bulwark of the Republic to join together to save it.

Stresemann died, of exhaustion, on October 3, 1929. Six months later parliamentary democracy came to an end in Germany, and the Weimar Republic entered its death throes. It fell to Dr. Heinrich Bruening, a leader of the Catholic Center Party, who was appointed chancellor in March 1930 at the insistence of the Army, to destroy the ailing system of representative government and thus pave the way for the coming of Hitler and the Nazi Third Reich.

Not that Bruening desired Hitler's advent. He was a creature of the Army and preferred the return of the Hohenzollerns, which he desperately tried to bring about. But it was his virtual dictatorship, aided by the world economic depression of the early thirties and his own bungling, which made Hitler's leap to power inevitable.

Bruening, like Schuschnigg of Austria, whom he resembled in his piety and his political blindness, became a great favorite in our democratic circles when he came to America to live, and I have heard him at home wax very eloquent on German democracy and Germany's will for peace in the last days of the Republic when he was chancellor. The facts, however, are that he deliberately stifled German democracy to death by ruling through emergency decrees under Article 48 of the constitution; and as the Republic tottered, most of his efforts were devoted not to saving it but to speeding up secret German rearmament, tearing down the last vestiges of the Versailles Treaty, provoking trouble with Poland and otherwise pleasing the Army, which was his real master.

It is true that the world depression increased his difficulties, as it increased Hitler's opportunities. And it has often been argued by non-Nazi Germans that it was the economic crisis which alone swept the National Socialists into power. But the depression was worse in the United States, where it brought not fascism but a liberal New Deal. It was equally bad in Great Britain, where it resulted in a stringent retrenchment in armaments and a wave of pacifism.

One can even admit with Bruening that the times were hard and recall that from 1929 to 1932 production in Germany fell by a half, prices by a quarter, while unemployment, the great curse of the depression, rose from two millions to six millions. The times were indeed difficult. But is it not the test of a system of government, as it is of a human being, that it prove itself not in fair weather but in foul, not when affairs go well but when they go badly? That test was at hand for the German democratic republic as the third decade of the century began. The Republic failed to weather it, and died.

Bruening ruled by presidential decree for six months in defiance of the Reichstag majority, though his dictatorship was tolerated by the democratic parties, including the socialists, who feared the alternative of the Nazis more than they disliked him. Then, in the hope of reaping a popular reaction against the extremists of both Right and Left, he called an election in September 1930. The result was a bitter disappointment to him. Whereas the Nazis had had only twelve members in the Reichstag when he became chancellor, the

September elections gave them 107. This goaded Bruening on to try to steal some of Hitler's thunder. He became as nationalistic as the Nazis, as intent as they in demanding the scrapping of Versailles, the building up of the Army and the armaments industry, and in kindling the agitation against the hated Poles.

In March, 1931, the Bruening government let it be known that Germany was negotiating a customs union with Austria —an announcement that brought instant storms of protest from France and the Little Entente, which saw in it a prelude to *Anschluss*. The French forced Germany to break off the negotiations. And they were probably right in suspecting that Bruening had set out to make a customs union with Austria not for any special economic benefits, which would have been relatively few, but as a demagogic demonstration to show Germans that he, as well as Hitler, had dreams of a Greater Germany which would include the Nazi leader's homeland of Austria, and that he too was ready to flaunt the once victorious Allies, who had specifically forbidden the *Anschluss*. What Bruening, a cold and scholarly figure, failed to realize was that he could not compete with Hitler in demagogy. Only when it was too late did he and the Army comprehend that German right-wing nationalism could only triumph on the basis of an outrageous but highly organized and developed demagogy which would attract the masses. Hitler alone could provide this.

Chancellor Bruening now made one last effort to bring back the old Germany he loved without having to debase it by surrendering to the Nazi gangsters. Though he had sworn an oath to loyally support the Republic, he conceived the idea of restoring the Hohenzollerns to their throne. The story of his efforts, and how they failed, is still little known, even in Germany.

The next year, 1932, President Hindenburg would be 84. His re-election for a second term of seven years was almost certain, and even more certain was it that he would not live through it. His senility, even now, was almost complete. Who would replace him when he died? Bruening saw clearly that Hitler would. No other figure in Germany could possibly defeat the Nazi leader at the polls. To prevent that, one means alone remained: to bring back the emperor.

What emperor? Wilhelm II, who had fled to Holland? The Social Democrats and the labor unions would never tolerate it. The Crown Prince? There were the same objections. But perhaps even the socialists would accept one of the sons of the Crown Prince—after all, the Social Democrats had wanted the Hohenzollerns to remain on the throne even in the revolutionary days of 1918 when the Kaiser's stock was so low. They had asked only that the new emperor rule as a constitutional monarch, as the king did in England. That was exactly what Bruening proposed: a constitutional monarchy. And not next month, or next year, but only when President Hindenburg died, so that the transition could be made with the least possible trouble. Until his death, the aged field marshal would act as president and regent, with the public knowing he would be succeeded by one of Wilhelm II's grandsons, as emperor.

In the autumn of 1931 the Chancellor broached Hindenburg with his plan. The old president exploded with indignation. He would welcome the return of Wilhelm II, indeed he considered himself, even though president of the Republic, the Kaiser's trustee. To pick a grandson would violate the sacred principles of legitimacy. He would not hear of it. If the German people wouldn't accept the return of the exile in Doorn, said Hindenburg, they would have to put up with their present president. Bruening tried to argue that unless

Hindenburg acceded to this plan, his successor would be Hitler and Germany would be taken over by the Nazi barbarians. But the stubborn old Titan remained unmoved.

The next year Bruening, with the backing of the democratic parties, again including the socialists—for the choices were narrowing in Germany—succeeded in getting Hindenburg re-elected with 19,300,000 votes against 13,400,000 for Hitler and 3,500,000 for Thaelmann, the Communist candidate.

Two months later, on May 30, 1932, the newly re-elected President dismissed Bruening from office. The Chancellor, to repay the socialist masses and Catholic peasants for their vote for Hindenburg and against Hitler, had revived a mild scheme for resettlement of ex-servicemen on some of the bankrupt Junker estates in East Prussia. The scheme, known as *Osthilfe*, had originally been supported by Hindenburg himself. But in the meantime the Junkers, with the financial help of the Rhineland industrialists, had presented the Field Marshal with an estate at Neudeck, in East Prussia, which actually, at one time, had belonged to Hindenburg's family. Feeling himself at one with the Junker landowners whose property was threatened, Hindenburg, at their urging, threw out of office the man who had just got him re-elected.

The last days of the Republic had arrived. For the next eight months a motley group of antiquated barons and ambitious army officers, without political sense or any other kind of sense, for that matter, made a silly and, of course, futile attempt to preserve not the Republic but the old order in Germany, hoping to achieve this without the troublesome support of the Nazis, who were clamoring at least to share power with them. We need not dwell on their follies. These were indulged in first by Franz von Papen, a former cavalry officer who, as German military attaché in Washington in

1915, had been expelled for espionage. Hindenburg appointed him chancellor on June 1, 1932, and he promptly formed a "cabinet of barons" which quickly became a joke even in Germany. With virtually the whole Reichstag against him—the Nazis, the Communists, the socialists, even the Catholic Center of which Papen was a member, at least were united on this—he ruled for a few months, as had Bruening, by presidential decree.

In December, von Papen, a master intriguer, was replaced by his intriguing Reichswehr minister, Kurt von Schleicher, a politically minded general who had enjoyed momentary success as a manipulator behind the scenes but who failed miserably as soon as he came out into the open as the last chancellor of the Republic. Schleicher's appointment meant that the Army, which had dominated all the governments of the Republic, would henceforth attempt to be the government—quite openly. To forestall the Nazis and capture mass support, General Schleicher proposed an alliance between the Army and the non-Communist Left, that is the Social Democrats and the trade unions. This was the very alliance which had been formed in 1918 and which had saved the old order in Germany from extinction. But having completed its task, it was of no further use to two pillars of the old order, the Junkers and the Ruhr industrial magnates. They were ready, as always, to accept the Army's leadership, but not in alliance with the socialists and the unions.

Whether Schleicher could have lasted in office any length of time is doubtful. But, like Bruening, he precipitated his fall by reviving the scheme for settling war veterans on the Junker estates in East Prussia. He even went Bruening one better in an effort to win over popular support. He promised to publish on January 29, 1933, a report of the Reichstag committee on the *Osthilfe*. The report, as everyone knew, revealed a scandalous misappropriation of government funds, which, instead of going for agrarian relief, had ended up in the pockets of the Junker landlords, the very men who now had old Hindenburg's ear. They were furious—and frightened. The report had to be suppressed or their reputations would be ruined. Again they appealed to their fellow Prussian landlord in the presidential palace. On January 28, Hindenburg dismissed General von Schleicher as chancellor. The publication of the report, due the next day, was "postponed."

Two days later, on January 30, 1933, Hindenburg named Adolf Hitler chancellor of Germany. The Republic was dead. The fifteen-year experiment of democracy in Germany had come to an inglorious end. The industrialists, the Junkers, the aristocracy, and the panicky generals, who had despised it, had made their decision. They could only obtain their nationalist aims—strict authoritarian rule of the nation, the removal of the last restrictions of Versailles, massive rearmament, revenge for the lost war, and eventual German supremacy upon the Continent—with the help of the one man on the extreme right who had a mass following and who had evolved a dynamic which appealed to the deep instincts of the German people.

To be sure, these representatives of the old order were confident that they could use Hitler for their own ends. No doubt they considered him a vulgar parvenu and his following an ignorant, misguided rabble. But they had made sure that he would have only two other Nazis, Goering and Frick, in a cabinet of twelve members. How could he really upset them when they outnumbered him in the government by 9 to 3? They did not remember—if they knew—that eleven years before, in 1922, Mussolini also had had but three Fascists in a cabinet of twelve. Majority rule, however, was a concept of democracy. It had no meaning and derived no power in an authoritarian government which ruled not by constitutional law but by the law of the jungle—the strong dominating the weak. This the would-be saviors of the old, traditional Germany did not realize, but Hitler did. Within a year and a half he would eliminate them from their seats of power, though he would continue to use them for his own purposes as they had intended to use him for theirs.

On the evening of the day Hitler assumed office, January 30, 1933, the brown-shirted Storm Troopers, a quarter of a million strong, paraded in triumph in a Wagnerian torchlight procession down the Wilhelmstrasse past the Chancellery, where Hitler, on one balcony, took the salute and President Hindenburg, on an adjacent balcony, stood in wooden silence. Probably the old field marshal scarcely realized what he had touched off. It is said that he looked down upon the marching columns and muttered: "I didn't know we had taken so many Russian prisoners."

His decaying mind lay buried in the past; Hitler's was focused on the future.

The next year I moved from Paris to Berlin to cover, as an American journalist, that monstrous future (or "wave of the future" as a famous American lady called it) which almost destroyed our world and which brought Germany to terrible ruin. In Berlin over most of the ensuing eleven years I was to witness the rise and fall of the Third German Reich, which Hitler boasted would last a thousand years. It was perhaps the high point of my own little journey through the first half of the twentieth century.

I have tried to chronicle it in some detail elsewhere[2] and will confine myself here to the reflections that came to me as I poked about the German ruins that midcentury year of a journey that was taking me over old, familiar scenes and pull-

[2]*Berlin Diary*, New York, 1941. *End of Berlin Diary*, New York, 1947.

ing me back, in my mind, through the desolate years more brimming with violence, intolerance, tyranny, massacre, bloodshed, and degradation for the human race than any other period in man's history.

It took Hitler little more than a year to exterminate freedom in Germany and liquidate the parties, persons, and institutions that stood in his way. The historical states such as Bavaria, the political parties and the trade unions, were all abolished. Trade, industry, banking, labor, agriculture, the schools and universities, the courts, the police, parliament, and even the seven lively arts were quickly "co-ordinated," as the process of nazifying was euphemistically called. What the Hohenzollerns, the Hapsburgs, and Bismarck had never come close to accomplishing was done by Hitler with the greatest of ease overnight. And the wonder—at least to a foreign observer—was that there was no genuine resistance to the destruction the Fuehrer wrought. "It was no victory," observed the philosopher Spengler, who had prophesied the Nazi triumph and who would soon sicken of it, "for the enemies were lacking."

The labor unions, whose general strike had squelched the fascist Kapp *Putsch* in 1921, accepted their forced liquidation and the confiscation of their funds with little more than a whimper. The political parties dissolved themselves without stirring up any rumpus at all. At the great universities, renowned for their learning throughout the world, there were no meetings of protest among the students or professors. A few of the latter, mostly Jews who knew they were in for it anyway, resigned and left the country as quickly as possible. The writers were perhaps the most courageous of all: the really great among them, such as Thomas Mann, declined to be co-ordinated and fled for the nearest frontier. Those who remained, with one notable exception—Gerhart Hauptmann —had the courage and the decency to remain silent.

It has often been reported that the Christian churches alone offered real resistance to nazism, but this is scarcely true. There were heroic pastors and priests and even bishops here and there who fought back against the persecution of their churches, though rarely against the other outrages of the regime. But their action, being individual, had little effectiveness. In July 1933, in the very first year of Hitler's rule, the Vatican made a concordate with Nazi Germany. Its terms were constantly violated by the Nazi thugs, but it was not until 1937 that the papal encyclical, *Mit brennender Sorge,* condemning the Nazi doctrines of state and race, was read from the pulpits of the Catholic Church in Germany. And it was noted by more than one disheartened Christian that after the great pogrom of November 1938, in which most of the remaining synagogues in Germany were sacked and burned by "mobs" organized and directed by this once great state, no Christian church of any faith opened its portals to give refuge to the persecuted Jews.

Why was there so little opposition and almost no resistance to Hitler? How could a people who considered themselves members of the civilized part of the human race, who had produced Goethe and Bach and Kant and Luther, who were perhaps more pious in their worship of Christianity than almost any other in Europe, submit so supinely to this Nazi barbarism? Not only submit to it, in the beginning, but soon embrace it with enthusiasm and even fanaticism?

The answer was—and it took some time for it to dawn on me —that national socialism expressed something that lay very deep in the German mind and soul. It may never have obtained an absolute majority in a free election—it did not (though it polled 44 per cent in the very last one)—but there

is no doubt that in the heady years of one foreign success
after another it enjoyed the loyal support of the overwhelming majority of the German people. Aside from the fact that
nothing succeeds like success, this was because nazism demanded, as did almost all the German people, revenge for the
lost war, an end to the restrictions of Versailles, and an assurance of Germany's proper place in the sun—the first place
on earth, that is. But the attraction of national socialism went
even deeper. In the very beginning of its rule it fulfilled for
the Germans a centuries-old longing for political unification.
This unity, which the other great races of Europe had
achieved, the British, the French, the Spaniards, the Italians,
had always eluded the Germans.[3] Hitler gave it to them immediately. It knitted the nation together and, coupled with
the successful defiance of the Versailles victors and the rebirth of a powerful army, which Versailles had forbidden, it
gave the German people a new self-confidence, a sense of
historical mission and of the growing strength to fulfill it. In
such an elated state of mind it was easy to ignore the barbaric nature of the regime and the character of the gangsters
who dominated it.

Part of the price for what Hitler gave the Germans was
the loss of personal freedom, but it cannot be said that they
unduly regretted paying that price. Many were more than
glad to pay it. For democracy, as I noted once in my diary in

[3] Even after Bismarck's "unification" of Germany in 1871, the new Reich,
under the provisions of the constitution adopted on April 14 of that year,
consisted of no fewer than twenty-five federal states: the four kingdoms of
Prussia, Bavaria, Saxony and Wuerttemberg, five grand-duchies, thirteen
duchies and principalities and the three free cities of Hamburg, Bremen, and
Luebeck. During the deliberations of the National Assembly at Weimar in
1919 the attempt of some of the members to transform Germany into a
single state was rejected and the Weimar Republic was formed on a federal
basis of seventeen states. One of Hitler's first acts was to abolish the federal
states and transform them into mere administrative units, each governed by
a *Statthalter* responsible to the Fuehrer.

Berlin, had forced them to live as individuals, to think and make decisions as free men. In the chaos of the twentieth century, this put too much strain on them. They preferred to let someone else, someone above, make the decisions and then tell them what to do. It was part of Hitler's genius that he understood this craving of the Germans for authority over them. He was quite willing to exercise it, for it enabled him to drive this hardy people like sheep toward the goal that soon became uppermost in his maniacal mind: a great war of revenge and conquest that would wipe out the stain of defeat in the last war and make the Germans the *Herrenvolk* of Europe and perhaps, if the Americans and the Russians could be brought down, of the world.

We know now from the secret German archives the precise moment when the die was cast and the mad *Fuehrer* made his irrevocable decision to plunge the world into war.

It happened on November 5, 1937. On that day Hitler summoned to the Chancellery in Berlin General von Blomberg, minister of war, General von Fritsch, commander-in-chief of the Army, Admiral Raeder, commander-in-chief of the Navy, General Goering, commander-in-chief of the Air Force, and von Neurath, the foreign minister. He harangued them from 4.15 P.M. to 8.30 P.M., with Colonel Hossbach, his aide, noting down his words. He apprised them definitely and without equivocation that he had decided on war. And he told them why.

The date, November 5, 1937, is a fateful one in our first half-century. Yet no one in the outside world, in those many countries which two years later would become the victims of the decision made that autumn afternoon in Berlin, knew it, or even suspected it, at the time.

Our minds were on other things. Just three weeks before, the German government had solemnly pledged itself to respect at all times and under all circumstances the inviolability and territorial integrity of Belgium, an act that convinced the blind men in Paris, London, and Washington that Hitler, despite his bombast, could be counted upon after all to preserve the peace. Lindbergh had just paid a much publicized visit to Germany, as had the Duke and Duchess of Windsor. All three had been received with great cordiality by the Nazi gangsters and acclaimed in the streets by the German people. Hitler and Mussolini were winning the Spanish civil war for Franco and fascism, and in London, Neville Chamberlain, who had become prime minister in the spring, was abetting them and considering, in his abysmal ignorance of foreign affairs, and especially of German affairs, how further to appease the German Fuehrer.

I myself spent the first days of November in Brussels, where the nine-power conference sat futilely trying, by means of empty words about peace, to end the war between Japan and China.

Hitler's words to his military chieftains on the afternoon of November 5 were not empty; they were very much to the point he had always had in mind since he was demobilized from a defeated army in 1918. "The German future," he began by saying, "is dependent exclusively on the solution of the need for living space . . . This can only be sought in Europe . . . History has proved that every expansion of space can only be effected by breaking resistance and taking risks . . . Neither formerly nor today has space been found without an owner; the attacker always comes up against the proprietor.

"The question for Germany," he put it bluntly, "is where the greatest possible conquest can be made at the lowest cost."

And the next question, he added, since German aims could

be achieved "only by force," was "when and how." There were three "cases," he said, "to decide upon."

Case 1 involved the period 1943-45. At that time the German Army, Navy, and Air Force would be at the pinnacle of their power. Their armaments would be superior to those of any other nation. But the time factor was all-important. After 1945 there would be the danger of German arms becoming out-of-date and the further one of other countries catching up. "What the actual position will be in the years 1943-45 no one knows today," he said. "It is certain, however, that we can wait no longer. On the one hand, the large armed forces, with the necessity for securing their upkeep, the aging of the Nazi movement and of its leaders, and, on the other hand, the prospect of a lowering of the standard of living and a drop in the birthrate, leave us no other choice than to act. If the Fuehrer is still living, then it will be his irrevocable decision to solve the German space problem no later than 1943-45. The necessity for action *before* 1943-45 will come under consideration in Cases 2 and 3.

"Case 2. Should the social tensions in France lead to an internal political crisis of such dimensions that it absorbs the French Army and thus renders it incapable for employment in war against Germany, then the time for action against Czechoslovakia has come.

"Case 3. It should be equally possible to act against Czechoslovakia if France should be so tied up by a war against another state that it cannot proceed against Germany."

Later remarks of Hitler's in the course of his extensive discourse make it clear that he hoped to embroil France, and possibly Great Britain, in a war in the Mediterranean against Italy. He felt that the Spanish civil war might bring about this desirable result. Here he overestimated the will of the

British and French governments to resist a Fascist dictator just as, two years later, he underestimated it.

At any rate, he told his military chiefs, "It must be our first aim . . . to conquer Czechoslovakia and Austria simultaneously in order to remove any threat from the flanks . . . Once Czechoslovakia is conquered . . . then a neutral attitude by Poland in a German-French conflict could more easily be relied upon. . . ."

Hitler was not thinking then merely in terms of local wars against his small neighbors, Austria and Czechoslovakia, but of a larger war, in which France would become involved, and possibly England and Russia. He did not think in 1937 that Russia would come in "in view of Japan's attitude." He felt fairly certain that Britain would not come to the support of France and that this would affect France's "attitude." And at the end he decided that Case 3 was the best bet. "Should it occur," he said, "I have firmly decided to make use of it anytime, perhaps even as early as 1938."

This time, at least, he was as good as his word. In 1938 he took both Austria and Czechoslovakia, but their conquest proved to be easier than he had anticipated. No war was necessary. The threat of war was enough. As it happened, I watched his goose-stepping troops march into both countries unopposed. In Czechoslovakia, it is true, his armies occupied only the Sudetenland in October of 1938. But this act, which was approved by Chamberlain and Daladier at Munich on September 30, destroyed the Czechoslovak Republic and Hitler's army occupied the rest of it, without opposition, in the following spring.

In his harangue on November 5, 1937, Hitler had been wrong on only one point: that he would have to go to war to conquer Austria and Czechoslovakia. But his appetite for war increased as his army, navy and air force grew in strength. A year and a half later he again convoked his military chieftains to the Chancellery in Berlin to impart to them a new decision that made war—a big war, a world war—as he fully realized, inevitable. This cold-blooded and fateful decision was announced to his henchmen on May 23, 1939.

Five days before, Franco had entered Madrid in triumph. The day before, Count Ciano, the Italian foreign minister, had come to Berlin to sign a ten-year military alliance which pledged Germany and Italy to come to one another's aid should either of them become involved in "military entanglements." But on Hitler's specific orders Ciano had not been told how near Germany was to "military entanglements." This information was reserved for the gentlemen who gathered in the Fuehrer's study in the new Reich Chancellery on the afternoon of May 23: Field Marshal Goering, Grand Admiral Raeder, Generals von Vrauchitsch, Keitel, Halder, Milch, Bodenschatz, and a half-dozen lesser military fry.

The minutes of this meeting, kept by Hitler's adjutant, Lt. Col. G. S. Schmundt, were later captured by the Allies. The mad Fuehrer, as was his custom, expounded at length, but we can note the essentials of what he said in a few sentences —words which an observer sitting a little beyond the charmed Nazi circle might have caught whenever the Commander-in-Chief raised his voice, shrilly, hysterically, for I quote him exactly:

Circumstances must be adapted to aims. This is impossible without invasion of foreign states or attacks upon foreign property. Further success cannot be attained without the shedding of blood . . . Living space is the basis of all power . . . Poland will always be on the side of our enemies. Danzig is not the subject of the dispute at all. It is a question of expanding our living space in the East. There is no other possibility for Europe. . . .

There is therefore no question of sparing Poland, and we are

left with the decision: *To attack Poland at the first suitable oppor-*
tunity. We cannot expect a repetition of the Czech affair. *There*
will be war.

A war just against Poland? Or World War II? Hitler leaves
no doubt in the minds of his listeners what kind of a war it
will be.

"I doubt the possibility of a peaceful settlement with
England . . . England is therefore our enemy, and the conflict
with England will be a life-and-death struggle.

"What will this struggle be like?" Hitler poses the question.
And he proceeds to answer it. He realizes the vulnerability
of the Ruhr basin, source of Germany's armaments. Therefore "the Dutch and Belgian air bases must be occupied by
armed force. Declarations of neutrality must be ignored. . . .
The war with England and France will be," he repeats, "a
life-and-death struggle. The idea that we can get off cheaply
is dangerous: there is no such possibility. We must burn our
boats. It is no longer a question of justice or injustice, but
of life or death for eighty million human beings."

No one, no nation, of course, was threatening the life of
eighty million Germans. But Hitler by this time had come
to believe in his own lies and there was no one left in Germany who dared even to argue with him, much less expose
his falsehoods. Only later, when all was lost, when they were
trying to curry favor with their conquerors, would the men
around him, the generals and diplomats who had helped
make his early conquests possible, contend that they had
differed with the Leader.

Hitler, then, would burn his boats. There would be war—
a world war. On the eve of it, he delivers a few more dia-
tribes to his chieftains in order, he says, "to strengthen your
confidence." There is a final war conference at Berchtes-

gaden on August 22, 1938, ten days before the scheduled attack on Poland. He lets the generals in on a secret: he is about to sign a pact with Stalin. "Stalin and I," he tells them, "are the only ones who see the future. So I shall shake hands with Stalin within a few weeks on the common German-Russian border and undertake with him a new distribution of the world."

The Fuehrer is afraid of only one thing: "that at the last minute some *Schweinehund* will make a proposal for mediation." He means Chamberlain, the man who appeased him at Munich. Chamberlain, he laughs, "will be thrown downstairs—even if I must personally kick him in the belly before the eyes of all the photographers.

"No," he says with finality. "For this it is too late. The invasion and the extermination of Poland begins on Saturday morning."[4]

His megalomania at this meeting reaches a high pitch. Everything, he says, "depends on me, my existence. Furthermore—probably no one will ever again have the confidence of the whole German people as I do. There will probably never again be a man in the future with more authority than I have. My existence is therefore a factor of great value."

This line of thought, incidentally, is continued in a harangue he makes to his generals two months later, on November 23, to celebrate the victory over Poland. "As the last factor I must, in all modesty, name my own person: irreplaceable. Neither a military nor a civilian person could replace me. I am convinced of the powers of my intellect . . . No one has ever achieved what I have achieved . . . The fate of the Reich depends only on me. I shall act accordingly . . . I

[4]The original date set by Hitler for the attack was Saturday, August 26. He postponed it until the following Friday, September 1, 1939.

shall shrink from nothing and shall destroy everyone who is opposed to me."

In all modesty!

At the Berchtesgaden war council on August 22, he had given one last word of advice to his generals: "Glory and honor are beckoning to you, gentlemen, as they never did for centuries. Be hard. Be without mercy. The citizens of Europe must quiver in horror . . . And now, on to the enemy! In Warsaw we shall celebrate our meeting again!"

And so the war came, on the morning of Friday, September 1, 1939—a gray, sultry day in Berlin, as I remember. I stayed on in Germany another year and three months, journeying now and then from Berlin to see at first hand such things as the annihilation of Poland and, in the spring of 1940, the Nazi conquest of the West.

At first the Germans were a little apathetic, a little disappointed that their leader, who previously had won such stunning victories (the occupation of the Rhineland, of Austria, of Czechoslovakia) without firing a shot had at last resorted to war. But the amazing victories, over Poland, over Denmark and Norway, over Holland, Belgium, and France, came so quickly and with such ease and with so few losses and such scant dislocation of civilian life, that their enthusiasm began to mount. Their dreams of German supremacy were coming true. No other German leader in history had ever achieved anything like this.

For a long time the Germans had believed themselves to be the victims of an unkind, unfair fate that had robbed them of the position in the world which was surely their due. Now, at last, they had, overnight, come into their own—they were masters of the European Continent, the heart of the world—and it made little difference to them that this mastery had been won at the expense of others and by methods more deceitful, more brutal and barbaric, than our times at least, when Western man was supposed to have become somewhat civilized and even Christianized, had ever seen. Had not other nations—most nations—risen to greatness through armed conquest? The history books were full of stories which said that they had. Every great nation—Greece, Rome, France, Spain, England—had had its turn. Now was Germany's.

In my own naïveté I sought in numerous conversations with many Germans in those heady days to ascertain whether they did not, perhaps, have any doubts of a moral or ethical nature about the course their nation and its leaders had taken and especially the means they had employed. But, with one or two exceptions, I could not find that they had. Later doubts would arise in quite a few German breasts and this would be taken as proof in America that there were many "good Germans" who had been against Hitler's war and the diabolical way he had waged it and also against the savagery of Germany's occupation of the fallen lands. But it must at least be noted that such doubts as did arise came in almost every case only after the realization that Germany would certainly lose the war and that the consequences would be catastrophic for the German people. As long as Germany was winning there were precious few—outside of the concentration camps, at least—who did not rejoice at Hitler's conquests.

I myself, departing from Berlin in December 1940, left Germany at a time when it seemed certain to nearly everyone—in Germany and out—that Hitler had won the war and that Europe henceforth would be organized under his New Order. That it would be a barbaric order, bringing forth again a new Dark Age, seemed obvious to me. But this view was not shared by the overwhelming mass of the German people. They—all of them—looked forward to it. It would be good; it would be the promised land that they, as a people, had looked forward to for more than a thousand years: a Europe united under Teutonic domination.

And if the others, the Poles, the Danes, the Dutch, the French, did not like it? I would sometime pose the question to my numerous German acquaintances. It inevitably drew the blankest of stares. They did not care how the others liked it. Most never gave it a thought.

I have frequently noted in this account of a journey back through the years and across the various frontiers the incredible changes that took place in some of the nations and among some of the peoples in the brief interval of time, as history goes, that I had known them. The contrast, however, between the Germany I left one snowy day in December 1940 and the Germany I came back to in the autumn of 1945 was so great, so overpowering, that it was—and is—beyond my powers to describe.

The great conquerors were no longer recognizable. The historic nation had crumbled into dust. The invincible armies that had fought their way triumphantly to the Arctic Circle, the Pyrenees, the Volga, and the Caucasus, and to within a few miles of the Nile had dissolved or surrendered or been slaughtered; the goose-stepping soldiers who had strutted through many a conquered foreign capital were now jamming the prisoner-of-war cages, their once smart uniforms reduced to tattered rags, the arrogance gone, erased, from their countenances. The great German cities, the beautiful towns, were in ruins, the rail lines shattered, the bridges down, the canals and rivers blocked by sunken ships and barges. There was no government, no state or municipal service, no economy, no communications, no transport. The whole framework of society had collapsed. It was a debacle without precedent in our experience. And Hitler, who had led the Germans to this dire end, was dead; and Goebbels, and Himmler. Each by his own hand.

Yet, Germany, as we know, did not die. Not even the old Germany, which we mistakenly believed had been destroyed in the first German war but which now, in 1945, we were certain was dead, buried forever under the ruins, died. It survived. Again, as in 1918, the much hoped-for "new" Germany failed to emerge from the defeat of the old Germany. The Germans had not learned the lessons one supposed they would have learned from such a catastrophe, the second in a quarter of a century and much worse than the first. Despite all that had happened they had not changed.

This soon became evident. You quickly learned when you went back to Germany that first grim winter of the peace that the Germans did not regret having started the war and having waged it so ferociously. They regretted only that they had lost it. Once again they had been unlucky, they said.

Not even nazism, though it had brought these folk to ruin, was dead. As early as December 1945, a team of public opinion experts set up by the American occupation authorities ascertained through a scientific sampling of the German mind that a clear majority of all Germans in our zone believed that nazism had been a good idea but had been badly carried out. They still believed in the evil principles of Hitlerism, that is. If those principles had only been better carried out, Germany would have won the war instead of losing it. And the majority of Germans who believed that increased constantly as the years went by and they pondered the past and remembered how close they had come to winning.

The answer the Germans gave to the question put by the American authorities as to their feeling about nazism was disappointing to some of our highest American officials who had never ceased to prattle about how Hitlerism had been destroyed. "The results clearly indicate," said the official report of our Reactions Analysis Staff, as it came to be called, "that the term, national socialism, has not come into disrepute to a majority of Germans."

Indeed it hadn't.

Nor had the conception of democracy come into any great repute. Our statesmen in Washington and our highly touted proconsuls in Frankfort and Berlin never tired of reiterating that the Germans had at last become truly "democratic." This was not true. The Germans, it seemed to me at least, were not much interested in democracy. Certainly they had no confidence in it. When our pollsters asked them flatly: "Do you believe that the Germans today could actually govern themselves democratically?" less than half answered in the affirmative. A third took an outright negative view; the rest said they had no opinion one way or the other. Perhaps the question bored them.

"Clearly," commented our analysts after studying the poll, "a large proportion of U.S. Zone Germans lack confidence in their ability to manage their affairs in a democratic way."

Perhaps they had more confidence in the undemocratic way? This was not a facetious question. In Bonn you could not help but feel that the Federal Republic, established in 1949, was a façade, as the Weimar Republic had been, behind which lurked the old Germany growing in strength from day to day. It could be argued—and was—by my German friends that the Republic's first parliament had been elected by 80 per cent of the electorate—a far higher percentage of voters than ever turned out in a national election in the truly democratic U.S.A. It could be added that the Germans showed an unusual sense of maturity and strength by casting 80 per cent of their votes for moderate parties. Both statements were true—and encouraging.

Nevertheless, the democratic parties were shadowy affairs. The principal ones had been resurrected from the Weimar era and were run by elderly men who had either capitulated or failed in 1933. Adenauer, the head of the largest one, and Schumacher, the leader of the second largest, conservative and socialist respectively, were able, fearless men. But did they not belong to the past? You got the feeling that many Germans thought so, especially the youth. The young voters were holding back, and even many who voted for one democratic party or another were really waiting, you felt, to see which way the wind would blow when Germany became really on its own. They did not ticket themselves by merely voting in the privacy of a polling booth. But they refrained from taking an active part in politics. It was too early to take a stand. Who could tell? Perhaps the Nazis would soon return to power. Or something like them. A new Hitler, possibly. It would not be prudent to risk charges of being called a traitor later on.

Already, these people could see, the old gang was back in control of German economy. The industrial magnates and financiers had made Hitler's rule possible and now they had become the darlings of the American and British. By law— Allied occupation law—most of them should have been in jail along with other major Nazi offenders. Instead the British and American officials had fallen over themselves in their haste to restore them to their old jobs and to control of their great business enterprises. The German people saw this and understood what it portended.

In 1948 they began to come out in the open with trial balloons for various neo-Nazi parties. The office of the U.S. High Commissioner for Germany itself listed more than half a dozen of these groups, which it called "extreme rightist." There were the German Reich Party, the German Rightist

Party, the National Rightists, the German Bloc, the Fatherland and Union, the Bruederschaft, and the Socialist Reich Party.

They all appealed to the multitude of dissatisfied elements: former Nazis, former generals and soldiers, refugees, the landed aristocracy, and the disgruntled and sometimes impoverished sections of the middle and upper classes. At first they didn't get very far. There were too many parties. There were too many petty organizers who, remembering Hitler's rapid rise from the gutter to the pinnacle of power in Germany, wanted to become Fuehrers. And, as anyone who has followed German politics would expect, they quarreled incessantly with one another.

But at the turn of the half-century the last-named group, the Socialist Reich Party, began to run away from the field. Entering an election for the first time, that for the state legislature in Lower Saxony on May 6, 1951, it polled 367,000 votes—11 per cent of the total—and elected 16 members to the legislature. A few months later this avowedly neo-Nazi party (the Nazi Party itself is still proscribed in Germany) made its bow in Bremen by winning eight seats in the state parliament, only one less than obtained by Chancellor Adenauer's Christian Democratic Party, though its percentage of the total vote was under 10 per cent. Still, Hitler's National Socialist Party did not make such an auspicious beginning as this when it first began running candidates for office back in the early twenties.

Even the U.S. High Commissioner's Office, which for years had been smugly telling visiting firemen that nazism was dead, awoke with a jolt. After the Bremen election the political adviser to the Commissioner exclaimed: "The success of the Socialist Reich Party is alarming."[5]

[5] N. Y. *Times*, October 8, 1951.

Alarming, but hardly surprising.

In its Seventh Quarterly *Report on Germany,* issued in June 1951, the Office of the U.S. High Commissioner had reported very frankly on the sudden rise of this neo-Nazi party.

The philosophy and tactics of the Socialist Reich Party (SRP) [it said] are in many respects indistinguishable from those of the Nazi Party before 1933. The party's espousal of totalitarian ideas is at times open, on other occasions thinly veiled. Meetings are replete with military music, strong-arm squads, insignia and emotional ultra-nationalistic appeals strongly reminiscent of the Nazi regime. SRP speakers have revived the "stab in the back" legend to explain the defeat of the Third Reich. They tend to castigate as traitors all Germans who opposed Hitler. The goals of the SRP do not differ materially from those of other parties of the extremist right. It favors a strong, centralized German government, the immediate evacuation of Occupation troops, the conclusion of a peace treaty, the immediate restoration of complete German sovereignty and the creation of Europe as a "Third Force" between East and West.[6]

At Potsdam the Allied Control Council had been instructed to destroy the Nazi Party, dissolve all Nazi institutions, and "ensure that they are not revived in any form." In its Seventh Quarterly *Report* the U.S. High Commissioner's Office reiterates that this has always been "one of the basic objectives of American policy in Germany." Yet in the same report it admits that both the philosophy and tactics of the Socialist Reich Party are in many respects the same as those of the Nazi Party.

Has it moved to squelch this neo-Nazi party? Not at all. It is alarmed at its rise. But it does nothing to stop it. Its policy, it says, is to leave that to the Germans. The matter, it says smugly, is "a major responsibility of the German people," the

---

[6] Seventh Quarterly *Report on Germany;* April 1-June 30, 1951; Office of the U. S. High Commissioner for Germany (p. 31).

majority of whom, as we have seen, still believe that nazism "was a good thing."

This majority, it might be added, understand perfectly well the significance of the leading figure in the Socialist Reich Party. He is Major General Otto Ernest Remer and he is known to all Germans for one single but mighty deed which he performed in Berlin on the afternoon of July 30, 1944. He saved Hitler. He preserved nazism. Almost single-handed he thwarted the plot of the generals and the field marshals to overthrow the Hitlerite regime. And he was only an unknown major of a guards battalion when he did it.

The attempt on Hitler's life that morning, to be sure, had failed. The bomb, planted at the feet of the Fuehrer at his headquarters in East Prussia by one of the conspirators, had gone off, but it had only slightly wounded its intended victim. Even then the plotters had a good chance to succeed. Hitler was far away in East Prussia and with him were all the members of his government save one. Goebbels alone of his ministers was in Berlin that day. And he was surrounded in the Propaganda Ministry by a guards battalion which had been sent to arrest him. The plotters, led by some of the most illustrious generals in recent German history, were in control of the Berlin garrison. They had the troops—the physical force—to occupy the capital and to proclaim the end of Hitler and his regime. Moreover they had well-laid plans—the product of a year's work of some of the best organizing brains in the German Army. But they had not considered the character of one, Major Remer, commander of the guards battalion which had been sent to arrest Dr. Goebbels. As it turned out this was a disastrous oversight.

Remer was not a Nazi, at least not a party member. He was simply an average German junior officer who had been neither nauseated by the nature of the Nazi regime nor disillusioned by the imminent prospect of military defeat. Like any other officer he did what he was told by his superior officers. He did his duty. His duty on the afternoon of July 30, 1944, was to follow the orders given him by his commanding officer: to surround the Propaganda Ministry with his guards battalion and arrest the Propaganda Minister. Hitler was dead, he was told. Supreme authority had been taken over by Field Marshal von Witzleben. Remer was no major to question the authority of a field marshal.

But when he got to the Wilhelmstrasse in front of the Propaganda Ministry a surprise awaited him. One of his lieutenants, a party propaganda officer attached to the battalion, suggested that he telephone Dr. Goebbels first, before arresting him. This he did, and the Minister invited him in to talk things over. After some hesitation, Major Remer accepted. He might as well carry out the arrest in a gentlemanly fashion. Goebbels was a cabinet minister, after all, and a great name in Germany.

Goebbels was also a great talker and at this crucial moment in his career, when his acknowledged talent for quick talking and quick thinking was all that stood in the way of the overthrow of the Nazi regime and his own arrest, words did not fail him.

Had not the Major, he asked, like all army officers, sworn a personal oath of allegiance and obedience to Adolf Hitler? Yes, replied the Major. But Hitler was dead.

Goebbels sprang to the telephone. General Fellgiebel, chief of the Signal Corps at Hitler's headquarters and one of the plotters, was supposed to have blown up the telephone line to Berlin. But despite his post, and the seemingly golden opportunities it offered, he had failed to do this.

In a moment Hitler's raucous, excited voice was barking over the telephone. Goebbels quickly handed the receiver to the young major. Then came the greatest surprise of Remer's life, one that conceivably may make him Hitler's successor in the new Germany we have built up from the ashes. One second at this fateful moment Remer was an obscure major of battalion. The next he was being hailed by the Supreme Commander himself, the Fuehrer of the Third Reich, as the savior of Germany! He was being told in the torrent of words which followed that the existence of the Fatherland depended on him, on his resolution, and that regardless of his junior rank his commands would now supersede those of the highest generals or even of field marshals and that, for the moment, he possessed full powers to crush the rebellion in the name of the Fuehrer and Supreme Commander.

That was quite a rise in the world for a battalion major, and no promotion ever came with more lightning speed. Before nightfall Major Remer rallied the Berlin garrison behind the Fuehrer and snuffed out the only serious revolt ever attempted against Hitler. He was more than a match for Field Marshal von Witzleben, Col. Gen. Beck, the brilliant former chief of the General Staff, and several other generals. Hitler immediately jumped him from Major to Major General.

You might have thought, if you had not known Germany and the Germans very well, that, after Hitler's fall and the utter catastrophe which befell Germany as the result of Hitler's rule, Major General Remer, Hitler's savior, would not be marked for any particular prominence in the new "democratic" Germany that was going to make amends for all the evil the Nazi Fuehrer had wrought. No German could forget the great and unique service he had rendered nazism in its hour of crisis nor the shattering blow he had deliberately dealt the "good Germans" who at the eleventh hour had striven to liberate Germany from the Nazi tyranny.

The Germans did not forget. They soon made Remer an authentic hero. Somehow, in the chaotic days that followed his great feat, he developed some of *his* hero's gift of rabble-rousing. He became an effective speaker, a tub-thumper whose voice and personality could arouse the masses. And he set about to organize the millions who had been convinced Nazis into a new Nazi party with the very aims, point of view, and tactics that Hitler had used so successfully on his road to power.

Admittedly, it is too early to say whether or not he will succeed. In a field that is still wide open, the odds undoubtedly are against him. But at the midcentury, five years after the fall of Hitler, at a moment when we were begging the "new" Germany to join us in the fight for freedom against Communist tyranny, it was significant, I thought, that this neo-Nazi party with this particular leader was, overnight, emerging as a political force to be reckoned with, strong enough to "alarm" our own complacent occupation authorities and to be considered by them, as the Seventh Quarterly *Report* put it, "a potential danger."

I myself was not surprised at this development. From all that I had seen and felt in Germany since the surrender, it seemed to me to be a most logical turn of affairs. The true Germany, the Germany we have come to know in two ferocious wars and then forgotten as soon as the shooting stopped, was emerging as it was bound to do—just as it had emerged after the First World War.

This Germany was not democratic and it was not the wiser for the two shattering defeats it had suffered in the two world wars that had dominated our time. Given the opportunity, it would undermine the West German Federal Republic as it had undermined the Weimar Republic. It stood for an authoritarian structure of government and society. It believed that this not only best suited the Germans but that the majority of them preferred it—in the long run—to any other system. True, this authoritarian Germany had failed twice—disastrously. Any other people, after such an experience, would have had enough, and out of sheer desperation rooted out the last remnants of the old nation that had brought it so much misery and set to work to found a new one.

The German people had not done this in 1918, and they were not doing it now. It was not they, but their enemies, their conquerors, who had overthrown the Hohenzollern dynasty and brought Hitler's savage rule to an end. It was not they but the victorious Allies who had insisted both times, in 1918 and 1945, that Germany try democracy. Left to themselves they would have gone along with the Kaiser or with Hitler and continued to accept meekly or even enthusiastically the way of life which these two rulers and their regimes imposed upon them.

But were there not, you asked as you roamed about Germany as the second half of our century was beginning, some new voices crying out, as Martin Luther once had done, for a new way of life for the Germans? Were there not at least some writers who could fire the imagination of the people for good as Hitler had for evil? Certainly in all the German land there was a poet, a playwright, a novelist who had remained silent during the Nazi tyranny and secretly written his heart out in the hope that some day his words would stir his people to seek a new path.

I, like many others, looked for him when I went back to Germany that first winter of the peace. The desk drawers could now be unlocked. And among the heaps of manuscripts that had been hidden in them from the Nazi censors and secret police certainly there would be a masterpiece or two, perhaps from a young, unknown author, which would light the way for the new, regenerated Reich. But the drawers turned out to be empty. Not a single writer of note or even of promise who remained in Germany during Hitler's rule had felt the call. The books that began to be published were from the old authors, the ones who had made their peace with Hitler or even actively supported him. Or they were from the pens of politicians, diplomats, and generals who had been members of Hitler's team. In both cases the books were little more than crude apologies, written in self-justification. Most of them offered lame excuses for Nazi excesses. Some of them defended Hitler's vilest deeds. Many of them blamed the democracies for Germany's plight.

Ernst Juenger, a staunch nationalist who had welcomed Hitler's coming to power, was perhaps the most popular writer in the years just after the defeat. A hero of the first German war, he had soured on nazism though he had continued to publish under Goebbels' strict eye and during the war had been given pleasant posts as an army officer first in Paris and later in southern Russia. His diaries of the war years, published under the title of *Strahlungen*, and a novel, *Heliopolis*, written just after the war, were best sellers and though they expressed a certain horror of the Nazi savagery they offered nothing better to replace it than a return to the old conservative, nationalist Germany. Juenger had no interest in democracy and it was not surprising that he attracted a following composed mostly of rightist extremists who longed for the good old days of Nazi dictatorships.

Of the other writers who published under Goebbels, Hans Carossa, Ernst von Salomon, and Hans Grimm enjoyed a certain popularity after the defeat. All were mediocre and none of them had learned anything at all from the Nazi disaster. Indeed they defended nazism, and von Salomon and Grimm were addicted to the old Nazi line that the Allies and the Jews must be held responsible for Germany's ills.

Some of the most popular authors in postwar Germany turned out to be the generals. The books of General Heinz Guderian, the great tank commander (*So Geht Es Nicht,* or "That Isn't the Way to Do It") and General Franz Halder, the brilliant chief of the General Staff until Hitler dismissed him in 1942 (*Hitler Als Feldherr,* or "Hitler as Warlord"), were best sellers. Both criticized Hitler for his mistakes—his errors in military judgment, that is. But they did not seem to feel any moral compunction about his wholly unjustified and unprovoked attacks on one innocent country after another nor about the inherent evil in a system which destroyed man's freedom and organized the massacre of millions of helpless human beings because of their race. Their message to the German people was that if Hitler had let the generals run the war, Germany would have won.

The youth of Germany, unlike that of America, felt no urge to commit its war experiences to paper. Perhaps the shock of defeat, of long years for many in Russian prisoner-of-war camps, of coming back to destroyed homes and uprooted families and unemployment, was too great. I sat up many a night during my journey talking with them, for they were Germany's only hope. They were still dazed and inarticulate and some were naturally bitter and cynical at the collapse of the world that had looked so rosy to them in the days of their service in the Hitler Youth. But it was remarkable, I thought, that none of them had sought to transform their thoughts and impressions, their hopes and disillusionments, into novels or plays or poems or essays.

Here and there, to be sure, as I moved around Germany that year I came across a German writer of courage and nobility whose voice was crying out in the wilderness. Such a

one was Eugen Kogon, a Catholic liberal, who spent seven
years in a concentration camp and survived to write a classic
—an amazingly dispassionate account of the concentration-
camp system set up by the S.S. (called in German *Der SS-
Staat* and published in America under the title: *The Theory
and Practice of Hell*). As editor and publisher of the *Frankfurter Hefte*, one of the finest literary and political monthlies
in the world, and chairman of the Executive Committee of
the German Council of the European Movement, Kogon was
one of the most decent and civilizing influences in Western
Germany. So was Arno Rudert, a physically shattered victim
of the concentration camp, who was coeditor and publisher
of the daily newspaper *Frankfurter Rundschau,* a courageous
anti-Nazi journal, and Karl Gerold, his partner.

Unfortunately, there were not many others in Germany
like them. If there were, there would be more hope for this
faltering land.

Hope? What hope was there? There was very little hope
that Germany would become democratic. But was there a
chance that she might at least become settled enough to stop
disturbing the peace of the world? At the very least, could
we expect her to pledge her undoubted strength to our side
in the struggle with the Soviet Union and its Communist
satellites?

One fine autumn day I sat on the banks of the Rhine above
Bonn, the capital of the Federal Republic, pondering these
things. The spot was actually the terrace below the Godes-
bergerhof, one of the pleasant inns of Godesberg that lie along
the swift-flowing river. The view was not entirely unfamiliar.
I had been there before—twelve years before, almost to a day.
Up the river a few hundred yards was the Dreesen Hotel,
where Hitler had stayed and where he had conferred with
Neville Chamberlain in those feverish fall days of 1938 just

before Munich. High above the far shore on the Petersberg you could see the Petershof, now the seat of the Allied High Commissioners. The British Prime Minister had stopped there and I remembered ferrying across the river and going up there to hear him in faltering sentences betray the bankruptcy of his policy and his mind. He was trying his best to sell Czechoslovakia, "that faraway land," as he had referred to it, down the river. But he was troubled and baffled to find that every time he made a concession to Hitler the German leader demanded another. A week later, at Munich, I would see him capitulate completely and thus take the step that made World War II inevitable.

Chamberlain, I recalled that fine fall day twelve years later, had gambled on Germany's siding with the West, in return for the concessions he was constantly making to her. He honestly believed he was pushing her into eventual conflict with Russia. Now, in the midcentury year, the United States, it seemed to me, was glibly making the same gamble. We were making one concession after another to the West German Federal Republic, restoring her sovereignty, her economy, her opportunity to rearm, in the complacent belief that she would side with the West and against Russia.

Perhaps she would. But could we count on it? Was it wise to risk so much on an assumption that might be false? Recent German history, it seemed to me, was not exactly reassuring. Bismarck, under the Hohenzollerns, had promoted friendship with Czarist Russia. The Weimar Republic had made a virtual alliance with Bolshevik Russia that lasted from 1922 to the coming of Hitler eleven years later. And Hitler himself, though he had impressed the Chamberlains with his rantings against communism and the Soviet Union, had made a pact with Stalin in August 1939 which had brought on World War II.

What reason did we have to assume, unless we were completely blind to history, that Germany, however the structure of its government and society might evolve in the second half of our century, would not line up with Russia again? At any rate, the idea that the Germans necessarily would sacrifice themselves for the defense of the West was to me a dangerous delusion. In 1870, in 1914, in 1940, great German armies had struck westward and two out of the three times overwhelmed France. Was this Germanic pressure from behind the Rhine toward the west forever stilled? I could find no ground for believing so.

It was not, of course, communism which attracted the Germans toward Russia. By the midcentury, communism was a spent force in Germany. In the free elections in the Western zones the Marxist party polled but 5 per cent of the vote. In the East zone its vote probably would have been less in a free election since the Germans there had lived under Communist rule for five years and had had more than enough of it. But the Germans did not have the delusion, so widespread in America, that in order to do business with Russia you had to sympathize with her ideology. Both the bourgeois-democratic Weimar Republic and the fanatically anti-Communist Nazi Reich had found they could make profitable deals with Bolshevist Moscow. Might not the latest of the Germanys—the one we were now building up—eventually find that it could too?

For the Soviet Union, as many a conservative German reminded me during my journey, had much to offer Germany. All Germans agreed on one thing: they wanted a united Reich. And only Russia, in occupation of the eastern part, could grant that—by getting out. Only Russia, the Germans emphasized to me, could give back the lost territories in the east, most of which had gone to Poland. And the day might come, they thought, when she might do so—for a price. After all, not only Czarist Russia and Imperial Germany had divided up Poland. Soviet Russia and Nazi Germany had parceled it out between them in 1939. It could happen again, my German acquaintances said. There would be a price, of course. The Kremlin was not giving anything away. The price would be a Russian-German alliance—a partnership which, as Stalin had frankly reminded the Germans after the war, would be dominant in Europe, as indeed it would be.

There was the other alternative, the one we were gambling on, that Germany would ally herself with us and furnish much-needed troops and arms to the Western coalition that was trying so desperately at the midcentury point to make itself strong enough to deter Russian aggression. I found little enthusiasm for this course among the Germans themselves. Even those who were for it attached a condition that the United States, Great Britain, and France could not readily accept. These Germans, and Dr. Kurt Schumacher, the fiery leader of the socialists, was one of them, were not much interested in an alliance for the *defense* of the West. They wanted Germany to participate in it only on the condition that its principal purpose be not the defense of the Elbe line but the taking of the offensive against the Red Army *beyond* the Elbe so that the eastern provinces could be reconquered and restored to Germany.

The logic of the Germans had to be admired. They saw only two ways of restoring a unified Germany and getting the lost territories back. One was by an alliance with the West, which would achieve these goals by armed might. The other was by an alliance with Russia, which alone had the power to satisfy these twin German aspirations by grant, and without war. The latter solution would satisfy the Russians. Neither solution was satisfactory to the West.

There by the side of the Rhine, which had once formed the border between the civilization of Rome and the barbarism of the Teutonic tribes and along which had been centered for two thousand years much of German history and German legend and German literature and song, I, who did not belong to this world but whose life, like that of so many other Americans, had been drawn into it and shaped by it, pondered the question: which way, then, would the Germans go?

I could not answer it. No one could for sure. But surely, I thought, it was as premature for our generals in the Pentagon to be counting up the German divisions which they thought would soon be at their disposal, as they were said to be doing that year, as it was for Molotov to be dreaming, as he was reported to be doing, of Russia's sharing the productivity of the Ruhr.

In the immediate years ahead the Germans would undoubtedly play off one side against the other in order to extract the maximum advantage for themselves. In the end their decision as to which way to jump would be governed by the consideration of which side could offer them the most. I saw I had been wrong in thinking that the Germans had not learned a single lesson from the two lost wars which they had fought virtually alone. They had, I realized, finally learned at least one lesson: that they were not quite strong enough to conquer Europe by themselves. In the future, they saw, they would have to ally themselves either with Russia or the West, whichever was stronger and promised most to Germany as a partner. No decision had yet been made. The choice was still wide open.

On the American plane from Frankfort to London, I picked up the morning newspaper, the *Frankfurter Rundschau*. On the front page was a headline: MANTEUFFEL DEMANDS FULLY

ARMED GERMAN WEHRMACHT. The famous panzer general had been addressing the magnates of the Rhine-Ruhr Club at their stronghold in Duesseldorf. The *Rundschau* reporter noted that it was an "overflow" meeting and that many former high-ranking German army officers were present. This was the combination—magnates and military—which had been the backbone of Kaiser Wilhelm II's Germany, which had sabotaged the Weimar Republic and brought Hitler to power. Since the second defeat they had not been much in the public print. The big industrialists had been busy, however, regaining control of the German economy. The generals had been thirsting for new armies to command.

Now both groups were confident enough to begin to come out in the open. On this day General of the Panzer Troops (as he was called) Hasso von Manteuffel was telling the members of the Rhine-Ruhr Club and their military guests that it was "high time" that the Federal Republic restored "fully armed German troops with equipment equal to that of other powers, including tanks and an air force." He and those behind him, the general said, were ready to defend "Western freedom."

Western freedom! Was it not the Manteuffels "and those behind him" who shortly before had come within an ace of destroying it?

I had heard when I was at Bonn of the so-called "Manteuffel Plan" which had been circulating up and down the Rhine. In it General Manteuffel had rejected Allied plans for the Germans to furnish just a few troops to the Atlantic Pact coalition. "They," he had argued, "would be no more than cannon fodder for the Soviet offensive. No military leader of any status would appeal to soldierly German youth to throw itself beneath the Soviet panzers at some Thermopylae be-

tween the Elbe and the Rhine—in order that our Western
neighbors might sleep in safety a few nights longer." Manteuffel considered that the minimum German contribution to
the defense of "Western freedom" must be, as he put it, "an
armored German core together with light forces for an over-
all total of thirty divisions." And "obviously," as he reiterated
to his audience in Duesseldorf according to the *Rundschau*
dispatch which I was now reading, the Germans must be
represented in the high command of the European forces.

I passed on from this account to another that caught my
eye in the morning journal. Dr. Hjalmar Horace Greeley
Schacht, it seemed, had just been cleared of any taint of
nazism by a German court—Schacht who had held two cabinet posts simultaneously under Hitler, who had plotted to
make him chancellor in 1933, and whose financial wizardry
had contributed immensely to the strengthening of the Nazi
regime and to its rearmament for war. Five years before, I
had seen him in the prisoners' dock at Nuremberg and heard
him deny he was a Nazi and claim that he had fought val-
iantly and tirelessly against Hitler. It had been a little difficult, though, to forget my earlier remembrances of him
sitting on the stage of the Kroll Opera House, where the Nazi
rubberstamp Reichstag gathered, with Hitler's other cabinet
members and grinning with pride and approval as the Fuehrer raved and ranted from the rostrum. Now he was cleared
by his own people of any guilt for his well-known past.

I put my newspaper aside. We were crossing the Rhine
and would soon be leaving Germany behind us. I had followed its fortunes for a quarter of a century, through the
last years of the Weimar Republic, the long years of the Nazi
tyranny, the agonizing years of the war, and the five uneasy
years of the second peace. In that time Germany had gone

full circle. When I had first gone there it was recovering from a lost war and now it was recovering from a second—both times with the liberal help of its conquerors. The first time it had shattered our hopes that it would become a democratic nation devoted to peace. Once again we had resurrected the same old hopes. Did they stand on any firmer foundation now? I myself could see few signs of it. The opportunity for Germany was still there. It was not too late for her to join the civilized world. But how many chances, I wondered, did a people have in history to make good? The Germans had squandered so many, used so many up. If they failed again might not their chances for survival as a great nation be exhausted? Germany's neighbors might not care to save her a third time.

The plane headed over the Channel and soon the cliffs above Dover hove into view. I had last seen them from this direction in the fall of 1940 when, with other correspondents, I waited near Calais with the German Army to cross over. The crossing never came off. England, as we know, was not conquered, as the Germans had been so sure she would be that autumn. She had changed a good deal, I knew. Like all the other countries through which I was passing on this journey, England had undergone incredible transformations in the second quarter of the century. London had been my initial stop when I had first come abroad in 1925. It was still the seat of empire then, a great citadel of conservative capitalism, in many ways the mightiest city of the world. Over its grimy, chimney-potted roofs lingered an aura of power— money power, political power, world power—which still enabled those who had it, and wielded it, to dominate much of this earth and to maintain for themselves a gracious, leisurely, commanding way of life that amazed and fascinated a hustling corn-fed youth of twenty-one from the prairies of Iowa.

And now—just twenty-five years later?

The plane came down at the London airport and I drove into the city in the rain to see.

5. WILL THERE ALWAYS
BE AN ENGLAND?

"This happy breed of men. . . .
This blessed plot, this earth, this realm,
this England."

—SHAKESPEARE.

"Poor England! Leading her free, careless life from
day to day, amid endless good-tempered parliamentary
babble, she followed, wondering, along the downward
path which led to all she wanted to avoid."

—WINSTON CHURCHILL.

"The advantages which position, coal, skill and enter-
prise won for us in the nineteenth century have been
liquidated . . . Most of us are not men or women, but
members of a vast, seedy, overworked, overlegislated,
neuter class, with our drab clothes, our ration books
and murder stories, our envious, stricken, old-world
apathies — a careworn people."

—HORIZON.

THE MERE THOUGHT of the profound changes that had taken
place on this island in so brief a moment of history was staggering, even to one at this closing stage of a journey that
had recalled the death or decay or overthrow of so many
venerable worlds, institutions, and ways of life across the
Channel on the Continent.

The British had emerged from the stern test of the First
World War in a position of supremacy never surpassed in

172

their history. They seemed to have proved once more the genius of a foreign policy that went back four centuries and which led Britain invariably to ally itself with the weaker powers of the Continent against any single nation which threatened to dominate it. This instinctive course had disposed in time of the challenge of Philip II's Spain, Louis XIV's France, and the French Empire of Napoleon. Now in 1918, it had successfully destroyed the aggressive aspirations of Hohenzollern Germany.

The British Empire was not only intact but larger by a million square miles and seven million persons, which had been added to a vast territory that before the war spread out over thirteen million square miles, a fourth of all the land there was on the planet, inhabited by 450 million people, one quarter of the earth's population. The world in all its time had never seen anything like it. It was the largest, the wealthiest, the most populous empire ever organized.

As late as 1925, despite the tremors faintly felt here and there, all seemed well with it. My first impression of London on my arrival that year off a cattle boat from America is of the British Empire Exhibition at Wembley which King George and Queen Mary had reopened with regal pomp and ceremony in the spring. A sort of Kiplingesque atmosphere clung to it, the ghosts of the great empire builders and viceroys—Ripon, Lytton, Lansdowne, Cromer, Milner, Morley, Minto, Zetland, Curzon, and others—hovered about although some of them were not yet dead; and crochety, pink-faced old gentlemen spoke reverently of being carried back to the golden time of Victoria and the Diamond Jubilee.

The mid-twenties were, in many ways, still a golden time in England. The curse of chronic unemployment was beginning to plague the country, to be sure. Gandhi was already awakening India, and there were rumblings elsewhere in the

Empire and in the world. The Germans had turned to their military hero, Hindenburg, and elected him president of the Republic. But in London these warnings that the victorious peace was far from secure were scarcely noticed, much less understood, and therefore never heeded.

The complacency of the small ruling class, even to one fresh from Coolidge's smug America, seemed monumental. There was no doubt that this amazing oligarchy, satiated as it was by its wealth and power, and blinded by it, was firmly in the saddle. Indeed, despite the growth and extension of political democracy, the upper class, comprising the people of position and wealth, had been in the saddle since the autocratic rule of the king had ended some three centuries before. After the First World War, democracy in Britain was as pure and as complete as in America, but one soon learned in London that democracy did not necessarily mean equality.

And therein lay, for me at least, one of the fascinating riddles of British life and politics. The men of means, the gentry and the aristocracy—all those who made up the upper class—had gradually extended the suffrage until it included all the people. But in so doing they had managed, with a genius that could only be admired, to persuade the masses, as Virginia Cowles[1] has pointed out, that the best way to use the political power which their massive vote gave them was to elect their "betters" to govern them. This the great body of the middle and lower classes had done, so that even in the twenties a foreigner was startled to see how great a number of men of title or of wealth were chosen in the rough and tumble of the elections to be members of the House of Commons.

The lower classes seemed to accept, as an established fact,

[1] *No cause for Alarm,* by Virginia Cowles; New York, 1949.

the assumption that the upper classes were born to rule. In the last election before the Second World War, in 1935, the people elected an overwhelming majority of 415 Tory members to Parliament, of whom more than half were either knights or baronets or related by blood or marriage to the peerage. Between them the Conservative M.P.'s held 775 company directorships and 279 were products of that bulwark of the upper class, the public schools, principally Eton and Harrow.[2] "It is as difficult for a poor man, if he is a Conservative," Duff Cooper, a Tory himself, wrote in the *Evening Standard* in 1939, "to get into the House of Commons as it is for a camel to get through the eye of a needle."

This mixture of aristocracy, gentry, and wealth not only dominated the Parliament and therefore the government of England but also its economy. Two per cent of the people owned sixty-four per cent of the national wealth—an arrangement which led John Gunther to observe that "these persons comprise a fluid and impregnable ruling class, or caste, which is one of the most remarkable phenomena in the world today."[3]

Few foreigners, unless they were business tycoons or otherwise wealthy or ambassadors or loaded with a Continental title, penetrated this charmed circle that dominated England. Those who belonged to it were aloof, to say the least, and my own knowledge of them (until the second war broke down the barriers temporarily) was mostly confined by what I read in the papers or heard in the gossip of Fleet Street or learned by an occasional metaphorical rubbing of shoulders when my journalistic assignments took me to Parliament or to such sporting events as the races at Ascot, the cricket at Lords and the tennis at Wimbledon. One became dimly

[2]*Ibid.*
[3]*Inside Europe*, by John Gunther; New York, 1936.

aware then of a still privileged world that moved between the great country estates and the town houses in London, its members living in a certain luxury with considerable grace and ease, absorbed in sports, in parties and hunting, in endless gossip about who was getting married or divorced or otherwise carrying on, eating well and drinking well, not taking business too seriously if they were engaged in business, but fascinated by politics, which they regarded as a splendid game, like cricket—and all the while, it seemed to me, woefully and disastrously oblivious to the currents that were rising to engulf them, rising not only in their own tight little land but across the narrow Channel on the European Continent and beyond the seas at the furthest outposts of the Empire.

For the eddies that in time would become whirlpools were already discernible to those who had the time and the inclination to look sharply around. Even some bare, hard fact stood out. One fact was that the very foundation of England's prosperity had been shaken by the first war and its aftermath. A billion pounds, one fourth of its foreign investments, had been liquidated to help pay for the victory. England's near-monopoly of shipping was being broken by the growing merchant fleets of the United States, Germany, and Japan. The production of coal, which had been one of the main props of the nation's economy, had fallen off sharply and its export had dwindled to disastrous proportions. First the United States and then Japan and Germany were capturing former British markets, especially in Asia and South America. Wall Street was replacing Lombard Street as the financial capital of the world.

Without these markets and the lion's share of the world's shipping and the profits from international banking and insurance and the production and export of coal, the British

Isles, small in themselves, overpopulated, and poor in natural resources, could not possibly maintain either the standard of living to which its inhabitants had become accustomed or its eminent position as a world power and empire. Everyone in Britain knew this instinctively. But throughout the twenties and early thirties they shrank from recognizing it or doing very much about it. Their prestige, which was still great, and their traditions, which were old and hallowed and had served well, would somehow, they seemed to think, carry them along and pull them through.

In the meantime, why worry? For those born to wealth or rank, or who acquired it, life was still good. It was a pleasure, a pleasant duty, to rule over so much of the world. Often it was profitable. Sometimes there were quite glittering awards beyond money: a brilliant career in Parliament and in government; or in diplomacy or the Army and Navy; or a governorship of an Indian province or of one of the colonies, or the viceroyship itself—posts where an Englishman was truly king and could live with all the purple trappings. In those years I came often to England in June, at the height of the "season," as the climax of the year for society was called. No doubt the great garden parties, including those given on the lawn of Buckingham Palace, were not nearly so dazzling as those in the gay, sparkling post-Edwardian days just before the 1914 war which Osbert Sitwell has described with such touching nostalgia in his memoirs. But they were elegant and colorful affairs and one still remembers the flowered dresses and ridiculous hats of the women, the fastidious attire of the gentlemen, the glittering jewels, the profusion of flowers, the procession of marble-faced, liveried servants, the sumptuous food and the champagne, and the cultivated air of social superiority and snobbery that permeated these occasions. During Ascot week the parties in the town houses and in the country at the week end would be especially gay and scintillating, as if the good people had few cares and many pleasures.

And what about the others in England, who had neither wealth nor rank? Those who belonged to the solid, stolid middle class on the whole approved of the privileged position and life of those above them. They had a deep pride in their country, its institutions and customs. They were proud of the Empire and admiring of those who had built it up; and they voted Tory. Some of them, by dint of amassing fortunes or reputations in the professions or in government service, graduated to the ranks of the upper classes, bringing new blood and sometimes brains and sometimes wealth to enrich and strengthen the upper crust.

And the others? The majority of the population—the great mass of the lower middle class and the workers? Over the years an awakening had come to them—and a discovery.

In fact they had stumbled across a secret of political power that is still hidden from Americans: *that since in a political democracy, which must by its very nature be dominated by those who hold the allegiance of the numerical majority, the people who work for wages and modest salaries outnumber those who don't, they can, by combining in one party, assume the political rule of a nation.* In a day of universal suffrage they have the votes to achieve this end.

This was foreseen in England long ago by a few eminent and farsighted Conservatives. One of them was appalled by the prospect; another took it philosophically and with good humor.

Walter Bagehot, the noted Victorian economist and essayist, and author of *The English Constitution*, was frightened at the very thought of the lower classes getting together for political action. It would be, he wrote, "an evil of the first magnitude" and would mean "the supremacy of ignorance over instruction and of numbers over knowledge. So long as they are not taught to act together," he said, "there is a chance of this being averted, and it can only be averted by the greater wisdom and foresight in the higher classes."

Some years later, in 1892, Lord Randolph Churchill, the father of Winston Churchill, took a less gloomy view. "The Labor community," he wrote, "is carrying on . . . a very significant and instructive struggle . . . for the practical utilization in its own interest of the great political power it has acquired."

It was merely doing, he saw, what other groups before it had done in *their* own interests when they ruled the nation.

Our land laws were framed by the landed interest for the advantage of the landed interest, and foreign policy was directed by that interest to the same end. Political power passed very considerably from the landed interest to the manufacturing capitalist interest, and our whole fiscal system was shaped by this latter power to its own advantage, foreign policy being also made to coincide. We are now come, or coming fast, to a time when Labor laws will be made by the Labor interest for the advantage of Labor . . . Personally I can discern no cause for alarm in this prospect. . . .[4]

Apparently, after the first war, a growing number of British citizens saw no cause for alarm either. The vote of the Labour Party increased rapidly. In 1910 it had totaled but 370,802. At the next election, in 1918, it rose to two and a quarter millions. In 1922 Labour polled four and a half million votes, elected 142 members to Parliament, and displaced the Liberals as the second party in Britain and as the official opposition. In 1929 Labour became for the first time the

[4]Quoted by Virginia Cowles, *op. cit.*

largest party in the Commons, with 288 members against 260 for the Conservatives and 59 for the Liberals. Twice between the wars, for the first nine months of 1924 and from 1929 to 1931, there were Labour governments under Ramsay MacDonald, but as they did not have a majority in the Commons, being dependent on the Liberals for their day-to-day existence, they were powerless to carry out any of the essentials of their party program.

With the exception of these two brief periods, the ruling force in Great Britain, from the fall of Lloyd George's wartime coalition in October 1922, until May 10, 1940, when Winston Churchill formed his coalition for the second war, was the Conservative Party. For a few months under Bonar Law, and then from May 1923 until May 1937 under Stanley Baldwin, and finally under Neville Chamberlain, the Conservatives determined the course of the nation for fifteen out of the eighteen years that led up to the catastrophic situation of May 1940. From 1931 on, to be sure, when MacDonald dumped his Labour colleagues overboard, there was a so-called "National Government." But its national aspect was only a façade. And though the ailing, tragic and—in the end—ridiculous MacDonald clung tenaciously to the office of prime minister until June 1935, the real power in Britain was wielded first by Stanley Baldwin and then by Neville Chamberlain and by the Tories, whom they led.

It is therefore the Conservative Party, the very bulwark of the nation and the Empire, on which most of the blame must be put for the disastrous course which Britain followed between the wars. During much of this time I observed its incredible policies with growing amazement from the vantage point of the Continent. Over there one derived not only a certain perspective but firsthand knowledge of the threat to Britain that was rising in Germany. The complacency, the stupidity, the sheer blindness of the ruling group in London which led it to throw away all the advantages Britain had gained from victory in the first war, to dissipate its strength, to decline to keep pace with German rearmament, to nag the French and flirt with the fascist dictators, surpassed my understanding, which was certainly not above the average.

We have seen how this complacency, this utter confusion of thought, this failure to face facts, corroded France and made it ripe for its defeat and downfall. But there was a fundamental difference between France and Great Britain. The French were weakened not only by their blindness but by their divisions. As regards foreign policy there was no comparable division in England. All three British parties seemed to have on identical blinkers when they looked out at the world. The Conservatives, Labourites, and Liberals vied with each other from the fateful year of 1933, when Hitler assumed power in Berlin, in their championship of retrenchment on arms and in their practical devotion to pacifism.

If Baldwin and MacDonald and Chamberlain were blind to reality, then so was the great mass of the citizenry of Britain. Never was a people so united in floating placidly downstream. It was one of those "awful periods," as Churchill would later say, when the British nation "loses all trace of sense or purpose, and appears to cower from the menace of foreign peril, frothing pious platitudes while foemen forge their arms."[5]

It was the period (1933) when the Oxford Union passed its resolution that "this House refuses to fight for King and country." It was the period (1935) of the National Peace Ballot in which eleven and a half million British citizens, 40 per cent of the electorate, "voted" for peace.

[5]*The Gathering Storm,* by Winston Churchill; Boston, 1948.

To me, in Berlin, all this made no sense. All the decent
men in the world were for peace; but Hitler was for war.
By 1935 he was rapidly forging a military machine to make
and win a war. The only recourse left for the nearby democratic lands—Britain, above all—was to build up a military
force to match Germany's. Its very existence might deter
Hitler from starting a war: if not, it would at least save their
countries from quick defeat.

The key to military supremacy at this time lay in air
power. Though Germany had been forbidden by the Treaty
of Versailles to manufacture military aircraft or to create an
air force of its own it was no secret that one of Hitler's first
acts on coming to power in January 1933 was to organize an
air force. By 1934, though its existence was never admitted
by the German government, it was firmly established and
rapidly growing. When Churchill called this to the attention
of Baldwin in March of that year, the Prime Minister gave a
solemn promise in the House of Commons that Britain would
at least maintain air parity with Germany. (Apparently
there was no thought of making Germany comply with the
Versailles Treaty, though Great Britain and France still possessed, in 1934, the military power to enforce compliance.)

Baldwin did not keep his promise. A year later he was
forced to confess that he had been completely misled by the
estimates of Germany's progress in the air. The Nazi Reich
had in fact, as Hitler told two astonished English visitors,
Sir John Simon, the British foreign secretary, and Anthony
Eden, in Berlin at the end of March 1935, reached air parity
with Britain. To Mr. Churchill, who almost alone in the Commons had prodded the government not to let Nazi Germany
get ahead of Britain in the air, this was "a disaster of the
first magnitude."[6] It would become an even greater one each

[6]Winston Churchill, *op. cit.*

year as the Luftwaffe continued to outdistance the R.A.F. When the war came, Britain had just half as many planes as the Germans.

In those years of the mid-thirties, I traveled not infrequently from Berlin to London and Paris. And just as the French capital grew more and more incomprehensible to me so did London. In Berlin I saw a constant stream of English visitors and I followed the course of British politics daily in the *Times* and other British journals. Moreover I kept in contact with the British Embassy in the Wilhelmstrasse. But one had to go to London itself to become completely confounded not only by the policies the Tory government was following in those years but by the attitude of the Labour Party and the Liberals. Some of my closest friends were rising young men in the Labour Party, and two or three were prominent as Liberals either in the House or in London journalism.

But they, like the Conservatives, seemed to move in a world completely devoid of reality, lost in a fantastic wilderness of their own making. There were some Tories, men of considerable power, who were inclined to approve Nazi Germany. But Liberals and especially Labour detested it. They yearned to see Hitler in hell. Yet they stubbornly refused to support any policy that might help to put him there. They declined even to back those measures by which Britain and France might have called Hitler's bluff when they were still able to—up to the Rhineland occupation in 1936, say. And to the bitter end they opposed even halfhearted efforts to make the R.A.F. as strong as the Luftwaffe and the decision of the government, on the eve of the war, to adopt conscription. The Liberals and the socialists hated Nazism, but they were determined not to do anything about it. No more than the Conservatives did they have the heart—or the wisdom—to face the consequences, for Britain, of Hitler's rule in Berlin.

I remember our complete bewilderment in Berlin at the reaction in London to a Parliamentary White Book published on March 4, 1935, which commented with almost unseemly moderation on the "anxieties" caused by German rearmament. It had been made public in connection with the scheduled visit to Berlin of Simon and Eden to discuss releasing Germany from the disarmament provisions of the Versailles Treaty in return for Hitler's assurances of his peaceful intentions. It was a most mild statement of British concern over Germany's secret rearmament, especially in the air, and with the aggressive spirit which Hitler was generating in the German people and particularly in the youth. The Fuehrer was furious. He asked Simon to postpone his visit. In Berlin we took Hitler's wrath with a grain of salt. There were well-founded reports that he was on the verge of a daring move and that he preferred to see the British statesmen after—not before—he had taken it. That he was angered by the British White Paper there was no doubt. But he had his mind on a more important matter, which he had long been preparing to carry out: the tearing up of the military clauses of the Versailles Treaty and the introduction of conscription for a new army of thirty-six divisions, which he proceeded to announce on March 16. A thousand White Papers emanating from Whitehall would not have made him any more determined than he was. Only a stiff British attitude backed by armed might would have restrained him.

This seemed obvious enough to any observer in Berlin. What we were not prepared for was the hysterical outburst in London against the moderate White Paper, which had merely called attention to a few well-known facts about what was going on in Nazi Germany. The National Peace

Council promptly called it "the most incredible document that has ever been published by any government." Lord Robert Cecil, the president of the Council, thought it "a deplorable document." Herbert Morrison, the Labour president of the London Municipal Council, who one day would be foreign secretary, believed the White Paper to be "one of the most tragic events since the Versailles peace."

The Liberal and Labour press, and even sections of the Conservative press, were outraged, rivaling Hitler in their fury. To the Liberal London daily, *The News Chronicle*, the consequence of the White Paper was "a catastrophic increase of Germany's suspicions and fear of encirclement. In twenty-four hours the British Government has immeasurably deteriorated the entire international situation. We hope," it concluded, "that the British Government will not spare any efforts to regain the ground lost by the publication of the White Book and assuage the anger which is aroused in Germany."

The Conservative weekly, *The Economist*, felt that "to publish such assertions makes Germany a scapegoat . . . The document," *The Economist* lamented, "does not take the German point of view into consideration and creates the impression that England has joined in the encirclement of Germany."

The *Daily Herald*, principal organ of the Labour Party, went even further in this orgy of incredible nonsense. "The White Book," it commented, "is not only an insult to Germany, it is also the rejection of the entire system of collective security . . . Germany is repeatedly accused of 'breaking the treaty,' of 'aggravating the situation,' and of 'bringing about a situation which imperils the peace' . . . Let us hope that the effects will not be catastrophic . . . But let the world understand—it is important for the world to understand —that this is not the voice of the English people."

Hitler was not easily given to laughter but if he saw these unbelievable outbursts from London, as there is reason to believe he did, he must have given in to the temptation. At any rate, a few days later, on March 16, he abrogated the military sections of the Versailles Treaty and thereby shattered the structure of the peace of Europe that had endured for sixteen years.

Three months later, in brazen violation of at least seven solemn undertakings and in defiance of the protests of its French ally, the British government entered into cahoots with Hitler to violate the naval clauses of the Versailles Treaty. It was perhaps the most shameful act of any British government between the wars. There were others of which few Britons should have been proud: Sir Samuel Hoare's attempt to sell out Abyssinia to Mussolini, and Neville Chamberlain's betrayal of Czechoslovakia at Munich.

Heretofore we have been concerned with the complacency with which Britain slid downhill between the wars. Now we come to the first of the essentially immoral acts which her Tory government committed in a desperate effort to appease the fascist dictators under the delusion that by so doing it was saving Britain from war.

During a visit to London in the spring of 1935, Joachim von Ribbentrop, Hitler's "special plenipotentiary," as he then was, had dangled a bait which the British Admiralty had promptly swallowed. He revealed that his master was ready to restrict the German fleet—"definitely and for all time to come"—to 35 per cent of Britain's total tonnage. Within that broad limitation Germany would be allowed to build 60 per cent of Britain's submarine strength and, in exceptional circumstances, 100 per cent. This, Ribbentrop explained, was a "one-time" offer. If the British government accepted it in principle, Hitler would be ready to negotiate the details immediately. If not, the offer would not be renewed—ever!

Prodded by the Admiralty, which thought Ribbentrop's proposal was a bargain compared to the situation before the war when British naval superiority was only 8 to 5 over Germany, the Baldwin government lost no time in negotiating a naval agreement on Hitler's terms. No matter that at this very moment Britain was joining with France and other nations in an appeal to the League of Nations against Hitler's unilateral violation of the military clauses of the Versailles Treaty. Britain now hastened to help Hitler violate the naval clauses of the treaty.

One of those clauses had forbidden Germany to construct any submarines at all. But the British government had no compunction in conspiring with Nazi Germany to break it. The morals of treaty breaking aside, it seemed incredible, from the standpoint of Britain's self-interest, that *any* British government would deliberately encourage the Germans to start building up a great U-boat fleet. The day the naval treaty was signed in London, June 18, I noted in my diary in Berlin: "The Wilhelmstrasse quite elated. Germany gets a U-boat tonnage equal to Britain's. Why the British have agreed to this is beyond me. German submarines almost beat them in the last war and may in the next."

Actually, as was to be expected, the Germans, as soon as they had built up to 60 per cent of Britain's submarine tonnage, invoked the emergency clause allowing them to construct 100 per cent. When the war broke out in 1939 they had 57 U-boats to Britain's 58. Within a year they constructed 58 more. The island kingdom was to pay dearly for this particular folly.

And yet it was stoutly defended by the British government

and overwhelmingly approved by the House of Commons. Sir Samuel Hoare, who had replaced Sir John Simon as foreign secretary on June 7, 1935, had the temerity to tell the House: "The Anglo-German naval agreement is in no sense a selfish agreement." And he made much of what he called "the very important statement of the German government" that "henceforth they would eliminate one of the causes that made the war so terrible, namely, the unrestricted use of submarines against merchant ships."

If the mind reels at such unbelievable naïveté, one must remember that at this time those in power in London had not yet had much experience in evaluating Hitler's word. Few, if any, members of the cabinet appear to have read *Mein Kampf*, in which Hitler warned the world of his contempt for solemn promises if they stood in the way of his own or Germany's advancement. The reoccupation of the Rhineland, the rape of Austria, the destruction of Czechoslovakia still lay ahead.

A crisis from another quarter was, however, presently at hand. On October 3, 1935, Mussolini's forces invaded Ethiopia. The League of Nations, under Britain's leadership, reacted with unaccustomed speed. By October 11, fifty out of fifty-four nations in the League Assembly had approved the Council's decision finding Italy guilty of violating the Covenant and asked for collective measures to be taken against the aggressor.

Economic "sanctions" was the watchword. It was confidently believed that they would soon bring a country as poor in natural resources as Italy quickly to her knees. They might have, had they been applied honestly and fearlessly by the nations banded together in the League. But they were not. Mussolini had warned that oil sanctions would mean war. And it was soon clear that none of the nations backing the League, Britain always at their head, dared risking war. Therefore oil sanctions, which alone would have made Mussolini's conquest of Abyssinia impossible, were not applied. Neither was the shipment to Italy of steel ingots and pig iron forbidden. The League's collective measures hampered Italy but did not seriously hurt her. The Duce's ragged, badly led armies conquered defenseless Ethiopia in seven months—between the rainy seasons.

But at first the hypocrisy of the League powers in applying partial sanctions was not apparent to the peace-loving citizens of their countries. This was especially true in Britain. The whole country had been aroused by the stirring speech made by Sir Samuel Hoare to the League Assembly in Geneva on September 11:

The British people are deeply and genuinely moved by a great ideal . . . and they are not prepared to abandon it . . . The ideals enshrined in the Covenant . . . have appealed with growing force to the strain of idealism which has its place in our national character . . . The League stands, and my country stands with it, for the collective maintenance of the Covenant in its entirety, and particularly for steady and collective resistance to all acts of unprovoked aggression.

To one delirious League delegate, Sir Samuel's eloquent words furnished "one of the great electrifying moments in the history of the League." But in truth they were mostly eyewash. Baldwin had no intention of risking war to uphold the League against the aggressor. He would not even hazard applying the sanctions that would ruin Mussolini's enterprise in Abyssinia. But he saw in the upsurge of popular feeling in Britain in support of backing the League against the aggressor an opportunity not to be missed. He therefore called an election for November 15.

Rarely has the British electorate been so hoodwinked. The Conservatives campaigned on the issue of peace and unstinted British support for the League against aggression. Said the government's election manifesto:

The League of Nations will remain as heretofore the keystone of British foreign policy. The prevention of war and the establishment of peace must always be the most vital interest of the British people, and the League is the instrument which has been framed and to which we look for the attainment of these objects. We shall continue therefore to do all in our power to uphold the Covenant and to maintain and increase the efficiency of the League. In the present unhappy dispute between Italy and Abyssinia there will be no wavering in the policy we have hitherto pursued.

The Labour Party jumped on the bandwagon. It too promised peace and support of the League against Mussolini's aggression. And it clamored against rearmament, though it was difficult, for an outside observer at least, to see how, without more arms and planes, Britain could give effective aid to the League's collective action against military aggression. The confusion and contradictory attitude of the Labour Party was summed up by its newly elected leader, Major Attlee, in the House of Commons, October 22: "We want effective sanctions, effectively applied. We support economic sanctions. We support the League system." But in the next breath he was crying for fewer tools to do the job. "We are not persuaded that the way to safety is by piling up armaments. We do not believe that (nowadays) there is such a thing as national defense. (!) We think that you have to go forward to disarmament and not to the piling up of armaments."

The election gave Labour three times as many seats as

it had held—154 to 52—but Mr. Baldwin gained a considerable triumph just the same. His "National Government"—for he still clung to the fiction—obtained a majority of 247 seats. The Tory Party alone elected 387 members to Parliament.

"Thus," as Churchill later commented (in *The Gathering Storm*), "an administration more disastrous than any in our history saw all its errors and shortcomings acclaimed by the nation."

The acclamation died suddenly, if only temporarily, less than a month later. The Conservative election manifesto, as we have seen, had promised that "there would be no wavering" in Britain's policy of upholding the League against Italy's aggression. But early in December, on his way through Paris to Switzerland, where he planned to pass a vacation ice-skating, Hoare saw Laval, the French foreign minister. He wavered. He agreed to a plan giving Mussolini most of what he wanted in Abyssinia without further fighting. It was the Hoare-Laval Pact of December 9.

The cabinet in London approved it on the same day. Its terms were to be kept secret until it had been submitted to the three parties to the dispute: the League, Italy, and Ethiopia. But Laval immediately leaked it to the French press. There was an uproar in England such as had not been heard for many years. It caught the government, basking in its great electoral victory, by surprise and caused great consternation in the ministerial ranks. At first the Prime Minister sought to evade the issue, at least until the official text had been published, by which time he apparently thought the storm would blow over.

"My lips are not yet unsealed," Mr. Baldwin exclaimed in the House. "Were these troubles over I would make a case, and I guarantee that not a man would go into the lobby against me."

The storm did not subside. Indignation was particularly great against Hoare, who in September had so roundly denounced Italy's aggressive intentions and then in December abetted them. But the outcry threatened to bring Prime Minister Baldwin himself down. Now it was his turn to waver. The cabinet which on December 9 had approved Hoare's handiwork decided on December 18 to reject it, and the harassed Foreign Secretary had no other course but to resign. On December 19 Baldwin made a curious apology to the House, frankly admitting in a manner that appealed to the British that he had not expected "that deeper feeling that was manifest in many parts of the country on what I may call the grounds of conscience and of honor." On December 22 the popular Anthony Eden, whose name had become identified with the League, succeeded Hoare as foreign secretary.

This instinctive flare-up in Britain against the Hoare-Laval plan showed that, as sometimes happens in a democracy, the people were ahead of the government, that they were not prepared to see their country knuckle down to a fascist dictator and abandon every precept of decency and honor. It was much to their credit. But it did not last long. Soon the British people, like the government, fell into a deep apathy from which they were not to be aroused, even by one act of Nazi-Fascist aggression after the other, even when their very security as a nation was gravely threatened, until the last possible minute. When they awoke from their apathy it was too late—or almost too late. To an American visitor to London in those days, it was beyond comprehension that the instinct of self-preservation in a great and powerful people who heretofore had shown a positive genius for looking out for themselves could become so extinct.

———

In Berlin during this time we were conscious that Hitler

was watching all these proceedings with the keenest attention. He did not expect that the League of Nations would
take any serious action against Italy but because of his own
plans he wanted to make sure. And he wanted to see what
Britain would do in the face of Mussolini's defiance. He felt
that events were playing into his hands. I remember spending the afternoon of October 4, 1935, the day after the
Italian legions attacked Ethiopia, in the Wilhelmstrasse getting an earful of the Fuehrer's thoughts from some of his
henchmen. They were in high spirits. I scribbled their opti-
mistic conclusions in my diary that day: "Either Mussolini
will stumble and get himself so heavily involved in Africa
that he will be greatly weakened in Europe, whereupon Hitler can seize Austria, hitherto protected by the Duce; or he
will win, defying France and Britain, and thereupon be ripe
for a tie-up with Hitler against the Western democracies.
Either way Hitler wins."

The course of events that fall and winter convinced the
German dictator of several things: that the League was dead
as a force in European politics; that the French had no stom-
ach for a fight; and that the British had lost the will to make
hard decisions which, as he showed in *Mein Kampf,* he had
so admired in them in the past.

Fortified by these convictions, he struck in the following
spring.

On March 7, 1936, he sent in the German Army to reoc-
cupy the Rhineland in violation not only of the Versailles
Treaty, which of course had been forced on Germany, but
of the Locarno Pact, which Germany had freely signed. Less
than a year before, on May 21, 1935, in a much publicized
"peace" speech to the Reichstag, but which was directed
especially to public opinion in Great Britain, Hitler had solemnly promised not only to respect the remaining provisions

of Versailles but had gone out of his way to assure the West that Germany "in particular will uphold and fulfill all obligations arising out of the Locarno Pact." He had even added: "In respecting the demilitarized zone [of the Rhineland] the German government considers its action as a contribution to the appeasement of Europe."

But the fiasco of the League and the paralysis of mind and will in London had led him to change his mind. On March 7, he staked his whole future on the gamble that neither France nor England would do more than verbally protest his reoccupation of the Rhineland. On the eighth, I learned that the German Army had been given strict orders to beat a hasty retreat from the West bank of the Rhine if the French Army opposed them in any way. Had this happened, Hitler would have been finished, and he knew it.

But he had calculated correctly. The French government and the French High Command hesitated. They appealed to London. His Majesty's government would not hear of taking any effective action. To be sure, Mr. Eden called in the German Ambassador to tell him Hitler's action was "deplorable." But as Lord Lothian said—and the British press and people echoed: "After all, they [the Germans] are only going into their own back garden." In fact British public opinion was inclined to sympathize with the Germans and to be annoyed at the French for becoming so excited.

Flandin, the French foreign minister, flew to London on March 11 to implore the British government to join France in taking military measures, if necessary, to drive the Germans out of the Rhineland. He told both Neville Chamberlain and Stanley Baldwin that if a firm Anglo-French front was maintained Hitler would yield without war. "You may be right," the Prime Minister retorted, according to Flandin's own account, "but if there is even one chance in a hundred that war would follow from your police operation, I have not the right to commit England." Mr. Chamberlain said: "We cannot accept this as a reliable estimate of a mad dictator's reaction."[7]

Neville Chamberlain was to prove himself singularly inadept at estimating this particular mad dictator's reaction to anything in the years to come. But this was not apparent in the balmy spring days of 1936.

Nothing was apparent. It was not apparent that this was the last chance for Britain and France to stop Hitler short of a long and costly war. No one in London except Churchill appears to have realized the *military* consequences of Germany's reoccupation of the Rhineland: that Hitler could now fortify the western German border opposite France so as to be free to move in the east and southeast.

The mad dictator actually did not move again for two years. In London it was noted that Hitler seemed to be settling down. Had he not shouted to the housetops in the very Reichstag speech wherein he announced the occupation of the Rhineland: "We have no territorial demands to make in Europe! . . . Germany will never break the peace"? I had heard the words myself, but I had also heard the words of General von Blomberg, the war minister, on the following day: "An enormous responsibility rests upon our shoulders. It is all the more heavy because *we may be placed before new tasks.*"

With Hitler quiet, Britain settled down and turned her thoughts to her own internal affairs. The much vaunted Intelligence Service does not appear to have learned of the historic meeting in the Berlin chancellery on the afternoon of November 5, 1937, at which, as we have seen, the German leader apprised his generals of his decision to go to war.

[7]*Life of Neville Chamberlain*, by Keith Feiling; New York, 1946.

A dictatorship knew how to keep its secrets. Perhaps even if the British had known of this one they would not have believed it, or at least done nothing about it. It was more pleasant to be preoccupied by less troublesome matters at home.

In May of 1935 the people of Britain had been happy to celebrate the silver jubilee of King George V's accession to the throne. There was a deep and genuine affection for this monarch whose quarter-of-a-century reign had encompassed so much stirring history. In a rapidly changing world that had seen so many thrones toppled into dust, he was the symbol of a very real stability and tradition. At his jubilee the people of the realm united to pay him and Queen Mary a warm and generous tribute.

King George V died on January 20, 1936. It soon became evident that his son, Edward VIII, would turn out to be a very different kind of king. For the next two years the British people were to be absorbed largely by his affairs, first by the unorthodox manifestations of his independence of mind and finally by his passion for an American divorcée, which shortly would cost him his throne. Once again, when the crisis caused by the King's insistence on marrying Mrs. Simpson reached its climax in December 1937, the British people showed that profound unity of feeling which is the admiration of the outside world. King Edward abdicated December 10, to be succeeded by his brother, King George VI, who was crowned in Westminster Abbey on May 12, 1937, amid a new upsurge of national sentiment and devotion to the throne.

A fortnight later, on May 28, Mr. Baldwin, who had handled the constitutional crisis with considerable skill and tact, stepped down from the high office he had held so long. He received an earldom and the highest honor in the land, the

Garter, retiring from public life in an atmosphere of public esteem such as has rarely been accorded a British political figure. He had personified what the British liked most in their public men in time of peace: moderation. He was the very embodiment of John Bull: ponderous, solid, dependable. He was not intellectual and never brilliant—qualities which the British are suspicious of in their politicians. But he was a shrewd judge of men and of domestic politics. Harold Laski, a socialist, noted that Baldwin had "the Englishman's genius for appearing an amateur in a game in which, in fact, he is a superb professional." And Mr. Churchill, who was at odds with him throughout the thirties, found him "a profoundly astute party manager" with "a deep knowledge of British party politics . . . a genius for waiting upon events." Kingsley Martin, the socialist editor, spoke of Baldwin's "reputation for simplicity and honesty" being "worth millions of votes."

His great weakness was that he thought too much in terms of "millions of votes" and not enough—though he was the staunchest of patriots—of the threat to Britain that was rising on the Continent, whose affairs interested him little, perhaps because he knew so little of them. His mind seldom roved beyond the narrow confines of the British islands. This handicap was to lead him toward the end of his career to make a devastating confession—one of "appalling frankness," as he himself said.

On November 12, 1936, in answer to a charge by Churchill that he had failed to keep his solemn pledge that Great Britain would never fall behind Germany in air strength, Baldwin told the House of Commons: "Supposing that I had gone to the country and said that Germany was rearming, and that we must rearm, does anybody think that this pacific democracy would have rallied to that cry at that moment? I cannot think of anything that would have made the loss of the election from my point of view more certain."

Mr. Churchill was stunned. "That a Prime Minister," he wrote later, "should avow that he had not done his duty in regard to the national safety because he was afraid of losing the election was an incident without parallel in our parliamentary history . . . It carried naked truth about his motives into indecency."[8]

If Mr. Churchill was stunned and the House, as he says, "shocked," it cannot be said that the rest of the country was quite so affected. Indeed it is a commentary on the inexplicable torpor in England at this time that Mr. Baldwin continued tranquilly in office. No more than the Prime Minister did the people and the press, regardless of party, wish to face the unpleasant facts of Nazi Germany's rearmament nor arouse themselves to do something about them. The Labour and Liberal Opposition was as blind and as irresponsible as the ruling Tories. Labour especially was obsessed by pacifism. All during the years when Hitler was racing to build up a mighty air force and army to carry out the objectives he had publicly proclaimed in *Mein Kampf* Labour demanded that Britain disarm.

In 1934, when the government came forward with a modest program of meeting the challenge of Germany's growing Luftwaffe by gradually increasing the strength of the R.A.F. over a period of five years, the Labour Party, backed by the Liberals, introduced a motion of censure. It expressed regret that the government "should enter upon a policy of rearmament neither necessitated by any new commitment nor calculated to add to the security of the nation, but certain to jeopardize the prospects of international disarmament and to

[8]Winston Churchill, *op. cit.*

encourage a revival of dangerous and wasteful competition in preparation for war."

Mr. Attlee, in support of this motion, had added: "We deny the need for increased air armaments . . . We reject the claim to parity."

A year later, after Mr. Baldwin had confessed that Germany had already caught up with Britain in the air, Mr. Attlee, for the Labour Party, was still reiterating his blindness to the House: "We stand for the reduction of armaments and pooled security . . . Our policy is not one of seeking security through rearmament, but through disarmament." And Sir Archibald Sinclair proposed on behalf of the Liberals in the same debate: "Let the government table detailed and definite proposals for the abolition of military air forces."

Up to the outbreak of the war, the Labour Party fanatically opposed conscription, which the government had finally—and reluctantly—pushed through Parliament in the summer of 1939. I remember arguing that year, whenever I was in London, with my Labour Party friends, particularly with men like Aneurin Bevan, whom I had known for years, that conscription was a necessary evil forced on them by Hitler and that it was not nearly so "undemocratic" as they supposed. The experience of Switzerland and the Scandinavian democracies proved that. But they turned on me in scorn and fury. "We have lost, and Hitler has won," Bevan exclaimed when the conscription bill was finally passed. Arthur Greenwood called it "criminal."

Neville Chamberlain, who now became prime minister, was a man of different stripe than his easygoing predecessor, though he was no less ignorant of what was transpiring in the outside world. One difference was that Chamberlain didn't realize it. Narrow and insular, with the outlook of a provincial businessman, which he had been most of his life, the new prime minister was a man of positive and stubborn opinions and considerable driving force. He easily convinced himself that he knew all about Europe, that he could handle the fascist dictators and make an honorable peace with them. Of his horror of war, his sincere desire for peace, there could be no doubt. But unfortunately, in the Europe which he faced, on becoming prime minister in May 1937, good intentions were not enough. And Chamberlain lacked the knowledge, the instinct, that, until this period between the wars through which we have been journeying, had enabled British statesmen for centuries to assess accurately the power and the direction of forces on the Continent and make the decisions which permitted Britain to ride out the storms and emerge on top.

With the coming to power in England of this limited if well-meaning man, there began the brief era of intensive appeasement which he initiated and led and which was to end so disastrously for him, his country, and the world. There is no parallel in British history to the catastrophic diplomacy which he pursued for the next two years and which led him inexplicably to encourage and strengthen the very enemy who was determined to destroy his country, and to betray or abandon or weaken the friends and allies, whose help might have enabled him to prevent the war he sought to avoid or to win it quickly and overwhelmingly if it broke out. In the foolish course which he now pursued he was not alone. Behind him was the almost unanimous opinion of Parliament, press, and people.

We come now to the climax of this account of a great nation caught in some historic force whose reason and logic escapes us but which inexorably propelled it downward to the edge of the precipice. The steps down, still fresh in the memory of many, may be briefly noted; they were landmarks in my own groping journey through our century.

Chamberlain's principal motive was pure. It was to avoid war. Like all decent men he loathed it. "War," he said before the war, "wins nothing, cures nothing, ends nothing . . . In war there are no winners, but all are losers." He recalled what a historian had written of the Greeks: "that they had made gentle the life of the world," and he said: "I can imagine no nobler ambition for an English statesman than to win the same tribute for his own country."[9]

Noble it might be, but was the gentle life possible in a world increasingly threatened by a mad German who believed that the future belonged to the tough and the brutal? Chamberlain believed so. In one of his first speeches as prime minister he said: "Are we to allow these two pairs of nations [Britain-France and Germany-Italy] to go on glowering at one another across their frontiers, allowing the feeling between the two sides to become more and more embittered, until at last the barriers are broken down and the conflict begins which many think would mark the end of civilization? Or can we bring them to an understanding of one another's aims and objects and to such discussion as may lead to a final settlement? If we can do that, if we can bring these four nations into friendly discussion, into a settling of their differences, we shall have saved the peace of Europe for a generation."

He lost no time in clumsily setting out to try.

His strategy was simple—and incredibly naïve. It was to court the two fascist dictators, to restrain France and keep her at arm's length and to discourage the United States and Russia from butting in to spoil his game.

Though the public in Britain and America did not learn

[9]Keith Feiling, *op. cit.*

of it until six years later,[10] Mr. Chamberlain found an opportunity to rebuff the very first serious effort made by the United States under the Roosevelt administration to intervene in European affairs and throw its not inconsiderable weight into an attempt to alleviate the crisis caused by the growing aggressiveness of Germany and Italy. On January 11, 1938, President Roosevelt in a secret letter to the British Prime Minister proposed to call a conference in Washington of the Axis and democratic powers to discuss the worsening international situation, if Britain would first approve and give its "wholehearted support." For the President this represented, given the isolationist state of American public opinion, a somewhat dangerous gamble. In his desire to head off war, he was willing to take it; but first he wanted Mr. Chamberlain's blessing.

Instead of a blessing Mr. Roosevelt promptly received a brush-off. Without even consulting Mr. Eden, his foreign secretary, who was away on vacation, the Prime Minister promptly replied suggesting that the President's proposal cut across his own efforts to reach an understanding with Germany and Italy. He divulged that he was prepared to recognize *de jure* Mussolini's conquest of Ethiopia as part of an over-all settlement with Italy. He asked if the Washington conference might not better be postponed. It was—forever. The President was disappointed, and also "gravely concerned" that the Prime Minister was ready to accept Fascist aggression in Abyssinia. Cordell Hull, Secretary of State, thought such acceptance would arouse "a feeling of disgust."

Ten years later, when he was writing his memoirs, Churchill would still be almost speechless at the mere thought of Chamberlain's having muffed this heaven-sent opportunity of getting America to intervene in Europe's growing mess.

[10]*The Time for Decision*, by Sumner Welles; New York, 1944.

"To Britain," he wrote, "it was a matter almost of life and death . . . We must regard its rejection—for such it was—as the loss of the last frail chance to save the world from tyranny otherwise than by war. That Mr. Chamberlain, with his limited outlook and inexperience of the European scene, should have possessed the self-sufficiency to wave away the proffered hand stretched out across the Atlantic leaves one, even at this date, breathless with amazement . . . Having neglected our defenses and sought to diminish the defenses of France, we were now disengaging ourselves, one after the other, from the two mighty nations whose extreme efforts were needed to save our lives and their own . . ."[11]

For Russia also proffered a hand and was likewise coolly turned down by the great Peace Maker.

In America at the midcentury it was difficult, I realized, to discuss realistically anything that had to do with the Soviet Union because of our disillusionment and consequent hysteria at Moscow's double-dealing since the war. Nevertheless in any honest account of this journey through the prewar period the facts concerning Russia's offers to collaborate with the Western democracies against Nazi Germany (whom she would later briefly embrace) must be set down. They impressed Churchill, who, wiser than we—and than Chamberlain—never let the distrust and hostility he felt toward the Soviets destroy his sense of reality in a power-dominated world.

There were four formal Russian overtures. The first came on March 18, 1938, a few days after the *Anschluss*. The Soviet government suggested to Britain and France that a conference be held to consider how best to implement the Franco-Soviet Pact within the framework of the League should Nazi Germany, whose troops had just occupied Austria, commit

[11] Winston Churchill, *op. cit.*

further aggression. The Russian suggestion was turned down. In the House of Commons on March 24, Mr. Chamberlain explained why: "His Majesty's government are of the opinion that the indirect but none the less inevitable consequence of such action as is proposed by the Soviet government would be to aggravate the tendency towards the establishment of exclusive groups of nations which must in the view of His Majesty's government be inimical to the prospects of European peace."

Again one is rendered speechless by Chamberlain's gullibility—or was this explanation merely a further example of an outrageous hypocrisy? For Germany and Italy had already joined together in an extremely close and exclusive group. In October 1936 they had signed a secret agreement which set up the Rome-Berlin Axis. Even before that they had joined together to intervene for Franco in Spain. And in the autumn of 1937 Italy had formally adhered to the German-Japanese Anti-Comintern Pact. Chamberlain was not alarmed at his potential enemies' ganging up. His only concern was to prevent his own side from doing the same. Churchill proposed a "Grand Alliance" of Russia, France, and Great Britain to balance the Axis as the Entente of these same three nations had offset the German-led Triple Alliance before the 1914 war. Chamberlain considered it and smugly rejected it as "impractical."

The second Russian offer of help against Nazi Germany came on September 21, 1938, ten days before Chamberlain sold out Czechoslovakia at Munich. Speaking to the League Assembly at Geneva, Litvinov announced that the Soviet government had reiterated to France and Czechoslovakia two days before that Russia would fulfill its obligations under its pacts to come to the aid of these two nations in case of a German attack. As proof of its readiness it asked for immediate military talks between the war ministries of the three nations. Chamberlain paid no attention to this offer from Moscow and proceeded to Munich to betray Czechoslovakia to Hitler.

Notwithstanding this further rebuff, not to mention her exclusion from the Munich conference, Russia proposed, on March 21, 1939, a conference of six powers. Hitler's troops had just occupied Bohemia and Moravia (March 15) and thus stamped out what was left of the Czechoslovak Republic. There was no doubt that Poland would be next on Hitler's list. But Chamberlain saw no use in a conference in which Russia took part. He not only had "a most profound distrust of Russia," as he said privately at the time; he had "no belief whatever in her ability to maintain an effective offensive, even if she wanted to."[12]

Being in this frame of mind, there is little wonder that the Prime Minister failed to grasp the last and final overture from Moscow. It was a formal offer, made on April 16 after a conference between Litvinov, the Soviet foreign secretary, and the British ambassador in Moscow. The Kremlin proposed three concrete things: a pact of mutual assistance against aggression between Great Britain, France, and Russia; a guarantee by the three powers of all states in Central and Eastern Europe against aggression; the conclusion of a definite agreement between the Big Three powers "on the forms and extent of the immediate and effective assistance to be rendered to one another and to the guaranteed states in the event of an attack by aggressors."[13]

No offer could have been more complete. All the agreements which Chamberlain was hastily making, or would

[12]Keith Feiling, *op. cit.*
[13]*Nazi-Soviet Relations 1939-41; Documents on German Policy 1918-45;* the State Department.

make, to come to the aid of Poland, Rumania, Greece, and Turkey in case of Nazi attack were useless unless he also brought in the only nation with substantial military power in the east. There could be, as Churchill tried to argue, no eastern front without Russia, and no effective western front without an eastern front. Therefore the Soviet Union must be brought into the anti-Hitler coalition at once. Churchill himself, as well as Lloyd George, thought Moscow's proposal was "a fair offer." He urged the Chamberlain government "to get some of these brutal truths into its head" and not reject Russia's overture.

Chamberlain stalled. He did not reply to the Soviet note of April 16 until May 8. Three precious weeks were lost. In that fatal time, as we know now from the Nazi secret archives, Stalin convinced himself that Chamberlain did not really want a military alliance with Russia. The Prime Minister, in Stalin's view, preferred to drive Germany, if he could, against Russia and thus save the West from Hitler's wrath and from war. If that were so, it was a game which two could play. Stalin proceeded to play it. Before the end of April he began feeling out Berlin to see what Hitler—as opposed to Chamberlain—had to offer. He began to play the kind of double game with which we became more familiar after the war. For a short time he was ready to jump either way—into the arms of the West or of Hitler. But for a short time only.

Five days before Chamberlain replied to the Russian offer, Stalin gave public notice of which way he was leaning. On May 3 he abruptly dismissed Litvinov as Russian foreign secretary. The significance of this move apparently was lost in London for some days or even weeks. But, as I recall, it was not lost in Berlin. Litvinov stood in the minds of the world for "collective security" against agression, for a Russian alignment with the League and with the West against the Nazi-Fascist Axis. His going meant that the Kremlin was changing the direction of its policy. Berlin was delighted. London seemed unmoved. Berlin and Moscow, in the greatest of secrecy, began to draw together in an evil conspiracy.

It is probable that, up to the end of May at least, if not a little bit longer, Chamberlain could have forged an alliance with Russia which might well have deterred Hitler from launching his war in the first place or which would have led to Nazi Germany's quick defeat if war had broken out. Perhaps the Prime Minister's insistence on sending a mere Foreign Office official, William Strang, to Moscow to negotiate with the Russians was the last straw to the Kremlin. Strang was an able permanent official and knew Russia. But did not the negotiation of a crucial alliance at such a strained moment call for a man of greater political standing—a cabinet member at least? Only a few months before, Mr. Chamberlain had thought it necessary for himself as well as Lord Halifax, his foreign secretary, to journey to Rome to discuss the European situation with Mussolini. Was it not slighting the Russian dictator to send such a subordinate as Mr. Strang to talk with him about so important a project as a military alliance against Germany? Did it not show that Chamberlain was not negotiating in earnest? Stalin apparently thought so. Perhaps he knew that Mr. Eden, whom he respected and admired, had volunteered to undertake the mission to Moscow and had been rejected by the Prime Minister.

The exact date on which Stalin made his decision to go with Hitler has never been definitely established, so far as I can ascertain. The first feelers were made in Berlin by the Soviet ambassador on April 17. By May 7 the French ambassador in Moscow was sure that the Germans and Russians were already discussing a rapprochement based on the partition of Poland. On May 30, we learn from the Nazi secret archives, the Wilhelmstrasse notified its ambassador in Moscow that "we have now decided to undertake definite negotiations with the Soviet Union." But as late as August 4, that ambassador was reporting confidentially to Berlin that his "over-all impression" was "that the Soviet government is at present determined to sign with England and France, if they fulfill all Soviet wishes . . . It will take a considerable effort on our part," he warned, "to cause the Soviet government to swing about."[14]

To give impetus to that effort, Hitler, unlike Chamberlain, did not make the mistake of sending an unknown permanent official of the German Foreign Office to Moscow. On August 15 he had his ambassador in Moscow inform the Soviet government that there were no questions "between the Baltic and the Black Sea" which were not amenable to settlement between the two countries and that he was now prepared to send Joachim von Ribbentrop, his foreign minister, to the Russian capital "to set forth the Fuehrer's views to Herr Stalin."

Exactly a week later, Ribbentrop arrived in Moscow and began his talks with Stalin and Molotov. The next evening, August 23, the infamous Stalin-Hitler Pact was signed. The published part was a nonaggression treaty in which the two countries pledged not only to refrain from warring on each other but to give no support to any third power which got involved in a war against either. The secret part divided up Poland and the rest of Eastern Europe.

Ribbentrop departed in triumph. His master could now push the button and begin the war. The bewildered members of the French and British military missions who had thought that *they* were negotiating with the Russians packed their bags and also departed. Stalin, puffing his pipe, must

[14]*Nazi-Soviet Relations, loc. cit.*

have felt very pleased with himself. Chamberlain had tried to sick the German beasts on Russia in the hope that Britain would be spared. But he, Stalin, had turned the tables. He had now made it certain that the Germans, after overrunning Poland, would *first* turn on the West. Let them fight it out with the decadent British and French. All three nations would probably destroy themselves in an all-out war. Then Russia could step in and be the master of Europe.

It was a clever, if cynical and cold-blooded, calculation. Churchill thinks it was, at that moment, "realistic in a high degree." But was it? In less than two years Stalin would learn how disastrous it had been. Chamberlain himself never made quite as monumental a mistake. Both men amply demonstrated that unbounded lack of knowledge of the Germans that has been—and still is—a phenomenon of our times. In their cases, the cost to their countries and their fellow countrymen was a dreadfully high price to pay for this ignorance.

To Chamberlain's credit, he did not panic nor flinch when the awful news from Moscow reached him. Precautionary measures amounting to partial mobilization were immediately taken. The Prime Minister himself promptly wrote Hitler a frank letter in which he warned that "no greater mistake could be made" than to believe that Great Britain would not honor its commitments to Poland because of the Soviet-German Pact.

It has been alleged that if His Majesty's Government had made their position more clear in 1914, the great catastrophe would have been avoided. Whether or not there is any force in that allegation, His Majesty's Government are resolved that on this occasion there shall be no such tragic misunderstanding . . . Whatever may prove to be the nature of the German-Soviet Agreement, it cannot alter Great Britain's obligation to Poland, which His Majesty's Government have stated in public repeatedly and plainly, and which they are determined to fulfil.[15]

This time Chamberlain was as good as his word—and it was to his honor, though it would lead immediately to the most devastating war in history and to an ordeal for his people more terrible than any they had been through. However honorably and courageously he acted in the end, Chamberlain could not escape a severe verdict from history. He and his predecessors at the helm of England had thrown away one advantage after another. The road they had taken for a decade was littered with milestones to disaster, as Churchill phrased it. We have seen in this journey what they were: the failure to keep Germany disarmed as stipulated by the Versailles Treaty; the conniving with Hitler to break the naval disarmament provisions of the treaty; the neglect in at least maintaining air parity with Germany; the refusal to join France in forcing Hitler out of the Rhineland in 1936; the bland acceptance of Hitler's criminal conquest of Austria; the betrayal of Czechoslovakia; the rebuff to America's attempt to intervene; and the brush-off of Russia—and all the while the asinine wooing of the two fascist dictators.

What logic or sense was there in Chamberlain's giving iron-clad guarantees to Poland after he had thrown so much away? He easily could have stopped Hitler, as we have seen, at the time of the Rhineland reoccupation—without having to fight a war. With the help of France and Russia, not to mention Czechoslovakia, with its thirty-five divisions and its fortress line, he could have brought overwhelming military power to bear to destroy Nazi Germany quickly in the fall of 1938. But each time he had recoiled in horror from taking any kind of action against Hitler. Now that Britain's military

[15]Nuremberg Documents.

position, as the result of his blundering, was almost hopeless —with Czechoslovakia gone and Russia lost and the United States uninterested and France at its lowest peak—he chose to stop Hitler by an action that made his involvement in war inevitable. There was no logic or reason in this last desperate step. It was forced upon him by his own folly and by that of those who had ruled Britain before him.

On September 3, 1939, Britain, true to its engagement to come to the aid of Poland if she were attacked, declared war on Germany. For five years its people fought and endured with the grit and gallantry which had raised them to such a high position over the centuries. But, as during the previous war, this magnificent spirit would not have been enough had not the United States and Russia been forced by German foolishness to join them in their struggle.

For the first time in its long history, Britain emerged from a war completely exhausted. Financially it was almost bankrupt. Economically it was run down. The Empire was in dissolution. The Commonwealth was in the process of great change. Ireland, whose strict neutrality during the war had endangered the very life of the mother country, would shortly proclaim itself a republic and abandon the Commonwealth. South Africa, under the domination of the majority Boers, would increasingly draw away. Even those dominions which remained staunchly loyal, such as Canada and Australia, looked less and less to London for guidance. The Canadian Prime Minister would ask "that every care should be taken" not only to leave each Dominion in unfettered control of its own affairs, but to avoid even the appearance of an explicit and unified Commonwealth point of view. In a similar vein the Australian Minister for External Affairs would speak (in 1948) "of an entirely new principle, namely that within the Commonwealth the leadership and initiative need not always rest upon Britain herself."[16]

It was this England, battered and weakened by war and adversity and ruled for the first time by socialists, which now concerned me on this midcentury journey.

At first glance London did not seem much different from the city I had known before the war. In appearance it had changed little since my first glimpse of it a quarter of a century before, except for the bombed-out patches that were most extensive around St. Paul's. It was raining, as usual. There was a bus strike, which forced one down into the underground to get about. It was in the subways that I noticed the first change—there and in the streets and in the parks. The ordinary folk looked healthier and better dressed. They had seemed to me a seedy lot before the war, with their sallow complexions, shabby clothes, and shoes worn down at the heels. Now they had a bit of color in their skin. They were certainly not fashionably dressed, but they were decently dressed; and so were their children. There were no urchins in the streets. There was a certain air of well-being about these common people that was exhilarating just to see. Could it be, I wondered, because they had captured political control of the nation and were helping themselves to a bigger slice of the economic pie?

What about the well-to-do? Had they been reduced under socialist rule to pauperism, as was rumored in certain drawing rooms in New York and Washington? I strolled past the Ritz down St. James Street to see. Obviously the revolution had not struck with much force here. Men in well-tailored dark suits, obviously from Saville Row or thereabouts, and

[16]*This Age of Conflict*, by Frank Pentland Chambers and others; revised ed.; New York, 1950.

bowler or Homburg hats and swinging tightly rolled um-
brellas (the rain had subsided) brushed by me and strode
into their exclusive clubs. Behind the window of one I noticed gouty-looking old gentlemen buried behind the *Times*.
They seemed not to have stirred from their comfortable old
black-leather chairs in the twenty-five years since I had first
looked upon them. At the door of the Ritz, the tweedy set
was getting into sleek motorcars, probably headed for a week
end in the country.

What about this socialist revolution we had heard about
in America? I walked down to Piccadilly Circus to buy a paper. Perhaps there was some further news of it. Maybe this
red revolutionary government of Britain, as a choleric con-
gressman in Washington had described it to me, was abolishing the monarchy and proclaiming a socialist republic, or
something. H. G. Wells, I seemed to remember, had advo-
cated this in his last bitter days. I bought a batch of papers
and went into the Café Royal to read them. Sure enough,
the headlines were all about the royal family. Was it in danger? No "FIRST PICTURES OF PRINCESS ANNE," the big type
said. She was, I learned, the month-old child of Princess
Elizabeth. Her baby face was spread all over the front pages.

I went back to my hotel in Kensington, a chilly and dark
hostelry which, I soon noticed, was full of people I imagined
had become extinct in this Labour-ruled welfare state. It was
teatime and I went into the great parlor to have some. It was
crowded. Whatever else had happened in England, this traditional hour was still sacred—and unchanged. In the vast
lounge, with a coal fire smoldering in the fireplace, every
nook and corner was occupied by what I took to be country
people come up to London for one reason or another. They
had not only survived, I saw, but seemed very much alive
and kicking: retired Indian Army colonels and colonial offi-

cials, country squires, Church of England rectors, and what not, the laymen tweedy and puffing pipes, the clergymen immaculate in black silk vests and reversed collars, and their womenfolk in loose-fitting woolly suits, knitting between sips of tea.

Snatches of conversation floated over to my eager ears. It had not changed among these people despite all that had happened. It was of the country life: flowers, gardens, horses, sports, food, rural inns, and the goings-on of people they knew. The only new note was the talk about putting up with government restrictions and of getting around some of them —of how to get a few extra pounds beyond the government allowance for a holiday on the Continent. These were the English who between the wars had filled the pleasant hotels in France, Italy, Switzerland, and the Tyrol. Now shortage of foreign exchange was keeping them at home, and they suffered.

But these sturdy folk hardly had the air of being dispossessed. They still struck me as being the bulwark of something in England that did not die out in a generation. Confused, I retired to my room to ponder what I had seen this first day.

First impressions, as I had learned in my profession long ago, are not always very accurate. As I began to burrow below the surface and check back on what had happened here, I became more and more conscious of what has turned out to be the theme of this book: the profound changes in so short a time in a civilization that for centuries—until we came upon the scene—evolved slowly, securely, almost imperturbably, like a great tree.

These changes, to be sure, had been for some time in the making. They were discernible at the start of the century and became almost predictable by the end of the First World

War. But it was the second war, in which this nation had to fight to the point of exhaustion merely to survive, which brought them to a head. The experience shook this ancient, tradition-bound society to its roots and quickly and radically transformed it. That this took place tranquilly, by democratic agreement, so to speak, according to certain rules which all respected and abided by, is a tribute to the collective character of this strange race. Is not history full of examples of a ruling class using the military and police illegally to retain power when its position is threatened from below? In England there was, of course, not the slightest thought of this. Those who lost their power and much of their private income and their comfortable old way of life accepted their fate calmly and even gracefully. In the game of life which the British played, the upper class might—and did—eventually win back some of its political power, but the rest was lost forever. Regardless of who ruled the government, a great leveling had come for good.

It was applied suddenly and drastically in the first summer of the war when Britain was down, and many, outside, thought it was out. On May 22, 1940, as France was being overrun and the British Expeditionary Force on the Continent destroyed, Parliament—the Commons and the Lords— passed unanimously, in a single afternoon, one of the most revolutionary acts in its history. It required "persons to place themselves, their services, and their property at the disposal" of the government. As Attlee, who supported the measure on behalf of the Labour Party said: "The Government demands complete control over persons and property; not just some persons and some particular sections of the community, but of all persons, rich and poor, employers and workers, men and women, and all property."

The conception of private property being inviolable, so

sacred in our Western democratic-capitalist world, was
knocked out for the duration of war. It was not to be restored
completely even when the war was over. Labour especially
approved such a step. If you conscripted human beings, it
argued, it was only fair to conscript wealth and property.
Labour had to swallow a bitter pill of its own: the forcing
of men and women to work where they were told. Regula-
tion 58A, under the Emergency Powers Bill, enabled the
Ministry of Labour to "direct" any person to perform any
service "which that person is, in the opinion of the Minister,
capable of performing." Midway through the war, men were
even "directed" to toil in the coal mines.

Not only the men but the women of Britain were conscripted. The thoroughness of conscription was indicated by
the figures for September, 1943. Of 15,920,000 men of working age, 15,000,000 were in the armed services, civil defense,
or industry; of 16,020,000 women of working age, 7,250,000
were similarly engaged—600,000 of them in uniform either
in the forces or in full-time civil defense.

Strict control of all business enterprises and a drastic system of price controls and the rationing of consumer goods
completed a regimentation of life such as Britain had never
before experienced and which went much further than that
attempted by any other democratic land during the war.
Even totalitarian Germany did not go to such lengths.

This Spartan system naturally had a profound effect on
the British people. Unlike in the first war, or in any other
time, the common people had the feeling that a good many
differences between the rich and the poor had been abolished, that everyone without exception was called upon to
make equal sacrifices, that the privileges which had hitherto
gone with rank and wealth were no longer recognized, and
that all citizens were being treated fairly by an all-powerful

government in which for the first time all classes were about equally represented. Britain, during the war years, became a truly egalitarian society.

Actually the workers fared better in many ways than ever before. Despite the shortage of food many of them had more to eat. Before the war, according to an estimate of Sir John Orr, nearly half the people of Britain did not have the means to provide themselves with an adequate diet. About a third actually were victims of malnutrition. The wartime ration gave them as much food as a lord—and sometimes more, if they were engaged in heavy labor. Steady employment at good wages gave them the money to buy it. For the first time in history it could be said that all the British people were on an adequate diet, though the rich were deprived of many luxury foods and visiting Americans, overfed as we were, found the fare monotonous.

Wages increased throughout the war, the index of weekly rates mounting from 100 in 1939 to 152 in December 1945, while the rise in the cost of living was only 31 per cent. Not only were individual workers thus enabled to increase their real income but labor as a whole made considerable progress toward one of its major goals: a bigger share of the national cake. Whereas in 1938, wages, after taxes, amounted to 39 per cent of the national private income, in 1945 they came to 44 per cent. Those who lived from profits and salaries got a corresponding smaller slice of the cake: profits, after taxes, over the same period dropped from 37 per cent of the total private income to 34 per cent; salaries from 24 to 22 per cent.[17]

But sharing the burden, while it enabled the nation to pull through, did not lessen the disastrous cost to the nation of fighting the war. In money alone the cost came to

[17]*Annual Abstract of Statistics*, No. 84, 1935-46.

$110,000,000,000; some 25 per cent of Britain's total capital was dissipated. But these figures did not begin to tell the story. For more than a century Britain had only maintained herself as a going concern by means of interest received on her large foreign investments, which until recently had comprised half of all there were in the world and which paid for one-third of her imports. During the first war she had been forced to sell a fourth of her foreign holdings—a billion pounds' worth—to help finance her military effort. By the end of the second war she had sold another £1,118,000,000 of foreign assets plus £152,000,000 in gold and dollars. In addition she had incurred a debt to sterling countries of nearly three billion pounds. This made a total of over four billion pounds of what the economists called "external disinvestment." Or put another way: the war for survival changed Great Britain from being a creditor to the world to the amount of sixteen billion dollars to being a debtor of some twelve billion dollars. As the conflict ended she was spending some five billion dollars a year more than she was earning. You could hardly count the cost, the Chancellor of the Exchequer commented in presenting his lopsided 1945 budget, "when you are fighting for your lives over three continents."

But that was not all. I doubt if more than a handful of Americans at home realized that an agreement between London and Washington had divided the joint war effort so that Britain would devote three-fourths of her resources to outright military production and the United States would furnish a large proportion of the food, clothing, and raw materials needed by her ally. This made for greater efficiency and effectiveness in the Allied effort to defeat the enemy but it left Britain in a serious predicament at the end of the war when President Truman abruptly, on August 21, immediately after V-J Day, canceled Lend-Lease. Mr. Attlee, who had just become prime minister, summarized the position to the Commons: "If the role assigned to us had been to expand our exports so as to provide a large margin over our current needs which we could furnish free of charge to our allies, we should, of course, be in an immeasurably stronger position than we are today."

Britain's situation was, in fact, disastrous. The nation faced bankruptcy; the people, starvation. There were still millions of soldiers overseas to be supported until they could be brought home and demobilized. The factories which had been pouring out guns, planes, and ammunition could not be converted to peacetime production overnight. Exports had dwindled to little more than a quarter of their prewar volume. Yet because of the loss of its foreign capital holdings and the incurring of its vast new sterling debt Britain would have to export 50 per cent over the prewar level merely to maintain the standard of life before the war. This also could not be done overnight. The troops would have to be brought home first, the factories reconverted, and some work done on the four and a half million homes which had been destroyed or damaged by the bombing.

In the meantime Britain was dependent upon the United States for the food and raw materials to enable her people just to exist. The sudden suspension of Lend-Lease meant these necessities would have to be paid for—in dollars. Britain didn't have the dollars. Its only recourse was to ask for a loan. Lord Keynes, the financial wizard and one of the truly great men of our time—though orthodox Wall Street frowned on his unorthodoxy—was dispatched hastily to Washington to get it.

This was the occasion when Keynes pointed out some truths about the relative sacrifices made by the two nations and their people during the war. Americans (and this author was certainly among them) had believed that Lend-Lease to Britain was a one-way transaction. Actually it had amounted to 1 per cent of our national production, or $13,499,000,000. But Britain had lend-leased to us 15 per cent of her total production, or $4,320,000,000. Her bomb-stricken people had raised 53 per cent of the cost of the war through their taxes; the figure for America was 47 per cent. Some 55 per cent of her total labor force was in the armed services or engaged in war production at the height of the war; in the United States 40 per cent were so occupied. British civilian consumption had decreased 16 per cent; American civilian consumption had increased 16 per cent. Britain's shipping had been halved during the war; America's had grown five times. Her national debt, as the result of the war, was 40 per cent higher proportionately than ours; the loss of her domestic investments thirty-five times ours; the deterioration of her capital equipment three times ours.[18]

Such was the position of Britain when, in the midsummer of 1945, to the surprise of everyone, Churchill, who had led the country from the dark days of Dunkirk when all seemed lost to overwhelming victory, was thrown out of office by the electorate and replaced by the first purely Labour government in British history. It was to rule for six years, and the changes it wrought, many of them irrevocable, though the Tories would return to political power under Churchill in the fall of 1951, must now be briefly noted. They constitute a climax to this midcentury journey through this land.

Whatever one thought of the results of Labour's rule, no one could deny that the party carried out its promises—a rare

[18]Virginia Cowles, *op. cit.* Also the British White Paper published at the time of the loan negotiations.

achievement in itself, in our imperfect democratic world, which was accustomed to seeing political parties promise much before elections and deliver little afterward. In its first fifteen months in office, covering the first session of Parliament, it passed eighty-four acts, breaking all records for the amount of legislation put through in so short a time. Before it was dismissed from power at the end of six years it had nationalized the Bank of England, coal mining, transportation, civil aviation, international telecommunications, electricity, gas, and the iron and steel industry, and had transformed the United Kingdom into the most advanced welfare state in the world.

It would be erroneous, however, to believe, as so many Americans appeared to believe, that the quasi-socialized welfare state was forced down the throats of the British people by a "red" socialist government. The truth was, as anyone who looked into the matter could see, that the kind of nation which Britain became after the war was in reality the result of a very fundamental collaboration between Labour *and* Conservatives. The origins of social welfare went back at least as far as the first years of the century, when the Liberal government, elected in 1906 and influenced by Bismarck, put through the first important "social" legislation. But it was the strain and the challenge of the second war which led the Tory Party to agree with the socialists on a degree of collectivism in peacetime unprecedented in any major democratic society. I do not believe that our American conservatives have understood this basic fact—or tried to understand it.

Certainly the British Conservatives made no secret of this collaboration: on the contrary. In 1949 after the Labour government had pushed through the revolutionary (to Americans, at least) compulsory National Insurance Scheme and the National Health Service (socialized medicine, as we called it at home) and had completed the nationalization program except for iron and steel, Mr. Churchill declared: "In the last four years they [the Attlee government] have carried out plans prepared by the National Coalition Government with its large Conservative majority, of which I was the head."

Mr. R. A. Butler, whom Churchill would make his Chancellor of the Exchequer in 1951, supported his chief in demanding credit for the Tory Party. Speaking on the same day he said: "The welfare state is as much our creation as it is that of the socialists." Indeed in the last two election campaigns the Conservatives outdid the socialists in promising to improve and extend social welfare. They went along, too, with the nationalization program except for iron and steel, which is the only industry they have promised to restore to private enterprise, and then only under strict government controls.

The reasons for this stand of British Conservatives on nationalization were not difficult to ascertain despite the fact that they stood traditionally for free enterprise. The industries taken over by the state had long been sick. Churchill himself had asked for the nationalization of the railways as far back as 1918. Sir Geoffrey Heyworth, chairman of the great industrial giant, Unilever's, had recommended nationalization of gas during the last war. In every case, except iron and steel, which was not sick, pressure for nationalizing came, in part, from Conservative circles themselves.

The most pressure from all sides was for the nationalization of coal, the sickest of all the industries and the first taken over by the government. For a century and a half, coal had been the foundation of Britain's prosperity. Between the wars, its production lagged and hit rock bottom at the end of the war. In 1913 Britain had produced 287,000,000 tons from the labors of a million miners and had exported 94,000,000 tons. In 1946 there were only 692,000 miners at work, production fell to under 170,000,000 tons, of which only 9,000,000 tons were exported. During the war a committee appointed by Churchill's coalition government under the chairmanship of Sir Charles Reid, an eminent mining engineer, assessed the situation and found there was too much separate ownership of too many small mines to enable the industry as a whole to function with even a minimum of efficiency. It became obvious to all that if coal mining was to be left to private enterprise Britain's recovery as an industrial exporter would be impossible. In 1947 coal was therefore nationalized with the blessings of both parties. Some 1,000 private companies, owning 1,500 mines, were paid by the government as compensation $658,400,000, a sum which the *Times* thought "fair and reasonable."

This did not mean that because the government assumed ownership it was going to run directly the coal business or any other which was nationalized. What the British did was to set up public corporations for each nationalized industry. These were run by boards of governors whose members received, by British standards, high salaries—usually £5,000 a year—and most of whom had had long experience as directors or managers either in the private industry or in similar businesses. Thus Lord Hyndley, who had experience as a coal owner and in the public service, became the head of the Coal Board, whose other members were made up of one coal owner, two trade unionists, a mining engineer, a scientist, a lawyer, a civil servant, and a chartered accountant.

It would take some time, of course, to learn how successfully the nationalization of the nation's basic industry would work out. It could hardly do worse than under the hodgepodge of private ownership which had all but wrecked the industry. Obviously, many bugs had to be ironed out. I heard considerable criticism of the Coal Board's management. Some thought it was too centralized, too lethargic, too rigid; and everyone complained about the rise in the price of coal. In the first two years the Board did increase production by 10 per cent though thereafter the rise was not all that had been hoped. However the British are a patient people, and one heard no talk of restoring coal to private hands. The general hope was that the nationalized industries would gradually increase their efficiency. At any rate, so far as one could foresee, they would stay nationalized. Both parties seemed to agree on that, except in the case of steel.

To Americans alarmed at such socialization, the British replied that they were only doing what we had done with the T.V.A., and that, anyway, only twenty per cent of the national assets had come under government ownership—proportionally about the same as in Switzerland, a country which fairly bristled with its devotion to conservative free enterprise. I found the Stock Exchange functioning as usual, privately owned and managed, with an authority over the accounts and public issues of all major companies that gave it a power which at home was divided between the New York Stock Exchange and the federal government's Securities and Exchange Commission.

The real revolution in the United Kingdom, I soon learned, was not so much economic as social. Since July 5, 1948, five acts of Parliament had come into force which made Britain truly a welfare state, entitling every man, woman, and child in the country, regardless of wealth, occupation, or social status, to free medical, dental, and hospital care and protecting every citizen, as a government statement said, against all major disasters or disabilities which economic ill fortune or mortality could inflict.

Four parliamentary measures provided what was called National Insurance and Assistance. The fifth bill set up the National Health Service, or "socialized medicine." However much Americans might dislike such "socialistic" schemes, or were taught to dislike them by our press and by such institutions as the American Medical Association, there was no doubt that the British people liked them immensely. There was no doubt either that the Conservative Party, with Churchill at its head, had collaborated fully with Labour in establishing them. Indeed the Tories had some claim to say, as they did, that they had initiated them.

In 1943 Churchill, as prime minister, had publicly declared: "You must rank me and my colleagues as strong partisans of national compulsory insurance for all classes, for all purposes, from the cradle to the grave." A Conservative minister of health had drawn up far-reaching plans for socialized medicine and had actually begun negotiations with the medical profession regarding them when the elections of July 1945 brought the Labour government into office. What the socialists did was to consolidate the previous plans for state insurance and free medicine, pass them through Parliament, and put them into operation. When the measures were debated, the Conservatives critized many details but on the fundamentals they were in general agreement with the Labour government.

The very comprehensiveness of these schemes for social security took one's breath away. The mere enumeration of the detailed provisions of the five acts would fill a long book. We have only time and space in this hurried journey to glimpse a few of the chief features.

The four Insurance and Assistance Acts were based on the monumental Beveridge Report of 1942. Sir William Beveridge, as he then was, had found that in Britain far too large a percentage of the premiums paid to private social insurance companies was soaked up by the cost of administration and much too little left for benefits. He concluded that here was a jog that the state would have to take over on a basis of compulsory contributions by individuals and employers, augmented, for a time, by supplementary grants from the government. Eventually the scheme should be self-supporting, without the need of government contributions.

Unlike medical care, national insurance is not free. Employed men over 18, for example, must pay 4s 7d weekly, and their employers 3s 10d. Since the average weekly wage is 140s the cost of the insurance comes to about 3 per cent of a man's earnings. Self-employed persons must pay 6s 2d weekly into the fund.

The benefits are many and would seem to take into account about every contingency thinkable. They cover: sickness, unemployment, injury, maternity, widowhood, guardian's allowances, retirement pensions, and death. In addition the Family Allowance Act grants out of the Exchequer five shillings a week for every child after the first until the children are sixteen years of age. Nearly 3,000,000 families are already receiving five shillings apiece for some 5,000,000 children. One family, with 14 children eligible, holds the record—a practically perfect record, it would seem to be. The Treasury pays it £3, 5s a week for its fertility.

Sickness benefits come to 26 shillings a week for the period of illness. If a man is injured at his employment he receives 45 shillings weekly. If he is permanently disabled he is paid the same. If he becomes unemployed he gets the same as if he were ill—26 shillings a week for 160 working days. This benefit can be extended up to a year in exceptional cases. After a year he must put his case before a local tribunal, which can extend unemployment payments further. Retirement pensions come to 26 shillings a week beginning at the age of sixty for women and sixty-five for men.

National Insurance benefits begin even before the cradle. There are special maternity grants which provide a gift of four pounds to the mother for each child born and a maternity allowance of 36 shillings a week for thirteen weeks (starting about six weeks before the expected confinement) for employed or self-employed women who give up their work. For other women an attendance allowance of 20 shillings per week for four weeks after confinement is paid.

When the English die the state insurance business also steps in to help the family of the deceased. Twenty pounds are paid toward funeral expenses. There are three kinds of widow's benefits. They are too detailed and complicated to go into here. Suffice it to say they range from 26 shillings a week to 36 shillings.[19]

The Legal Aid program lies outside the insurance scheme but perhaps deserves a word in passing. Backed by both parties and made an act by Parliament in 1949, it provides

[19]Because of the arbitrary nature of the exchange rate and the differences in wages, and costs of living between the two countries, it is difficult to transform these figures into American equivalents. In 1950 the average weekly earnings in our manufacturing industries were $65, or about three times those in Britain at the present rate of exchange. On the other hand, the cost of living for a British worker, if calculated in dollars, was much less than for an American, though certainly not three times less. If one takes percentages of wages to calculate contributions to, and benefits from, the state insurance system and assumes that its cash benefits buy approximately 50 per cent more in goods and services in Britain than at home, a rough estimate in American terms would be as follows: Employees would have to pay into the fund out of their $65 a week wage about $2.00; employers about $1.65 for each employee. The sickness or unemployment benefit would come to $19.50 a week, and for those disabled at their work it would amount to $30 weekly. Old age retirement pensions from the state would be $19.50 a week. Mothers would be paid a maternity allowance of $7.60 a week for thirteen weeks, and each family would receive from the fund a weekly stipend of 75 cents per child after the first. To the expense of a funeral the state insurance fund would contribute $90, assuming that its cost, too, is 50 per cent less in Britain.

government funds to lawyers representing clients at court who cannot afford legal fees. Though the government expects to put up as much as 8 million pounds a year for this, the system is run by the Law Society, an ancient and private body of lawyers who can be counted upon to steer clear of state interference. The program eliminates the necessity of charity among the barristers and solicitors, who formerly had to serve the poor free, and guarantees that every citizen can have adequate legal representation regardless of the cost.

We come now to the other half of the social revolution in Britain about which there has been such an uproar in America —or among some in America, at any rate. Fresh from a stiff dose of medicinal propaganda from the American Medical Association on the unspeakable evils of "socialized medicine," I arrived in England on this journey to find to my astonishment that the National Health Service, which gave all citizens medical, dental, and hospital care free of charge, was easily the most popular of all the accomplishments of the British government since the war. Moreover, the Conservative Party was as warm in support of it as the Labour Party, if not more so.

In the 1950 general election the Tory campaign guide had reminded the electorate of the party's position: "It can never be too often stated that the Conservative Party is wholeheartedly in favor of a National Health Service available to all."

Judging by what the A.M.A. at home had said I expected to find the British medical fraternity in open revolt and probably engaged in a sit-down strike. But this was not at all the case. Not that all of them had liked the National Health Service. The majority, at least in the beginning, had not. The facts, so far as I could get them, were as follows:

Britain had had a form of state health insurance since 1911, in which the state paid private doctors to care for those insured. But this covered only a small minority of the population. Between the wars, in response to public demand, the British Medical Association had seriously taken up the whole matter of a general medical service to the nation. In 1938 it issued one report, and in 1943 another, with its suggestions. Some of these were eventually accepted in the National Health Service Act; some were not. The Labour government put in quite a few ideas of its own. The doctors did not like them. They were not, they said, against the idea and the objectives of a national health service. They merely couldn't accept the government's plan.

Their fears were quite understandable. They were afraid they would lose their freedom by being transformed into government civil servants, under the constant orders of the state. They saw the age-old intimate relation between physician and patient destroyed by the interference of a third party—again the state. They also had some more practical objections. The government scheme offered them a basic salary of 300 pounds a year plus a per capita fee for each person on their list of patients of approximately one pound. The maximum number on a list would be 4,000. Thus a doctor with 4,000 patients on his roll would receive roughly 4,300 pounds a year, which was well above the average physician's income heretofore. But the British doctors didn't want any basic salary. It was the opening wedge of slavery to the state, they said. They also objected to restrictions on the buying and selling of practices. The Health Ministry desired to prohibit the buying or selling of that part of the good will in practices which in the future accrued from patients registered in the health service. It did offer, however, to compensate for any loss by establishing a fund out of which the capital values of the existing practice would be repaid to doctors losing by the transactions.

In 1947 the British Medical Association held a vote of its members on the Health Act, which had passed the House the year before. They voted 17,037 to 2,500 not to participate in the National Health Service. They thought they had killed the bill. But they hadn't. Public opinion was turning against them. The fiery minister of health, Aneurin Bevan, was no man to give in easily. He threatened and cajoled. He made some minor compromises and reminded the profession that its members, according to the terms of the act itself, were free to come in or not; they were not being forced into socialized medicine. They could stay out of it if they wanted to. There was a great deal of bluff in this, of course. How could you run socialized medicine without any doctors? In 1948, shortly before the new act was to go into effect, the B.M.A. held another vote. It declared that if 13,000 or more general practitioners were still against it, the Association would advise all its members to remain out of the scheme altogether. The vote was 9,558 to 8,639 against going in. But since the number of those opposing the plan was far short of 13,000, the B.M.A., true to its word, advised its members to join and co-operate with the government.

Most of them did. Between 18,000 and 19,000 out of 21,000 in England and Wales joined; in Scotland 2,400 general practitioners, or almost all, joined. Of the 10,000 dentists in England and Wales 9,470 signed up; in Scotland, 1,255, or almost all.

The people, who had naturally welcomed the prospect of not having to pay doctor, dentist, or hospital bills (though of course they paid them in taxes which furnished almost the entire revenue for the Health Service) signed up to the extent of 95 per cent. This made it almost unanimous: for the patients and the doctors.

An American had to rid himself of many misconceptions when he saw this dread "socialized medicine" in practice. You did not, for instance, as I had been told at home, have to take any doctor the state assigned you. As before, you could choose your own family doctor. He, in turn, was not forced to take you. If he didn't want you on his list, you would have to seek another. But if you became dissatisfied with your doctor, you could change—also just as before. What about specialists? Here again you could choose. The only limitation, as with the family doctor, was the size of the physician's list. If he already had as many patients as he could handle you would have to go elsewhere. But was this not the case before?

The age-old relationship between doctor and patient had not greatly changed. True, the physicians and dentists became greatly overworked and the hospitals overcrowded. This was because millions who had never had proper care in their lifetime now asked for it and received it. There were abuses. People who were not really ill took valuable time from the doctors. But was this abuse unknown among the rich in the old days? There was a genuine fear in the profession that the specialists would be so hamstrung by the bureaucracy and so discouraged by lack of incentive that they would fail to push ahead and break new ground in their ever advancing fields. An effort was made to remedy this. Many specialists, by joining the Health Service only on a part-time basis, were able to enrich themselves by fat private fees from those able and willing to pay them. Specialists working full time on government salaries were certainly not reduced to poverty, their payment ranging, according to age and experience, from $5,600 to $11,000 a year. But for these, it was

quickly recognized, special financial inducements were necessary. So a system of awards was established to be administered by a committee of eminent men selected largely by
the Royal Colleges. Specialists who distinguished themselves
in their field would receive awards which would bring their
salaries up to $20,000 to $25,000 a year. At that level they
would not starve.

The dentists of Britain, for a time at least, fared fabulously
under "socialized medicine." The Health Act provided that
they were to be paid not by capitation fees but according to
the work they did: a dollar for looking at a patient's mouth,
so much for fillings and extractions, and so forth. What happened was that the Ministry established the fees at such a
high level that at first dentists made a great deal more money
than ever before. Dentists who had averaged from $5,000 to
$15,000 a year found themselves taking in $20,000 to $60,000.
One busy practitioner earned $96,000 during his first year
under "socialized medicine."

It was not only the high fees fixed by the government but
the flood of patients to the dental chairs which brought such
sudden prosperity to the country's dentists. I remember myself being appalled, when I first arrived in England, at the
condition of British teeth. It was indescribable; it was a
scandal and a shame. The only time most persons visited a
dentist was to get their aching, rotting teeth pulled. Preven-
tive dentistry was almost unknown, or rarely practiced. The
neglect of children's teeth was a national crime.

Little wonder then that when decent dental care was
offered free of charge millions of Britishers stormed to the
dentist. I am told that the dentists themselves, who are not
a particularly emotional set, were aghast at what they saw
in the mouths of the millions. They worked overtime to do

something about it, and the government fees naturally piled up.

However, Health Minister Bevan soon reduced them. He halved everything a dentist made over $20,000 a year. Then he cut the fees, first by 20 per cent and later by a further 10 per cent.

There were, then, many "bugs" in the National Health Service, and abuses, and a great deal of confusion and irritation, as there is bound to be when so far-reaching and monumental a project is suddenly put in operation. (There were 200,000,000 free prescriptions filled at a cost to the government of $128,000,000 the first year, but this astronomical figure would drop when a charge of one shilling per prescription was made.[20]

The fact remained, and the British people did not forget it, that until the year 1948, in their long history, the majority of the population had never been able to afford adequate medical, dental, and hospital care; now everyone, without exception, had it. In these circumstances frantic cries from across the Atlantic that this was "socialism" and "slavery to bureaucracy" left them rather cold. Sometimes they would ask their American visitors, as they asked this one: Even in fabulously rich America can you honestly say that *all* the people today can afford to receive—and do receive—all the medical and dental and hospital care that they need? Do we?

The aggregate cost was immense, and of course the free Health Service was not really free. The people in Britain did not kid themselves that it was. They knew that they had to

[20]On January 29, 1952, the Chancellor of the Exchequer announced to the House of Commons that he proposed to put the shilling (14 cents) charge on prescriptions into effect. He also introduced legislation calling for a maximum fee of one pound ($2.80) for dental services. Patients would also be asked to pay part of the cost of wigs, hearing aids, braces, and trusses.

pay for it through their taxes—a billion and a half dollars a year, 5 1/2 per cent of their national income. But most of them seemed to agree with the *Manchester Guardian,* itself anti-Labour, when it said: "The cost is high. Was ever public money better spent?"

In this land, then, where so much had changed, people were guaranteed by the state a certain economic and social security from the cradle to the grave. Is that wrong? Is the craving of ordinary people in the Western world for security sapping the strength and energy of their society? Does having security thwart enterprise and reward the shiftless and result in drab mediocrity and bring decay? Or does it, by freeing people from material worry, release them the better to develop their talents and exercise their creative energies and live richer, fuller lives? The answer, I found in this journey, often depended upon one's background. Curiously, those who had always enjoyed security scoffed the most at others, who had not had it, wanting it. There was no doubt that the latter desired it. Was that unreasonable, and even perverse? It was not for me to say.

One Labour leader in London assured me that having security had given the working class an entirely new life. Before the war, he explained, the average laborer's family skimped and hungered in order to save a few pounds against the rainy day of unemployment and sickness. He does not look forward to that contingency today, but also he does not fear it so. Hence he spends much more money on food, clothing, entertainment, sports, and even vacations.

Somewhat to my surprise I found that even many of my middle-class friends, pinched as they were by the drastic taxation and all the other restrictions, had been given a new lease of life by the social security benefits which covered them—especially "socialized medicine." How often a serious illness, a major operation, a complicated child birth, had ruined their finances and plunged them into debt. At least they were free of that worry.

And the really well-to-do? They cursed and complained, of course, and no wonder. Where 7,000 of them had earned, after taxes, £6,000 or more in 1938, only a bare 70 persons in all the land had been that lucky in 1948. (£6,000 in 1938 was $30,000; today it is $16,800, because of the devaluation.) But the figures were misleading. Most of the fortunes of the rich were still intact and many of them were great enough to allow the family to live well off a little of the capital without reducing it by very much. Also, there were two other opportunities. The businessman could deduct several thousand dollars a year from his personal income tax for "business expenses." The ingenuity of British businessmen in this regard has confounded even the severe and eagle-eyed tax collector. Finally, not even the socialist government taxed capital gains, as capitalist America did. Thus many an enterprising entrepreneur managed to make a handsome annual income not only by wisely playing the stock market but by purchasing run-down enterprises cheaply, building them up, and then selling them for a gain. On such a profit he was not taxed.

No doubt the rich have been soaked. And they have lost a good deal of their political power. But the good life, so far as I could see, has not entirely eluded them. In the country, especially, to which many of them have retired, they manage to get along—rather graciously and well.

One could imagine them and all the others with the illustrious family names and the ancient titles sitting in their still spacious drawing rooms, gathered perhaps before a fire or looking out on the garden landscape that had not changed much in centuries and asking the question which, in truth, concerned everyone in the realm: Can England ever recover her former greatness?

I wondered myself. As my plane took off for the journey home, the question kept turning over in my mind. It did not seem likely that England could ever be again what she had been.

The sources of power and wealth which had made her supreme so long were no longer there. They had been dissipated by two destructive world wars and by the upheavals of our revolutionary era. The Empire, with India gone, had shriveled into a few colonies, mostly in the African jungle, and some island dots here and there. The Dominions of the Commonwealth no longer looked to the mother country, from which they had now become completely independent. In 1936 some 45 per cent of their trade had been with Britain. In 1945 this had shrunk to 23 per cent. Gone, too, were most of the lucrative foreign investments which formerly had brought so much prosperity to the British Isles. Even the great oil concessions in the Middle East region which Britain had controlled so long were being threatened by the wave of rising nationalism that had swept over Asia. The nationalization of the greatest of them, in Iran, had been a severe blow to the British Treasury. The billboards all over England carried in giant letters the grim warning: "Export or Die!" But this was a desperate task against the competition of the American industrial giant in a world more and more dominated by the dollar.

It made little difference that the Conservatives would return to political power. They could scarcely undo history. Indeed when they were returned to office in the fall of 1951, their first acts were not, as their conservative American friends had hoped, to get rid of some of the restrictions to private enterprise clamped down by the socialist government but to add new restrictions of their own. Tory austerity became even more severe than Labour's had been.

The truth was that Britain was living beyond her means—by more than two billion dollars a year. R. A. Butler, the Tory Chancellor of the Exchequer, in his very first speech after the Conservatives resumed power in 1951, warned that this could not continue: "If we do not find means to correct the disparity between what we earn and what we buy . . . we shall, in fact, be bankrupt, idle, and hungry."

Mr. Churchill did not try to disguise the danger in his opening remarks to the new Parliament: "We must all be conscious of the realities of our position. Fifty millions of people are now crowded in our small island which produces food for only three-fifths of them, and has to earn the rest from over the seas by exporting manufactures for which we must also first import the raw material. No community of such a size, and standing at so high a level of civilization, has ever been economically so precarious . . . In the present year we are running into an external deficit at the rate of £700 million [$2,100,000,000] a year . . . These figures mean, in short, that we are buying much more than we can afford to pay from current earnings, and this can lead to national bankruptcy."

It could; but would it? That remained to be seen. The deficit was due almost entirely to the staggering burden of rearmament which Britain had shouldered on a scale equal to that of the United States though she was not in our fortunate economic and financial position.

Fortune, one might say, which had smiled upon the British Isles so long seemed now at the midcentury to have turned its attentions elsewhere, casting its favors in other directions. This had been the experience in the past of all great nations and empires and had brought their eventual decline. What stirred this traveler was that with Britain it had happened so quickly, within one's own brief lifetime, so that one could say, however sadly, what none could have said in Roman times: that he had seen with his own eyes the dissolution of a fabulous empire and the steep and dizzy descent from the heights of a great nation.

The irony—and the tragedy—of it was that it had come at the very moment when for the first time a goodly measure of social justice and of economic democracy had been achieved, giving the common people, who constituted the overwhelming majority in Britain as elsewhere, a fair share of the wealth and an equal share of the opportunities. The nation's pie was being divided more equitably than ever before; but the pie was shrinking and the decent life that at last had been opened to the masses was threatened. Perhaps that was the luck of life. Perhaps it was the rule—the way life was, a part of its tragedy.

There would be an England, of course—if not for always, at least for much time beyond our own. The indomitable spirit of this unique island race would certainly long endure. But I could not help thinking as I departed, that midcentury year, that I would never again see England as it had been when my own little journey through the second quarter of our century had first taken me there. The majesty of empire, the splendor, the grandeur, the power, the solid wealth— were they not lost forever?

6. THE PROSPECT OF
EUROPEAN UNION

"A day will come when all of you, nations of the Continent, will, without losing your distinctive qualities and your glorious individuality, be blended into a superior unity and constitute a European fraternity, just as Normandy, Brittany, Burgundy, Lorraine, have been blended into France . . . A day will come when bullets and bombshells will be replaced by votes, by the universal suffrage of nations, by the venerable arbitration of a great sovereign senate, which will be to Europe what the Parliament is to England, what the Diet is to Germany, what the Legislative Assembly is to France."

—VICTOR HUGO, in 1849.

THERE WERE two places in Europe that year I did not get to: Geneva and Strasbourg.

There was a great deal in the newspapers about the meeting of the Consultative Assembly of the Council of Europe in the beautiful old Alsatian city, but somehow I could not quite bring myself to go there. I judged by the press that a number of fine speeches were being made about the desirability of Europe's uniting. Churchill made one, and Reynaud, of France, another. A series of resolutions were passed which my friend, Russell Hill, who was present, assured me would represent a great step toward the unification of Europe—if anything were done about them.

That was the trouble. Nothing much was ever done about

them. In Strasbourg the earnest men of Europe indulged in talk of a very high level. They were men of good will, fiercely proud of a common European culture. Their aspirations for European unity were noble. But they had no power, no authority to do anything about them. All they could do was talk. And they spoke only for themselves, as individuals.

I had followed with interest and anticipation the evolution of the Council of Europe from its birth. It was born amid considerable enthusiasm at a meeting of representatives of private organizations working for European unity at The Hague from May 8 to 10, 1948. The delegates were a distinguished lot. Churchill was there, and Léon Blum and Spaak and a number of other former prime ministers of their respective countries. Eminent churchmen, lawyers, industrialists, trade unionists, professors, and men of letters completed the roll. They quite realized, as one of their resolutions said, that "the time has come when the European nations must transfer and merge some portion of their sovereign rights"; and, as another resolution stated, that "no attempt to rebuild the economy of Europe upon the basis of rigidly divided national sovereignty can prove successful."

The idea was perfect. How was it to be carried out? The good Europeans decided to appeal to the five governments which had signed the Brussels Pact: Britain, France, Belgium, Luxembourg, and the Netherlands. Four governments were sympathetic; the Labour government of Britain was cool. Prime Minister Attlee explained in a letter to Mr. Churchill in August 1948 that if a European Assembly were convened "this must be done by governments." The time had not yet come for that, he said. Governments were already too busy with other "urgent and difficult problems." To which Mr. Ernest Bevin, the British foreign secretary, added in a speech to the Commons: "Only when governments have settled the issues of defense, economic co-operation, and the political developments which must follow, will it be possible to establish some kind of an assembly. To create an assembly at this stage is like putting on the roof before building the house."

There was some sense in this position, but it was not very popular, and under the pressure of the other governments and of Mr. Churchill the British government finally gave in and agreed to erect a roof before building the house. On May 5, 1949, the foreign ministers of the five Brussels nations and of five others, Norway, Sweden, Denmark, Ireland, and Italy, concluded an agreement to set up the Council of Europe. It was to consist of a Committee of Ministers, made up of one cabinet minister from each state; and a Consultative Assembly the members of which would be selected by the respective states. In practice they are drawn from the parliaments of each nation. The big powers send 18 members each of the Assembly; the smaller powers from 3 to 8, depending roughly on their population.

So here at last as the Council of Europe met for the first time on the eve of the second half of the century in Strasbourg, its permanent seat, there seemed to be in the making Europe's first supranational government. There was the European parliament (the Assembly) and the European cabinet (the Committee of Ministers).

Unfortunately the Council had no authority, no power. The Committee of Ministers, which met in secret, alone was empowered to take any action whatsoever, and then only in the form of recommendations to member governments which those governments were perfectly free to disregard. The Consultative Assembly was purely a debating chamber. It had none of the legislative powers of national parliaments. Its resolutions might be gems of wisdom, produced after the most brilliant and high-minded debate, but not even the Committee of Ministers, let alone the member governments, were obligated to pay the slightest attention to them.

Perhaps it was a beginning; but it was a pitifully feeble one. Turkey, Greece, and Western Germany ultimately joined the Council. But more members merely swelled the chorus of the harmless if well-meaning words which echoed over Strasbourg. It was easy to talk big when one had no responsibility. No less a person than Winston Churchill gave eloquent testimony to this. Sometime during my journey that midcentury year he had gone to Strasbourg and on the floor of the Assembly had made a ringing appeal not only for European union, which was a general idea, but for the formation of a European army, which was a specific idea, and a good one, that thrilled the Continent.

The French government took it up enthusiastically for it opened the door to the solution of one of Western Europe's (and General Eisenhower's) most difficult and pressing problems: how to get German troops for the defense of the West without allowing the rebirth of the Wehrmacht and the dreaded German General Staff. As contingents in a European army, the Germans would not become a military threat. The United States backed the idea, and Belgium and Holland accepted it.

But when the North Atlantic Council met in Rome a year later, Mr. Churchill, with the responsibilities of a prime minister again on his shoulders, had lost his ardor for a European army. He commanded Mr. Eden to tell the NATO meeting in Rome, and Sir David Maxwell Fyfe, his home secretary, to tell the Consultative Assembly in Strasbourg that Britain would not contribute troops to any such force. Without British participation it was questionable whether a European army was possible.

My friend Russell Hill, in Strasbourg, was sad and chastened. The British position, he reported, "did not suggest that Mr. Churchill, the prime minister, would take the leadership in uniting Europe as he had done when he was a private individual with less authority and less responsibility. It may be doubted that Mr. Churchill was ever very serious about the European army. When he made the proposal last year he had not thought it out carefully. He wanted to make an inspiring speech, to liven up the assembly debate, to embarrass the Labour government."

Strasbourg, seemingly abandoned by its old champion, became thick with gloom. The dream of European Union, of a United States of Europe, evaporated into the fog that floated over from the nearby Rhine.

At home many well-meaning Americans (Governor Dewey was one) who apparently remembered little of history—either their own or others'—became impatient and sternly lectured the Europeans on the urgent necessity of their getting together in a United States of Europe just as the thirteen American colonies had done to form a United States of America. But the parallel, if there was one, was nebulous, distant, and misleading.

In America in the eighteenth century a completely fresh start with a federal government for a continent had been possible. Most of the vast region from ocean to ocean was uninhabited (except for a few Indians) and thus there were no established vested interests which would be hurt by political and economic union. The thirteen colonies were in no way comparable to the ancient states of Europe with their differing languages, customs, traditions, and cultures. It was relatively easy for the American colonists, knitted together by a common language and by the experience of already having been united under one crown and over-all rule and

244 Midcentury Journey

then further united by a revolution and a revolutionary war, jointly made and fought, to combine in a federal union; though even with all these advantages the joining together was not achieved without bitter controversy and years of untiring effort.

The economic problem was not comparable at all. In Europe the national economies had evolved slowly over the centuries. There were no vast open spaces to be developed. Each country, especially after the industrial revolution, built up various kinds of production in which a great deal of capital and labor skill was invested and which became the solid foundation of each nation's economic life and prosperity. At the midcentury every one of these nations in Europe feared that to surrender authority to a supranational federation would risk undermining the very basis on which their economies, often highly competitive, rested.

This concern was expressed by the National Executive Committee of the British Labour Party in a manifesto issued in 1950: "It is highly doubtful whether at the present time any European government would submit to a majority ruling against its profound conviction on an issue vital to itself."[1] A British Labour delegate to the Council of Europe at Strasbourg in August 1950 was more specific: "We could not accept the creation of a supranational authority. We could not agree that the fate of Britain's coal and steel industry should be decided outside Britain, perhaps against the will of the British people."[2]

British capitalists and Conservatives agreed. An American could see their point. I myself could not imagine either the owners or the workers at home agreeing to the fate of our

[1]*European Unity. A Statement by the National Executive Committee of the British Labour Party;* London, 1950.
[2]The London *Times;* August 28, 1950.

own coal and steel industries being decided, say, by some
United Nations authority, especially if it came to the matter
of lowering prices, profits, and wages to conform with those
abroad.

Did the failure—or, as some said, the fiasco—if the Council
of Europe at Strasbourg mean that no important unification
of Europe could take place in our time? No. By a curious
irony of fate a great deal of unity was being achieved as the
result of a mixture of pressure and material help from the
United States. This development constituted, it seemed to
this observer, one of the most encouraging, if bizarre, hap-
penings in the strange world of the midcentury. Nothing
quite like it, I believe, had ever occurred before. The Americans were obviously more concerned about European unity
than the Europeans; and they were more confident that it
could be achieved. Despite the fact that every nation in the
Council of Europe except Britain, Turkey, Sweden, and Ireland had been conquered and occupied during the war, despite the probability that if Europe did not unite it could not
remain free, the Europeans themselves did little toward getting together until the brash and wealthy Americans came
along and practically insisted on it in return for their billions
of dollars of aid.

We did not, to be sure, act out of any particularly char-
itable instincts, though these, I suspect, played a greater part
than most Europeans realized. Our main concern was, first,
that the free countries, ravaged by war and German occupation, be made stable enough, economically, socially, and
politically, so they would not succumb to communism. When
this was achieved, as it was rapidly and to a considerable
extent by Marshall Plan aid, we were determined, in our
own long-range interests, to make Western Europe strong

enough militarily to discourage Russian aggression and, if it occurred, to resist and repel it.

Unfortunately—since you cannot often have it both ways, that is, have both guns and butter—the necessity to rearm administered a severe blow to European economic recovery. Just when the nations of free Europe were getting back on their feet, they began to stumble and stagger under the burden of rearmament. It was at this point that the United States stepped in with a proposal which, if it proves successful, will not only make free Europe strong enough to resist the Russians but will inevitably unite her to an extent not thought possible a few years ago.

This was the significance of the organization which grew out of the North Atlantic Treaty signed in Washington on April 4, 1949 and ratified for the United States by the Senate by a vote of 82 to 13 on July 21. From it sprang the North Atlantic Treaty Organization, or NATO—the most remarkable and hopeful organism to be developed in the Western world since the end of the war. Unlike the Council of Europe it had power—military and economic. Also it took in the United States and Canada. And as the fateful last half of the century began, its member states were starting to yield to it, however reluctantly, some of the historic sovereignty which they, as nations, had guarded so long and so jealously for themselves.

Even before NATO, a process of unification among its European adherents had set in under the impetus of American aid. The Organization for European Economic Co-operation (O.E.E.C.) had been formed in 1948 by the sixteen countries receiving Marshall Plan help. Its purpose was to co-ordinate the division and the administration of the funds and materials received from the United States. For a time the American officials of the Economic Co-operation Administration (E.C.A.) hoped that the O.E.E.C. would become the foundation for a sort of European Economic Union. Under its aegis a European Payments Union, for example, was set up which, partially at least, restored the convertibility of currencies which had scarcely been exchangeable since the war and which thus stimulated foreign trade.

My own impression, shared by most Americans in E.C.A., was, however, that the O.E.E.C. would only hold the European nations together as long as American aid continued to flow. Once it stopped, they would resort to their old, nationalistic, selfish ways.

But NATO was different. Here was an idea translated immediately and with the minimum of bickering into an international body with flesh and bones and with the means to act. Its Council was a sort of parliament of the Western nations which, as was shown in the initial meetings of 1951, not only debated but resolved problems in such a way as to make its decisions binding on the national governments. Its Defense Committee, consisting of the defense ministers of the participating states, and which, in turn, ruled over the Military Committee, composed of the chiefs of staff of the various nations, knitted the Atlantic countries together for mutual defense in a manner never before attempted or achieved in peacetime.

This process was carried much further with the setting up in Paris at the end of 1950 of SHAPE—the headquarters of the Supreme Command in Europe of the North Atlantic Treaty powers—under General Eisenhower. Here was not only a close military collaboration between Western Europe and the United States for the first time in peace; it marked the first effective effort of the Western European powers themselves to fuse their military strength under one supreme command in time of peace.

It went further than mere collaboration and co-operation. Out of Churchill's mind (as we have seen) and General Eisenhower's headquarters and the ministries of the French government in Paris came the idea of the first European army in history. This would not be a coalition army made up of separate Allied armies, as in the past. It would be a truly supranational force, a unity in itself, with troops from a dozen European nations forming its larger units, and officers of all the nations constituting its general staff.

Such an army would, as we have observed, solve the problem of having much-needed German troops serve in the defense of the West without incurring the danger of resurrecting the Wehrmacht and the German General Staff. It would also be a vital step toward European federation. Perhaps the possession of a common army would do more than anything else to bring the nations of Europe together. And incidentally it might bring to a close that long and tragic chapter of history which had seen so many Franco-German wars. Without a national army of its own, Germany would no longer attack and overrun France or vice versa.

One other idea, originated by the Europeans themselves, promised to contribute toward Franco-German peace and toward the economic federation of Europe. That was the Schuman Plan, which would consolidate the production and sale of the coal and steel of Western Germany, France, Italy, Belgium, the Netherlands, the Saar, and Luxembourg under joint management. If the basic industries of Western Europe were combined, would it not be fairly easy to go on and unify the lesser enterprises, thus merging the economies of the six states? If economic union were achieved would not political union be bound to follow?

It was at least possible, especially if the pressure of the United States, operating through the North Atlantic Pact Organization and E.C.A., were continued. One drawback, to be sure, was Great Britain's refusal to join either the Schuman Plan or the European army, and its coolness toward the Council of Europe and the whole conception of European union. Britain, whether under Labour or the Tories, remained distinctly isolationist when it came to the Continent of Europe. Its leaders believed, perhaps with reason, that a too close association with the Continent would inevitably lead to the loss of the advantages that still obtained from its close ties with the Commonwealth and with the United States. Whatever the future of Britain might be, it lay not in being a member of a United States of Europe but a partner in the Commonwealth and the Atlantic Union.

European Union would have to be achieved without it. The London *Times* summed up the British attitude in the winter of 1951-52: "The most important thing for the governments and peoples of Europe to realize is that if they wish to federate, they must do so without Britain."

I did not go to Strasbourg, and I did not go to Geneva, where as a raw young American my hopes for the successful transformation of Woodrow Wilson's dream into reality had once risen high. On and off over the second and third decades of the century I had journeyed to Geneva to cover the meetings of the Council and the Assembly of the League of Nations. Gradually the hope for it dimmed and finally became extinguished. When, in 1938, I began to make in Geneva such a home as a roving correspondent had during those last frantic days of the peace, nothing was left of the League but a sad memory and a sprawling marble palace which looked over Lac Léman toward the snows of Mount Blanc—a vast and stately tomb in which lay buried so many decent hopes and aspirations that war-weary men had dared to entertain.

I had thought for a moment, that year of my journey, that Geneva would be a good place to stop for a few days to collect my thoughts and to ponder why the League of Nations had failed and whether the United Nations, whose permanent abode was rising along the East River a stone's throw from my New York home, would go the way I had seen the League go. But I abandoned the idea. It was easy enough, without going to Geneva, to recall why the League had failed. I could do it—and did—in the plane plodding through the night somewhere south of Iceland across the North Atlantic toward the Newfoundland shore—and home.

The League had failed largely because the two great Western democracies which were its main props, Britain and France, had not had the wisdom nor the courage to live up to its covenant. The League had floundered and sunk when Britain and France declined to back it in taking collective action against the aggressor states: first Japan, then Fascist Italy, finally Nazi Germany.

Would I live to see along the East River, I wondered, a repetition of the tragedy whose unfolding I had watched over so many years along the shore of the Lake of Geneva? Already a good many hopes in the U.N. had been dashed. It had not brought a very stable or a very decent peace. Yet in the June before, prodded by the United States, which had remained aloof from Geneva, the U.N. had taken the one step which the League of Nations had never dared to take: it had called the bluff of totalitarian aggression: it had dispatched troops to stop the armies of an aggressor, and those troops would shortly drive him back to where he had come from. The failure to take such action against Japan in Manchuria, against Italy in Ethiopia, against Nazi Germany in the Rhineland, in Austria, and in Czechoslovakia, had doomed the League. The United Nations had taken it in Korea and by showing that aggression did not pay had saved itself from the League's sorry fate and perhaps saved the world from World War III.

———————

One winter night over the North Atlantic at the end of the first half of the century our west-bound plane from Europe reached the point of no return and, after the usual calculations of fuel supply and headwinds had been made, continued on its way toward the American shore. Personally I had reached a point of no return myself. I would never again see Europe as my home, as the center of my life and work, which it had been for the past quarter-century. I was returning for good to where my roots were, even though for a time I might be, like all former exiles, voluntary or otherwise, a bit of a stranger in my native land.

This midcentury journey, I began to realize, had turned out to be not only a sort of recapitulation of the world one American approaching the age of fifty had lived through; it had been, too, a farewell to Europe.

I felt a certain aching, a certain sadness at the leaving of so many familiar places. It had been a lucky experience to have lived and worked in so many ancient and varied cities —London, Paris, Vienna, Berlin, Geneva—and to have been given the opportunity to absorb some of the spirit which each of them imparted. My debt to them, to all of Western Europe, was beyond calculation.

Now that I was gone I could see more clearly the incredible changes that had taken place in so brief a moment of time, as history went, since my first crossing. Europe then was still the center of the world, as it had been since the Renaissance. It still dominated our planet—militarily, financially, economically, and culturally. But years of savage war had dethroned it from its supreme position and all but ruined it. Now not even the Great Powers in Europe, despite their eminent civilization and the glory of their long history, were strong enough to stand on their own feet. The center of world power had shifted out of Europe, a part of it to the East, a part to the West, to be split up between two non-European giants: America and Russia. The struggle between these two superpowers would be dominating the rest of our days. Western Europe could not stay out of it any more than the United States had been able to remain out of Europe's two world wars. The realization of this frightened the Europeans, who knew that if the conflict degenerated into another war it would be fought on their soil to their utter and final ruin. Hence their despair and their feeling of frustration that after such a glorious and civilized past they were now helpless to decide their own destiny or even to do very much to ward off the catastrophe which, if it came, would snuff them out.

I took leave of them, depressed by the thought of how far they had fallen in the few anguished years I had known them—and yet not without hope that they would somehow rise again. Even an American knew that a world in which the genius of Western Europe had been stilled would be a poor place in which to dwell—poorer in many ways than before, drabber, less civilized, more spiritless, and rather desolate.

At the same time an American could feel a certain pride that his country had finally awakened, grown up, shed its narrow provincialism and begun to assume not only its proper role in world affairs but a deep interest in keeping European civilization alive.

When I had first crossed the ocean in 1925, the United

States was not taken very seriously in Europe, and Americans were still regarded there as rather uncouth, uncultivated nitwits who knew how to make money but who knew little else. The gaping American tourist, plodding dutifully through the art galleries and past the ancient monuments, uttering inanities in a high-pitched nasal voice and impatient to be back home in the bosom of the brother Elks and the Rotarians, was taken by the Europeans to represent the finest flowering of American civilization.

At the midcentury it could not be said that we were especially loved over there[3]—no foreigner ever was, especially if he and his country were the objects of envy, as we were— but we were respected and in us reposed most of the hope that was left in Europe. There was gratitude, to be sure, for the generous help we had given but even more, I think, for the fact that we constituted a hope. There was also genuine anxiety that we might betray the hope and the confidence, not willfully but as the result of our shortcomings.

There was fear that we might blunder into a war with Russia. A few could imagine us even precipitating it during one of our attacks of hysteria over communism or the latest Soviet provocation. Others thought our patience was too thin, our tolerance too easily undermined, our excitability too easily kindled—in short, they lacked confidence in our stability. And in our intelligence. They welcomed our dollars and our arms but at the same time wished that we would also export ideas. You could not, they said, buy converts any more than you could kill an idea like communism with guns or bombs—even atom bombs. They did not believe that we

[3] I was always puzzled that this hurt so many Americans. Was David L. Cohn right when he wrote in the *Atlantic* (September, 1951): "A puppy-friendly people with warm luncheon-club hearts, we want to be loved"?

were winning the war for men's minds. The Voice of America was a little shrill when it was not feeble.

Despite our shortcomings, however, an American could feel elated at the progress we had made. What had puzzled and frightened me in the past was that in the three decades between 1910 and 1940 we had not had the gumption to play any part in the events which landed us in two world wars. Had we done so, both of those holocausts might have been avoided. Perhaps in the years that led up to 1914 we did not have the power to influence decisively the course of history, though the fact that our intervention in 1917 proved decisive in determining the outcome of the first war indicates that we did have the power.

There is no question that we had it between the two wars. But we didn't have the sense to use it. We have seen in this journey some of the events that the United States might have influenced: the Japanese occupation of Manchuria and China, Italy's conquest of Abyssinia, the Spanish civil war, Hitler's various *coups*—the occupation of the Rhineland, the rape of Austria, the destruction of Czechoslovakia.

Had we joined in time the coalition we were eventually forced into by Hirohito and Hitler, either none of these outrages against the peace would have been attempted in the first place or, if they had been, they would have been swiftly undone by a combined force which later proved it had the military power to undo them by its eventual victory in the second war. I was sure in my own mind all through the late thirties that if the United States would let Hitler and Mussolini know that it would come to the aid of Western Europe if they dared to start a war, neither would have dared.

We know now from the German secret archives that although Hitler always calculated on Britain, France, and Russia eventually joining against him in the war he was plotting, he never gave a thought to American intervention. The United States, as a military factor against him, was never even mentioned in the numerous talks he had with his generals. Had Hitler been forced by us in advance to consider it, it is doubtful if he would have gone ahead with his plans. Certainly the German General Staff would not have followed him so docilely into a disastrous war. Had we in September 1938 informed Hitler that if he attacked Czechoslovakia we would join in a coalition of Britain, France, and Russia to stop him, there undoubtedly would have been no Munich, no destruction of the Czech nation, and therefore no world war the following year.

But we were still babes in the woods of foreign politics, with a Congress dominated by isolationists who were unpardonably ignorant not only of the world beyond our American shores but of the true self-interests of the nation which demanded that we cease sticking our head in the sand, ostrich-like, and begin to play an intelligent and forceful part in the world's doings.

No one, however unfriendly to us, can say that we are not doing that today. At least we have learned some lessons and are diligently trying to apply them. And we are endeavoring to avoid the mistakes which between the wars brought the other chief Western democracies, Britain and France, to the brink of the abyss.

We proved that during the midcentury year of my journey. A great test suddenly confronted us. There was an act of premeditated, totalitarian aggression in Korea. In Europe the people as well as the statesmen wondered what we would do. Cynically, they doubted whether we would do anything. History, they were sure, would repeat itself. The United States, like Great Britain and France in the thirties, would show in a crisis that it did not have the guts, let alone the wisdom, to take a bold lead in encouraging the world organization to stop the aggressor's attack by military measures, if necessary. It would be Manchuria, Abyssinia, the Rhineland, the *Anschluss*, Czechoslovakia all over again. There would be some loud and indignant verbal protests, perhaps even a ringing U.N. resolution, after which the aggressor would get away with his bloody deed.

The Europeans were at first stunned and then immensely encouraged by the swiftness with which the United States moved in the Korean affair. That summer as an American moved about the Continent he could not help being exhilarated by the reaction of the people. America's resolute stand, her skillful prodding of the U.N. to act, had not only restored their confidence in the United States and indeed raised it to a new high level. It had injected them with a new faith in the ability of the Western democratic world to survive in the struggle against Soviet imperialism and the relentless pressures of world communism.

Moreover it awakened them to the realities of Russian foreign policy and to the bankruptcy of the Communist idea. A great many European intellectuals who had convinced themselves that the Soviet Union stood for peace and that neither it nor the Communist satellite nations it controlled would ever resort to armed aggression lost, overnight, their illusions; for it was obvious to all that the Kremlin had given the green light to North Korea. And they were outraged by the brazen lies which poured out from Moscow justifying the Communist attack in Korea. They recognized them as no less false than those they had heard previously in similar circumstances from Hitler, Mussolini, and the Japanese warlords. The so-called Stockholm Peace Appeal, which millions of Europeans were signing in good faith that summer, was at once recognized for what it was: a swindle perpetrated by

Moscow to lull the decent folk of the world into a false sense of security. The stock of the Soviet Union and of communism, which had been rather high in Europe, where millions of persons had freely and sincerely embraced Marxism and joined the Communist Party, fell with dizzy speed. Russia became as discredited as Nazi Germany had been—and for the same reasons.

The free countries of Europe, rubbing their eyes and at last opening them wide, realized finally that they would have to unite and rearm to survive. For the first time they saw across the ocean a free, democratic land that would lead them and help them. Could an American, remembering all the past follies of the Western world—the ones recorded in this journey—not be proud that this had taken place?

7. A COMING HOME

"America! America!
God shed His grace on thee."

"America, you have it better."

—Goethe

"The land of the future."

—Hegel

"The hope of the world."

—Turgot

"The fairest experiment ever tried in human affairs."

—Richard Price

"To be an American is of itself almost a moral condition, an education, and a career."

—Santayana

"Why, in fifty years of progress, such as no nation in the world had ever known, did disillusion overtake the American mind and heart?"

—Lloyd Morris, in 1946

"A great nation busily engaged in fumbling its destiny during a preposterous generation."

—Henry Morton Robinson

"When, in our country, since the passage of the Alien and Sedition Acts, have so many people so arrogantly assumed the right to tyrannize over the minds of men, dictating what they shall think, what they shall speak, how they shall vote, with whom they shall associate, and imposing moral obloquy, if not the pains of the law, upon any who dares to question the dictum that all is for the best in the best of all possible worlds?"

—Gerald W. Johnson, at the midcentury

"You would suppose, to listen to these people, that the American Way of Life consisted in unanimous tribal self-adoration. Down with criticism; down with protests; down with unpopular opinions; down with independent thought. Yet the history and tradition of our country make it perfectly plain that the essence of the American Way of Life is its hospitality to criticism, protest, unpopular opinions, and independent thought."

— ROBERT M. HUTCHINS, in 1949

"It is all too easy to be wrong about the United States."

— CLYDE KLUCKHOHN

On us, of course, and on our land, fortune had smiled. Fortune and God and climate and soil and geography had all been kind.

The last night of the journey, as the plane droned westward over the ocean, I fell to thinking of it: of the luck, the accomplishments, the failures, the purposes and hopes and prospects of the America I was coming home to.

It had certainly changed—almost beyond recognition—in the quarter of a century since I first took leave. But where in the Old World from which I was now departing the changes had been toward decline, here in the New World they were the opposite; they were part of an advance, a progression.

As a people we were better off than we had been in 1925. We were wealthier, better educated, better housed, better clothed. As a nation we had grown up. And for better or worse we had become the most powerful country on the planet.

These changes had occurred while I was away. Because of this, perhaps, I was more struck by the contrasts than had I remained at home. I was continually thinking of how far we had come since that summer I left a mere quarter of a century before. We had come a long way, leaping from one era to another, and though we had had to hurdle many obstacles no one could say we had not got over them with dizzy speed.

I myself had missed the two fundamental experiences which shaped the lives of Americans during the thirties—until the war came: the great depression and the administration of Franklin D. Roosevelt. There had been no inkling of them when I departed in 1925.

That year all was well with the Republic. Or so it seemed to those who ran the country or edited its newspapers and magazines or siphoned off the lion's share of its ever growing wealth. I do not recall any word of warning from these sources that we were riding hell-bent for a terrible fall. Under the beneficent influence of Coolidge prosperity, the great god business had become, as Frederick Lewis Allen said, supreme in the land, almost the national religion; and the businessman, as Stuart Chase saw him was, "the dictator of our destinies," replacing "the statesman, the priest, the philosopher, as the creator of standards of ethics and behavior" to become the "final authority on the conduct of American society."[1]

Certainly the businessmen had in Coolidge a President they liked and who liked them and who left them alone to pursue their business and their profits. They seemed to be pretty good at this. American prosperity was fabulous. Only later, when I looked into the matter, did it dawn on me that this prosperity did not go down very far.

At about the time I left our shores three-quarters of our people were economically insecure: almost half of them

[1] *Only Yesterday,* by Frederick Lewis Allen; New York, 1931.

lived in actual poverty; one-third had to raise their families on an average income of $450 a year. But those at the other end of the scale had it good. Some 700,000 of them managed to procure as much of the national income as the 70,000,000 at the bottom. Some 25,000 of them, with incomes ranging from $75,000 to $500,000 a year, had as big a slice of the nation's pie as 12,000,000 of the poorer citizens. A mere 200 families owned or controlled nearly half of the nation's wealth.[2]

Yet I do not recall many Americans griping at this singular division of the spoils. I do not recollect that any of our great newspapers or mass-circulation magazines registered any complaints. The farmers out my way in Iowa and union labor in the big industrial cities were not entirely content, I remember. But they were weakly organized at the time and lacked the vociferous champions in Congress they later acquired. Inequalities in income had given great impetus in Europe to the rise of socialism, but no such thing had occurred at home. Most Americans, however impoverished, regarded Socialists as crackpots, and socialism always remained a dead duck in America. We took this for granted, but it puzzled the Europeans.

Was it not, however, this very inequitable distribution of wealth which, by failing to expand mass purchasing power to soak up the increasing production of our industry, brought on the worst depression in our history? Being abroad I had never been caught up in the orgy of playing the stock market which gripped millions of Americans in the late twenties. The Big Bull Market was beyond my comprehension and interest. I noted only that it seemed to provoke a strange national mania, and the many American visitors to Europe I saw in those days made little sense to me, with their

[2]*Fantastic Interim,* by Henry Morton Robinson; New York, 1943.

feverish gibberish about how American Can or A.T. and T. or G.M. were skyrocketing and how much easy money they were making. As luck would have it, I went home on my first leave in the fall of 1929 and was there when the stock-market crash came. But the hysteria was so great that I could not get clear just what had happened and why, and it was only years later, while trying to report various phases of the European depression, which though bad enough was not so severe as the one at home, that I came upon some ideas, necessarily sketchy, that explained in part (at least to me) the causes of the debacle in America.

I do remember from my visit in 1929 and from subsequent ones, short as they all were, what a cruel blow it was to our people, how it shook their confidence in businessmen, bankers, and the Republican Party and—what was more important—in their very economic system, whose basic tenets up to that time had seemed above criticism. I remember, too, the blow not only to our confidence but to our collective optimism. Even such a young and buoyant people as we could not laugh off the spectacle of 14,000,000 persons, a fourth of our working population, unemployed, 5,503 banks in trouble, and a sickening slump of wholesale prices by one-third, of the national income by one-half, of the value of merchandise trade by two-thirds, and a decline of factory payrolls to one-third of what they had been just before the bubble burst. What made it worse was the terrible sense of frustration of the hitherto most unfrustrated people on the planet. We did not know what had hit us or why, or what to do to fight back to our feet or whom or what to fight. The enemy who had laid us low was invisible. We were down but we did not understand why. Indeed it was difficult to comprehend why, in the midst of such plenty as this nation had, in the food its farmers raised and the goods its factories turned out in such abundance, millions had to hunger and live in such abject poverty. A simple citizen could be pardoned for wondering why crops were being plowed under and hogs slaughtered by the millions while so many stomachs were half empty. Obviously our system of distributing what we produced had broken down. The goods were there, and the demand. But tens of millions of citizens lacked the money to purchase them. Something was radically wrong. What was it?

Later, part of the answer, at least, would come to us.

We think of the great Bust as having been due mainly to the mad speculation of the late twenties which saw, between 1925 and 1929, an increase in stock shares from some 450 million to four and a half billion and a fantastic rise in their prices which had no relation to the real earnings of the companies that had floated them. This development undoubtedly helped to precipitate the crash and to make it so terrifying and complete. But the fundamental reasons for the depression went deeper.

There was first of all—and long before the stock-market debacle in 1929—a warning that all was not well with our economy. Production of capital goods, which by their very nature tend to be subject to the traditional business cycle (determined by the time consumed in wearing out machines, in the deterioration of buildings, etc.), began to slacken in 1927. That year investment in producers' goods dropped by three-quarters of a billion dollars. The building trade slacked off; fewer homes and factories were constructed. Production of automobiles, the most flourishing of our new industries, dropped 22 per cent below that of the previous year. The stock market did not reflect this slowing down of our creation of tangible wealth; just the opposite. Prices of stocks continued to soar. Even the most solid and conservative financiers and industrialists began to believe, like medieval peasants, in miracles.

They might have considered another warning, but they didn't. This was the drop, in 1927, of consumption. Ever since 1921, with the exception of one year, 1924, salaries and wages had been increasing annually by a billion and a half dollars, providing that much more purchasing power to buy up the increasing production of our factories. In 1937, wages and salaries increased by only $400,000,000. Purchasing power began to lag behind the supply of goods on hand. Between 1921 and 1929 we nearly doubled the volume of what we produced; but in that time salaries and wages increased only 40 per cent. The farmers fared even worse. I used to hear from some of them in my native Iowa. They complained they were caught in an unholy squeeze. Actually the share of the farmers in our national income dropped from 16 per cent in 1919 to below 9 per cent in 1929.

Only the holders of stocks and bonds were better off. Dividends went up in those eight crucial years by 100 per cent. The price of many stocks doubled and trebled. All through that time 90 per cent of our liquid wealth was concentrated in the hands of 10 per cent of our people. It was a physical impossibility for the 10 per cent to spend it all; they could not, if they had wanted to, buy all the goods that were pouring from our factories, or eat all the food being produced on our farms. Apparently it never occurred to them that it would be good business, in the long run, to increase wages and salaries, lower prices, and invest more in capital equipment so as to provide adequate purchasing power for the nation's magnificent output. Instead they poured their money into the stock market, sending up stock prices to ever more unrealistic levels; or they let their funds stagnate.

Years later, Barbara Ward, the English economist, would sum up the reasons for our debacle: "wild speculation on Wall Street fed in part by the undistributed profits of business, a marked falling off of production in the capital goods sector spreading to other sections, a decline in purchasing power and in employment, and a government committed by temperament and philosophy to non-intervention."[3]

Only when the country was prostrate, the banks closed, the factories stilled, the most elemental trade all but halted, business facing general bankruptcy, and millions wondering where the next meal was coming from did the American people, the most conservative and wealthy on earth, turn to a government with another temperament and philosophy. The nation and the people have never been the same since, nor are they ever likely to be. I will always regret that I missed the experience of living through those first heady years of the New Deal and of Roosevelt, for they transformed us as a people and as a nation, shaping our society and our civilization in a new mold. Perhaps an American abroad could see more clearly, if only because of the perspective that distance gave. At least he was relatively free of the prejudices which naturally affected the judgment of those caught up in the struggle, especially of the leaders of finance and industry who had collectively failed but who, notwithstanding, found it difficult, if not impossible, to adjust themselves to the mighty new currents which swept across our continent.

The year it all began, 1933, I happened to be taking time off from my professional duties in a little fishing village in Spain, where I found the time and the peace of mind to get caught up on some reading of history and literature and to reflect amid such idyllic surroundings on the meaning, if any,

[3]*The West at Bay,* by Barbara Ward; New York, 1948.

of the turmoil into which not only Europe, about which I had been writing for eight years, but America, which had been so serene and confident when I departed, had fallen. In truth I was a little weary of Europe's troubles, some of which I have tried to chronicle in this journey. I was therefore all the keener for news from home which came to our fishing village that year in countless letters and in innumerable papers and magazines and in the bewildered reports in the European press.

Some of the fishermen and peasants in the village, many of whom had relatives in America and all of whom believed that the United States was populated by a race made up exclusively of millionaires, used to ask me what had happened at home. They said they could not believe what they read in their newspapers or heard from the village priest: that in the American paradise millions were out of work, business and trade at a standstill, and the banks closed. Even in Spain, which was impoverished, that had not yet happened. I didn't try to explain. I didn't know the answers myself.

That year and in the years that followed, I sought answers, like everyone else. In time I came to believe, despite the scoldings, and worse, which I got from my banker friends and many captains of industry, that Roosevelt had really saved and preserved our capitalist, free-enterprise system. What puzzled and even astonished me was that he was never forgiven by those he had rescued and whose banks and businesses and fortunes he not only saved but, in the end, helped make stronger and richer. After all, it was not "socialism" or even government interference and control which brought about our economic debacle in the thirties. That failure was the responsibility of private enterprise. It simply didn't do the job the citizens had the right to expect from it. It will never get the opportunity, by itself, to try again. This is one measure of the changes we have been noting in this journey. The world of unfettered free enterprise that seemed so promising to us in 1925 is dead beyond recall.

Not that the mixture of private initiative and government support and control which we have had since 1933 has achieved any permanent solution of our basic economic problem, which is how to create enough mass purchasing power to absorb the ever increasing product of our factories and farms. Roosevelt and the New Deal accomplished a mighty repair job but they did not solve our problem; nor did private enterprise. We are rightly ashamed to admit it, but the sordid fact remains: our problem was solved temporarily only by the timely assistance of that greatest of all evils, *war*.

Do our faulty memories recall that the depression was not licked by the time the Second World War came? By that date our production had merely crept back to the level of 1929, we still had eight million unemployed, and our annual national income, in terms of 1939 prices, was more than ten billion dollars less than it had been the year the stock market crashed and the depression began.

Whatever the arguments may be against government butting into business—and they are many and we are constantly reminded of them—the stark fact remains that it took the government, acting under the dire pressures of war, to show that our economy was capable of achievements not dreamt of in those halcyon days when Coolidge and Hoover kept the Federal state strictly out of business. Between 1940, when our economy was still in the doldrums, and 1944, at the height of the war, we doubled our production and doubled our national income. The feats of our private industrialists, engineers, and workers in those years were prodigious. But they were stung into doubling our economy by the much despised government, which invested tens of billions of dollars in capital equipment, paid many billions more for goods actually produced, and created a new mass purchasing power among the people. Profits during those war years were not bad either. In fact, they constituted quite an incentive. Corporate profits rose from 6.5 billions in 1939 to 24.3 billions in 1944—an increase of four times—and though wartime excess-profit taxes greatly reduced them, they actually jumped, after the taxes had been deducted, from five billions in 1939 to 10.8 billions in 1944—or just double.

Whether or not our economy would have sagged after the pent-up demand for civilian goods following the war had been exhausted, we will never know. There were signs in 1948 and 1949 of a "recession." There were breaks in the market and in the price of wheat; and there was a rise in unemployment from two million in 1948 to over four million in 1950. Roger Babson, who had predicted the 1929 crash, again became bearish. In 1949 he foresaw a new depression on the horizon for 1953 because "the last one was never cured." Leon Keyserling, of the President's Council of Economic Advisers, saw "elements of increasing danger for 1949." He thought "the bright prospects could change to gloom within a year." There was evidence that purchasing power was drying up. National income in 1949 dropped by seven billions. Corporate profits, before taxes, were down five billions. It was estimated that the majority of low-income families had cashed in their war-bond savings accumulated during the war. More than eight million families and single individuals received less than $1,000 cash income in 1948."[4]

Once again the necessity to arm and to furnish our allies with arms intervened to save us. Communist aggression in

[4]Report of the Subcommittee on Low-Income Families of the Joint Committee on the Economic Report, November, 1949.

North Korea in June 1950 awakened the country to the danger. Immediately a vast program of rearmament was instituted and the economy, which had limped a little in 1948 and 1949, began again to boom. By the middle of 1952 this country would be spending 65 billion dollars a year for its security. A fifth of our entire national output would be going for arms.

Personal income by the middle of 1951 had risen to a new high, a total of 250 billion dollars a year, compared to 46 billions in the depression year of 1933—an increase of five times. The total national product was even higher than the peak previously reached at the climax of the war. In 1944 it amounted to 316 billions. In the middle of 1951 it was 328 billions, an all-time record.

Corporate profits kept pace. In the first half of 1951 they reached a new record annual rate of 50 billion dollars. Even after the higher taxes had been deducted they came to 22 1/2 billions compared to 19 billions in the same period the year before.

Once again our fabulous American economy was in full gear, producing more than ever before, a marvel of the world, a matter of pride to every citizen.

But was it also not a matter of concern that it took war, or the threat of war, to achieve this result? Was there not something radically wrong with an economic system that could only function well under the unholy stimulus of making guns and planes and tanks and atom bombs to kill people? We had solved the problem of production. Our plants and our land could produce enough to give every last one of our citizens an abundant life. Yet we had not learned how to distribute our products once peace set in and human beings settled down to live normal, decent lives. This, it seemed to me, was a shattering shortcoming, an example of the folly and the blundering inadequacy of the human race.

The challenge remained. Would we have the guts and the intelligence, the burning urge and the honesty, once peace came again, to meet it?

I wondered, that midcentury year I came home. To complete my journey I set off across the country, roaming across the plains and mountains from coast to coast, riding trains and planes along the Canadian border to the north and the Mexican border on the south, stopping off at cities on the Gulf—Galveston, New Orleans, Mobile, and even getting to that Mecca of the sun, Miami.

There was so much in the land that was sheer wonder. In the ignorance of my long exile I had scarcely realized how bountiful nature had been not only in such prosaic matters as climate and soil and mineral wealth but in the grandeur of the scenery it bestowed upon us. What a feeling of wonderment came over you when you watched the sun set over the Golden Gate at San Francisco or over the desert and the distant mountains of Arizona, or when, from a train plowing through the snow, you saw a blizzard rage in the high Rockies! Where else in all the world could you lounge in a plane and between dawn and dusk pass over a continent from one ocean to another, gazing upon the infinite variety of a land, its forests and cultivated plains and deserts and mountains, the mighty rivers, the lakes that were like oceans, the jungle swamps, the sprawling cities under a pall of smoke, the neat little towns assembled around a church steeple, the great highways and rail lines, winding like ribbons and interlacing it all?

Where else could you gaze upon the likes of the man-made skyline on Manhattan Island when your ship from Europe came up the river at dawn, or at dusk when a million lights shone high above the city? Where else the exhilaration that came when you were up and about a snow-bound New England village on a sunny, frosty morning?

You found beauty and even splendor wherever you went—and ugliness too, of course, where greedy or careless men had despoiled the land. And you found the people bursting with friendliness, cordiality, hospitality. They were better off, materially, than any other you had ever seen, a bit unmindful perhaps of their good luck, a little apt to take too much credit for themselves and grant too little to God and fortune. Yet surely they had the right to be proud of what they had built and of the life they had made. I myself was filled with excitement and joy and relief to be home among them for good.

And yet . . .

Some things puzzled me. Two things, principally: first, a curious schizophrenia in popular thought; and second, an inexplicable atmosphere of intolerance, suspicion, fear, and even hysteria, which threatened our freedoms and formed a relentless pressure toward conformity of opinion.

Schizophrenia was perhaps the wrong word for what I thought I saw. What I mean is that a good deal of the thinking of some of the people I met seemed to be divorced from reality. Perhaps this was merely a symptom of the confusion into which all of us had fallen. But it perplexed me.

The businessmen, for example, complained that the nation had succumbed to socialism. On February sixth of the mid-century year the Republican Party proclaimed that the major domestic issue of the 1950 Congressional elections would be "Liberty against Socialism." The implication was that America, under the Democratic administration, had become a socialist society. It was specifically charged that the government's program was "dictated by a small but powerful group

of persons who believe in socialism." Most of the businessmen I saw actually believed this, or said they did.

Was it true? Socialism, by any definition, is a system based,
as Webster puts it, "on collective or governmental ownership
and democratic management of the essential means for the
production and distribution of goods." Socialism does away
with private profits. Had that happened in America?

I could find no evidence of it. The facts and figures—the
truth, that is—pointed to just the opposite. In 1932, for example, the last year under Republican administration, which
presumably subscribed completely to untrammeled private
enterprise, the nation's corporations didn't make any profit
at all, taken as a whole. In fact they lost money that year—
3 1/2 billion dollars in all. After four years of the first Democratic administration, which even then, I am told, was being
called "socialistic," private profits of our corporations were at
least of moderate size. In 1937 they came to $6,200,000,000
of which $4,700,000,000 was left after taxes.

But during the year of my journey, corporation profits
were the highest in the history of the Republic. They
amounted to $41,400,000,000 of which $22,800,000,000 remained after taxes.

How could you call a system "socialism," I asked my
business friends, when it enabled privately owned enterprise to make more profits, even after whopping taxes, than
ever before in our entire history? How could you say we
lived under socialism when at the midcentury mark General
Motors did well enough to be able to report the highest net
profit ever recorded by an American corporation—the tidy
sum of $834,044,039, which was nearly two hundred million
dollars more than it had made the year before, when it had
also set a record for the greatest profit any company had
made up to that time and which, that year of 1949, repre-

sented an increase of 49 per cent over its previous peak, in 1948.

If private profits were the basis of our free-enterprise system was not the foundation stronger than ever? The figures said it was. Where was socialism, then? Could it be that it existed only in the mind, that it was in truth merely a hallucination, a devil conjured up out of the imagination and which one cursed and fought, as if in a dream, but which in reality did not exist?

There was another aberration which confounded me. The most eminent Americans talked in grave tones about the evil influence of "alien philosophies" which, they said, were corrupting the American Way of Life. Former President Herbert Hoover warned against them as did General of the Army Douglas MacArthur. I gathered that if a philosophy were "alien," it was *ipso facto* bad for an American.

But were not almost all of our philosophies and our very religion, from which we received so much of our philosophy of life—were they not "alien"? Christianity certainly was. It came from a foreigner in the faraway Near East. The Roman Catholic version came from a foreign source—from Rome. The Protestant interpretation came from "aliens"—Luther and Calvin. The concept of the life of reason came to us from over the seas—from the "alien" Greeks. We got something else from the Greeks—democracy. Should we abandon it because it was "alien"?

And what, I wanted to know, was all this strange talk about un-Americanism? There was a body of the House of Representatives in Washington called the "un-American Committee." There were similarly named committees in some of the state legislatures. They seemed to be busy ferreting out citizens they said were "un-American." But on what authority and on whose definition? The Constitution did not give such specific power to anyone. It did not define "un-Americanism." Nor did our illustrious founding fathers. Judging by what they said and wrote—in the Declaration of Independence and in the Constitution, for example—the very idea would probably have struck them as preposterous.

No other healthy modern democracy that I knew of had hit upon such a curious idea. There was no "un-British Committee" in the House of Commons, no "un-French Committee" in the Paris Assembly, no "un-Swedish Committee" in the Stockholm Riksdag. The very suggestion would have been howled down with derision or at least with amused laughter.

I could understand that a Communist who accepted the orders of Moscow could not possibly be considered a good, loyal American. But our un-American committees went much further in their efforts to label citizens as "un-American." Most of their victims were not Communists at all, but non-Communists, or anti-Communists, who held minority or unpopular views or who were suspected of holding them.

It did seem a little pretentious for one group of Americans to set themselves up as judges of the Americanism of others. What was an American? Was he not an infinite variety of persons, good and bad, virtuous and wicked, wise and foolish, liberal and conservative, practical and visionary, shortsighted and long-sighted, extravert and introvert, learned and illiterate, wealthy and poor, Democrat and Republican, employer, worker, farmer, lawyer, doctor, writer—Debs and Judge Gary, Colonel McCormick and John Dewey, Senator McCarthy and Senator Margaret Chase Smith, Tom Dewey, Norman Thomas, Willkie, Walter Reuther, Tom Girdler, John L. Lewis, Rockefeller, the president of C.I.O. and the president of N.A.M.—and holding a thousand differing, opposing, contradictory views and opinions about his coun-

try—how to save it, how to improve it, how to run it—and
yielding to no man or group of men, official or unofficial, the
right to judge him "un-American."

The hue and cry about "un-Americanism," it seemed to
me, was most un-American. It was foreign to our deepest
American traditions, and certainly not worthy of them.

There was something else. There was an atmosphere
throughout the land that year of suspicion, intolerance, and
fear that puzzled me. I had seen those poisons grow into ugly
witch hunting and worse in the totalitarian lands abroad but
I was not prepared to find them taking root in our splendid
democracy.

I had always boasted abroad that Americans were the
most carefree, ruggedly independent-minded individuals on
the face of the earth, never afraid to say what they thought—
and seldom backward in saying it, either, no matter who, or
how many, disagreed. Our fearlessness, our almost fierce independence of mind, were among the things that made us
great and that qualified us, after the war, to champion freedom in a world that was being darkened by totalitarian
thought control.

At first, that year, I could not believe my eyes, or my ears.
Everywhere I went a surprisingly large number of people
seemed afraid. Of what, in God's name? Of becoming involved in controversy, they said, of getting into trouble by
expressing an opinion that someone might not like.

That WHO might not like?

Well, they said, hesitantly and usually in a whisper (was
I back in Germany under the snooping nose of the Gestapo,
I wondered), the government, or the F.B.I., or some loyalty
board, or the University Board of Trustees, or Senator
McCarthy, or the un-American Committee, or the moguls in

Hollywood, or the sponsor of a T.V. or radio program, or the local newspaper, or any one of a hundred groups of self-appointed vigilantes—or even your boss at the office or your next-door neighbor.

"You will be destroyed if you don't watch out," they warned. And they mumbled something about smears, black lists, character assassination, guilt by association, and other sinister practices that I had never heard of in America though I was not unfamiliar with them after a long sojourn in the totalitarian dictatorships.

"The best thing," they said, "is to keep your mouth shut—and your thoughts to yourself. It's safer that way."

Americans talking about playing it safe! It was absurd. I refused to believe it. These good folk, government officials, teachers, professors, writers, actors, broadcasters, preachers, lawyers, labor leaders, small businessmen, chairmen of civic forums, politicians, diplomats, judges—they were surely seeing things, like my friends in business who, staggering under the load of mounting profits, thought, mistakenly, that it was "socialism" which was weighing them down.

For a long time I hesitated to accept what looked like evidence piling up. Then corroboration began to appear from some very high and eminent sources. I did not yet trust my own judgment; I hadn't been back long enough. But could I deny what those with the highest authority were beginning to say they saw?

One day in Washington the President of the United States spoke out. I happened to be listening to the radio when his voice came on. He was, it developed, dedicating the new Washington headquarters of the American Legion, whose members were pledged, in the preamble of the Legion's constitution, to "uphold and defend the Constitution of the

United States . . . to safeguard and transmit to posterity the
principles of justice, freedom, and democracy."

Those noble principles, the President thought, were in
danger; so was the Bill of Rights, which protects our individual liberties and is part of the Constitution we are all
pledged to uphold and defend. Coming from so high a Constitutional authority—the top one, in fact, under our system—
the words that now poured forth struck me with a strange
impact. I began to note them down:

*Americanism is under attack by communism, at home and
abroad. We are defending it against that attack . . . But Americanism is also under another kind of attack. It is being undermined by some people in this country who are loudly proclaiming
that they are its chief defenders. These people claim to be against
communism. But they are chipping away at our basic freedoms
just as insidiously and far more effectively than the Communists
have even been able to do . . . They are trying to create fear and
suspicion among us by the use of slander, unproved accusations,
and just plain lies.*

*They are filling the air with the most irresponsible kinds of
accusations against other people . . . These slander-mongers are
trying to get us so hysterical that no one will stand up to them
for fear of being called a Communist. Now, this is an old Communist trick in reverse. Everybody in Russia lives in terror of
being called an anti-Communist . . . In a dictatorship everybody
lives in fear and terror of being denounced and slandered. Nobody dares stand up for his rights . . .*

*Yet this is exactly what the scare-mongers and hate-mongers
are trying to bring about in this country. Character assassination
is their stock in trade. Guilt by association is their motto. They
have created such a wave of fear and uncertainty that their
attacks upon our liberties go almost unchallenged. Many people
are growing frightened—and frightened people don't protest.*

Stop and think where this is leading us.

*The growing practice of character assassination is already
curbing free speech and it is threatening all our other freedoms.*

I daresay there are people here today who have reached the point where they are afraid to explore a new idea. How many of you are afraid to come right out in public and say what you think about a controversial issue? How many of you feel that you must "play it safe" in all things—and on all occasions? . . .

Slander, lies, character assassination—these things are a threat to every single citizen everywhere in this country. When even one American—who has done nothing wrong—is forced by fear to shut his mind and close his mouth, than all Americans are in peril.

To hear a President of the United States speak such words troubled me. I myself had come to similar conclusions from my own hasty observations, and though I revolted at accepting them, I was afraid that they were true. However, I sought more light from other sources.

One was the Republican Governor of Maryland, Theodore R. McKeldin. Some time after my return he addressed the annual convention of the Maryland State Teachers' Association.

I have witnessed with deepening concern the development in recent months of this new danger to personal freedom. It is not the danger of forcible repression by government; it stems from action by individuals or groups exercising a pressure not less powerful than that of government . . . Its method is not direct interference with freedom of expression but it is not less destructive of that freedom because it intimidates men.

The threat is not that they will be arrested, but that they will be stigmatized. Duress by name calling is more cruel and unjust, for while arrest leads to trial under legal safeguards, the smear is employed without restraint or responsibility and the victim is punished in the very process of being accused . . . The result is that men who cannot be silenced by authority are gagged by fear, for they know that ofttimes the penalty of forthrightness is character assassination, economic ruin, and social ostracism.

The tragedy is that the attack on freedom is often made in the guise of a defense of freedom, and Constitutional rights are destroyed in the name of patriotism . . . I am thinking not only of revolting instances of men being publicly called Communists or Fascists without proof and other men not daring to speak in their defense. There is a deplorable intolerance which characterizes much of our so-called public discussion. It is conducted not on the level of debate; it descends to name calling and mud slinging.

Related to the technique of the smear and the big lie is the sly innuendo sowing suspicion against the integrity and good faith of the opponent. This, too, is a method employed by the Fascist and the Communist to discourage independence of thought. This alarming totalitarian tendency to inhibit free expression can be halted if the people are aroused to its inherent danger . . .

One encouraging sign was that an increasing number of eminent Americans were commencing to try to arouse the people to the danger. As the second half of the century began, voices which had been too long stilled could be heard rising across the country. I kept my ear to the ground and listened.

Paul G. Hoffman, automobile magnate, administrator of the Marshall Plan, president of the Ford Foundation:

The nation's fight against communism is being weakened by the use of methods that tend to make criticism socially dangerous and that force conformity through fear . . . Some of our people — often good people — are ready to pillory anyone who holds an unpopular view or supports an unpopular cause. As a result too many of our fellow citizens have been afraid to speak out. In far too many cases decisions, often in high places, have been influenced by fear. In short, the danger of Communist penetration and disruption has been compounded by the spread of panic . . .

Robert M. Hutchins, chancellor (as he then was) of Chicago University, at the 237th convocation:

Every day in this country, men and women are being deprived of their livelihood, or at least their reputation, by unsubstantiated charges. These charges are then treated as facts in further charges against their relatives or associates. We do not throw people into jail because they are alleged to differ with the official dogma. We throw them out of work and do our best to create the impression that they are subversive and hence dangerous, not only to the state, but also to everybody who comes near them . . .

The cloak-and-stiletto work that is now going on will not merely mean that many persons will suffer for acts that they did not commit, or for acts that were legal when committed, or for no acts at all. Far worse is the end result, which will be that critics, even of the mildest sort, will be frightened into silence. Stupidity and injustice will go unchallenged because no one will dare to speak against them.

To persecute people into conformity by the nonlegal methods popular today is little better than doing it by purges and pogroms. The dreadful unanimity of tribal self-adoration was characteristic of the Nazi state. It is sedulously fostered in Russia. It is to the last degree un-American.

There were many other respected and distinguished citizens who spoke out: Lloyd K. Garrison, saying that:

. . . Americans, in their zeal to defend themselves against foreign agents, espionage and sabotage, have gone far toward reviving the hated inquisitions of the Middle Ages. We have passed from guarding against overt acts to punishing people for beliefs, both real and imaginary, and in our zeal to stamp out the heresy of communism, we have let loose forces that are threatening the very freedoms we seek to save.

And Henry Steele Commager, saying in the New York *Times:*

. . . We are now embarked upon a campaign of suppression and oppression more violent, more reckless, more pervasive and ultimately more dangerous than any in our history.

There were others still, but these voices were a fair sample.

Was this, I wondered, what the United States of America had come to at the pinnacle of its greatness and when all over the world it was presuming to champion individual freedom against the threat of the Communist totalitarians to destroy it?

If so, was there not something wrong? And how soon would we right it? No one that year seemed to know. My friends assured me that we would recover our senses in due time as we had on previous, similar occasions.

According to the historians whom I consulted we had lost our heads at least four times in the past and given in to fear, suppression, and oppression: toward the close of the eighteenth century, when the Republic was young and the Federalists, panicky over the excesses of the revolutionists in France and of Jefferson at home, put over the Alien and Sedition Laws; again in the 1850's when the South, alarmed by the growing threat to slavery, ousted those who opposed it, censored the press and the mail, purged the colleges, and finally withdrew from the Union; again in the 1890's when our good and prosperous conservatives, especially in the East, became frightened of the Populists and tried to suppress them; and finally after the First World War, when we persuaded ourselves that the nation was about to be taken over by the local Bolsheviki, and to save ourselves deported hundreds of innocent aliens, sent Debs to jail, purified the legislatures of Socialists, instituted teachers' oaths, and thanked God for the "Palmer raids" on "radicals" which, as Frederick Lewis Allen would later say, "set a new record in American history for executive transgression of individual Constitutional rights."[5]

In not one of these cases, as Henry Steele Commager has

[5]Frederick Lewis Allen, *op. cit.*

remarked,[6] was there a real threat to the Republic, the Constitution, or our democracy. This we later acknowledged, eventually repealing the Alien and Sedition Laws, abolishing slavery, enacting into sedate law most of the program of the dreaded Populists, and repenting of the folly into which the silly "red scare" of the 1920's had thrown us.

Was our American society at last threatened in the midcentury years so that the hysteria, the fear, the repressions, were justified, or at least understandable? Were we so disunited and weak that we had to silence criticism, and make everyone conform, and smear and ruin those who did not, those who still insisted on speaking their honest thoughts, however erroneous? It did not seem so to me. The military power of the Soviet Union was a threat, as was the world Communist movement. But the first came from without, and almost all the strength of the second lay beyond our continent. Few citizens seemed to realize how lucky we were that communism had not caught on over here as it had, say, in France, where, as we have seen, it was the largest and the strongest single political party. Here only an insignificant handful were Communists. They were too small in number, in caliber, in appeal, to frighten a hundred and fifty million prosperous, vigorous people out of their wits or to endanger the security of the mightiest nation on earth. The F.B.I. and the processes of the law were more than adequate to handle them. They could safely leave the rest of us to regain our wits and our old American virtues.

I wondered what the youth of America thought of the frightened antics of their elders. I took to the campuses to find out. Here, surely, in our great universities and fine colleges, which were the envy of the rest of the world, one

[6]The New York *Times*, June 26, 1949.

would find that the traditional citadels of free inquiry and free expression had not been breached. I approached these institutions bursting with anticipation and hope. I came away chastened. Our campuses turned out to be but a reflection of the nation, or so it seemed to me. Perhaps, though, I was wrong. Again I could not quite bring myself to trust my own judgment. Again I must be seeing things, my accuracy of observation of the American scene warped by so long an absence in foreign parts.

But again corroboration kept popping up. Finally the eminent, respectable, conservative New York *Times*, one of the pillars of the nation, looked in on seventy-two major campuses, more than I had been able to visit, and harshly confirmed my worst suspicions.

A subtle, creeping paralysis of freedom of thought and speech is attacking college campuses in many parts of the country, limiting both students and faculty in the area traditionally reserved for the free exploration of knowledge and truth.

These limitations on free inquiry take a variety of forms, but their net effect is a widening tendency toward passive acceptance of the status quo, conformity, and a narrowing of the area of tolerance in which students, faculty, and administrators feel free to speak, act, and think independently.

A study of seventy-two major colleges in the United States by the New York Times showed that many members of the college community were wary and felt varying degrees of inhibition about speaking out on controversial issues, discussing unpopular concepts, and participating in student political activity . . . Such caution, in effect, has made many campuses barren of the free give-and-take of ideas, the study found . . . It has brought to many college campuses an apathy about current problems that borders almost on their deliberate exclusion.

The names of most students, teachers, and administrators

interviewed were withheld for fear, the *Times* said, of reprisal or criticism. (Was I back in Nazi Germany again?) But they had plenty to say.

The *Daily News* of Yale University:

> *We cannot believe that the American people will indefinitely tolerate this control over youthful lives by looming up before them the spectre of the "loyalty check." We cannot believe that this virtual blockade of the market place of ideas to young men can go on for a lifetime.*
>
> *And yet, despite hope, we see the sky growing darker, the night of thought-conformity closing in. We see college men growing more and more docile, more and more accepting the status quo, paralyzed by the fear of their futures. . . .*

It was naturally accepted that the F.B.I. was keeping a check on Communists but the students, professors, and administrators felt that our secret police was also snooping into the "liberalism" of the young men on the campuses. At the University of Michigan, Dean Erich A. Walter explained to the *Times:*

> *. . . that students were quite obviously more careful in their affiliations, recognizing that Federal Security officers were making careful checks of the memberships of liberal organizations.*

At the City College of New York a student editor held:

> *. . . that his fellow students were unwilling to speak out, particularly in engineering, where, he said, "the wrong word at the wrong time might jeopardize their futures." He said agents of the Federal Bureau of Investigation were constantly inquiring about students applying for Government jobs, and that some graduate schools, with Government-classified projects, were extremely reluctant to accept students who had committed themselves to an unpopular point of view.*

Not to a Communist view, note, but to an *unpopular* view. Abroad such pressure was called thought control and that was what it was, wherever it was exercised. Thought control in the United States! It seemed too fantastic to believe. And fantastic, too, were some of the consequences.

Dean Millicent C. McIntosh of Barnard told the *Times* she found:

> . . . *some girls held that anything identified with peace, freedom of speech, or negotiation to resolve differences was suspected of Communist influence. "Girls are becoming afraid to advocate the humanitarian point of view," Dean McIntosh declared, "because it has been associated with communism."*

One student in the same institution said:

> . . . *that students were fearful of joining any political clubs on the campus, because they were afraid that such affiliations would hurt them in Government work. In the college placement office, Miss Ruth Houghton, director, said the word "liberal" was a "poisonous word" to many would-be employers, who conceived of the "liberal girl" as an "obstructionist" and "organizer against employer interests."*

And so this lamentable tale told by the *Times* went. The president of the student body at the University of North Carolina said:

> . . . *The growing fear of new ideas, largely a consequence of the McCarthy witch-hunts, has had its effect on students, as on citizens everywhere.*

Another student leader at the same university said:

> . . . *There is an atmosphere on the campus, as in most of the*

country, which tends to equate criticism with disloyalty and liberalism with communism.

At the University of Wisconsin the president of the student body said there had been:

. . . a general tagging of the student board as "subversive" because it had issued a statement opposing the views of Senator McCarthy.[7]

If the students were paralyzed with fear of exercising their constitutional rights and of following the old traditions of fearless, free expression of opinion which I had always thought were part of the glory of America, the professors were even more so. They resented being singled out from other citizens and made to sign a special loyalty oath. They considered themselves to be as loyal as anyone else, but as Harold Taylor, president of Sarah Lawrence College, said, they did not believe that a man could be made loyal by administering an oath to him or that the oaths were a measure of a person's loyalty. Professor Commager, of Columbia, thought the loyalty oath was "a fat-headed, feeble-minded attempt to find an easy solution to a complicated problem." There was little doubt in my own mind from what I had seen on the West Coast that the University of California, one of the truly remarkable institutions of higher learning in the country, had suffered in declining morale from the battle over the loyalty oath between its faculty and the Board of Regents. The professors—all but a few, that is—eventually signed it because they could not afford to be unemployed, but their resentment and bitterness permeated the eight campuses of the university, leaving an ugly scar that would not be healed for a generation and that marked a sickening

[7]The New York *Times,* May 10, 1951.

setback to the progress of education and learning in one of our greatest states.

Still, our educators kept up the fight against hysteria, thought control and conformity. I think Dean Wilbur J. Bender of Harvard University spoke for them when he said:

The world is full of dangerous ideas, and we are both naïve and stupid if we believe that the way to prepare intelligent young men to face the world is to try to protect them from such ideas while they are in college. Four years in an insulated nursery will produce gullible innocents, not tough-minded realists who know what they believe because they have faced the enemies of their beliefs.

As long as such men—and there were hundreds of them on our campuses—did not crack or surrender, our colleges and universities, it seemed to me, would eventually regain their position as a bulwark of the free spirit in our civilization.

——————

As a people, I gathered, we could all stand a little more education. I may be wrong, but I did not get the impression in my travels up and down the country that year that we were very well informed either about the world or our own land; nor did we always grasp the very issues on which our existence depended. The public opinion polls piled up evidence of our ignorance. Even Dr. Gallup, the prince of the pollsters, confessed that "today for the first time I am concerned lest lack of information lead the American people to decisions which they will regret."[8]

His pollsters found five areas of ignorance in which large segments of our population wallowed. One area was foreign affairs. Dr. Gallup put some fairly simple questions, it seemed to me, to the citizenry: Where is Manchuria?

[8]The New York *Times*, November 4, 1951.

Formosa? Will you tell me what is meant when people refer to the 38th Parallel? Will you tell me what is meant by the term "Atlantic Pact"? Will you tell me who Chiang Kai-shek is? Will you tell me who Marshal Tito is?

Only 12 per cent of the adults questioned could answer all six correctly. A larger number—19 per cent—flunked all six.

"The amazing thing," exclaimed Dr. Gallup, "is that virtually all of these people read a newspaper and listen to their radios daily."

I was a little amazed myself at Dr. Gallup's amazement. Perhaps the amazing thing was not that the good people could read a newspaper and listen to the newscasts daily and still be so ignorant, but that their daily journals and news broadcasts were of such an amazingly low quality that the millions who read and listened were bound to be left in almost total ignorance of what was going on in the world. Given the caliber of our information mediums there was nothing very amazing at the results. Later on in his article Dr. Gallup came around to recognizing this.

He had, he said, conducted a small survey among copy-desk chiefs in newspaper offices asking them to rate the way our daily newspapers treated world and national news and issues compared with other fare. The working newspapermen rated the handling of such news lower than that of any other. Our press, it seemed to the experts who made it, was doing a pretty poor job in furnishing readers with news from home and abroad.

Have our newspapers lost a sense of their historical function to keep the public informed about issues of the day? asked Dr. Gallup. "Have they begun to worry too much about having the most popular comic strips and the most complete sports pages, and too little about keeping their readers interested in, and informed about, the important problems of the day?" he asked again.

From the little I had observed since my return I suspected that Dr. Gallup had put his finger on something.

To be fair, we had no right to put the entire blame for our ignorance on our press and radio. Even when they gave the news we demonstrated a meager capacity to absorb it. Certainly the press and radio had not been silent about such public figures as Secretary of State Acheson and Senator McCarthy. Yet after Mr. Acheson had been in office for two years, 34 per cent of the American people, Dr. Gallup found, could not identify him as Secretary of State. But there was a certain balance in our ignorance. About the same percentage didn't know who Senator McCarthy was either.

And six out of ten didn't know what the Reconstruction Finance Corporation (R.F.C.) was all about, even after all the headlines about the mink coats and other scandals connected with it. I found many people kicking about the size of the national debt, but Dr. Gallup reported that when he asked the public how much it thought the debt amounted to the average guess was 150 billion dollars short of the mark.

In the other three areas, the Gallup pollsters found respectively that, as a people, we had an appalling misconception of (1) the destructiveness of the atom bomb, (2) the awesome effect of another world war on our present civilization, and (3) the alternatives to a shooting war.

Perhaps some of our ignorance, it occurred to me, was due to a lack of a sense of history. We were living, as the scholars never ceased reminding us, in a great revolutionary era. Yet I did not get the impression that many of us in America were aware of it. An instance was our attitude toward events in Asia, especially in China.

Asia had been in revolt for forty years. In China, Sun Yat-sen had launched a revolution before the First World War and Chiang Kai-shek had carried it on through the twenties and thirties. As the first half of our century neared its end Chiang was driven out by a Communist revolution. The State Department was not responsible for this. The Chinese themselves were. A good many factors contributed to the unfortunate result: eight years of Japanese invasion and occupation of China, the eventual defeat of the Japanese by the United States, four years of devastating civil war, the inefficient, unpopular, repressive and corrupt rule of the Kuomintang, the effective exploitation by the Communists of a general antipathy for the West, of the hatred of the peasants, who comprised most of the population, for the landlords, and of the promise that communism had a cure for the wretched poverty that was so widespread, and finally the success of the Communist armies.

These were the essential facts of the Communist revolution in China. They were matters of history. The State Department had nothing to do with them. No doubt it was displeased with the course of events, for they led to disaster so far as American interests in China were concerned. But China, really, had never been ours to keep or to give away. Our government had done what it could to maintain Chiang in power, first against the threat of Japan and then against the threat of the Communists. It had poured billions into the country. It had armed thirty-five Nationalist divisions. It had used United States Navy ships and Army planes to transport Chiang's troops to key points as soon as the Japanese were beaten. It had, in sum, given him far more aid than his Communist opponents ever received from Russia.

Yet most Americans I met during my journey that year sincerely believed that the State Department alone was responsible for the success of the Communists in China. They knew little of the efforts their government had made to prevent that success; they knew less of the intricate history of events in China itself which had led to it. More than one politician made political capital that year out of the charge that the administration had turned China over to Stalin. I held no brief for the administration, whose mistakes in foreign policy, it seemed to me, were many. But the charge that it had "sold out China to the Russians" was absurd and those who made it showed little knowledge of, or respect for, the facts of history, let alone for the truth. With all our power we were not strong enough to dominate the course of events all over the world. China was a reminder of that—and of how helpful it would be to our understanding of a complex, erring world if we could develop a sense of history.

No doubt it would have been helpful to my understanding of my own country had I spent more time in Washington after my return. I kept shying away from it. The shadow of Senator McCarthy lay so heavy over the capital that I found it tempting to slip away after a day or two to fresher, cleaner, saner air. I had seen the likes of McCarthy come to prominence in the totalitarian countries. He struck me as a second-rate Goebbels, possessing something of the German propaganda minister's disregard for truth or fair play or elementary decency and his flair for the lowest forms of demagoguery, but lacking the German's brain, which was above average. I wondered how so many decent Americans could be fooled by the Wisconsin senator's technique of the big lie and the smear, which I had seen Hitler and Goebbels develop in Berlin to such a high and disgusting art and at which the Muscovites were such masters. Few citizens who fell for McCarthy's line seemed to remember that though he had been quoted as publicly stating he knew of 205 "card-carrying

Communists" (later he reduced the number) in the State Department he never revealed the name of a single one.

I gathered, though, that the public at large and even the Senate began to sense McCarthy's true stature when he stood up in the highest legislative body in the land and charged that General Marshall, one of the most distinguished citizens of our time, had been part of a "conspiracy so immense and an infamy so black as to dwarf any previous such venture in the history of man." At any rate some time later Senator William Benton of Connecticut would charge under oath that McCarthy had lied to the Senate and deliberately attempted to deceive it, and would ask for his expulsion from that august body.

Washington was not a very pretty place that midcentury year. Compared to the war years, when it was full of brilliant, dedicated men, it now seemed to be taken over by a host of petty individuals dedicated to their own advancement, or their party's, but not their country's, of stunted mind and character, ignorant and hysterical and altogether inadequate for leadership of the greatest nation on earth confronted with the most difficult and baffling problems in its history. It was a depressing place but also, I must admit, fascinating. Regardless of how puny the men there were and of how they floundered, it had to be admitted that their decisions in the next few years would probably determine the fate of a large part of the human race. It was a place to go back to soon for a more lengthy and enlightening sojourn.

In the meantime, my midcentury journey over, I returned to New York.

On that teeming island I had found a permanent home at last. Gradually the feeling I had had so long that Paris was home, and Vienna and Berlin and London, faded. I found

myself settling down in what was surely the most fabulous
city of them all. In Chicago, where I was born, the leading
newspaper, for which I had worked during my first years in
Europe, maintained that New York was not part of the Union,
that it was really a foreign city. But this was said in fun, or
perhaps in envy. New York was not America—a fact which
its inhabitants often forgot; for America was a continent, the
sum of all its varying cities and the land between. But surely
New York was the glory of America. It was a city so unique
you could say that nothing quite like it had ever existed
before—anywhere.

On the whole, it seemed to me to reflect the country—its
hopes and fears, its aspirations and ambitions, its restlessness
and drive, its mixture of races and peoples, and, above all,
its incomparable achievements. Each section of the land
offered its special contributions to the nation, but here in
this island metropolis was the concentrate, the distillation,
of all that was good and bad—and great. And here was the
fountain of our creativeness. New York gave the nation its
fashions, its plays, most of its books and magazines and its
greatest newspaper. It originated most of its radio and television programs, provided the lion's share of its leading
sport events, and channeled most of the news that appeared
in its newspapers or was heard over the air. It was the financial center of the last great citadel of capitalism in the world;
it was the earth's greatest port, from whose 1,800 docks in an
average year 13,000 ships departed carrying 60 million tons
of goods, or nearly half the foreign trade of the country. And
though it was neither the capital of the nation nor even of
the state which shared its name it could be said to have
become, that midcentury year, the capital of the world when
the United Nations began erecting its headquarters on the
banks of the East River at the end of Forty-second Street.

Above all, New York was pre-eminent in art. A traveler gallivanting about America might not get the impression that art was taken very seriously or considered very important in a civilization whose leading members seemed to be preoccupied with making money. Be that as it may, art, in many of its wonderful forms, was enshrined in this city. It was an object of respect, of love, of passion, even of worship; and it was created, practiced, and appreciated according to tastes and standards as high as any I had known in the Old World cultural capitals of Paris, Vienna, Berlin, and London. What made New York so incomparable to me in this respect was that it combined in one city the eminence in the arts which was scattered over the capitals of Europe. Each of them had been famous for the high state of one art or another. But in New York, at the midcentury, anyway, you could see more than one of them practiced superbly; opera at the Met, symphony music at the Philharmonic, ballet at the Ballet Theatre and the New York City Ballet, chamber music from the Budapest Quartet. Though we lagged behind the European centers in not having a state-subsidized national theater, Broadway could, when it had a worthy play, provide as imaginative and finished a performance as was to be witnessed anywhere abroad. No other great American city, no matter how wealthy, even attempted to maintain a theater of its own. In New York most of the nation's book publishing was concentrated and to it or its neighborhood the majority of the writers came and settled down. Likewise with the painters, for the Art Students' League was one of the world's best art schools, full of fine ferment, and it was in the city's private galleries and exhibitions that most painters' reputations were made. We had no Louvre, but New York's Metropolitan Museum was perhaps next best, and I recall seeing in no other city such a succession of exciting temporary exhibitions of both modern and classical paintings.

The critique of art and literature was centered in Manhattan. It pretty well set the tastes of the nation and was on the whole, it seemed to me, of an excellent standard, at least equal to that of Europe and usually more objective.

I do not mean to overdo the comparisons with the Old World. I began to love the city for itself, for its own creativeness. But since I had lived most of my life in a Europe which insisted on judging America and Americans by such native products as chewing gum, Coca-Cola, comics, and the more silly Hollywood movies I fell naturally, I suppose, to making comparisons which were a little more fair and of which almost all Europeans were ignorant.

There were plenty of things in New York, of course, not to be complacent about or even admiring. It reflected the nation's anxieties and uncertainties, and since it originated so much of the material which shaped our culture and our way of life as a people, its failings were all the more important and depressing. One could feel this, for example, in the theater and in the weird world which gave America its daily fare of radio and television entertainment and enlightenment.

I was obviously not a competent judge of the American theater. But as a mere theatergoer, I was surprised to find that it had so little to say at a time when we were more beset with problems than ever before. As one settled down for the second half of the century the theater in New York seemed undistinguished. Almost the only thing that saved the season that first year from complete banality was the revival of plays by Shaw and Shakespeare, both deceased, neither American. Where were the American playwrights who had made the previous twenty-five years on Broadway so exciting? Apparently they were tired, or at least had said all they had to say.

And they had few successors. But was there more to it than that?

One day toward the end of 1951, Brooks Atkinson, New York's most discerning and fearless dramatic critic, offered an answer in the *Times* that stuck in my mind.

Something elusive and intangible seems to have drained the vitality out of the theatre and perhaps out of other American arts as well. No one knows the reason exactly. But could it be that the spiritual climate in which we are now living smothers art that is really creative, and that the emphasis on public expression of all kinds is toward meekness and conformity?

Here was a reiteration from an unexpected source of a theme that had so puzzled me when on my return I had heard it enunciated by so many, from the President of the United States on down.

Mr. Atkinson went on:

People are playing safe. They hesitate to say what they think. The intellectual and artistic life of the country has been flattened out. The ignorant heresy-hunting and the bigoted character-assassination that have acquired the generic title of McCarthyism are succeeding. The hoodlums are in control here as well as in Russia, and the theatre begins to look as insipid in the one place as in the other. . . . We cannot expect to have vital art in our theatre if we emulate totalitarian countries and yield the control of cultural life to the Yahoos and hoodlums.[9]

Was not that, I sometimes wondered, what those who furnished us our daily radio and television programs were also doing—yielding the control of their great popular medium to the Yahoos and hoodlums who were loose in the land?

[9]The New York *Times*, December 2, 1951.

That the network executives, and especially the advertising men, who dominated radio and T.V. because they controlled its purse strings, should tend toward "meekness and conformity" in our present uneasy climate was not very surprising. It was good business not to get involved in controversy. And when they looked around they saw all the other pillars of society conforming and taking no chances. Why should they be more courageous, more imaginative, than the next fellow in business? Their attitude was certainly understandable, unless you sought perfection itself.

But they went much further. They demonstrated what John Crosby in the New York *Herald Tribune* (November 19, 1951) called "an appalling moral cowardice" and what seemed to me to be a despicable disregard for the most elementary American principles of civil liberty, freedom, fair play, justice, and decency in knuckling under to an unofficial and private blacklist compiled in a vicious and irresponsible publication called *Red Channels*.

It contained the names of 151 radio and T.V. artists, directors, writers, producers, and commentators who allegedly had leftist or Communist or Communist-front affiliations. Judging by my own name appearing in this list, most of the allegations were patently fraudulent and deliberately misleading.

But the charges, unjustified as they were in most cases, were not important. After all, in a free country anyone was free to make the most asinine accusations. The radio and advertising executives, however, never bothered to investigate the charges. The fact that one's name was on the list was enough. He was, with a few exceptions, automatically barred from employment on radio or T.V. He was given no chance to defend himself.

The courage of those who provide our radio and T.V. could

be gauged by the fact that while not a single one of them ever publicly defended the *Red Channels* blacklist or even admitted that he paid any attention to it, few of them, especially in the advertising agencies, dared to hire anyone on this infamous register.

"The plain fact is," commented Mr. Crosby, "that *Red Channels*, which almost nobody in the business approves of or trusts, is still in the secret library of all the ad agencies, is still at the elbow of casting directors for T.V. and radio, and has immeasurably damaged the reputations, livelihoods, and careers of the people listed in it . . . The *Red Channels* blacklist is employed simply as a device to stay out of trouble with everybody, as a matter of—in the most cynical use of the phrase—public relations."

This was brought out in the case of Elmer Rice, Pulitzer prize playwright, who terminated his association with a well-known television program when the advertising agency handling it refused to approve an actor suggested by Mr. Rice for one of his own plays. The refusal was based not on artistic grounds, said Mr. Rice, but on "public relations." What this meant in effect, the playwright said he found, was that an attorney of the advertising agency conducted "an inquiry into the alleged political opinions and activities of the actors and bases his acceptance or rejection upon his judgment of the propriety of their political beliefs."

This smacked to me of the way artists were handled in Russia and in Nazi Germany, or in any other totalitarian country. But the president of the advertising firm stoutly defended the practice. "When you get somebody who may cause a lot of bad publicity for your program," he argued, "you do have to be a little careful. It's an ordinary business safeguard."

The trouble with that argument, it seemed to me, overlooking the fact that the *Red Channels* publishers made a practice of organizing "bad publicity" by getting a handful of people to telephone or write a protest, was that radio and television were not an ordinary business. By law the air waves belonged to the people. Wavelengths and channels on them were granted by the government to private concerns to exploit for their private profit, but *in* the public interest. Radio and T.V., because of their semimonopolistic character (there were only a few wavelengths and channels for the government to pass out) were quasi-public businesses whose leaders were, in a sense, trustees of the public with certain obligations which did not obtain for men engaged in "ordinary" private enterprise. The question was: were the men who were making good profits from the use of publicly owned channels living up to their obligations to the citizenry and the nation when they obeyed crackpot blacklists, submitted to all sorts of private censorship, and denied the people the right to hear and see a number of eminent artists and broadcasters?

America was the only major country in the world in which the government had turned over radio and television to private enterprise for private profit. Certainly our entrepreneurs had many notable achievements in both fields. Some of them were men of vision and integrity and unsurpassed technical skill. Millions of dollars had been invested by them in the industry, as they called it. Most of it had paid off, or promised to pay off. Few objected to that. But a lot of people, I gathered, expected the networks, stations, and ad men to show some responsibility for the trust they had received from the public and, at the very least, not to abuse it.

Perhaps a straw in the wind was a bill sponsored in the Senate by Senators William Benton, Leverett Saltonstall, Lester C. Hunt, and H. Styles Bridges—two Democrats and two Republicans—calling for a National Citizens' Advisory

Board on Radio and Television. The board, to be composed
of eleven outstanding citizens, would serve as a sort of public
watchdog and would report annually to the Congress on how
radio and television were serving the public interest. It interested me that the mere announcement of the proposal of the
bill aroused a storm of indignation among the broadcasting
executives. According to one of their spokesmen, Senator
Benton (a former advertising head himself) "has the opera-
tors on the nation's radio and T.V. stations in a towering
rage."

But support for the bill came from other sources; from Ray-
mond Rubicam, a retired advertising tycoon, for one, who
wrote: "Radio broadcasting in the United States has come
nowhere near serving the American people as well as it ought
to have served them. I am convinced that a large part of the
reason lies in the domination of radio by the advertiser . . .
What I am opposed to is what amounts practically to a mo-
nopoly of radio and television by advertisers to the point
where the public's freedom of choice in programs is more of a
theory than a fact, and to the point where the public service of
the two media is only a shadow of what it could be."

Mulling over these unexpected words from the founder of
one of the world's largest advertising agencies and for long a
power in radio, and having had a certain experience in the
medium myself, I could not quarrel with what he said. In fact,
I thought it made much sense.

————

There was a good deal of sense abroad in the country, I began to see, as well as nonsense; much to praise and love and
be proud of as well as to criticize and condemn—or have
honest differences over. The American citizen may have had,
as Gerald W. Johnson[10] said, too many flatterers, telling him

[10]*This American People,* by Gerald W. Johnson; New York, 1951.

what a great and glorious thing it was to be American, but never mentioning how difficult and dangerous it was. But Johnson himself, one of our Baltimore sages, and those I have quoted in this chapter, and others with courage and intelligence, were proof that our tendency toward self-flattery, self-righteousness, and conformity would not go unchallenged.

For all our shortcomings, of which the temporary manifestation of fear, intolerance, and witch hunting was the worst, the America I returned to at the midcentury was an infinitely better land than the one I had left in 1925. It was genuine progress to have grown up, to have come of age, to have shed the incredible provincialism of the twenties, its infantilism and insipidity, the blind worship of business and money, and the mawkish hypocrisy of Prohibition. It was progress to have left behind forever a period that was rightly called the Era of Wonderful Nonsense, in which the citizens, when they were not madly chasing the dollar, abandoned themselves to such weird trifles as pole sitting, bunion derbies, egg-eating contests, long-distance fiddling orgies, juicy murder trials, and the doings of such persons as the comely Peaches Browning and her senile Daddy with his toy goose.

It was a growing up when we abandoned isolationism, assumed our responsibilities as a world power, and made good our shortsighted refusal to join the League of Nations by taking the initiative in founding the United Nations, in which we were to play a leading part. It was progress when the nation doubled its productivity and gave its farmers and workers a standard of living far above that of any other country; when a foreign economist, who was not blind to our failings, could exclaim: "The United States in 1946 and 1947 was without peer in the world and its economic strength was unique in the entire history of mankind. No community had ever accumulated such wealth. No people had ever enjoyed such a standard of living . . . a phenomenal, astronomical prosperity compared either with the contemporary standards of the non-American world or with levels reached by any past age."[11]

The creation of the Tennessee Valley Authority, of Boulder Dam and Grand Coulee, was progress too; and so was the discovery in America of how to harness atomic energy, a secret which had eluded man for at least two millenniums. And whatever might be said abroad—or at home—about our lack of spiritual qualities, the fact remained that we had shown not a little generosity after the war in shelling out billions of dollars and a vast amount of food to help less fortunate countries abroad, including our recent enemies, to get back on their feet. (For UNRRA alone, we had furnished 72 per cent of its operating funds and 90 per cent of its supplies.) True, we had also acted out of self-interest, since we stood to benefit from a stable, decently prosperous world. But I could not recall any other nation in the past ever having acted similarly, even out of enlightened self-interest. I could find no record that Great Britain, for instance, had made such lavish gifts to others in the days when it owned half the foreign investments of the world and enjoyed from its enterprise and its fabulous empire a prosperity not approached by any other land.

Though our material well-being was the wonder—and the envy—of the world, no American in his right mind believed there was not room, even in this sphere, for much further progress. There was the challenge of the 8,000,000 American families and single individuals whom a joint Congressional committee revealed in 1949 to be receiving less than $1,000 cash income a year. Many of them, the committee reminded us, were forced "to live below even the most conservative

[11]Barbara Ward, *op. cit.*

estimate of the minimum necessary for health and decency," and not a few of their households had become demoralized by "low wages, broken work, broken health, broken homes."

With a little more effort on the part of the nation as a whole, could not these hapless millions also be given the opportunity to enjoy the vaunted American standard of living? The experts believed so. According to an exhaustive survey of our needs and resources made in 1949 by the Twentieth Century Fund, an increase of only 8 per cent in what we were likely to produce in 1960 would enable us to turn out enough goods and services to provide adequate food, clothing, housing and medical care for every living American, get rid of our slums, and take our children through at least two years of high school.

That was the material prospect for America that midcentury year. The spiritual prospects were something else. Admittedly, I had not been back long enough even to try to assess them.

There were some, I found, who believed that we had sacrificed the needs of the spirit to the demands of materialism, that we had needlessly surrendered the dream of the good life, as Lloyd Morris put it, for the illusion of material success.

That no doubt was partly true. And yet, moving about the country again in the winter of 1951-52 and in the spring that followed, after all but the closing lines of this book had been written, I gathered that the American dream was far from extinguished. Many a night after a public lecture I sat in simple, wholesome homes and listened to earnest, decent, average citizens pour out their views of life. These views were not always, by any means, concerned with dollars, gadgets and mechanical pleasures. Often they were mature, reflective, spiritual, denoting man's eternal concern with life's problems and mysteries. True, there was grumbling

about the state of the world, as there must have been since
time immemorial among human beings who were not spirit-
ually and mentally dead or hopelessly smug. But surely this
was a healthy sign. There were complaints, especially among
the well-to-do, about "ruinous taxes" and fears that the country was "going to ruin." But it was, as Lewis Gannett said,
hard to believe in ruin when you traveled around America
those first days of the second half of the twentieth century.

No great age was easy or comfortable to live in. "On the
whole," Alfred Whitehead, one of the more penetrating minds
of our epoch, once observed, "the great ages have been unstable ages." A people proved its greatness not in easy times
but in difficult times, in adversity, when the going became
rough and uncertain. That was when the test came. It had
come for us before—at our birth as a nation, during our Civil
War, and, in our own lifetime, in two world wars and in the
depression between the wars. Each time, thanks to our guts
and our faith—and (can we say it humbly?) our greatness—
we had emerged triumphantly from our ordeal. Now, so soon,
a great testing time had come again.

The inner meaning of our age of conflict, if it had any,
remained largely hidden from us. It was difficult to fathom
the reason or logic even in what we have seen on this brief
and cursory journey through a mere quarter of a century of
life in the Western world. Perhaps the best we could do was,
as in this peregrination, to apply what insight we had as
erring human beings toward the understanding of how and
why we had arrived at our present situation.

This journey had reminded me that the world I had been
born in at the beginning of the twentieth century was gone—
its stability, its relative simplicity, its firm beliefs, its peace of
mind, and all. But if these travels had also recalled that the

times of my adulthood had been full of darkness, disbelief, strife, hate, violence, tyranny, intolerance, war, suffering, and drawn, anxious faces, I must never forget that they had been full, too, here and there, now and then, of hope, love, charity, courage, decency, and a touching human craving for light and reason and justice and peace and God.

On the whole there were advantages in being alive, in being a witness and a participant, in what the historians assured us was one of the epochal transformations of history. There were moments even when you could feel proud and glad, and certainly stirred, to be living at this tumultuous time in so great an age.

ACKNOWLEDGMENTS

This book was written largely out of my memory, refreshed from notes jotted down over the years. But to refresh it further and to buttress it with a good many facts, figures, and quotations which my porous mind, at least, does not retain for ready use, I did a bit of reading, both of a general and a specific kind. When it was necessary I drew freely from the labors of others, as is evident from the footnotes—though they do not indicate my entire debt to all the writers I consulted.

For perspective, data, and a mood that I found surprisingly close to my own, *This Age of Conflict*, by Frank Pentland Chambers, and others (New York: Harcourt, Brace; revised ed., 1950) was most valuable. So was *The Gathering Storm*, by Winston S. Churchill (Boston: Houghton Mifflin, 1948) especially in its masterful description of the Europe between the wars, in its insight into German affairs, and its authoritative account of British foreign policy during the crucial decade that led up to the second war. For the flavor of the world of the well-to-do in Europe before 1914 I turned to, among others, Marcel Proust's monumental novel, *A la recherche du temps perdu* (Paris: Librairie Gallimard, 1927) and the memoirs of Osbert Sitwell—especially *Great Morning* (Boston: Little, Brown, 1947). Lloyd Morris' admirable *Postscript to Yesterday* (New York: Random House, 1947) recreated the mood of America before the first war, as did Charles and Mary Beard's already classic *The Rise of American Civilization* (New York: Macmillan, 1930).

Other books read for general background and data included: *A History of Europe,* by H.A.L. Fisher (London: Edward Arnold, 1936); *The World Since 1914,* by Walter Consuelo Langsam (New York: Macmillan, 1948); *Glimpses of World History,* by Jawaharlal Nehru (New York: John Day, 1942); *A World History of Our Own Times,* by Quincy Howe (New York: Simon & Schuster, 1949); *The Condition of Man,* by Lewis Mumford (New York: Harcourt, Brace, 1944); *The Crisis of Our Age,* by Pitirim A. Sorokin (New York: E. P. Dutton, 1943); *A History of Western Philosophy,* by Bertrand Russell (New York: Simon & Schuster, 1945); *Reflections on the Revolution of Our Time,* by Harold J. Laski (New York: Viking, 1943); *On Living in a Revolution,* by Julian Huxley (New York: Harper & Bros., 1944); *The West at Bay,* by Barbara Ward (New York: W. W. Norton, 1948); and *The State of Europe,* by Howard K. Smith (New York: Alfred A. Knopf, 1949).

Often I checked my memory and notes against standard reference works such as *The World Almanac; Information Please Almanac; The Statesman's Year-Book; Encyclopædia Britannica; Britannica Book of the Year; Facts on File; Encyclopédie politique* (A French publication); and the files of the New York *Times.*

For the various countries which figured in the journey, a number of books helped to bolster or correct my own impressions. Among them were: *Wien,* by Hans Tietze (Vienna: Verlag Dr. Hans Epstein, 1931); *The Hapsburg Monarchy,* by Wickham Steed (London: Constable, 1919); *The Social Revolution in Austria,* by C. A. Macartney (Cambridge: The University Press, 1926); two books by G. E. R. Gedye: *Heirs to the Hapsburgs* (London: Arrowsmith, 1932) and *Fallen Bastions* (London: Victor Gollancz, 1939); *Austria,* by F. H. Buschbeck (London: Oxford University Press, 1949); *The Book of Austria* (Vienna: Oesterreichische

Staatsdruckerei, 1948); *Legend of a Musical City,* by Max
Graf (New York: Philosophical Library, 1945); *Salzburg,*
by Hermann Bahr (Berlin: Verlag Julius Bard, 1914); *The
Course of German History,* by A. J. P. Taylor (New York:
Coward-McCann, 1946); *The German People,* by Veit Val-
entin (New York: Alfred A. Knopf, 1946); *History of Germany,* by Hermann Pinnow (London: J. M. Dent & Sons,
1936); *World in Trance,* by Leopold Schwarzschild (New
York: L. B. Fischer, 1942); *Germany: A Self-Portrait,* edited
by Harlan R. Crippen (New York: Oxford University Press,
1944); *Germany: Promise and Perils,* by Sigmund Neu-
mann (New York: The Foreign Policy Association, 1950);
Documents on German Foreign Policy—1918-1945 (Washington: Dept. of State); *Reports on Germany,* published
quarterly by the Office of the U. S. High Commissioner for
Germany, Frankfurt; the Nuremberg Documents, published
by the U. S. Government under the title *Nazi Conspiracy
and Aggression.*

Others: *The Grave-Diggers of France,* by Pertinax (New
York: Doubleday, Doran, 1943); two books by Henri de
Kerillis: *Français, voici la vérité!* (New York: Editions de
la Maison Française, 1942); *De Gaulle, dictateur* (Montreal:
Editions Beauchemin, 1945); *Pierre Laval; La France trahie,*
by Henry Torres (New York: Brentano's, 1941); *Modern
France: Problems of the Third and Fourth Republics,* edited
by Edward Mead Earle (Princeton: Princeton University
Press, 1951); *France: Setting or Rising Star?* by Saul K.
Padover (New York: The Foreign Policy Association, 1950);
The Reshaping of French Democracy, by Gordon Wright
(London: Methuen, 1950); *Gallic Charter,* by J. C. Fernand-
Laurent (Boston: Little, Brown, 1944); *French Personal-
ities and Problems,* by D. W. Brogan (New York: Alfred

A. Knopf, 1947); *Ordre et désordre de la France, 1939-1949* (Paris: La Nef, 1949).

Others: *The Foreign Affairs Reader,* edited by Hamilton Fish Armstrong (New York: Harper & Bros., 1947); *Tito and Goliath,* by Hamilton Fish Armstrong (New York: Macmillan, 1951); three books by John Gunther, all published by Harpers: *Inside Europe* (1936); *Behind the Curtain* (1949); *Inside U.S.A.* (1947); *Can Europe Unite?*, by Vera Micheles Dean and J. K. Galbraith (New York: The Foreign Policy Association, 1950); *The Nine Lives of Europe,* by Leo Lania (New York: Funk & Wagnalls, 1950); *No Cause for Alarm,* by Virginia Cowles (New York: Harper & Bros., 1949); *The Cautious Revolution,* by Ernest Watkins (New York: Farrar, Straus, 1950); *The English People,* by D. W. Brogan (New York: Alfred A. Knopf, 1943); *The Decline and Fall of British Capitalism,* by Keith Hutchison (New York: Charles Scribner's Sons, 1950); *Britain, 1949-1950,* and *Britain, 1950-1951* (London: The Central Office of Information); *British Security* (London: Royal Institute of International Affairs, 1946).

Others: *America's Economic Supremacy,* by Brooks Adams (New York: Harper & Bros., 1947); *Roosevelt: From Munich to Pearl Harbor,* by Basil Rauch (New York: Creative Age Press, 1950); *Roosevelt and Hopkins,* by Robert E. Sherwood (New York: Harper & Bros., 1948); *The United States in World Affairs* (Annual Volumes published for the Council on Foreign Relations by Harper & Bros.); two books by Walter Lippmann: *U. S. Foreign Policy* (Boston: Little, Brown, 1943); *The Cold War* (New York: Harper & Bros., 1947); *The Roosevelt Era,* edited by Milton Crane (New York: Boni and Gaer, 1947); *Only Yesterday,* by Frederick Lewis Allen (New York: Harper & Bros., 1931); *Fantastic Interim,* by Henry Morton Robinson (New York: Harcourt,

Brace, 1943); *The Turning Stream,* by Duncan Aikman (New York: Doubleday, 1948); *Twentieth Century Unlimited,* edited by Bruce Bliven (Philadelphia: J. B. Lippincott, 1950); *This Was Normalcy,* by Karl Schriftgiesser (Boston: Little, Brown, 1948); *Paths to the Present,* by Arthur M. Schlesinger (New York: Macmillan, 1949); *The Economic Reports of the President Together with the Reports by the Council of Economic Advisers* 1947 to 1951 (Washington: U. S. Government Printing Office); and *America's Needs and Resources,* by J. Frederic Dewhurst and Associates (New York: The Twentieth Century Fund, 1947).

Finally, I have checked back on several years' issues of that excellent quarterly *Foreign Affairs* and on the splendid pamphlets published by the Foreign Policy Association.

INDEX